ORWELL CALLING

A NOVEL

PETER HODGKINSON

Paperback ISBN: 978-1-7391237-0-3
Ebook ISBN: 978-1-7391237-1-0

Cover design by BespokeBookCovers.com

For Jackie

PROLOGUE

I AM NOW DEFINITELY AN EMPLOYEE OF THE BBC ... WE ARE IN for a long, dreary exhausting war, with everyone growing poorer all the time. The new phase which I foresaw earlier has now started, and the quasi-revolutionary period which began with Dunkirk is finished. I therefore bring this diary to an end, as I intended to do when the new phase started.

Orwell's Wartime Diary, 28th August 1941

ORWELL RESUMED his diary on 14th March 1942. What follows could have taken place in the intervening six months.

PART I

1

THERE HAD BEEN NO AIR RAIDS DURING THE NIGHT AND FOR the first time in weeks he had managed to sleep between his usual fits of coughing. With the prospect of yet another torturous planning meeting, he braced himself with a cold scrub, a shave, two cups of strong tea and a roll-up of pungent Turkish tobacco. It was 8am on a bright, unseasonably cold day in late October 1941. George Orwell closed the front door of his fifth-floor flat in Langdon Court and set off for his office at the BBC. It was his first day back at work after taking two weeks off sick. Eileen was still asleep.

Taking the stairs, he made his way to the ground floor, stopping on every landing to clear his lungs. This also gave him time to think about his work at the BBC, E.M. Forster, the price of a pint, the scarcity of bananas, Japanese advances, German retreats and today the state of Langdon Court itself. Before the war, the building had been a genteel, upper middle-class enclave and a haven of polite respectability. The lifts had always been in working order, or so he imagined, and only now were they traps for the unwary. Most of the small and ordinary things in life – the electricity and gas supplies, water for the bath and toilet, the post and rubbish collections, milk deliveries and much else besides – had become either unreliable or non-existent. Only the rag-and-bone man was dependably frequent. In wartime nothing could be taken for granted and everyone expected the worst. They were seldom disappointed.

Reaching the fourth floor, he concluded that war, like a cancer, killed you from both the outside and from within. Two young boys carrying violin cases rushed past, obviously late for their lesson, completely ignoring him as if he were the Invisible Man.

Orwell checked to see if there was any sign of 'Joe' in his handkerchief while continuing to reflect on how the flats had changed in what felt like just a few months. They had become occupied by refugees from mittel Europe, Jews for the most part who, having escaped the fascists, now found themselves in either East or West London depending on their previous profession. In Langdon Court they were mostly professional folk: journalists, composers, artists, musicians, instrument makers, scientists and doctors, all of whom had lost the tools of their trade in their exodus and appeared to be scraping a living doing whatever they could. This was seldom what they had practised in their former lives and most were now downwardly mobile tutors of one sort or another. Eileen had complained that the communal stairway perpetually reeked of garlic, which in England was taken as the scent of the alien. Orwell simply noted her observation on the 'pong ' as he liked to call it. As someone fixated with smells of any kind, he didn't in fact mind the odours or the discordance of foreign tongues as they reminded him of his times in Paris and Barcelona. Instead, while sympathetic to their plight, what really grated was that whenever he passed these new neighbours on the stairs, they failed to bid him good morning, good afternoon or good evening. It was this lack of basic English manners, he thought, that set them apart and lowered the quality of the building. It never occurred to him that he might be thought of as a hostile presence.

On the third-floor landing he stopped for breath once more and as he did so caught sight of a poster peeling off the wall. It must have been there for some time but he had previously failed to acknowledge it. It was in the Primitive style and depicted an industrial scene of billowing smoke stacks and heroically muscled proletarians, all conveyed in the obligatory red colour stamp. It was a production of the People's Convention, a proxy organisation for the Communist Party of Great Britain (CPGB), and it called for a 'popular front' with the USSR against all 'imperialist aggression'. Making sure he was not being observed, Orwell took a corner of the poster and tore it from the wall. He paused for a moment and looked at the large piece of paper in his now shaking hand. It was the first time he had ever done such a thing. He then let the scrap fall and continued his descent.

On the first floor he tried to repeat the violation, but this time the poster refused to surrender and half of it proclaiming the need for 'Friendship with the USSR' stubbornly remained. Since the German invasion of Russia in June of that year, the party line had changed on Stalin's orders and the CPGB's opposition to the war had metamorphosed into unconditional support. As such, and by way of a justification for his actions, Orwell decided that if the 'People's Peace' had become the 'People's War' he had licence to remove one, if not both, of the offending posters.

In the lobby, he relit his roll-up, coughed up yet more mahogany-coloured tea and tobacco phlegm and set off for work. Exiting the building, he thought this was going to be just another day at the office.

George Orwell had a presence, especially in the street. At six feet and three inches tall, somewhat emaciated and wrinkled, he resembled a half-completed sketch. He had an outline but no substance; he had grown upwards but his body had yet to be filled out. His shock of greasy black-brown hair was parted down the centre, creating two waves that added inches to his already considerable stature. His top lip was hardly discernible under a pencil-line French-style moustache that added little to his masculine appeal, if indeed that had been the intention. In fact, it made him look like a wartime spiv. His crevassed face suggested thirty-eight years of physical and mental struggle and the deep furrows in his cheeks and forehead simply accented the current conflict-ridden times. It was his piercing blue eyes in their deep hollow sockets that drew people in. That, and the fact that he seldom blinked, appeared to give him a permanent stare, one that froze friends and foe alike.

Orwell loped at a gentle pace in his oversized shoes and securing decent replacements for his size twelves had been a major challenge since the start of the war. His rough tweed sports jacket with leather-patched elbows and grey flannel trousers were supplemented by a dark-blue shirt and woollen tie. The entire outfit appeared as if it had been carefully orchestrated to convey an image of the struggling writer. Today, despite the state of his lungs and the bitter weather, he'd forsworn his trench coat and refused to wear a hat or cap. The effect was a blend of a country squire, a middle-class private-school teacher, a Bohemian and a proletarian in his Sunday best. This marked him out as a non-conformist, or at least someone who had perfected the art of classless dressing. Orwell confused people and that, indeed, was his intention. His muddled wardrobe spoke too of his status as a writer. He was a respected essayist and competent journalist, yet, by his own admission, only a mediocre novelist.

Smoke from his roll-your-own – a constant companion suspended from the right-hand side of his mouth – coiled above his funnelled head, contriving to make him appear as a chimney of some sort. He removed the cigarette only to cough its consequences from his already ravaged lungs. Making sure that no one was looking, he spat the dense, opaque phlegm into the gutter and followed up with a cursory inspection for any tell-tale signs of 'Joe', his internal blood-red assassin.

There was no disguising the fact that the man was ill.

Blitzed London was still a long way from recovery. Though the last major raids had taken place months earlier, the streets were still strewn with the devastation. Whole sections of road were impassable and the newly formed gaps between the houses rendered the once neat, regular terraces into a mosaic of shattered shells. They reminded Orwell of the state of English teeth. He stopped and stared into the living room of one of the bombed-out dwellings – it conjured up something akin to a stage set with three standing walls, a proscenium, containing the scene of a tragedy, save the remains of its leading actors. All the furniture and other removable items had long since been fetched or more likely looted. A thought amused him: perhaps it was the hideous wallpaper and colour scheme – both crimes against good taste – that had offended German sensibilities and attracted the fatal bomb? The whole scene also spoke of the absence of domestic comfort that was now all too common. The authorities, wearing an assortment of uniforms, told him to move along. As he continued his journey he began thinking about what life in England was like before the war.

Before the war normality had been numbingly conservative and in some cases as violent as any war for its individual victims, especially for many working-class women. Poverty, a mundane factory existence, multiple childbirths and years of abuse at the hands of brutal husbands had often rendered normal life a slow, lingering and painful journey towards a premature death. And the lives of menfolk had been little better – for the 'proles' had been at war, class war, since time immemorial. Yet in its predictability, their lives or existence had also been relatively stable insofar as 'settling down' had been the sole ambition of most. Orwell knew that, in reality, for the vast majority of the working class this meant being resigned to one's place and not having ideas beyond one's station. This was still a country steeped in deference and that might explain why working class people often avoided eye contact and stepped aside when he approached them on a pavement. The middle class, on the other hand, waited to see who would make the first move. Today, Orwell was going to intentionally reverse the custom whenever he could. Sociologically, it would make the journey more interesting.

As he continued to peer into the bombed-out dwellings, he saw not only the past but also the possibility of a brighter future rising out of the ruins. It wasn't just the taste in décor of the country that was in need of transformation, it was the entire rotten system. That what had passed for normal, everyday life had been ruptured and was seen by Orwell as both an offence but also an opportunity. He had a sizeable foot in both camps. Like many, he sometimes longed for a routine existence with all the comforts of home and it was the wartime destruction of these that he considered criminal. Yet he also recognised that change was both inevitable and necessary. Hitler's ambition had seen to it that normal life could and would never be the same again and there was, he hoped, to be no turning back. It was an opportunity for the radical societal change that he had long wished for. However, first there was a war to be won.

He arrived at 55 Portland Place shortly after eight fifty, but not in time to avoid the soot-filled rain that had begun to fall heavily. In the absence of hat or umbrella, his hair had subsided and its bi-sectioned waves collapsed under their sodden weight. By the time he passed the uniformed BBC commissionaire on duty at the reception desk, he resembled an upturned mop.

The rotund, ebullient sentry saluted him. 'G'morning, sir. Blimey, it's coming down now all right.'

'Good morning, Arthur,' Orwell said as he shook off the rain.

'It's Godfrey, sir. Arfer's the other one, 'e works here on Tuesdays and Thursdays,' the commissionaire replied, sounding apologetic about his own existence.

'Oh, yes. Good morning all the same, Godfrey.'

'And 'ow are you today, sir? Well I 'ope.' His cockney accent rang true to every music-hall caricature Orwell had ever heard.

'Wet—' Orwell collapsed into a fit of coughing.

'Blimey, you'd better take care of that, sir. That's a nasty cough you got there. There's a lot of it about. My missus—'

Orwell didn't wait to hear the folklore and quickly moved off, still rendering his congestion. Before attempting the stairs, he looked back at the commissionaire, who was standing stiffly, staring at him. The poor man was clearly indignant at Orwell's lack of basic civility.

On the first landing Orwell rested in order to regain his

breath. Joe had left a small black-red spot on his handkerchief. He thought about his behaviour – it was just like that of the refugees in Langdon Court, the type he despised for their woeful lack of manners. What was happening to him? He relit his roll-up. Why had he acted so crassly? Perhaps it was the current superficial, class-free friendliness with its plastic and insincere exchanges that had become commonplace since the Blitz? Especially the caricature of the plucky cockneys, such as Godfrey and/or Arfer, who were being constantly inscribed on the public consciousness by the newspapers and newsreels. They were everywhere being portrayed as bridge builders between the social classes: *We're all in it together*, the posters lied. The Queen had been to Whitechapel: *Pearly kings and queens all,* the newsreels exclaimed. Yet any fool could see that class divisions were as wide as ever, if not more so. All one had to do was visit Oxford or Regent Street in the West End and Whitechapel and Commercial Road in the East to see that there were two distinct wars going on – one for the workers, and another for the middle and upper classes. Orwell was having none of it and knew full well it was all bunkum and baloney. After all, he was now in the propaganda business himself. Nevertheless, he still felt guilty about how he had acted towards poor Godfrey downstairs.

Portland Place had been Orwell's place of work for the past two and a half months. His office was no larger than the average toilet cubicle and appeared far too small for its current occupant. He felt cramped, both physically and intellectually.

The Eastern Overseas Service India Section was responsible for broadcasting to India, Malaysia and Indonesia, and his job was to counter the German and to a lesser extent Japanese propaganda being broadcast to the sub-continent.

At the beginning of the war, the Nazi propagandists had provided the equivalent of political high explosives to the Indians whilst the BBC had served tea and cucumber sandwiches. It was all so very, very British and Orwell detested it. Indian listeners had been subjected to something akin to an English vicar's newsletter, with the births and deaths of minor British notables, the cricket results and especially the comings and goings of blue-bloods, no matter how diluted their royal lineage. In other words, nothing that would be or could be of any interest to budding Indian intellectuals and those destined, one day, to manage the affairs of that great country. Orwell – or Eric Blair as he was known at the BBC – had been hired as an Empire Talks Assistant to vary this paltry diet by producing radio programmes about 'British civilisation'. Whilst these Talks were intrinsically interesting, they were also part of a strategic attempt to quell the possibility of Indian sedition. Truth and lies were the salt and pepper of this propaganda and Orwell's job was to season the dish. Thus the distinction between 'white' and 'black' propaganda was very important to him. The white variety involved telling the truth, or at least a carefully crafted version of it, whereas black propaganda was always lies. He had convinced himself that he was in the business of making the white variety. He achieved this by taking on the mantel of a modern Enlightenment Encyclopaedist and constructing a schedule of radio Talks that encompassed both the arts and the sciences, as well as some political and social commentary. Literature was to the fore and his own contribution to the Talks was not insubstantial.

In many ways, Eric Blair revelled in the role of BBC producer, whereas George Orwell was struggling to maintain his political principles in the face of censorship and political interference from the Ministry of Information.

MinInform effectively governed the BBC's output on a daily basis and every broadcast was subject to a double-lock censorship process, once for security and once for policy. Every script had to have the double imprimatur of unseen censors and nothing was to be spontaneous, unplanned or unvetted. This meant the talks were pre-scripted and had to be adhered to, even where a seemingly natural discussion or dialogue was being enacted. To ensure no departures from the approved script, a switch-censor was also present in the studio to turn off the microphones should anything not previously sanctioned slip out. As a result, Orwell went about his business with the feeling that someone, somewhere, was always looking over his shoulder and about to stamp on any indiscretion he might commit. He felt like a caged bird: as Eric Blair he could sing his own songs but as George Orwell the bars on the enclosure meant he had no freedom to explore. Staff member Eric Blair 9889 was trapped, albeit in a somewhat gilded cage and a regular income of £640 a year. This was far more than George Orwell could ever hope to earn as a writer in such bleak times.

As he made his way along the corridors of Portland Place, he could see that the broadcasting beehive was in full motion. The drones even had their sleeves rolled up. He thought it odd – did anyone really believe that they were making a contribution to the war effort that was as important as that of the workers in the munitions factories or those down the mines? Yet his own position had been classified as 'essential war work'. At first, he had tried to convince himself that that was indeed the case. However, as the months moved on, he was certain his status was totally unwarranted. His contribution was neither important nor effective and he had come to the conclusion that he was wasting time that could and should otherwise have been spent writing.

This morning another programme on British poetry beckoned and its efficacy in terms of stopping the Japanese advance on Calcutta seemed to be a case of surrealism made real. The idea that the Indians, as a result of hearing the verse of Eliot or some other poet, could stop the Japanese in their tracks was so outlandish, insane even, it could be something out of a very dark comedy. Yet, as bizarre as it surely was, might it not be worth doing anyway? Orwell found that he had little choice but to apply himself to the impossible as though it were probable. What else could he do in this war? He was in no condition to fight or lay down his life and his yellow exemption card felt like a badge of dishonour. The lunacy of his situation demanded that he simply do his best. Such was his inner turmoil and, on some days, the pointlessness of the whole exercise seemed to overwhelm him. Today felt like one of those days. He had a Planning Committee meeting at 9am in Room 1-01.

2

'MEETINGS ARE MURDER! MONDAY-MORNING MEETINGS ARE double murder! Monday-morning planning meetings are serial murder.' Orwell chanted this mantra under his breath as he made his way to the dreaded room. He tried but failed to think of a suitable music-hall tune to accompany the verse before reaching the door.

The Indian Section Planning Committee (ISPC) meetings were purgatory. He would often quip that the bullet that had ripped through his neck in Spain had been less excruciating and that having knitting needles pushed into one's eyeballs would even be less painful. Only a pack of rats gnawing one's bare flesh would be more hideous than the torture he was about to be subjected to. What could and should have been an interesting and engaging intellectual discussion of programme content invariably turned into a mechanical dirge of the how rather than the why any subject was to be broadcast. That was the usual and only substance of these meetings. And this was not altogether surprising since the ISPC was constituted mostly bureaucrats and technicians whose bureaucratic diahorrea and robotic whining numbed him to the bone.

The BBC bureaucrats were short bespectacled people in dull suits who appeared to carry identical Corporation briefcases. Orwell thought they always looked and acted significantly older than their years and probably lived in some middle-class suburban desert such as Raynes Park, Surbiton or even Cheam. Whereas the technicians had assorted waistcoats or knitted tank tops, unruly curly hair and, as a mark of their practical bent, rolled-up sleeves. They seldom made eye contact. In this way it was a simple task to identify the role of any speaker in these meetings. While the technocracy offered latitude in so far as his choice of material was seldom interrogated, Orwell had long since concluded that they simply didn't care enough about the substance to have an opinion. Form over content appeared to be their guiding maxim. As for the bureaucrats, oversight of the ISPC was held at a distance by a more elusive, unknowable and unseen body – the College. Everyone knew this was a part of MiniForm. On the odd occasion when Orwell overstepped the mark and invited proscribed speakers onto the programmes, such as Bertrand Russell, the firm boot of the all-seeing College had quickly stamped all over his intentions. Just to add to the dire proceedings, his immediate boss, Z.A. Bokhari, chaired the planning meetings.

Sitting at the head of the table, Bokhari was as dapper as ever in his Savile Row styled pinstripe suit, which had in fact been cut and tailored in Bombay. Orwell thought it looked far too flimsy for the autumn weather. His shirt and tie were however in perfect solidarity and unlike Orwell he looked every inch the English gentleman. The secretaries were exiled to the fringes of the room and held their notebooks as they would their purses. Orwell's shared secretary, Miss Elizabeth Thomas – Betty as she was known – seemed not to have noticed that Orwell had entered and had made his way around the table. Standing directly behind her, he gently tapped her on the shoulder and in an exaggerated shrill voice that ensured all could hear, announced his presence.

'Good morning, Miss Thomas! Are you looking forward to this *very* important meeting?'

He surveyed the attendees for any sign they had savoured his sarcasm. There was none, save Bokhari, who raised a bushy eyebrow and tapped his pencil on the table.

'Oh ... good morning, Mr Blair! I didn't see you come in,' Betty replied.

Orwell leaned over and whispered in her ear, 'Betty, get me out of here. Save me from this torture. Please ... think of something, anything.'

'But Mr Blair ...' Betty looked flustered and consulted her notebook. 'Oh, Mr Blair, you have a call from Mr Forster at 10am. He said it was *very* important,' she said loudly to ensure that Bokhari heard.

'Did you hear that, Z.A.? Forster at ten. I'm afraid I must take that call.' Orwell smiled, raised his hands in supplication and leaned back over to Betty. 'You're an angel. 4.30?' he whispered.

Betty looked embarrassed but nodded. Orwell continued his tour of the table and came to sit at his chair on Bokhari's immediate right. As he sat down he spotted a new body. She was young and Indian. Oblivious to his ogling, she arranged some papers on the table in front of her.

Orwell broke his stare and nudged Bokhari. 'Who's that?'

Bokhari was seemingly not on the same wavelength. 'Who?'

'That girl ... the young woman.' Orwell nodded in her direction.

'She's your new assistant.'

'My new assistant? No one told me,' Orwell replied in half-hearted indignation. 'I already have Miss Doshi.'

'Her name is Miss Mukurjee and she's here for six months. She's just been approved by the College. She's very bright and most willing. I thought she'd be a very good addition to your section. I think you'll appreciate her work,' Bokhari replied quietly.

'How can you take on another assistant ahead of Miss Doshi? I need Jahida. It makes no sense. Make Jahida full-time. Give her a contract.'

Orwell looked to Bokhari's left where Jahida Doshi sat. She had clearly sensed they were talking about her.

'Please, keep your voice down, Blair. We cannot keep using Miss Doshi on the current basis, but for the moment she'll continue to help out. We can discuss this later.'

Officially, Jahida Doshi was a freelance contributor with no full-time BBC contract but, unofficially, she was Orwell's assistant and fairy godmother. She was forever mitigating his behaviour towards others and generally saving him from himself. In return, Orwell had tried desperately, though without success, to get Bokhari to promote Jahida to a full-time post. She also acted as chief mediator between the various political, ethnic and religious factions within the section. Her voice was treasure itself: deep, expressive and quite beautifully enunciated. It was to Jahida that people turned whenever an announcer was required. She was the section's mother-figure, although she had a youthfulness that belied her thirty plus years. Short in stature, rounded even, she exuded energy that emanated from some unseen dynamo. Despite the horrors of the war and what was happening in India, she managed to radiate joy. She smiled constantly and her cheeks puffed out animatedly during conversation. She chewed words as if they were beetle juice before spitting them out into the world. Unlike most of the other Indian women in the section, and in contrast to the dowdy attire of most women in the BBC, she wore traditional colourful saris. It later transpired that she changed from her Western clothes every day after stepping over the BBC portal. Highly organised and intelligent in both a cognitive and emotional sense, she was also politically astute and, unlike many of her Indian colleagues, was prepared to listen to all sides in any argument. It was often said, especially by Orwell, that the talks between the Indian Congress Party and the Muslim League would have benefitted enormously by her presence.

Bokhari drummed his porcelain tea cup with a pencil and called everyone to order.

'Ladies, gentlemen, please. If I can have your attention.' The assembly quietened.

Orwell had often mulled over Bokhari. He was an interesting character, an intellectual who had taken the managerial shilling. He was certainly no bureaucrat and operated an 'If I do it, it will get done' management style. He was undoubtedly a workaholic and could be counted on being in his office whenever he was needed. Indeed, the man never seemed to leave the building. Like Orwell, he was tall, with a distinctive head of hair. Bokhari's was a tsunami of epic proportions – a veritable headpiece comprising a black-and-grey wave that stood two to three inches high and threatened to engulf his golden-skinned brow. He bore an almost feline elegance, gracing the office with sylph-like movements. He was about the same age as Orwell, and spoke impeccable King's English in the best, or perhaps worst, traditions of the BBC. It was the one thing Orwell could not stomach. He despised the BBC way of speaking and the crime was somehow made worse when it came from the mouth of an Indian. Orwell thought it patronising, outdated and grating that everyone had to mould their natural voice to be accepted at the BBC. No one spoke like that in the real world, least of all their audience. It simply reproduced the deference that arose from associating a posh voice with knowledge and authority. Only Orwell had little grounds for this criticism: his own voice, a high-pitched upper-class crackle, a product of his Spanish neck wound, was weak and generally thought unsuitable for radio.

Bokhari was punctilious. He missed nothing and it was for this reason that the meetings descended into interminable dissections of the minutiae of every broadcast. Fastidious and parsimonious, he was never one to initiate an original idea. In many ways he was the perfect radio producer and made the programmes run, and run on time. In that regard, Orwell had a lot of respect for his management of the India Section. Yet, there was also something about Bokhari that made him feel uneasy. The man had no discernible political beliefs, although Orwell suspected he was tepidly pro-Indian independence. To uncover the real Bokhari, Orwell often made salacious suggestions regarding possible speakers or topics on the theme of independence. However, no obvious conclusions could be drawn as Bokhari was always scrupulously impartial. The politics of independence was kept within acceptable bounds or else firmly off the agenda.

Orwell returned his focus to the new addition and he watched her until she raised her head and their eyes met.

She appeared to know who he was and a very tight smile crossed her face. He returned the gesture and blew a plume of smoke into the air. Only then did she look away. It was unusual for the junior assistants to attend these meetings and he was intrigued by her presence. Ten minutes in and already bored rigid, he looked around the table.

His only true friend among his Indian colleagues was Mulk Raj Anand, a successful and well-liked novelist. Anand moved in the Bloomsbury circles only without being taken in by what he considered their effete politics and pretensions. He was too much of a realist and this is what had attracted Orwell. They had met briefly after Spain, where they had both shared a commitment to the lost Republican cause during the civil war. Anand had been reporting on the war whilst Orwell was actually fighting. It soon became obvious that they had many other causes in common. Both were writers who had made the plight of the poor and dispossessed a major theme in their work. And both came from relatively privileged backgrounds, without being part of the ruling class of their respective societies. Both were socialists of sorts, though neither had been drawn into the Left intelligentsia set. They were, however, most unalike physically. Anand was dashing, upright and well dressed and made Orwell feel like one of his tramps from *Down and Out in Paris and London*. After returning from Spain they had an acquaintance at an anti-fascist meeting and their friendship had been almost immediate. In particular, Orwell shared Anand's cynicism concerning the intentions of the British in relation to India. However, they violently disagreed on Gandhi and the role of non-violent action in the struggle for India's independence. Anand was agnostic regarding pacifism while, from the start of the war, Orwell had completely rebuked non-violence as an effective response to fascism. Indeed, he had upset a number of people, not just Anand, by suggesting that pacifism was in effect akin to being pro-fascist. Pacifism was also, in Orwell's opinion, never going to deliver India's independence. Nevertheless, Orwell and Anand's friendship had endured, albeit with the occasional spat and the extended silences that invariably followed.

Sitting directly opposite Orwell was Maharajkumari Indira Devi of Kapurthala, the so-called Radio Princess. This one-time aspiring movie star was an enigma. Despite her glamour, Orwell could only assume that someone had decided she couldn't act and had seen to it that she missed out on being a star of the silver screen. Known simply as the Princess, she was the Eastern Service's Westminster correspondent and the only woman to be found in the Parliamentary Lobby. It was entirely baffling how she had come to occupy this role and he doubted whether even she knew how it had come to pass. Regardless of her lack of qualifications, he had come to admire her tenacity and skill in overcoming her limitations as a political correspondent and broadcaster in what was an entirely male preserve. He had classified her politics as 'woolly feminism', his code for a suspected lesbian. As a result, he remained smitten by her beauty, grace and stature, but considered her off limits.

Next to the Princess sat a somewhat furtive character, another would-be actor called K.S. Desai. An otherwise charming and eloquent man in his early thirties, Desai had immediately fallen into Orwell's category of 'not to be trusted'. Desai appeared as gentle as he was transparent, yet Orwell thought him too much so. Later, when he discovered that Desai had come to Britain only weeks before the outbreak of the war, and that he had since changed his name from Dasai to Desai without explanation, Orwell's suspicions were heightened. When he also learned that Desai was also working for MinInform, it was all the confirmation he needed to justify his initial categorisation.

Next came the altogether more amenable young husband-and-wife team, Balraj and Damyanti Sahni. He had taken an immediate shine to them because they were approachable, innovative and easily the most energetic members of the India Section. Above all, he envied their zest for life. Unlike many of his Indian colleagues, he found it easy to discuss his ideas for radio drama with the Sahnis as they were always willing to explore new projects. Their burning ambition was to return to India and set up a touring theatre company, and it was obvious to all that they were counting down the days until the war ended. They had little or nothing to say in such meetings.

At the far end of the table sat Virat Baghat. Orwell had no idea what Baghat did apart from the odd Marathi translation. He was the silent one.

It was difficult for Orwell to identify with his Indian colleagues and they, no doubt, felt the same towards him. The assortment of personalities and political viewpoints meant they were not a uniform collective. Even their Indian heritage was as heterogeneous and heteroglossic as India itself. He had concluded that the negatives arising from their constant disputes and petty squabbles far outweighed the virtues of such a diverse group. Most disagreements appeared at first to be trivial cultural differences, albeit later turning out to be proxies for the real political and religious tensions that lay just below the surface. Yet their disparate views were seldom if ever over whether India's independence was their goal, it was more about *when* and *how* it might be achieved. He had quickly recognised that these differences were dependent upon their view of their colonial masters. As far as he knew, there were few, if any, openly hard-line nationalists who hated the British and viewed the whole race, including himself, as being beyond redemption. For these, anyone and anything that hastened the end of the Raj was to be supported regardless. Orwell suspected that Desai, for all his affability, might be in this camp. Milder nationalists were more nuanced and differentiated the colonial elite from ordinary British folk. Indeed, they thought most of the British population shared something of their yoke. Jahida appeared to be in this mould. Then there were the followers of Gandhi, such as the Sahnis, who fell somewhere between these two positions. Meanwhile the Princess gave the appearance of being agnostic. Regardless of their place on the continuum, most of the nationalists inhabited the Congress Party in various guises and their periodic splits notwithstanding. In contrast, most of the Muslim opinions and sympathies found their home in the Muslim League, who, for the most part, appeared to be more accepting of British rule, at least for the duration of the war, and lived in hope that their loyalty would be recognised and eventually rewarded with a separate holy land, Pakistan. Orwell suspected Bokhari of being in this camp but could not prove it. Finally, on the fringes of both main parties were the socialists and communists, who thought the end of British rule in India would be a rehearsal for the main event, a world-wide proletarian revolution. Mulk Raj Anand could be counted in their number.

The Indian Section had members of all persuasions and as the situation in India became more volatile, the staff became ever more fragmented. Being the only British member of the section meant Orwell was sometimes the focus of all their enmities. Only Bokhari appeared to stay aloof and untainted by any of the labels. By studiously avoiding any expression of opinion about independence, he managed to walk the tightrope of political neutrality. Given the intensity of the views held by most of the section, this was an act of forbearance that would have tested many a saint. Orwell had a natural aversion and suspicion of such piety.

At 9.50am, Orwell left the meeting to take the faux call from E.M. Forster. He made for the canteen, where he rolled a cigarette and a took a moment to make notes of his morning's observations. An hour later he returned just in time to hear Bokhari's closing remarks. The only item on the agenda of any note appeared to be the problem of Talks over-running and hosts not keeping to the authorised script. No names were mentioned, although Orwell knew that the key offender was Lady Sutton. Her weekly Talk was a broadcast disaster every week, yet no-one had had the nerve to confront her, not even Bokhari.

3

After the planning meeting, Orwell deliberately delayed his exit, hoping his new assistant would do likewise. She did and he waited for the room to clear before he circled the table. Only Jahida spoke to him before leaving: 'We need to talk. Don't!' was all she said. Orwell was sure he was being forewarned, but chose to defy his guardian angel and made his way towards the young woman. She didn't look up until he was almost upon her.

'Hello', he said, standing directly behind her.

He towered over her and forced her to turn and look up. She was clearly uncomfortable and went to get to her feet, but he placed a hand on her shoulder.

'No, please. Sit.'

He pulled out the chair next to her and sat down, all the while staring at her. Half-smiling, and with a cigarette unusually absent from his mouth, Orwell fiddled nervously with his tie and straightened his collar a number of times.

'I'm George Orwell, and I believe you're to be my new assistant.'

'George Orwell? I mean, I know you are ... but everyone

called you Blair. I'm a little confused,' she said softly in a broad Indian accent.

He smiled at her. 'It's Eric.'

She looked even more perplexed.

'You can either call me Eric, which is my proper name, or George, which is what my friends call me. Or Blair, which is what I'm known as here. And I suppose, as I'm to be your boss, it should really be Mr Blair in the company of others.'

The young woman seemed struck by his forwardness. 'But I'm not your friend, Eric, George, or —'

'I'm hoping you will be, Miss?' He tilted his head in an expectant manner.

'Mukurjee.'

She nodded and Orwell focused on her silken black hair.

'Do you have any other names Miss Mukerjee?'

'No. Everyone seems to have two names here. I've seen so many people with two names. Like yourself. It's very confusing.'

'The others are mostly single names but double-barrelled.'

'Pardon me?'

'That's what we say when people hyphenate or join up their family names. For instance, Thompson-Green, Bowles-Norton, Radcliff-Watts or Chipping-Norton and Trumpet-Player. That's quite common around here.'

She failed to register the joke and Orwell continued his attempt to lighten the mood.

'Some even have three names, although they daren't let on. Just like everything else, they ration them in wartime.'

'Really? That's very interesting. So you might be Mr Eric George Blair-Orwell? It doesn't sound right. I'm just Mukurjee. I have one family and one name,' she said matter-of-factly.

'But what do people call you?'

'Miss Mukurjee or just Mukurjee.'

'No, I meant what do your friends and family call you?'

She paused before reluctantly responding. 'Rana.'

'That's pretty. What does it mean?'

'Nothing. It's just Rana', she replied and looked down at her notebook. Orwell could see she was uncomfortable and moved the conversation on.

'I understand that you're to be my new assistant. An assistant to an assistant, so to speak.'

'I'm afraid I really don't understand.What do you mean?' She threw her head back and held her hair behind her neck.

'I'm officially a Talks Assistant. That's my designation, my job title. So that would make you an assistant to an assistant. That's the way the BBC works, it seems. Perhaps we should try to get you an assistant.'

Again, his humour seemed to pass over her head. 'Will I need one?' she asked quite innocently.

Orwell was charmed by her naiveté and let out a wheezy chortle. 'No, no. That was a joke.'

His attempt to reassure her failed and a small furrow appeared on her otherwise untrammelled brow. The joke had obviously missed the target.

He took out his tobacco tin and began to roll a cigarette.

'Would you like a smoke?'

'Smoke? No, I don't ... thank you.' Her disapproval was obvious.

'I didn't think so. It's a filthy habit, I know, but I enjoy it nevertheless. I can't stop even though I know I should.'

'If you thought I would not like a cigarette, then why did you ask?' There was no malice in her enquiry. Rather, she appeared to have a genuine interest in the social mores involved.

'I was just being polite, that's all.'

'To offer me something I wouldn't like? And something you call *filthy*?'

'I didn't know you didn't smoke.'

'But you said you thought I wouldn't and you said it's filthy. Why would you offer me something like that?'

'Yes, but I wasn't to know for sure. That's why I offered. It's considered polite to do so.' Engaging this young woman was already beginning to feel like trying to explain the rules of cricket to a Frenchman. Something he had in fact once tried and failed miserably. Nevertheless, and exasperating though she was, it somehow only added to her attractiveness.

'Let's go for tea ... or coffee, if you like.'

'But shouldn't we be working Mr Blair?'

'We will be. We can discuss what you'll be doing. I'm your boss, after all. It'll be a business meeting. Come. I'm dying for a tea...Please don't take that literally!'

He rose from his chair and stood behind Rana. As she stood, he slid her chair out from behind her, an action befitting an English gentleman.

Rana was dressed as demurely as any novitiate. Her cardigan was a shade of mahogany brown and underneath was a navy-blue shirt buttoned to the collar. Her grey skirt was well below the current knee-length fashion and her stockings, what little he could see of them, were of the thick, coarse, wartime variety that, as women had informed him, itched like mad. He couldn't help but wonder what type of suspenders she employed. Despite her natural beauty, she looked frumpish, school-mistressy and certainly older than her actual years. He tried to imagine what she might look like in half-decent clothes. She was also short and, as they made their way through the labyrinth of Portland Place, he thought she looked like a little girl at his side.

'Where are you from?' he asked as they negotiated the umpteenth corridor.

'Stepney Green.'

'No, in India.' He chuckled and this brought on a cough which he tried to stifle.

Rana waited before replying. 'Calcutta. Have you been there?'

'Stepney Green? ... Oh, Calcutta! Yes, briefly. I was born in Mothari, in Bengal. And I was in Burma a few years back.'

'Oh, yes. Now I remember.'

This struck Orwell as a somewhat odd reply. 'What do you mean?'

'I remember reading about you. You were a policeman of some sort. And I've read your book.'

'My book?'

'The Burmese one. Miss Doshi suggested I read it. So I did. She loaned me her copy. Which reminds me, I need to return it.' She made a note in her notebook as they walked.

'And what did you think?' There was a long pause.

'The book? I didn't like it. Not at all.'

Orwell stopped in his tracks and stood, mouth agape with a cigarette now hanging loosely from his lower lip. It was not the answer he had either expected or hoped for. They looked at each other and Orwell appeared irritated.

'Oh, I'm sorry. What, may I ask, didn't you like about it?'

'I just didn't,' she said, quite unapologetically, and resumed walking. Orwell caught up with her and gently placed a hand on her shoulder. They stopped once more.

'You must have a reason. You can't just say "I didn't like it" What specifically didn't you like? The characters? The story? The writing? What was it? I'd really like to know.' His voice rose beyond its normal squeakiness. Rana looked away and said, quite emphatically, 'Everything. All of it. I didn't like *any* of it.'

He turned and looked her in the eye, shook his head slightly and waited for her explanation. Seeing two people approaching along the corridor, they paused the interrogation until the passageway was clear.

'You asked for my view. I'm sorry but that is what I thought.'

'Thank you!' Orwell replied sardonically.

'You're welcome,' she said, seemingly unapologetic regarding the offence she had caused.

They entered the canteen and Orwell ordered two cups of coffee, despite Rana's protestations that she would rather have water. They sat at a table that looked as though it had not seen a cloth since Hitler's invasion of Czechoslovakia. Their cups were cracked and stained, and the poor lighting, rather than hiding the potential threat to their health, only added to the general griminess of the place. Orwell thought that the coffee tasted even more like rabbit droppings than usual, although on this occasion he didn't seem to mind. Along with her rather dismissive comments on *Burmese Days*, this had not been an auspicious start to their relationship, working or otherwise. After a long pause he broke the silence.

'All of it?'

'Pardon me?' Rana held her coffee cup in mid-air.

'*All* of it?'

'Oh, your book. Yes, all of it. I've read better books.'

Orwell couldn't believe his ears. This was insubordination. He was now her boss and she had to like his book. Even if she didn't, it was impolite and downright rude of her to say what she had already said. All of it? He wished he had a copy in front of him so he could read it aloud and ask her what exactly it was she didn't like. He had to make do with a viva voce instead.

'Was it Flory? Did you not like the character?' he said, almost pleading with her.

'Flory? Oh, yes, the very weak man. Hardly a man at all, in my view. A coward in so many ways, I thought. You can't really like a coward. So I didn't like him. But not just him, it was all your British ... or Europeans ...as you called them. They were all awful people.'

'Flory didn't like them either. And he didn't like himself. That was the whole point.'

'Then why was he there?'

'He was lost and confused. He went to find himself. To become someone.'

'But you gave him extremely poor judgement. He was socially – how do you say – inept, in addition to being a coward. I don't like cowards or inept weaklings. No one does, do they? So why did your opponent of British Rule have to be so weak?'

Orwell had no answer.

'It was a pity because, in my opinion, it spoilt the whole book.' Rana took another sip of the insipid coffee and pushed it aside. 'That, and the way you wrote about the Burmese of course.'

There was no inflection or hesitation in her verdict, and her criticisms were given as if they were indisputable. Her voice had become deeper, harsher and more mature. Orwell felt there was a coldness in her contempt for him and his writing. She was so different to the demure young woman he had just met. He tried once more to retrieve the situation.

'He was young and naïve. Just as I was when I went to Burma.'

'It is you then? Flory is really you?'

' No. I don't consider myself a coward or inept. It's fiction. It's not me. And in case you hadn't noticed, unlike Flory, I'm still alive. Albeit barely, some might say.'

'Do you know that your book is banned in India?'

'Yes, the authorities believe it to be seditious, and that it might inflame the natives. The few that read such stuff, that is.'

'Sedition? I really don't think that is very likely. Having read it, I can't see how it would encourage them or anyone at all. In any case, aren't those Indians who read already inflamed? I'm sorry, but in my opinion they would not be taken in by it.'

Orwell was taken aback by this unforgiving assertion.

'Taken in? What do you mean? I never intended for it to do anything of the sort.'

Rana looked away briefly. 'Flory, he's not innocent. He's obviously the product of your imperialism, as well as being a racialist.'

Rana stared at him and he felt compelled to return her gaze.

'He's fiction, an invention, a character. He's not *me*. If you know anything about me it is that I'm totally against imperialism and I'm certainly not a racialist! I think you must have misread or misinterpreted Flory.' His emphasis only served to make him sound like a Pukka Sahib.

Rana looked frustrated. 'Perhaps I didn't understand. But I can only tell you what I think. If it had been better, perhaps I would not have been so confused? I don't believe I am, by the way.' She waited for his response but again he found himself lost for words. Something extraordinary was happening in this moment but he couldn't quite decide what it might be.

'As I see it, your book is part of an imperialist tradition. All the ingredients are there: some guilt and anger and the usual excuses for treating the '*natives*', as you call them, very badly. It's all there in your story. I think it's a reflection of the different kinds of imperialist men. There's the old gentlemen of the Raj and the new impotent ones like Flory. It's very simple really. It's the end of Empire. You said nothing about the people that you dominate, other than their obvious inferiority, which you do not hide. The Doctor ...Veraswami, for example. The man is a complete fool. He could never belong to the Club as an equal and you should never have encouraged him.'

Her eyes lit up and she looked him in the eye, unblinking.

Orwell sat astonished by the stridency and comprehensiveness of her comments. It was though she had prepared a list. Not even his harshest critics had had the courage to confront him like this. Even Eileen usually softened her critiques of his work or, when she thought they were particularly bad, said nothing at all. Rana had no qualms about telling him, undiluted, what she thought. Or was she? Had she been schooled? Were these really her words? He was at a loss to know how to address the admonishment, the demolition, coming as it did from someone so young, so articulate and so beautiful. He needed time to reflect on what had just occurred.

'Have you read anything else that I've written?'

'No.'

'Just Burmese Days?'

'Yes.'

'And you judge me on that alone? Would you read some

of my other work? I'd like to correct your view of me. I have two quite short pieces that I think will give you a very different impression of my views on Imperialism and the Empire. I can give them to you.'

'Are they also fiction?' There was a barb in the way she said *fiction*.

'Yes, and no. They are based on my experiences in Burma. One is '*Shooting an Elephant*' and the other is '*A Hanging*'. They might give you a better idea of where I stand. Will you read them?

'If I have time. They don't sound promising or something I'd really like to read about.' Rana did not look as if she was interested in changing her opinions of Orwell.

They quickly finished their coffee and returned to his office. Rana went off to a BBC induction meeting and Orwell was left alone in his cubicle.

Jahida soon found him, daydreaming.

In the short time she had been working for him, Jahida had come to know all about both Eric Blair and George Orwell. She had accumulated an extensive knowledge of his affairs, both literary and personal, and was a critic of both. She knew he was seriously unwell. She had had personal experience of his predatory instincts with women. His current 'thing' with Betty Thomas was no secret, and neither were his difficulties with Eileen and their desperation to have a child of their own. And while she admired his politics and had read many of his books and essays, she was far from being a devotee. She saw that he was riven, contradictory, angry, and disinherited by choice. As well as being something of a social and literary outcast, she thought he was, nevertheless, an English gentleman. A charming reprobate. She watched over him as an elder sister might, despite being nearly ten years his junior.

Jahida could match Orwell blow for blow in being abstruse, impolite, demanding and blunt if the need arose. She could not, however, be as self-serving. This was a woman who gave herself to others and demanded little, if anything, in return. She was the perfect secretary in the original sense of the word – a keeper of secrets. Everyone confided in Jahida. She was the hub of the section and the person to go to if there was something to be known.

Yet, no one really knew her because she was discreet and intensely guarded, especially regarding her relationships. The fact that she had never married was a complete mystery. Men should have been falling over themselves to marry such a woman. Orwell's own clumsy advances had been met with a solid rebuff, an indifference that bordered on contempt. She had simply donned her elder sister face and that had been enough to deter the lecher. Thereafter, Orwell had treated her with an unusual degree of respect. She knew that he knew that he couldn't survive the BBC without her.

'You can't help yourself, can you?' she said in a tone that left no doubt as to her disappointment, even despair.

'What d'you mean?' Orwell's attempt to feign innocence was unconvincing.

'She's just a young girl. I beg you, leave her alone George. No good can come of it. Think of Eileen and don't be such a damn fool!'

This was no longer the elder sister speaking, it was Mother.

He tried not to snigger. 'I don't know what you mean.'

'You know damn well what I mean! I saw your eyes. I know that look.'

'Still not got the foggiest '

'Damn you George! Just listen for once. That young

woman is going to be trouble. She may not be what she seems and you should not get yourself involved. Mark my words, and I say this as a friend: leave her alone! Please, do not get involved.' Jahida left the office.

Orwell sat motionless and tried to fathom what Jahida had just said. Was she really upset for Eileen? Or, as usual, was she simply looking after him for his own good? And what exactly did she know about Rana? And in what way is she not what she seems? Far from deterring him, Jahida had merely whetted his appetite to know more about his new assistant.

4

Meeting Betty had never been easy. She would leave Portland Place before him and they would rendezvous at Waterloo station. He had grown rather tired of the subterfuge and increasingly uneasy about their relationship in general. Betty had been good for sex, but out of bed she bored him. Now, even when he was making love to her, he sometimes wanted to hate her. Instead, he ended up hating himself for wanting to hate her. In fact, he had been semi-loyal to Betty and had maintained a semblance of interest in her, mixed with a growing amount of self-pity.

He imagined that Betty had enough plans for both of them. Once he had finished with Eileen, or she was hit by a bomb, they would retire to The Stores, his little shop in Wallington. There she would have his children. He envisaged her in her pinny, making apple pies and breast-feeding their three, four or even five children. In this version she would nurse him back to full health and look after him forever. The sun would always be shining and he would be in the garden tending the vegetables. Of course, he would write and become rich and famous and she would accompany him to the BBC and watch as he recorded programmes on matters she neither understood nor cared for. It didn't matter. He would be hers and it would be The Golden Country.

Orwell watched Betty standing under the monumental station clock as it struck 4.30 pm and just for one moment imagined it falling on her. It would be over and he could resume his life in the knowledge that there would be no squealing, disruption or lasting consequences. And if Eileen ever found out, he thought she wouldn't mind ... if the fling was over.

The affair needed to end.

Betty was overly made up as usual. Her powdered cheeks and bright-red lipstick made her look like the worst sort of tart. It both excited and repelled him. He wanted one of the passing soldiers to stop and proposition her. He imagined her taking off with some G.I. on the promise of silk stockings and chewing gum for life. No such luck. It was probably the teeth: the Yanks liked their women to have perfect teeth and Betty's were typically English.

Every now and again, she glimpsed up at the clock. Orwell waited for something or someone to take her out of his life. He acknowledged his own cowardice and was about to break the deadlock when a young woman approached Betty. It was one of the other secretaries at the BBC – a large, buxom girl who always seemed to be bursting out of her frock. He couldn't recall her name.

Eventually, he decided to leave while they were otherwise engaged. It was difficult for a man of his height to slip away unnoticed and he knew that he had to choose his moment carefully. Should Betty ask – and no doubt she would – the fact that he had seen the busty girl would vouchsafe the fact that he had made the effort. He resolved to end the affair at another time.

He decided while south of the river to visit the market in The Cut. After days working in the closeted atmosphere of the BBC, he missed the feeling of being amongst 'real' people, the types he had experienced on his tramps around the depressed areas of the north of England, Paris and Barcelona. He wanted to breathe and smell the working classes, the proles, and digest their lives. The Cut was his ideal place to do this.

The market next to Waterloo station had become a haven for London's ever-growing bombed-out, dispossessed and those who were 'down on their luck' as they say. These were the capital's untouchables, who flocked like the pigeons, more in desperation than hope, to the vegetable stalls around four o'clock each afternoon. Their quest was the 'mainders', the bruised, battered, perished and discarded remnants of the near-inedible and unsellable fruit and vegetables. The scene was pure Dickens and Orwell could imagine Bill Sykes or the Artful Dodger passing him in the street. Fagin was no doubt just around the corner and Oliver Twist would be begging for more somewhere among the throng. The deeper he descended into the market the more it reeked. He itched to put his gas mask on. Instead, he lit up a cigarette to disguise the odour of putrefying matter, piss and human despair. It reminded him of the markets in Burma, only worse. At least in India and Burma, the caste system was transparent and had no pretence of being otherwise. Here, class divisions were only visible in their effects and their causes remained mostly hidden. There was nothing of the colour of the Orient, just a suffocating dark bleakness beneath the already damp skies of the cold, late afternoon.

Standing head and shoulders above the scrummaging mass, his voyeurism gave way to a fit of coughing. He bent nearly double as Joe squeezed his lungs hard. His chest felt ready to explode and for one moment Orwell lost all sense of where he was and what was happening. He soon recovered enough to feel at one with the crowd. He was one of them despite the pain and a body that was giving up on him. No one attempted to speak to him or help him. So much for wartime camaraderie and cockney bonhomie, he thought.

When his lungs had relented and half-relaxed he made his way back to Waterloo Bridge. He crossed over the river, wondering how long Betty had waited for him under the clock. Each step raised another question. How would he end the affair? He didn't want to get her sacked but he couldn't carry on working with her.

The khaki and grey masses were mostly walking in the opposite direction, towards the station, and he was swimming against the tide.

Might he try to get her transferred? Bokhari would help. But what reason could he provide as justification? Incompetence? There were no grounds.

'*Standard*. Get your *Standard*!' a paper-boy shouted. He read the headline ... something about a crucial advance but he couldn't make out for which side. In that moment it didn't make any difference. Tomorrow the same headline would be used for the opposite side.

He stopped to re-light his cigarette and resumed the Betty question. It had to be promotion as she was simply too good to be wasted on him. He would give her a glowing reference and insist that Bokhari find her a better position in the BBC.

Suddenly, there was an almighty crash. The shell of a bombed-out building was being demolished and as the building collapsed some navvies stood around admiring their handiwork. A huge plume of dust hit the street and Orwell covered his nose and mouth with his handkerchief.

All things must come to an end. How would Betty take it? Why, in any case, would promotion end the affair? Surely she would want to carry on when their daily contact was less public? It would be easier to have an affair if he was not working alongside her. How could he end the relationship?

ORWELL ARRIVED home to find Eileen sitting in the dark. It was her weekly remembrance for her brother, Laurence, who had been killed at Dunkirk the previous year. 'Eric', as he had been known, though no one knew why, had been her confidant and inspiration. She couldn't call Orwell Eric as a result and he was always and forever to be George. The once bright and lively woman he had married sat on the floor with a small candle flickering next to the unlit fire. The room was freezing cold and he knew not to disturb her.

He watched her, thinking about how she had once been his lighthouse and illuminated any room at any time with her good looks, wit, common sense and a practical intelligence. That Eileen, the one he loved at first sight, was no longer in the room. Instead, this Eileen had not been in his thoughts all day. All he could do was remind himself of how things had once been. He blamed himself and then the war for bringing her to this sorry state. To make matters worse, she would never be the mother of his child.

There was only one other woman who had come anywhere near to his ideal: dear Ethel Mannin. An attractive, intelligent and uncompromising author of progressive ideals, she had once told him to 'fuck off' in front of a whole crowd of onlookers. Her Irish working-class heritage was seldom far from the surface, despite her success. The intelligentsia, communism, the middle class - she had never got into bed with any of them. Nor indeed Orwell, whom she corresponded with sporadically about each other's writing: she was an ardent admirer of his realism and he applauded her commitment to various causes. However, privately, both were circumspect about the merits of their respective efforts as novelists. They had shared a sojourn into pre-war pacifism but he had left her 'bitched, buggered and bewildered' when he told her he wanted to enlist and fight in the war. He loved that turn of phrase and repeated it to himself whenever he thought of her.

Ethel had no time for what she called his 'dilettantism' with the working class and his 'pretend socialism'. That was when she told him to fuck off back to Southwold. When she married Reginald Reynolds, the Quaker pacifist and Gandhi's intermediary in Britain, Orwell knew he had lost her forever. A subsequent review of a well-known British pacifist who he deemed to be objectively pro-Nazi had not helped matters. The argument that meeting force with force was the only effective response to fascism was now his mantra. Nevertheless, they maintained their correspondence and when their paths crossed, Orwell found himself still besotted by her.

Orwell looked at Eileen and thought that Ethel had had something of the life that Eileen was once promised. Perhaps that was at the heart of the difference between the two women.

'You stink.' Eileen rose slowly from the hearth and switched on the table lamp. 'Where've you been?'

'To the pub, to hear the news.'

They had no wireless and the Fox and Horses provided their night-time broadcasts. Orwell tended to the fire.

'You stink,' Eileen said again. 'Beer and cigarettes. George, when are you going to stop?'

He ignored her and stalled a cough his throat. This was not the time to affirm her concerns.

'How are you? Did you have a good day?' The cough burst out on the last syllable.

Eileen sat at his feet. 'Please, will you stop smoking?'

'Shall I light the fire or is it too late? We could just go to bed. Have you eaten?'

He was concerned about her health as much as she was about his.

'Have you?'

He wheezed. 'I had lunch in the canteen.'

'What was it?'

'I couldn't make out what it was – even after I had eaten it! Bully beef maybe, but it could have been cat or dog! Have you noticed how few there are around these days?'

'But you ate it?'

'Of course. Yet another of my sacrifices to the war effort!'

Eileen struggled to stand. Her tiny frame was diminishing each day and her eyes seemed to be growing out of proportion to the rest of her face. She was chalk white.

'I've some demonstration stuff Lettice dropped off. She had to do it a few times today, round and about. She didn't cook it herself, of course, but saw it being done. It's not bad. I'll put it on for you.'

'Only if you have some.'

She was not looking after herself and he wanted her to eat.

Eileen's friend Lettice Cooper worked at the Ministry of Food and she had been a godsend. Her contribution to the

BBC's Kitchen Front programmes meant she sometimes had access to the dishes she recommended on air. Each recipe needed to be trialled and tested in the BBC kitchens and Lettice was never slow in claiming her just desserts. It meant the Orwells could eat at least one half-decent meal a week. Orwell repeatedly joked about her name and couldn't help but laugh no matter how many times he spoke of Lettice serving lettuce at the ministry.

Eileen left for the kitchen. Orwell rolled himself another cigarette but thought better of lighting it and returned it to his tobacco tin.

It occurred to him that Rana had something of both Eileen and Ethel. She had Eileen's once beauty and Ethel's belligerence.

'How was your day?' Eileen shouted from the kitchenette.

Orwell got up and moved to the open adjoining door. '1-01.'

'That bad, eh?'

'Worse. Bokhari has insisted that we not only follow the belt-and-braces censorship rules, but we also submit scripts to him so that he can send them to the delegated censor in the BBC, who then sends them to the ministry – your lot. I suggested you just took them to work to save everyone the bother. "No!" he screamed, you know, in that Indian way. "The Ministry of Information insists we have the dual channel." So – and you will not believe this – not only will Bokhari see them beforehand, but so will Collins!'

'Dennis Collings? Your Eleanor's man? I didn't know he was at the BBC.'

'What do you mean, my Eleanor's man?'

'Eleanor, the great crush of your life! Your first love, or so you told me. I sometimes think she still is.'

'No! It's Norman Collins. No 'g' and no guts. The little shit from Gollancz! The one who's turned down every book I've sent them. That man has a way of getting in the way of everything I do and now he's my censor at the Corporation! What must I have done to deserve this?' He broke into a coughing fit and returned to his chair in the living room.

Eileen brought in a cup of water. 'My poor darling. You have had a bad day!' Eileen went to comfort him but he continued coughing so she held his hand. He could feel her bones and tendons through the skin. Her hands were dreadfully cold and painfully blotched purple. At last he stopped coughing and grabbed her around the waist, not wanting to let go even though she no longer felt the same way. It was though she was disappearing piece by piece, in mind and in body. He held her tight against him. Her breasts against his face had all but gone. It was his fault; he had brought this upon her.

Eileen moved away as if sensing he was exploring her curves and finding them missing. Her womanhood seemed to have abandoned her in the recent past. It was as if she no longer felt attractive and resisted the thought that he might still be aroused by her.

'Get off you daft bugger!' There was both play and order in the command.

'Why?'

'That's the why, as my mum would say. Anyway, I'm doing your supper.'

'Our supper. You need to have some as well. I'll not eat if you don't.'

Eileen avoided his look and headed for the kitchen. 'Don't be such a Jess!'

'I mean it. You have to have some.'

'All right, I will, but not much. You need all you can get to fill those boots of yours.'

'But I've been told no one can fill my boots! I'm one of a kind!' Orwell broke into a broad grin, conscious of his tea and tobacco-stained teeth that usually remained hidden.

'Too right. You're a unique silly bugger! Sit down and I'll bring it in.'

5

The thought of a nine-to-five existence had always been the antithesis of Orwell's conception of life as a proper writer. That one should submit to the discipline of an institution or work to instruction was something he had set himself firmly against from the outset. How could a writer be creative to order, work to someone else's timetable and deliver stories as if they were birthday or Christmas presents? Yet, in the routine and sheer mundane regularity of his job at the BBC he had somehow come to mitigate these previously held notions. Quite unexpectedly, as Eric Blair, he found himself becoming accommodated to the organisation and actually gaining some form of comfort from the institutionalisation of his creative drives. Planning, deadlines, schedules, censors, accountants, having too small an office, sharing a secretary and having to be nice to prospective contributors, no matter how obnoxious, had become part of his world. All these impediments did little to undermine his sense of purpose and he worked prodigiously at his task, Monday to Saturday 8.30am to 5pm, with only the occasional Tuesday taken off in lieu. A curious, symbiotic mixture of intellectual and bureaucratic energy had overtaken him and as a result his productivity was the subject of much praise and not a little envy among his colleagues, though this view was not shared by Eileen. He found himself taking some pleasure from the daily challenge of trying to be innovative whilst at the same time satisfying his immediate masters, Bokhari especially. He liked his work and sometimes enjoyed it, although he was loath to admit this to anyone, least of all to himself. He had gone native and took to the trade with all the enthusiasm of an apprentice, although he knew that there was no possibility that this would be his destination.

Whether his new energy was the product of wanting to do his best in all things or simply working alongside Rana, he could not decide. It had been over a month since she had come into his life and the nature of their interaction had already changed dramatically. She had transformed his outlook from one of endurance into one of positive appreciation of his labours. As a result he had an extravagant need just to be with her. For the first time he felt that he could cope with any amount of maladministration, pettifogging and back-stabbing malarkey that came with working at the BBC. A kind of foolishness had entered into him. Rana had become more approachable and occasionally laughed at his poor jokes. She had also shown a keen interest in his ideas, so much so that he had to keep reminding her to concentrate on the task in hand. The intensity of her interest appeared to be without limit and it concerned him. She appeared to have become infatuated with him and that was something he had never envisaged.

Despite his initial aversion to her candour and aloofness, his attraction grew ever more intense as the days went on. It was both troubling and invigorating in equal measure.

There was an inexplicable chemistry between them. Given their age difference, the burden of Joe, the fact that he was her boss, Jahida's wrath and Eileen's depression, he knew that any relationship with Rana would inevitably end in tears or worse. Despite this, he began to hope that he could be more than a father figure to her.

She was the one who suggested they meet. They had been discussing the possibility of a programme on war poetry and the topic of 'love in times of war' arose quite spontaneously. Orwell was once more thrown by her outspokenness – especially the notion that free love was a welcome product of our increasingly uncertain mortality. War, she suggested, was a perfect excuse to make love to as many people as one could, in the knowledge that you might have neither the opportunity nor the ability to do so again. In other words, war gives us a licence for licentiousness, and not just for the combatants. There was no hint of shyness or reticence in her references to sex and her explicitness left him blushing and searching for a response.

Rana's transformation was both unexpected and inexplicable. It was not just what she said and the words she used, it was that she was using a form of verbal foreplay. It was then, just when his imagination was most aroused, she had proffered the invitation of a date, although she had not used that term. That was his prosaic translation, one that seemed wholly inadequate since what she was proposing was an altogether more serious and grown-up entity, a relationship of some sort.

Throughout the remainder of that fateful day he was both excited and perplexed by her sudden forthrightness. He reflected on her tone and thought that she had sounded rather too calculating. Had the whole discussion been designed to lead to the one outcome, a sought-after relationship, or had she just seized the moment? Either way, what could she possibly find attractive in him? This was not some form of self-effacement on his part, as he had always found it difficult to understand why women were attracted to him. Even Eileen had not been able to articulate the matter to his satisfaction. He was enough of a realist to recognise himself as gaunt, sick and a bit of a bastard most of the time. Anand had once described him as 'a man's man' and Orwell mistakenly took this as some oblique reference to his sexuality and had admonished his friend severely. The last thing he wanted to be thought of was 'Nancy queer'. For all his positive qualities, such as his intellect and political astuteness, his physical negatives were high hurdles for any woman to negotiate, especially one nearly half his age and as beautiful as Rana. Little wonder he was reticent to believe that she might find him suitable as a lover. In his previous affairs he thought he had known what both parties wanted, but with Rana he had no idea. What ulterior motive might she have? He was fearful of her. She was a danger, but he didn't know why.

The practical issues involved in an affair were hardly new to him. Apart from the fling with Betty, his previous liaisons had been with women of a certain class who often had both the means and wherewithal to share the running. They also tended to pay for the necessary accoutrements and all he had had to do was make an appearance. Being seen having high tea at the Ritz with a woman writer was socially acceptable, even if it was often a precursor to supper in the bedroom. Brenda Salkeld in Southwold had been the first. Then the love of his life, Eleanor Jacques, followed by Eileen's friend Lydia Jackson and more recently Inez Holden, Stevie Smith and Hetta Crouse. His affairs nearly always started as friendships that slipped into amore, then back into either companionship or mutual recrimination. He had been completely obsessed by Hetta and had refused, in his mind, to let her escape his longing. He had even offered to leave Eileen if she dropped her proposal to wed one of his regular radio contributors, the poet William Empson. Just as with Ethel Mannin, Hetta had managed to elude the Orwell 'pounce', only in her case it had not ended in reproaches. His short *affaire amoureuse* with Stevie, another poet and novelist, told a similar tale. Stevie had thought that, in return for her intimacy, he would let her broadcast some of her poems on air. He hadn't recollected any such bargain and they had argued. She promptly withdrew access to both her work and her body.

Betty Thomas had been an altogether different proposition. She was his first and only working-class mistress. As such he had had to make the running and attend to all the practicalities – arranging liaisons in seedy hotels, day-trips to dingy seaside B&Bs under the pretext of meeting various contributors, as well as the occasional day out in the countryside, weather permitting. Luckily, Betty had not been choosy and Orwell's only rule had been to abstain from using his cottage, The Stores, in Wallington or the London flat.

With Rana there could be no question of using hotels or friend's flats. He had to find an alternative and it had to be out of the way, a place that both friends and colleagues, even enemies, would never think to venture.

He made his way to The Cut and enquired about rooms. After a half dozen fruitless efforts, often met with unrestrained incredulity that someone of his class was seeking accommodation in the area, he chanced upon a rather large costermonger. The stallholder looked at him and said nothing. Orwell, in turn, stood his ground and waited until the man's customers had gone.

The short, stocky man wiped his hands on a dirty apron, tipped his flat cap and attended to his piles of dubious fruit and vegetables.

'And what can I do you for, guv?'

'Do you know anyone with a room?'

'What, to rent?'

'Yes.'

'Round 'ere?' He raised his eyebrows and broke into a broad smile, juggling a turnip in his filthy hands.

'Yes,' Orwell said timidly.

A knowing smile crossed the greengrocer's face, revealing missing teeth on one side. A leery look took over his salmon-pink face.

'A Love-a-Duck Hotel you after?'

Orwell did not understand.

'Try Dick Crow's. He 'as a junk shop on Short Street. Just round the corner there. The ol' boy will 'elp yer.' The man tapped his nose. 'If you've the means, that is.'

Orwell thanked him but the stallholder looked somewhat aggrieved at their one-way exchange.

'Is that all?'

Orwell took the hint and pretended to be interested in the rotting fruit. 'I'll take two apples.'

'Just two?'

'Make it four – why not?'

He made his way through some of London's poorest inhabitants and, after donating the maggot-ridden apples to an unsuspecting beneficiary, escaped into Short Street. This little byway was as run down as The Cut. Small, dilapidated terraced houses competed with workshops and lock-ups for the cold, coal-stained air. The Nazis couldn't be held responsible for the misery that confronted him because the dereliction obviously pre-dated the war and was entirely home-grown.

The huge, grey blimps tethered overhead were threatening rather than reassuring and hung in the sky like giant prison wardens watching over their inmates to ensure none escaped to the more respectable areas of the City. Mothers, daughters and grandmothers – it was difficult to discern which was which – stood on the doorsteps, swapping hard-luck stories. They were mostly short, squat women with turban-style headscarves and chequered aprons. Some had their stockings around their ankles and were still wearing their slippers. A few smoked and had cups of tea in their hands. All seemed oblivious to the swarm of grubby children who played at their feet. Orwell thought the absence of their femininity was paradoxical; how could they have produced so many offspring? Who, apart from the inebriated, would want to make love to them? As he passed the throng, they stopped what they were doing and followed him with their stares, as if they had never seen a man in broad daylight, especially one so tall. A buzz went up when he had moved on a suitable distance. He realised it would be impossible to walk down this street without being noticed. Everyone probably knew everyone else's business. As such, it was hardly the best place for a secret rendezvous. Was he insane or just insanely bewitched to think otherwise?

Crow's was the only shop remaining in the street. All the others were either boarded up or falling down. The door bell clanged ferociously as he entered. The Emporium was a junk shop in everything but name, and was cluttered and bursting with all manner of wartime plunder. It did not take long to realise that the bulk of the pickings were the remains of what had been left courtesy of the Luftwaffe. Orwell was immediately struck by awful irony of someone actually benefitting from the murderous productivity of the Nazi bombers. Then again, he thought, the black market was awash with such profiteering, not to mention the arms manufacturers.

Crow was nowhere to be seen and Orwell began to inspect some of the goods. A small, carved wooden box took his attention and he lifted it up. It was made of hard wood, teak he thought, and the pattern of the carving suggested it could have been of Indian or Burmese origins. He took it to be an omen. Then, as if having crept out of the woodwork, the shopkeeper was standing next to Orwell.

'Two bob,' Crow whispered.

Orwell was taken by surprise. He turned and nearly dropped the little wooden box.

'I was just looking.'

'Nice little box that. Worth more, but special offer – today only.' Crow moved to the front of the shop and stood across the doorway as if to prevent Orwell leaving without a purchase.

The man was short and round, with a straggly grey beard, and a bald pate laced with long wispy strands of hair. His age was indeterminate. He was dressed completely in black, save a white collarless shirt. Orwell noticed how shiny his shoes were.

'Is it Indian?'

'Could well be. One and eleven and it's yours.'

'Where did you get it?'

'That's for you to ask and for me to know. A bargain, whatever its provenance.' Crow raised his eyebrows.

'One and eleven, you say?'

'Two bob.'

'But you said—'

'It's just gone back up. The price for answering all your questions.' Crow moved back into the shop and sat on a high stool behind the overflowing counter.

'I'll give you one and ten. That's all I've got.' It was an obvious lie.

'You must be a little mutton.' Crow said. It took Orwell a moment to translate the Cockney slang.

It seemed Crow would not be beaten down. In any case, Orwell wanted to get on with his main business.

'The reason I'm here is ... well, I'm looking for a room. I was told you might be able to help.'

'I might. What sort of room you looking for?'

'Occasional. For when I come to town. I sometimes have to stay over and I need a place.' It sounded even less believable than the first lie.

Crow held up his chin and looked at Orwell. '*Occasional*? Now how often would that be?'

'Weekly ... once or twice a week... at most.'

'Get a B 'n' B. You'd be better off.'

'I'd rather not. I need to come and go. You have to be up and out in a B and B.'

'An hotel then? Are you going to buy that little box?' Crow placed the box on the counter and sat on his stool.

'Do you know of a place?'

'I might do. It's still two bob, the box I mean.'

'Is the room near?' Orwell could hear the desperation in his own voice.

'Could well be. When would you want this *occasional* room?'

'Now. Well, not today, but soon. This week perhaps.'

Crow got down from his chair. 'Shut the door. Lock it,' he barked.

'What?'

'Shut the door, lock it and turn me sign! There's a lot of thieving bastards round here nowadays. Lock it and I'll show you what I got upstairs. It might interest you. Come on. I haven't got all day!'

Orwell put the latch down, pulled the bolt across and reversed the sign to CLOSED. He followed Crow through a curtain and into the back of the shop. They negotiated more detritus and went up some narrow, unsteady stairs to a small room off the landing. The door was open, revealing the grime within. It stank of damp and years of neglect. Dust covers stood in for curtains-cum-blackouts and the small fireplace had not been cleared of ash. The bed had a noticeable sag and its covers were grubby and thinning. It was probably full of fleas and other unwelcome bedfellows who had no doubt feasted on the previous occupants. What could be seen of the carpet was soiled and an undressed light bulb swung by a cord in the centre of the room. Crow turned on the hazy light and the full sordid horror was revealed in all its glory. A few mass-reproduction paintings hung drunkenly on the walls and offered a grain of respectability, though what deprivations they covered could only be guessed at. Their bucolic landscapes were as distant from the reality of the room as the moon.

'Ten bob a week and it's yours,' said Crow. He ran a finger through the dust on the mantelpiece and appeared to acknowledge the miserable state of the room.

'Ten shillings?'

'Ten bob. And use it as you will.'

'Seven?'

''Arf a knicker. That's ten shillings in your money. Take it or leave it. I've plenty of takers.'

'And I can come and go? No questions?'

'Whenever you like, with whoever you like. You're a gentleman, I can tell. But it'll still be ten bob. Now, do you want it or not?'

'Yes, yes, I'll take it.'

'And the little box?'

'That too,' he replied, and regretted the words as soon as they left his lips.

'In that case, it's just gone down again. One and ten pence ha'penny.' For the first time Crow smiled and the full glory of his jumbled yellow teeth was exposed.

'Fine,' said Orwell.

'The ten bob's up front for the room. I'll get the key. It opens the back door, down and around the side alley, if I'm not around that is. I will be, mind yer. So you can come in the front most of the time. Unless, that is, you want to mind your own ... a little privacy and all that.'

6

Crow was on his perch when they arrived and he said nothing. Rana feigned looking over the junk while Orwell went to the counter.

'Mr ... Smith, I wondered whether you were ever coming back. I was just about to re-let the room.'

'Mr Crow.'

'Please, everyone calls me Dick.' He looked away from Orwell and began a close examination of Rana – feet, legs, torso to head and back again.

Rana returned his gaze and a salacious grin spread across the old man's face. She nodded her head by way of an admonishment, then averted her eyes. Crow raised his head and pointed towards the curtain. Orwell followed his beckoning through to a passage leading from the shop to the rickety stairs. They remained silent as they negotiated the hazardous climb. Crow stopped to let them pass and retired downstairs.

Remarkably, Crow had cleared some of the junk and the fire was primed and ready to be lit. The naked light bulb continued to illuminate the cold, tawdry space. In one corner, and taking up much of the room, was the large double bed covered with an indeterminately coloured eiderdown. There were no pillows, two slush-coloured cushions had been thrown next to the wall as a substitute for a headboard. In a corner, a very small table and a solitary wooden chair stood on a mosaic of threadbare carpets and exposed floorboards that were liberally covered with paint, no doubt spilt many years previous. A muslin cloth was tacked over the small window overlooking the backyard and provided a musty veil of privacy. The very idea of making love in this soiled room only deepened the sense of squalor. Rana's disappointment was obvious but there was little Orwell could do or say that would be of any comfort. The walls echoed her disgust. Their affair, like the room, seemed destined to be a crude and demeaning experience. He quickly lit the fire and removed a bottle of red wine from his briefcase. He thought they could ignore the surroundings if he turned the light off after the fire had developed a flame.

'I'm sorry. It was the best I could do.'

'It's not what I expected,' Rana whispered.

'Or hoped for?'

'Yes, to be honest.'

'I'm sorry. It's difficult to find a place where we can come and go whenever—'

'Don't worry. I understand. I do. You did your best.'

Rana's attempt to hide her disbelief left him feeling tainted. How could he have brought her to this awful place? What had he been thinking?

He placed the solitary chair by the fire and offered it to her. As she sat down he caught her shoulder – a spontaneous attempt to make bodily contact. She took his hand. Her fingers felt warm against his. He twitched and slid his hand free. Momentarily, he felt old, vulnerable and uncharacteristically nervous. He went in search of glasses for the wine. There were none, only two tea cups from Crow's war bounty. Orwell took his pen knife from the front pocket of his briefcase and struggled with the corkscrew attachment. With the faintest of protest the cork popped and he poured the wine. He handed Rana a cup. A small piece of cork floated on the surface and she dipped her little finger into the wine to retrieve it.

'Sorry,' he said. 'I'm always doing that. I should have—'

She wiped her finger on the side of the chair. 'Don't worry so. It's only—'

'Are you warm enough?'

'Yes, are you? Your hands felt cold.'

'Nerves I reckon.'

'Nerves? Are you nervous of me?' Rana giggled. 'Let's drink. Cheers!'

They sipped the wine. It tasted cheap and bitter and Orwell noticed Rana wince as it found her taste buds.

'I'm sorry ... it's rough stuff.'

'I've had worse,' she replied. Her tone suggested his excuses were beginning to grate on her.

They stared at the fire, which was at last beginning to throw out some heat. Orwell fed it a log from the grate.

'How long have we got?' she asked.

'I have to be back at eight. We have guests and Eileen's cooking.'

Rana took another swig of the foul wine – medicine for the unease that had crossed her face.

'What time is it now?'

Orwell looked at the watch that, for once, he had remembered to wear. 'Five thirty.'

The log sparked and crackled, filling the silence for a moment.

'Shall we ... shall we get into to bed?' Rana suddenly suggested.

Orwell, taken by surprise, took a large slug from his cup. 'Yes, I'd like that.' As soon as the wine hit the back of his throat he began to cough.

'I thought you might.'

Rana went over to the bed and pulled back the covers. There were no sheets and only an old soiled, ribbed counterpane lay over the blankets. She ran her hand over the bedding, then examined her fingers. Seemingly content that there were no obvious villains, she took off her coat and hung it over the back of the chair. Orwell poured himself another drink.

'Should we wait until the bed has aired a little?' he said, trying to buy time for a smoke. The tobacco tin was already his hand. That his craving had greater weight than the yearning to make love disappointed him. It was as if the combination of the squalor and fear had all but paralysed his desire.

'Have a cigarette. It will calm you down,' Rana said. 'Is there a toilet?'

He had not thought to ask Crow and was unnerved by the question. He paused for a moment, then said he would go and enquire. Taking a roll-up from his tin, he went to the door.

Rana heard Orwell climb down the stairs and made out a muffled conversation. She looked under the bed and was relieved to discover an antiquated chamber pot. After quickly unhooking her stockings from her suspender belt and pulling down her knickers, she sat on the cold-rimmed pot and willed the flow, hoping he would take the opportunity to finish his cigarette before returning. She peed in spurts, stopping whenever she thought she heard the sound of encroaching footsteps. She wiped herself on a handkerchief and inspected the contents of the vessel. It was tinged red.

Orwell returned with a bag of wood for the fire. Rana was sitting on the bed, still dressed.

'He said we can use his lavatory. It's up the stairs on the next floor.'

'No need. I found a pot. I was desperate. I just need to empty it,' Rana said.

She reached under the bed and lifted the pot, then walked towards the door. 'Up the stairs?'

'Yes. He said you can't miss it. And make sure you pull the chain. He insisted.'

'Of course.'

Rana left the room and after a minute or two Orwell heard a flush. She returned and stood before him.

'Time of the month, I'm sorry. I'm menstruating. Not much, but it could be messy—'

He was shocked by her candour and then the realisation that he might be denied.

'Oh. Really, I —'

'It's light. We can still ... if you like. There's no need for a preventative. Every cloud?'

'Every cloud ...' he said, relieved. He had of course not thought about any contraception.

'Do you?'

'Do I what?'

'Do you still want to?'

'Of course, but—'

'But you don't want the mess? I understand'

Her demeanour was devoid of anything approaching romance and, even less, longing. The situation was beginning to annoy him. It had suffocated the adolescent-like lust he'd had for her thirty minutes ago.

'We could still go to bed .'

'If you want.'

'Let's just lie down.' Rana began to undress. 'Could you turn the light off first?'

He went to the light switch, then to the fire and poked a flame into life. It threw its shadows around the room. Some landed on Rana as she stood in her slip before climbing quickly under the covers.

He was now on show.

'I need a pee,' he spluttered, and left the room, trailing smoke.

When he returned, he turned his back on Rana and undressed slowly, deliberately folding his clothes before placing them on the floor in a neat parcel. He was wearing semi-long johns that hovered above his chalk-white knees. He kept his underpants on and almost toppled in his haste to get into the bed.

They lay still and for a full minute observed the flickering, orgiastic shadows dance around the ceiling. Rana took the initiative and her hand moved to capture his. He was still cold and struggled to find purchase on her curves as she slid his hand first to her hip, then up over her breast. She moved her hand down to his crotch and his only semi-erect penis awakened. He jolted at her discovery. Rana sat upright and pulled her slip over her head, revealing her breasts. He stared and then, when she noticed his gaze, quickly averted his eyes. She rolled herself on top of him and sat across his groin, still with her knickers on. Tentatively, almost unwilling, he fondled her breasts as she leaned over to kiss him tenderly on the cheek and then on the lips. She must have tasted the cigarettes and cheap wine because she recoiled and raised herself. Her hands moved inside his pants and felt for his erection. Thereafter, she controlled every move until he climaxed, coughing violently. By then he knew that she was experienced.

He began to get dressed. Rana was turned on her side and watched as he put on his Home Guard uniform.

'Why are you putting that on? She sat up in the bed and pulled the cover up to her neck.

'I said...to Eileen...I was on duty tonight. I had an early shift.

'You lied?'

Orwell didn't answer and reviving the fire, he spat into it and it hissed disapprovingly. Joe had begun to show his displeasure. 'Did you read the pieces I gave you?' he spluttered.

'Yes. The Hanging was rather oblique, if it was meant to be a critique of the colonial system that is. We don't know why the prisoner was being executed. What if he had killed his wife, his daughter or any other woman? Are we supposed to feel sympathy for him? If you are the witness, which you probably were, is it you we are meant to feel sorry for, for having to witness the barbarity?

'It was our common humanity that I was trying to get across. You obviously don't think I succeeded.'

' Not really. I'm sorry.'

'And Shooting the Elephant?'

Rana had read the story but didn't feel it was the moment to continue to criticise him.

'I'm still thinking about it. I thought you had to go?'

He quickly dowsed the fire with the remains of the wine and directed a look at Rana as if to say, 'you need to get up.' Rana took the hint and began to dress.

'Take the day off. Come to Wallington.' He regretted the

words no sooner than they were spoken. Still, there was no going back.

' Walling...Where's that?'

'I've a little place. It's not far but it's a bit of a trek. You catch a train from King's Cross to Baldock ...in Hertfordshire, and then a bus. You could be there by lunchtime. It's out of the way and we can have some peace and quiet. If the weather's fine, we can go for a walk in the country. I'd love to show you around.'

Rana nodded.

7

Orwell arrived back at Langdon Court at 8.30 pm. As he was late, he chanced the erratic lift. Goldstein, his elderly neighbour from the fifth floor, was already occupying the cage. Smelling of borscht or some such dish, the old man said nothing and repeatedly tucked his upper lip into his lower in a movement of manic mastication.

After just a few seconds, the lift shuddered to a halt between floors. The two men stared at each other, silent in their common plight. They waited for a minute, then Goldstein repeatedly pressed the fifth-floor button hard. It did not light up. He looked as though he had been stricken with some form of claustrophobia and began gasping and shuffling his feet. Orwell caught the smell of fear in the man's breath and withdrew to a neutral corner of the lift. Was the old émigré afraid of the uniform or dying in a cage? Perhaps both. Orwell had already reckoned that each minute spent confined with his unwelcome detainee constituted a bone fide excuse for his tardiness. He was therefore content to wait a while. Goldstein, his face now puce, looked helplessly at Orwell, as if to say, 'You're a soldier – do something!'

Orwell reached across and pressed the button once more. It lit up and the lift began to rattle upwards.

The old man looked to the heavens and mumbled a prayer of thanks. Orwell decided some unseen, benign controller was at work, one that, in his omnipotence, knew he desperately needed an excuse for being so late. He allowed Goldstein to exit and the little man scurried off, still without saying a word other than to his god. That was the difference between them. As a matter of principle, he shouted after him, 'And good night to you.' It elicited no response. Goldstein was already safely behind his front door.

Orwell stood outside the door to his flat and heard voices, although it was difficult to make out whose they were. Their high spirits would be dampened by his entrance soon enough. He itched for a cigarette but his watch told him to face the music.

'George, where have you been? We're all here, waiting.'

Eileen was unusually lively. He suspected she had already opened the wine he had been saving for a significant occasion.

'I got stuck in the lift. Didn't you hear me shout?'

'No—'

'Yes, we did but we decided to leave you there!' Mulk Raj Anand poked his head around the door.

'Bastard!' Orwell said, and began to cough.

'Did you really get stuck, *Sergeant*?' Anand saluted and held out his hand.

'Why did you take the lift? You told me not to!' Eileen said.

'How long were you in there for, old boy?' Anand asked.

Orwell thought for a moment. 'A good twenty minutes.'

'By yourself?'

'No, Goldstein was with me.'

Eileen laughed. 'Goldstein! Oh, poor George.'

Orwell raised his eyebrows, shook his head and held his nose.

'Who's Goldstein?' Anand asked.

'Our neighbour!' chorused Eileen and Orwell.

'Did you have a good chin-wag?' Eileen was smirking behind a tea towel.

'Yes, we did. After he's finished writing his fifth symphony and collected all the major art treasures of Europe, he has plans, as a Red, to take over the banks and dominate world trade. Can I get a drink now?'

'But did he really smell, George?' Eileen giggled as she poured some of the Reserve.

'Yes, he did ... like a new-born baby.'

'How would you know? Now I know you're lying!' Eileen looked him straight in the eye, then Anand. It was as if an invisible curtain had descended and her transformation was both abrupt and complete. He sensed the barb but was unsure whether it was the mention of a baby or her suspicion of his lie that had upset her. He turned to Anand, who looked away guiltily and quickly left the kitchen.

Eileen knew something and he had hit a nerve of some sort.

'And get that stupid bloody uniform off,' Eileen said.

He went to the bedroom and changed into his day clothes. A worn tweed jacket replaced the khaki tunic, transforming him from the disciplined to the dissident. The voices of the guests in the sitting room became more animated and, not being able to delay any longer, he went to investigate the commotion.

The conversation ceased with his entrance. Stevie Smith was already semi-comatose as she had a habit of dozing off at every opportunity. Indeed, to see her awake at this hour was something of a rarity. Stevie grizzled perpetually, especially when, often disparagingly, Orwell referred to her as the bard of Palmers Green, that frayed hem of London's skirt she inhabited. Their falling-out had definitely soured relations even more of late. Yet, she always returned to the fold whenever invited by Orwell, who still felt a pang of guilt over their tryst. Keeping Stevie in the inner circle was a sort of penance.

Eileen, on the other hand, did everything she could to exclude Stevie from the guest list. Too depressing, she complained, especially when Stevie arrived in one of her regular bouts of self-obsessed morbidity. Why did he insist she be invited? she asked. In Eileen's opinion only George appeared to appreciate her artistic or literary merit.

Stevie was indeed dressed in her inimitable schoolgirl style – dark pleated skirt, white blouse and ankle socks. She half-tumbled as she greeted Orwell and he only just managed to catch her before she fell.

'Oh, George, anything for a fondle!' she said as she rearranged her blouse and pecked him on the cheek.

Inez Holden looked on, seemingly trying not to appear embarrassed. It was Inez who had introduced Stevie to him the previous year, though he sensed she now deeply regretted it. A competent and articulate woman, Inez was also a writer and journalist. She'd been a willing victim of what she had coined the Orwell 'pounce'. For nearly six months they had been meeting regularly, and this was known to Eileen, or at least Inez had been led to believe that was so. Orwell had explained his desire for other women and insisted that Eileen was party to his needs and had no objections to his seeking fulfilment in that regard. Although Inez had not been entirely convinced by this explanation, she had only diluted the relationship rather than dissolved it. Their liaisons were now far less frequent and more fleeting, and the sexual element was becoming secondary to their companionship.

Orwell surveyed the remainder of the assembly.

'Inez, Bill, Hetta ... Where's the little lady, Mulk?'

'Kathleen's pregnant,' Anand announced sharply.

Now Eileen's earlier caustic comment made sense. He tried to put that aside and act as normal.

'Who's the father?' Orwell smiled. 'It wasn't me, I promise! Congratulations ... and commiserations. Did you hear that, Eileen? Kathleen is pregnant? And there's a vicious rumour that Anand is the father!' he shouted towards the kitchen.

Eileen came into the sitting room. She was back to her sullen self. 'Yes, he told us earlier, when you weren't here. And stop teasing him, George. Everyone knows *you* couldn't be the father.'

Bill Empson got up, saying he had to relieve himself. He gently touched Hetta's face and, as he passed Orwell, held out his hand.

Orwell looked him in the eye and reluctantly shook Empson's hand. 'I believe congratulations are also in order.'

'Thank you, George, for the knife and fork. It was very thoughtful of you.'

'Knife and fork? What the bloody hell are you talking about?' Stevie Smith shouted.

'George's wedding present to us,' Hetta said, in her thick Afrikaans accent.

'I'm sorry I couldn't make the wedding.'

'He was too jealous,' Eileen snapped.

'Jealous?' Stevie asked, sounding completely confused.

'He wanted to marry Hetta himself.' Eileen poured herself a drink and took a large swig.

Anand tried to divert the conversation. 'I think we should just congratulate Hetta and Bill. To Hetta and Bill!'

Stevie Smith raised her glass and spilt some of the contents. 'Jesus, what a waste! Oh, not Bill! I meant the wine.'

'To Hetta and Bill ... Oops, shouldn't we have waited?' Anand looked towards the door. There was a frozen pause as Bill Empson returned, clearly registering the distinctly saturnine air in the room.

'What's up? Are my flies undone?'

There was a slight crack in the atmosphere and a few strangled laughs before the silence resumed.

'To Hetta and Bill!' Anand said again.

'And the BBC for bringing these lovebirds together!' said Orwell.

Anand waved his hand towards Stevie. 'Give us something for Bill and Hetta.'

Stevie rose and looked directly at Orwell. 'It was my bridal night, I remember ... I can't bloody remember ... oh, yes, I'm going to call it "I Remember". And this is a slight adaptation because I can't bloody remember! Here goes, a new poem. "It was my bridal night, I remember. An old man of forty or fifty or so. I lay with my young bride in my arms. A man with TB. It was wartime, and overhead the Germans were making a particularly heavy raid on ... St. John's Wood? George – no, Bill – Bill, do they ever collide? I do not think it has ever happened. Oh my bride, my bride."'

There was another embarrassed silence as Stevie flopped back into her chair. Anand broke into a round of applause and the others followed, if only to break the silence. Orwell felt the need to say something.

'An adaptation? I'm sure Bill and Hetta appreciated it nevertheless. Thank you, Stevie.'

Eileen looked distinctly unimpressed.

Orwell hoped the irony had not been detectable in his voice but Inez, who had been sitting impassively throughout, had recognised it. Orwell gently touched her shoulder as he passed her on his way to his captain's chair at the head of the table. She had more than suspicion in her eyes. Although she could not possibly know about Rana, he sensed she had somehow intuited he was involved with another woman.

'Were you working, tonight?' Inez asked without a shred of innocence in her tone.

'Home Guard. I was on duty.'

'Are you busy at work?'

'Yes, very. It's a madhouse. I think we should rename it The Bedlam Broadcasting Corporation.'

'And have you a secretary?'

'Yes, I share one.'

'Very pretty too,' Anand added unhelpfully. 'I've seen her. Betty, isn't it?'

'Pretty is she, George?' Inez smiled falsely and knowingly.

Orwell did not answer.

'And he also has two or three very pretty Indian maids working for the Pukka Sahib,' Anand added mischievously.

Inez looked at Orwell and raised her glass. 'To the leopard that never changes its spots. Happy hunting, George.'

Eileen had sat down on an easy chair by the hearth. She stared into the fire, which was barely managing to stay alive. Anand went over and filled her glass.

'Thinking of Laurence?' he asked.

Eileen looked as if she were about to cry. She sipped the wine and held out her hand. Anand took it and crouched down next to her.

'I'm pleased for you and Kathleen. Is she happy?'

Anand did not answer. Instead, he filled a small coal shovel with some nuggets of anthracite from a nearby bucket. He stoked and poked the fire.

'Are you happy?' Eileen asked.

'How can anybody be happy in wartime?' Anand replied. 'It's no time to be bringing children into the world, especially here of all places, and now of all times.' He looked at Eileen, then averted his eyes.

'Mulk, how can you say that? You know George and I have been trying.'

'Yes, I know. I'm so sorry. It was callous of me. I didn't think.'

'Are we going to eat?' Orwell demanded, half-expecting Eileen to spring into action.

'It's ready … in the oven,' Eileen replied wearily, and remained seated.

'I'll get it then.' He reluctantly raised himself from his chair and went towards the kitchen.

'I'll help you,' Inez said, and followed him.

Orwell donned an oven glove and grabbed a tea towel. He lifted out a large casserole dish. It was piping hot and steam quickly enveloped the room and misted the window. Inez stood and watched.

'You bastard, George.'

'What?'

'Look at Eileen. Have you no heart? Look what you're doing to her.'

'She's unwell and she's drunk,' he said as he gathered the plates from a rack above the stove.

'You're playing around again.'

'Who told you that?'

'No one. I don't need to be told. I can see it. It's written all over your face and the way you act. I've seen it for myself.'

'Well, you're wrong. I'm not having an affair.'

'And you're a rotten liar! What about me? What do you call what we've been doing? And now there's someone else. I can tell, George. What's more, I think Eileen can as well. Open your eyes.'

Inez grabbed the plates off him and went back into the living room.

He stood by the stove, wanting to be somewhere else, anywhere. He gathered himself and took the casserole into the living room.

'What have we here? Smells divine and I'm starving,' Stevie Smith burbled, just managing to prop herself up at the table.

'Hot-pot,' Orwell said.

Hetta leaned towards the table. 'Hot-pot?'

'It's Lancashire hot-pot, but only mutton. It's impossible to get lamb, except on the black market, and the price is ridiculous. So I'm afraid it's mutton dressed as lamb tonight.'

Anand rose and stood next to Orwell. 'Behold the mighty Englishman. He rules the Indian small, because being a meat-eater he is five cubits tall.'

'Bollocks, Mulk. You eat meat as much as I do so let's have less of that,' Orwell said sternly.

'Just being polite to my hosts. When in Rome ...'

Eileen picked at her food, pushing vegetables around her plate and only occasionally lifting a half-empty fork to her mouth. She continued to drink and, before the others had finished eating, lit a cigarette and allowed some ash to fall into her food. Orwell noticed but continued eating. Stevie Smith appeared barely conscious, yet somehow managed to clear her plate, then helped herself to Eileen's left-overs, seemingly ignorant of their cigarette seasoning. What little Bill Empson said seemed to drift off like thought-balloons into the ether. No one appeared to be interested in his proselytising for something called Basic, a truncated form of English comprised of only 850 words. Stevie Smith thought the whole idea philistine – not only would it diminish the language but murder the whole notion of beauty, truth, pain and emotion. It would be the language of machines, she declared.

'There would be no need for poets or writers,' Inez added.

'The fascists would love that,' said Anand.

Orwell sat and said nothing. He was thinking about someone else.

Surprisingly for an aesthete and poet, Empson continued to make the case for the synthetic language. Only Hetta remained attentive and held his hand as though to prevent him from floating off along with his abstractions. Anand stared at Orwell knowingly and when their eyes met, they both looked down at their plates.

As the evening progressed and the drinks flowed, the talk was mainly of the immanent fall of the East and the Japanese treatment of the Chinese, about which Empson had particular knowledge in his role as a producer in the China Section of the Empire Service. He was doing for China what Orwell had been tasked to do for India, only with far more success, it was generally felt. Hetta chipped in with an account of her recent Afrikaans broadcast, intended to counter Nazi entreaties to the Boers. If Orwell felt he was wasting his time, Hetta's task seemed even more pointless and it was by no means clear what, if anything, she might have said in the programme that could possibly have turned any South African blockheads.

As they moved on to the whisky Empson had provided, Orwell got into his stride and went into a long diatribe about under-population, an inopportune topic at the best of times, let alone with Eileen's current state of mind.

'There should be a tax on childless couples. The country needs children. We should throw abortionists into the sea and abolish contraception,' he suggested.

'Just because you have no need George, doesn't mean everyone fires blanks,' Eileen replied caustically.

'Are you a Catholic?' Empson asked naively.

'Am I fuck. No, we have a population shortfall and we need to do something about it. There aren't enough Roman candles to make up the numbers we need. In any case, there's too many Catholics already,' Orwell shouted, his voice hitting a new pitch.

His proposals were met with derision by the women around the table. Stevie Smith even likened him to Hitler. That was not enough to stop the tirade.

'And the Yanks. Their women are now so obsessed with their figures that they aren't having kids as a result. It's madness. And the bloody feminists—'

'Nonsense, George,' said Inez. 'You're drunk.'

'Women, women who wear scanty panties have never had a comfortable fire burning in the hearth, or a baby, or a cat or a dog.' The thought had come to Orwell from nowhere.

Stevie Smith stirred for a moment and added dryly, 'Or a canary. I've never had a canary.'

Everyone found this amusing, except Orwell who was

revelling in the outlandishness of his argument and deliberately stirring up controversy.

'And everyone knows that all scout leaders are homosexual. And priests masturbate more than any other men.'

The comment was met with even louder rebukes from around the table.

Eileen became ever more morose and reprimanded him. 'What evidence have you got for any of this, George? None. None at all. It's just your fantasy and fears, if you ask me.'

Orwell became silent and sullen. The tension between them was palpable.

No one mentioned the India Section, not even Anand.

8

ORWELL WAS TAKEN ILL WITH BRONCHITIS AT THE BEGINNING of December. Joe was also attacking his lungs and as a result he had to take two weeks sick leave. Consequently, Rana's visit had had to be postponed. Against both his doctor's and Eileen's advice, he went to Wallington rather than a TB sanatorium to recuperate and was soon over the worse. He arranged to meet Rana while Eileen was staying with her sister in Greenwich.

Rana arrived in Wallington and almost immediately was the subject of curiosity and not a little suspicion. There she was, a young Indian woman arriving alone without a suitcase in a comatose patch of the Home Counties, mid-morning in November and during a war. It was as good a recipe for attracting attention as one could possibly devise. As arranged, Orwell was not there to meet her – on reflection a rather odd and unnecessary precaution for there was only one topic of gossip in the village the minute she got off the bus – '*what with his wife being away and all*' – and headed towards The Stores.

There was a little bell on the otherwise bare counter and

when Orwell failed to appear, she gave it a gentle ring. Nothing. Then a louder ring. A minute or two later he ducked under the low door. His shirt sleeves were rolled up to his elbows and braces held up his dark-green corduroy trousers. He wore muddy Wellington boots, indicating he had been in the garden. A roll-your-own cigarette was stuck to his lower lip as he broke into a sheepish half-smile.

'You've found me then?' he said.

'Yes, I'm here. Did you think I wouldn't come?' There was more than a hint of rhetoric in her response.

'I had no idea. Really, I didn't know what to expect but I'm glad you've come. Come on through.'

There was something different about her: she was wearing makeup – dark eye liner, rouge and her lips were a brighter red than usual. He wasn't sure whether he liked the effect. Did it cheapen her? Did Eileen wear makeup?

He showed Rana into the main living room where, on first encounter, the low ceiling incubated an overpowering odour of tobacco. Rana stopped herself from pinching her nose and instead took a deep breath. He led her through to the small scullery where another, less powerful but vaguely familiar, smell was present.

'It's Muriel, the goat. That's what we call her.'

'I thought it might be – a goat that is.'

'Do you like goat's milk?'

'No. Not really. It reminds me too much of home.'

'Stepney Green?' he replied and grinned.

Rana felt edgy and elected not to respond.

'Can I get you some tea?'

'Yes, thank you. But no milk, please.' She broke into a smile-cum-grimace and nervously looked away. He went to the sink and filled the kettle. He was too thin, though his arms at least were still quite muscular. He reminded her of one of those station porter wallahs in Calcutta whose strength belied their emaciated appearance.

'Sit down. Make yourself at home. It's not a castle but it's home. My country retreat.'

'Not your only house though?'

'No ... well, yes, in the country it is, actually. The London flat is temporary and it's rented. This is where I'd live if I didn't have to work in town. Sugar?'

Rana noticed the singular possessive and wondered how Eileen felt about the place. There was little evidence of a woman's touch.

'You have some?'

'It's The Stores. I think I have some.' He fumbled around in the cupboard next to the stove and took out a brown paper bag. 'Ah, here we are.'

'Three then, please'.

'You like it sweet, the Indian way.'

'Yes, thank you.'

Rana looked around the room, surprised by how sparse and ramshackle it was. Uncomfortably dirty too. He had trodden muck from the garden into the mat by the stove and vegetable peelings, old boxes and buckets of waste surrounded the kitchen table. Newspapers lined the floor leading out to the back door and a cold draught ran through a clearly cracked pane of glass in the window. The only heat came from a small wood-burning stove and she caught sight of her own breath. He brought two large, sturdy mugs over to the table.

'Our best China.'

'Aren't you cold?' Rana asked.

'Are you? I'm sorry, I should have realised. When you're digging out there, you don't notice it. In fact, you don't really notice anything. It's my escape from everything, even when the ground is as hard as rock. We've had some hard frosts. After two weeks out here I think I care more about my vegetables than what's happening in the war! Here, pull your chair up to the stove. I'll light the fire inside.'

He went into the living room and Rana heard him clearing his lungs. She cradled the hot tea and noticed a picture of Eileen above the hearth. She rose to inspect it. Eileen was younger than she had imagined, also prettier. The sun disappeared behind a cloud and for a moment threw the room into semi-darkness. Rana took it as sign that she should leave. She thought about what might become of the remainder of the day and realised she had no idea when the last train for London departed. Neither was she sure that she had the nerve to go through with this.

'Come on through,' he shouted from the living room.

Rana took both their teas with her. The living room resembled a ransacked library. Books lay strewn everywhere. He was drawing the flames by holding a sheet of newspaper up against the fireplace. As soon as he had a blaze he withdrew the browning paper and threw it onto the fire. He then moved the two-seater settee closer to the heat.

'What time is the last train back?' Rana asked.

'Four fifteen, I believe,' he said softly and with a hint of disappointment. 'You've only just got here and you're thinking of going?'

'No, it's just that ... well, you know how busy we all are at the moment.'

There was a silence while he tended the fire. It gave her time to think.

'Then why did you come?'

'You asked me,' she said abruptly.

'Is that the only reason? That I asked you?'

Rana paused and drank some of the treacle-brown brew. 'You like your tea very strong. It's not to my taste.'

'Yes, I'm sorry. It's an old habit. I forget sometimes. And Eileen ... she's always reminding me to cut down on the leaves. Are you sure you'll have no milk?'

'I'm sure, thank you. I saw the picture next door. I presume that's Eileen.'

'Yes, well, it was. It was taken some time ago now.'

'She's very pretty.'

'Yes, she was. Well, she still is of course. Only she's not been too well lately. That's why she doesn't like coming here.'

He reached for his tobacco tin and Rana hoped he would not smoke.

'What's wrong with her?'

'Physically, you mean?' The half-joking face had returned. 'Sorry, no, we don't know what's wrong. She's having all sorts of tests. They can't decide or she won't tell.'

He rolled his cigarette between his fingers and took a taper from the grate to light it. Almost immediately the acrid smell of his strong Turkish shag ascended and he began to smother another cough.

'And you're not well.'

'No, but I never have been. Not to worry though. I can still write! Joe hasn't killed me yet.'

'Joe?'

'My nemesis. It's my pet name for whatever it is that's eating my lungs.'

'Why Joe?'

'Uncle Joe ... Stalin. I thought it appropriate.'

He allowed himself a catarrh-filled cough. 'Yes, these bloody lungs have never quite done their job. I'd love to trade them in for some new ones. I sometimes think we should all be born with spares. I could open a shop. Just think how much we'd make in wartime!'

The casual way he discussed his predicament seemed to confuse her. Her usually terse, sometimes officious BBC boss was obviously more relaxed in this environment, almost as though his accursed cough was occupying an entirely different person.

She appeared to be studying him as he took another long drag on his roll-up and exhaled the smoke through his nose.

She looked older, perhaps more mature, he thought. Her complexion was even darker in the muted fire light and her normally bright eyes were less prominent despite the makeup. Through her unbuttoned coat her conservative dress sense was still apparent. He noticed her hands were beginning to shake.

'Are you still cold?'

'A little. I'll be fine soon. That's a good fire.'

'Would you like some whisky in your tea?'

'Do you have any? I don't usually drink so early but I might try. Thank you.'

'Let's say for medicinal purposes.'

'No, I'm most well.'

'I know. We just say that as an excuse sometimes. I wasn't suggesting you're ill.'

'I don't really have to have an excuse, do I? Can't I just say I'd like to try it?'

'Of course you can. I'll find it.'

He went to a small side-board and brought out a bottle. He poured a small measure into Rana's tea and a larger glug into his own. He stood by the fire and raised his tea mug.

'Cheers. Bottoms up!'

'Cheers.'

She took a sip and her face contorted. 'It's good. I think I like it. Goodness, it warms you up right here.' She slid her hand from her throat to her stomach, following the heat.

'What shall we drink to?' he asked. 'India? Independence?'

'Yes, to India and independence!'

'And an end to the war.'

'Most certainly. To all wars.'

They sat for what seemed like minutes and studied the flickering fire in silence. Neither exchanged glances. Eventually Orwell broke the impasse.

'Let me show you around.' He went to the kitchen and returned before she had chance to move. He had donned an old grey greatcoat and held a pair of Wellington boots.

'You'll need these,' he said.

'Eileen's?'

'Yes. There should be socks in them.'

Rana obviously had no wish to wear his wife's socks or boots, even less to take a tour of the cold English countryside. But she put on the Wellingtons all the same while he went back to the kitchen and returned bearing more attire, this time a hat, scarf and gloves.

'You'll also need these. The sun has gone and it gets perishing.'

As they walked the country lane to the village, he wasted no time in impressing Rana with his detailed knowledge of the flora and fauna. Every living thing was identified and classified. He seemed in his element.

He smoked and coughed, giving any animals or humans within earshot plenty of time to hide themselves. As a result they saw neither on their tour. It was as if the entire village had gone into hiding. The net curtains were undoubtedly twitching as they arrived at Main Street with its row of country cottages, a garage with a solitary pump, and two small public houses. Including The Stores, this appeared to be the sum total of civilisation in Wallington. By the time they reached the village green, Rana understood how completely immersed he was in this rural idyll.

'We can get some grub in The Plough if you like.'

'Is that wise?'

'What do you mean?' He seemed puzzled by her question.

'Your neighbours. They'll see me.'

He chuckled. 'They've already seen you. Nothing and no one passes them around here. It's impossible to have a pee in private! Metaphorically speaking, that is.'

'Won't they talk?'

'Of course they will. You'll be the subject of every conversation for at least the next month.'

'And what will they say?'

'The usual.'

'And what's that?'

'You know, he's having an affair, or worse.'

Rana paused as they got to the door of the pub. 'The usual?'

'I meant that's what their small minds would naturally conclude. Why? What else did you take it to mean?'

'The word implies regularity or normality' Rana tilted her head, awaiting his response.

'I didn't mean it like that. It's interesting, isn't it, how you thought that? Would you be jealous?'

Rana looked away and stood with her back to him.

'Or worse – and what did you mean by that?'

'If you want, let's go back.'

'What did you mean?'

'They probably think you're ... a prostitute or something like that.'

'Do I look like one? Too much makeup?'

'No, of course not. Come on, let's go back. I'll make you some lunch at the shop.'

Rana turned and faced him. 'No, let's go in. I'd like to go in.'

The pub was no bigger than his living room. Two customers sat on a bench adjoining an open fire and the landlord was at the bar reading a newspaper and smoking – a gross man with unkempt black, greased-down flecks of rapidly disappearing hair, wearing a collarless shirt and waistcoat. He looked up, effecting a show of minimum interest before averting his eyes to the two regulars and throwing a knowing nod.

'Mr Orwell, good to see you again.'

'Nelson.'

'What can I get you, sir? Or rather, where's me manners, what can I get you, miss? Ladies first!'

'Have you any food?' said Orwell.

'I think we can do you a sandwich, sir. We've ham and cheese and onion. But we've no eggs today. The missus hasn't laid any!'

Orwell ignored the humour and looked at Rana. She thought for moment.

'Cheese and onion. And I'll have a gin with lemon, thank you.'

'Sorry, miss. No lemons.'

'Tonic water?'

'Not at this time. Lemonade?'

'Thank you.'

'That'll be one cheese and one ham with mustard. And I'll have a pint of your best.'

'Righty oh. Is that it?'

Orwell nodded and the landlord went to deliver the order to the kitchen. Rana and Orwell moved two stools to the end of the bar, away from the landlord's perch. The two men by the fire occasionally stole glances their way. Rana watched Orwell go through the rolling ritual – the plucking of the tobacco, the laying out on the paper, the initial forward roll, then the reverse, the moistening of the gum side with his tongue, and finally the snipping of any escaping strands. He smothered small coughs as if in anticipation of the cigarette's effect.

The landlord delivered their drinks. Minutes later his wife came through the curtain separating the bar and kitchen. She was as large as her husband, ruddy, and with pendulous breasts. A headscarf captured her hair. She carried two plates on which the huge sandwiches competed with her breasts.

'Ham?' she asked, in a shrill voice.

Orwell indicated.

'Is that all?' the buxom woman asked.

'Desperate Dan would be proud.'

'I beg your pardon?'

Orwell thought for a moment. 'I said, they'll do us proud.'

The landlady stood and stared at him, as if computing what to say. 'It's Mr Orwell, isn't it?'

He nodded and the landlady looked directly at Rana.

'And how is *Mrs* Orwell?'

'Very well. I'll tell her you enquired.'

'Is there anything I can get for you, young lady? You don't look like you're from 'round here.'

'No, I'm from India. I work at the BBC in London with Mr Orwell.'

'Yes, Miss Mukurjee is my assistant. We work on radio programmes together. We have some business to attend to now so if you would excuse us. And thank you for the sandwiches.'

The landlady was obviously smarted by Orwell's curt response. 'Of course. Enjoy your lunch.'

Just before the landlady disappeared behind the curtain she turned and said, 'You're the second dark— Indian here today.'

'What do you mean?' Rana asked.

'A gentleman, Indian by the look of him, like yourself, I mean. Dark skinned. Really dark. He was in earlier. Wanted a cup of tea. So I gets him one. No milk but he wanted a heap of sugar. I says it's rationed and I only gave him one. Turned 'is nose up, he did, the cheeky blighter.'

'What time was this?' Rana said, agitated.

'Just as we opened. Twelve it must have been.'

'Did he say why he was here?' said Orwell.

'No. He just wanted a cuppa tea.'

'What did he look like?'

'Told yer, Indian looking. Darker than the young lady though.'

'What else?'

'I dunno. Youngish. Twenty or so. They always look younger than they are. Black hair though, lots of it. Very oily and needed a cut. And dark eyes.'

'Was he tall or small?'

'Short, about the young lady's size, I'd say,' said the landlord.

'Short?' Orwell repeated.

The landlord guffawed. 'Certainly shorter than yerself!'

'And he didn't say what he wanted or what he was doing here?'

'None of our business,' the landlady said as she went through the curtain.

Orwell turned to Rana.

'Could be Anand.'

'Were you expecting him?'

'No, but he's been here before. Once. I wouldn't describe him as young though.'

'Then where is he now?'

'Probably at the shop.'

'Do you want to go and find him?'

'Yes, I'll go. You stay here. I'll bring him back if he's there.'

'But ... do you want him to know that I'm here?'

'It'll be all right. He's a good chap. I won't be long.'

He returned fifteen minutes later and longer than it should have been, thought Rana.

Orwell came through the door, shaking his head. ' No one. Not a sign. No note. Nothing. If it was Anand, he would have left a note or come back here to the pub and waited. It's a complete mystery.'

'I was thinking, why are we assuming, just because he's Indian, he's looking for you or me?' Rana asked.

'It could be a coincidence, I suppose.'

'Yes, why not?'

'It's strange though, two Indians in Wallington on the same day. What are the chances of that? Did you see anyone Indian on the train?'

'No, and I was the only one to get off the bus here.'

They settled down to their drinks and sandwiches. Rana tried to rationalise the incident but she was unsettled.

In a whisper, he suddenly asked, 'Why did you tell her that?'

'Who? What?'

'The landlady ... that you worked with me at the BBC.'

'I *do*.'

'But why tell her?'

'Why not? Doesn't she know you work there?'

'No'

'Why not?'

'They think I'm an author.'

'But you are an author and you work at the BBC.'

'But they think I'm *just* an author.'

'I'm sorry, but what difference does it make?'

This whole exchange felt like a pretext for an argument and Rana suspected he wanted her to leave. They continued to eat but their efforts left little impression on the plate. Not much of consequence passed between them over the remainder of the lunch – a few asides about the forthcoming programmes and the various contributors, some gossip about colleagues and some common complaints about the rationing situation.

As they left the pub, Orwell turned to Rana. '3.15.'

'I'm sorry?'

'There's an earlier train, at quarter past three from Baldock. I can get a local to run you there.'

'Do you want me to go?' Rana said.

'No, it's just that... I just thought you might want to get back early.'

'Do you want me to stay?'

'Do you want to?'

'I do, but only if you want me to.'

'Stay. We can finish our discussion about Shooting the Elephant.'

9

An emergency meeting of the Eastern Services Indian Section Planning Committee had been called for 9am in Room 1-01. It was 2nd January and Bokhari was insistent that, Hitler or high water, all were to attend. Extra chairs had been arranged around the fringe of the meeting table. The heating had not been on since Christmas and the room felt as cold as an ice store. The usual participants filed into the freezing chamber, their breath visible as they exchanged salutations on the New Year. By 9.15 the room was full and Orwell, late as usual, took his place.

The cold air hit him and he smothered a cough. There were some familiar and not so familiar faces in addition to the usual corridor acquaintances. Betty had made sure she was not directly next to Orwell and Rana was seated on the perimeter.

The meeting was called to order by Professor Rushbrook Williams, the Eastern Services director.

'Gentlemen, please may we begin? This is a very important meeting and I would ask that you please pay close attention. No doubt you wish to know why you have been called to this meeting. You will find out shortly.'

With a balding pate and crinkled skin of burnt ochre, Rushbrook Williams bore all the hallmarks of an old-school India time-server. As an academic, fellow of All Souls Oxford and Professor of Modern History in Allahabad, he had spent much of his professional life serving the Raj. He was everything Bokhari aspired to be. So it was with obvious pride that Bokhari was asked by Rushbrook Williams to make an initial statement.

Bokhari stood, face ashen. His opening words had a gravitas that signalled a mournful message was to follow.

'Thank you, Professor Williams. I will try to be as succinct as your good self.' Bokhari's obsequiousness was never more in evidence. 'Gentlemen, ladies, this meeting has been convened at the behest of Mr R.A. Rendall, the Director of Empire Services here at the BBC. Unfortunately, Mr Rendall is ill-disposed and cannot be with us today. Colleagues from the Ministry of Information, the India Office and our own Home Service are also in attendance. You are all most welcome, gentlemen. Without further ado, may I introduce Mr Robert Brock of the Indian Section of the Ministry of Information. Mr Brock has oversight for our broadcasts and he wishes to inform you about a very important and disturbing development that occurred yesterday.'

Brock sat next to Bokhari. He was middle-aged, very short, stocky with flat, oiled grey hair. He was dressed quite anonymously and when he stood it made little impression due to his diminutive stature. Orwell could hardly believe he was face to face with a member of the College. This was the man who, for the past three months, had vetoed and proscribed any number of his scripts and initiatives. And Brock was just how Orwell had imagined the MinInform censor to be: one of those nonentities you could quite easily pass in the street without changing one's step.

'Gentlemen, may I have your attention, please? Sorry, *Ladies* and Gentlemen ...'

Orwell detected an accent, and muttered loud enough for those around him to hear, 'He just had to be a Scot.'

'Yesterday, we received confirmation from your Monitoring Service here at the BBC that the fugitive Indian nationalist, a Mr Subhas Chandra Bose, who some of you will be familiar with, has started to broadcast from Berlin. Yes, it appears that he has thrown in his lot with our enemies. His radio station is called Azad Hind—'

'Free India,' Bokhari interjected.

'Yes, indeed, Free India. We now know it is in fact an Axis-Nazi front. They are putting out pure propaganda designed to inflame the sub-continent precisely at this time of rising tension. The Japanese threat should not be underestimated. Singapore, Malaysia, Burma are all in their sights and, if they do fall, India will surely follow. This blackguard Bose wishes to encourage mutiny in the ranks of those Indians who have come to the aid of the empire in this, *our* moment of greatest need. Currently, there are at least two million Indian volunteers fighting for the Allied cause ... our freedom and theirs.' Brock paused and read from his papers before proceeding. 'Bose's words are crude and his message is very simple: he wishes to see us defeated so that India may gain its independence *today*. Thus he believes that by allying himself to the Nazis and the Japanese he can achieve that end sooner rather than later. If I may, I will give you a flavour of his approach. This is from his New Year broadcast, just yesterday "*The world is divided into two parts, one containing the healthy advancing nations of the world, and the other containing the idle, boastful and wealthy. Only those who are prepared to sacrifice their lives unstintingly will be victorious. The price of freedom is sacrifice. Japan has shown India that the wealthy and strong British are, after all, not very strong.*" I'll not continue. I think you all can gather from that what this evil little man is trying to provoke. Which is where we come to your contribution. We need to redouble our efforts to counter his vile propaganda. We need to keep the Indian people, at least the ones that matter, on our side. And I have it from the highest authority, the prime minister himself, that under no circumstances must India be lost. The entire empire is at stake, gentlemen ... and ladies, of course.'

Brock stopped, and looked around the room, seemingly to gauge the reaction. There was none. Most of the assembly sat with their heads down and eyes averted.

'Just because Bose is an Indian does not make him less of a threat. Yes, Bose calls himself a nationalist, but as of now he is also a Nazi, a fascist and a supporter of the Axis powers. He is a traitor to India's cause and he deserves whatever we can throw back at him. For that reason, we need you to sharpen your response and fight fire with fire. Your work has become not just useful to the war effort but absolutely vital. I trust you will respond to this threat with an unbridled commitment to our mission. Together, we can defeat this black angel. Heed his own words, I beg you: "The price of freedom is sacrifice." Indeed, not just India's but our own freedom requires your sacrifice. Thank you for your attentiveness and good luck! I'll not detain you any longer from this essential task. Mr Bokhari will co-ordinate our efforts.'

Orwell was taken aback by the sheer effrontery of the man. 'The black angel'! Had he no conception of his audience? This blue-pencil wielder obviously had no idea who he was addressing. There were brown and black faces all around and all were Indian nationalists of one hue or another.

As Brock resumed his seat, a discordant hum went around the room and clusters of whispered conversation broke out. Bokhari called the meeting to order as Orwell looked at Rana. A broad smile crossed her usually beatific face, one that broke with her usual inscrutability. He thought it odd and wondered why she was so pleased with what she had just heard? Was it that she agreed with Bose that the world was indeed divided between the idle rich imperialist powers and the poor trying to escape their yoke? He hoped so. He would love her if that were so. But what if she agreed with Bose's alliance with the Nazis as a means to achieve India's independence? He would have to hate her if that were the case. In fact, he would hate her with all his being. Come what may, he was determined that today was the day he would find out what she really thought.

Before Orwell could leave his seat, Bokhari was upon him, pressing his shoulder to restrain him from leaving. 'Blair, may I introduce you to Mr Guy Burgess?'

A tall, lean, inordinately smiley and youthful looking man stood to the side of Orwell's chair. An overpowering smell of aftershave filled Orwell's lungs and made him wheeze. Burgess had to step back to allow Orwell to stand to his full height. They shook hands, very lightly. Orwell immediately noticed the tie: Burgess was an Old Etonian. He averted his eyes before Burgess noticed his recognition.

'Mr Burgess is doing your job in the Home Service talks,' Bokhari said. 'I suppose he's your opposite number over there.'

'George Orwell, isn't it?' Burgess almost giggled through a cut-glass accent.

'Yes, but I'm also known as Eric Blair – my real and sometime BBC name.'

'How splendidly confusing! Your nom-de-plume or rather nom-de-guerre at the BBC? What shall *I* call you?' Burgess smiled and stood expectant.

'Whatever you want,' Orwell replied gruffly.

'We must meet sometime ... to swap notes on this rum affair with Bose. We, or rather the War Office chaps, had no idea where the man was apparently. My friends over there thought he was already in Japan or Bangkok or some such place. Turns out he's living the life of Riley on Sophienstrasse, which I seem to remember is a very pleasant and respectable part of Berlin. They say the Nazis are bankrolling him majestically. Looks like 1857 all over again!'

'1857?' Orwell had lost the thread of Burgess's declaration.

'The Great Indian Mutiny,' said Bokhari.

'Oh, yes, of course. I wasn't quite with you there for a moment. I'm sorry, you'll have to excuse me. There's someone I need to catch.' Orwell tried to look flustered rather than ignorant.

Burgess stood in his way. 'I seem to recall that in the '57 – and you might be able to help me here Bokhari – it was also in the propaganda put about by the agents of – what's his name? Goodness, I can't remember. Wait. Oh, yes, Wajid Ali – that the British were weak and not invincible. Which, as we just heard, is precisely Bose's line today. And it was true then, of course, that we had in fact just been humiliated in Afghanistan. Our Singapore of tomorrow perhaps? Bose must be reading his history books – but only those written by Wajid Ali, I'd suggest.'

Burgess paused and looked at Orwell, who still shuffling and eager to depart. Their eyes met and he resumed.

'All propaganda, or effective propaganda at least, is based on at least some atom of the truth, wouldn't you say, Orwell? Mind you, ignorance also plays an important part. They also said – Ali's men in '57, that is – that Britain only had a population of a hundred thousand at the time! And, to cap it all, that Russia had taken over Britain following our defeat in the Crimea! Imagine if that were true. We could all have been Russians by now! Comrade Orwell? Comrade Burgess? Comrade Bokhari? Comrade Churchill!'

Burgess seemed to be fishing, and Orwell said reluctantly, 'You seem well informed.'

'I did something on '57 at Trinity ...Cambridge.'

'Of course, Cambridge,' Orwell replied sardonically.

Burgess, clearly registering Orwell's disdain, quickly changed the subject. 'I thought we might double up on some of the contributors to our respective broadcasts. I hear you're doing some pretty interesting programmes and I'd be interested to have your views on a number of items. Can't say I've read your books though! Perhaps I will now. What would you recommend? I'm an Eliot man myself. Not the poet chappie, who I know you have something to do with. Oh no, it's George Eliot for me, *Middlemarch* and all that. I also adore Balzac, he's a great favourite of mine. I've also recently taken a liking to Forster, whom I'd *love* to meet.'

'Really?' Orwell went to look at his watch, only he was not wearing one.

'*Burmese Days* is my favourite,' said Bokhari. 'You might start with that one.'

'Let me make a note of that.' Burgess wrote on some papers he was carrying then handed Orwell a sturdy embossed business card. 'Here.'

Mr Guy Burgess
Radio Talks Producer
British Broadcasting Corporation
55, Portland Place
London
Telephone: Whitehall 4468

Orwell had never seen such a card in the hands of a BBC employee and could not reciprocate even if he had wanted to.

'I'm afraid I've left my cards in my other coat,' he lied deliciously and looked at Bokhari, who quickly turned away in mild embarrassment. Orwell felt quite pleased with this riposte to the brio of the young imposter.

'Never mind. I'm sure our paths will cross around here. I'll be in touch in any case. I might have even read your book by then! I hope we meet soon. Cheerio then.'

Burgess left with his broad smile still etched onto Orwell's grave face, and his perfumed miasma lingered.

'Who is that man?'

Bokhari seemed confused. 'He just gave you his card. Burgess of the Home Service.'

'I know that – but who is he? What's his background? Eton and Cambridge but what else?'

'Eton? More than likely. I wouldn't know his school but I do know he was here before.'

'At the BBC?' said Orwell.

'Yes. He told me so himself, earlier. Before the war he did *The Week in Westminster* programme. They say he was very good. Then he went to the War Office. Something in propaganda, I assume as he appears to know quite a lot about the subject.'

'He told you that? Do you believe him?'

'Why ever shouldn't I? He seems a nice sort and a gentleman, I would say.' Bokhari began to pack his papers into his pristinely organised briefcase.

'Eton, Cambridge, the BBC and the War Office. And he's my opposite number?' Orwell snorted then wheezed.

'I thought you went to Eton.' Bokhari said, shaking his head vigorously as he walked off.

Bokhari classified all public-schoolboys as gentlemen and Burgess was obviously approaching his apotheosis.

Orwell set off to find Rana.

She was in the canteen, as was Burgess, who was sitting with Brock.

'Let's go,' he commanded.

'But I haven't finished my tea. It's too hot.'

He took her cup and poured some of the tea into the saucer. 'There.'

'I will not drink it like that!'

'I do.'

'I'm not you. And I will not embarrass myself. That is not how civilised people drink their tea.'

'No, but I do.'

'Where are we going?' Rana looked worried, even frightened.

'Out of here. I'll buy you tea somewhere else. Come.'

He went to grab her arm but thought better of it when, out of the corner of his eye, he noticed Burgess and Brock watching. And then, to his horror, Burgess made a beeline for their table.

'Oh, George – can I call you George? I forgot to say, I'm trying to line up a Professor Bernal for a talk on the Soviets and Science. I had heard you have something similar in mind. Perhaps we should meet sooner rather than later and discuss.'

'Bernal? Do you know him?'

'Sage? Yes, we've met a few times. He did a talk for me some time ago. I thought he might be a contributor you'd be interested in. Do *you* know him?'

'No, I just wondered.'

Orwell had been trying for weeks to get the scientist and known communist sympathiser to contribute to a forth-coming series he had planned on Science and Politics. That Burgess had already had Bernal do a talk came as a bitter disappointment.

'Could you introduce me to this charming lady, George?' Burgess took Rana's hand and shook it ostentatiously. 'Guy Burgess of the Home Service. How do you do?'

Rana seemed stunned by his flamboyance and didn't try to withdraw her hand.

'This is Miss Mukurjee, my assistant,' he said hastily.

'Mukurjee. Bengali, I presume? And George's assistant! He's a very lucky chap, I'd say.'

'We really must be going now.' Orwell went to pull back Rana's chair but Burgess got there before him.

'Allow me,' Burgess crooned.

Rana rose and looked at the tea in the saucer. Burgess had noticed and Rana looked embarrassed.

'Thank you, Miss Mukurjee, but I'll drink my tea later.' Orwell took a sip from the saucer, spilling some in the process. Burgess would surely recognise the chivalry, as the cup and saucer had been in front of Rana the whole time, but at least he had tried.

'Brock is right – we need to think very carefully about what we do with India. Bite the bullet! 1857 and all that. If you recall, the Sepoys refused to bite the bullet because of the pig and cow fat on the cartridge paper we supplied them. Hence the expression, I assume. I think it's a salutary reminder to imperial masters, if they're not careful, they can be the architects of their own downfall. If I were you, I wouldn't ask them to bite the bullet in your broadcasts!'

'Yes, I see what you mean. We don't want a repeat of '57 in the age of radio, do we?' Orwell replied sarcastically. 'Well, thank you for that. We really must be going. You know how busy we all are at the moment. I may call later ... maybe next week, if that's okay by you, Burgess?'

'Call me Guy.'

Orwell took Rana by the arm and left at a pace. He turned and as he did so he saw Burgess pointing to the saucer for Brock's delectation. Bose was right about one thing: sacrifice was indeed the price of freedom.

'WHO IS THAT MAN? And what was all that business with 1857?' Rana asked as they stood on the pavement outside Portland Place.

'The Great Mutiny in India.'

'I know that!' she said indignantly. 'But why were you talking about it with him?'

'He does what I do, for the Home Service. He's, well, he knows something about Indian history and he thought Bose's propaganda was all old hat.'

'Old hat?'

'That we've heard it all before.'

'In 1857?'

'Yes, as it happens, it's the same old game. The same tropes in nationalist propaganda designed to provoke a mutiny among the Indian troops. You heard Brock: Bose thinks that, by defeating the British, they – you – will gain your freedom. In fact, we've heard it all before and Bose has nothing new to say by the sound of it.' Orwell paused, allowing for any passers-by to move out of earshot. 'Why did you smile at me in the meeting, when Bose's speech was being read?'

Rana looked surprised. 'Did I?'

'Yes, you were smiling for some reason.'

'Perhaps I saw your face. You were also smiling.'

'Grimacing more like. Do you agree with Bose?'

'About what exactly?'

'That the empire is finished and British rule in India is on the brink.'

'Is it?'

'I'm asking you. Do you think that parleying up to the Germans and the Japs will help India get its independence?'

'Do you?'

'You never give a straight answer!' She was exasperating. 'As it stands, no, I don't think it helps India to throw us out at this time. It might just let the Japanese be your next masters. Would you prefer them? Do you have ambitions to be a geisha girl?'

'My ambition is to have no master.' Rana turned and walked away.

He thought for a moment and then went after her.

'Wait! Wait up. Please, Rana,' Orwell spluttered, swallowing a rising cough. 'I think we need to talk. We must. Come to dinner? Please?'

Rana did not respond and looked at him. He wanted to hack the contents of his mouth onto the pavement but checked himself just in time. He felt a rather pathetic figure and the wheezing and half-digested cough forced him to look away.

'Just biting the bullet!' he spluttered.

'When?'

'Tonight? No, let me think ... not tonight. I've a shift in the Home Guard. How about Thursday?'

'What time? Where shall we meet?' There was an insistence in her voice.

He had not expected such a prompt response and the nervous cough descended once more.

10

Listener research was the latest thing at the BBC, or so Orwell had been told. Therefore his idea was rather simple: Bose's propaganda could be assessed using his India Section colleagues and their responses would be employed to develop counter-arguments for future broadcasts. He would justify this on the grounds that it was necessary for the war effort. Of course, the idea was bound to lead to all manner of trouble for everyone concerned. However, and like all dangerous ideas, it would either be a roaring success or blow up in his face. It was also another ruse to flush out Bokhari's position on Independence.

'Who better to try it out on?' he did his best to sound persuasive, but Bokhari seemed unconvinced. In fact, the senior man looked more than disdainful, annoyed even.

'You are simply asking for trouble!'

'What have we got to lose? If it works, we'll have a more effective programme. If it doesn't, nothing's lost.'

'You'll cause a good deal of anxiety. It's a very sensitive issue.' Bokhari was definitely agitated.

'Anxiety? Sensitive? For goodness sake, Z.A., the future

of India is at stake! We're at war. A little anxiety is surely worth it?'

'I don't think India will be lost or won by some propaganda trick. Furthermore, your colleagues won't appreciate being used like this.'

'I really think you're missing the point. It wouldn't be a trick or using them. We'd be testing out our broadcasts, our own propaganda. At the moment, we just assume it has some effect. But how do we know? Maybe we're just wasting everyone's time. This would be a chance to test it before we broadcast. You heard what the higher-ups said – we've been asked to redouble our efforts.'

'Have you thought through what it might do to the section?' Bokhari asked, almost pleading.

'What do you mean?'

'You're assuming we're all the same. All Indians are like those next door.'

'You're precisely the type of Indians we need to reach.'

'And what type is that?'

'Educated, middle-class Indians. Owners of a wireless.'

'Is that a type? What about our political differences? There are, as you are well aware, a spectrum of views among our educated, middle-class colleagues who own a wireless. Have you considered that?'

'That's why we need to test the broadcast material. We need to appeal to a whole range of political views to see if we can we find some common ground. That's what we'd be looking for.'

Bokhari paused, turned in his chair and stared at the wall for what seemed like an age. Orwell took out his tobacco tin and rolled a cigarette. Was it his own views that Bokhari wished to keep undisclosed? He waited for his boss to say something.

Eventually he turned in his chair and faced Orwell. 'One try. That's all. And on your head be it.'

'Of course. I'll set it up. Everyone to be invited?'

'It has to be everyone,' Bokhari said. 'The results would be invalidated if you only had volunteers. You need the spectrum. I'll send out an instruction. It'll have to be Monday morning and you'll have to prepare the necessary scripts.'

THE FOLLOWING Monday morning Orwell waited for Anand at reception. His friend eventually appeared and, in the lift, quietly confirmed that he had not been to Wallington. Orwell declined to say why he had asked and Anand was obviously puzzled by the question.

The section gathered in Room 1-01. Bokhari, Baghat, Jahida, Desai, the Princess and the Sahnis had all taken their seats. Confusion, expectation and not a little of Bokhari's predicted anxiety were etched across their faces. Rana was conspicuous by her absence and Orwell felt he should wait for her, but the others were already restless. He needed to start the proceedings.

A spontaneous hush came across the meeting-room table and Orwell took this as his cue to begin. He outlined the aims of the meeting and the process he intended to use. He asked if anyone had any questions. Anand immediately raised his hand.

'I think some of us might object to being your laboratory rats.'

There was a light murmur, even the odd forced chuckle, which helped defuse some of the tension.

'I prefer to think of you more as pointers,' Orwell replied with a smile.

'Dogs?' Anand broke into a broad grin. 'You have just doubly insulted us, Mr Blair!'

'Can we get started?' Orwell took up a sheet of paper and explained that he was going to ask Desai to read Bose's New Year wireless broadcast. That Desai as an actor would lend some authenticity to the piece, he suggested.

'But I've never heard the man,' Desai said.

'Neither have we, but I'm sure you'll do a better job than I at sounding like Bose!' Orwell handed him the paper. 'Now, if you please, could you read us the script? And the rest of you, you have to imagine you're in India, listening to the broadcast. And please, no notes. It should be as natural as we can make it. You are listening in on your wireless.'

'But that's absurd! We're here in London and we're all exiles, not listening to the radio in Bombay! We can all see it's not Bose. It's a completely artificial situation,' the Princess exclaimed.

'Yes, but use your imagination. Put yourself in Bombay, Calcutta, Delhi, Madras or wherever, and imagine you've tuned your wireless to Azad Hind and Bose comes on. Please, just try. Pretend.' Like a school teacher with an unruly class, he pleaded with them to behave.

'But if we pretend, it will not be real. And if it is not real, then the results will be worthless. In any case, I would never tune to Radio Hind or whatever it calls itself!' the Princess replied, to the acclaim of most of the others.

Orwell stared at the assembled company and was becoming increasingly frustrated. Bokhari sat motionless and raised his eyebrows. Near to resigning, Orwell decided to have one more try.

'This is not about you, Desai, tell them, please. You are being asked to play-act. I'm asking you to take the part of someone, perhaps like yourself, in India today. And you need to be as real as you possibly can. You need to become them for the moment. We shall then gather their – your – responses and try to assess the impact of the propaganda. It is not scientific, I grant you, but it is a pointer, an indicator, as to how Bose's broadcasts might be received by educated people like yourselves. And that is all we're trying to assess. Now, Desai, could you please start?'

Before Desai could say a word, the Princess intervened once more.

'But what is our role? Are we to be ourselves, only transported back to India, God forbid? Or are we to be someone else – someone whose views we might not share? Please tell us, Mr Blair, as I am very confused by this whole business. Why are we being asked to be actors?'

Orwell took a deep breath and forced himself not to swear.

'Either. Be yourself back in India. Or take on the role of someone you might know in India, someone not unlike yourself, or even someone completely different if you so wish. Soon, I hope, we'll pick up on the type of person you've chosen.'

Bokhari, with both palms pressed on the table, came to Orwell's rescue. Orwell couldn't work out whether he was concerned by how things were developing or revelling in Orwell's discomfort.

'Ladies, gentlemen, please, this is an experiment. Let us at least try to do as Blair suggests. Afterwards, we can go through any issues or concerns. Mr Desai, please read the speech.'

The voice of calm and authority did the trick. Desai stood up and read in an exaggerated Indian accent.

'The Russians have been so soundly defeated by Germany ...so Europe has nothing more to fear from them. And in this destruction the small nations of Europe took an active part with Germany—'

'Please, please Desai' said Bokhari, 'it really doesn't help if you try to sound too Indian. Your natural voice, please.'

Desai resumed reading. 'Romania with confidence sent her young men to fight on the side of Germany. Volunteers from practically every part of Europe fought. The Conference of Small Nations held at Berlin showed that Europe is fully prepared for a New Order.'

Desai paused and Bokhari thwacked the table.

'Continue please. And, remember, this is a wireless broadcast. You do not wait for the audience to respond! Slightly slower, too?' said Bokhari.

'Japan's entry into the war has turned the eyes of the world towards the New Order. The world is divided into two parts, one containing the healthy advancing nations of the world, the other the idle, boastful and wealthy. Only those who are prepared to sacrifice their lives unstintingly will be victorious. The price of freedom is sacrifice. Japan has shown India that the wealthy and strong British are after all not very strong. Not only India, but all the other countries who have been oppressed by the British were shown the way to freedom in 1941.'

Desai took another deep breath and waited. Bokhari and Orwell gestured for him to continue.

'All those Indians who have lived in exile because of British oppression are now prepared to sacrifice their lives for freedom. Swami Satia Nanda, an Indian leader for the past twenty-eight years, exposed the British deceit to the Indian people. He warned the Indians that they should not be deceived. In a speech on the radio, he added that only

Britain dislikes India. It will be dangerous for India if she is controlled by the British any longer. If the Indians unite, they can throw off the shackles of slavery. The 400 million people of India can produce an army that can be matchless.'

Desai looked about the room and raised his eyebrows. No response was forthcoming.

'One can only achieve freedom by struggle and this is the best opportunity for India to achieve her freedom. We pray to God that the Indian desire for freedom may be fulfilled in 1942.'

There was a long silence as Desai sat down.

'Thank you, Desai,' Orwell said, and waited for the others to respond. They sat in silence and avoided all eye contact.

'Can I have your immediate thoughts, please?' Orwell asked.

After another long silence, Anand said, 'The man is clever.'

'In what sense?' Orwell was thankful for his friend's contribution.

'He's an opportunist. He deliberately conflates everything. That India's independence is linked with the demise of the British Empire is not in doubt. I think we would all agree that is correct. Most educated Indians would agree. Writing-off Russia is perhaps too glib and may also be premature, as is Japan's supposed success. But how can one disentangle all this? It is far too complicated to unpick on just hearing this broadcast.'

'Is that your interpretation, Anand, or the man in the street in Calcutta?' Bokhari asked.

'Sorry, that's my interpretation. If I were the man in the street in Calcutta, I would say the only message I would glean from all this is, fight the British. Get rid of them, now.

Kick a man while he's down – why not? It's not cricket we're talking about here!'

'Or not to fight the Japanese? Indeed, to support them,' Jahida interjected.

'Yes, I agree,' Anand replied. 'Or, at least, not to oppose the Japanese should they come. If the present war is being fought to create a new world order based on democracy and freedom, and if the Allies aim to liberate the ninety million peoples of Poland and Czechoslovakia, Holland, Belgium, or wherever, writhing under the oppression of Hitler, then let them begin, as a token of their earnestness, by liberating the 400 millions of India held under British rule.'

Most of the congregation tapped the table and nodded.

'Is that what most Indians would be thinking?' Orwell asked, looking directly at Jahida.

She was leaning with her elbows on the table and her head in her hands. Her fingers were covering her ears as if she had no wish to engage any further in the discussion.

'And what would the woman in the street think?' Orwell said.

Still she didn't say anything.

'It is quite irrelevant,' the Princess said.

'Irrelevant?'

'Yes, it is quite irrelevant what *we* think. Women will not be listening to this. To us, it matters not one iota whether it is true or false, right or wrong. Bose is not talking to us. It's the men – always the men – that these things are aimed at. We are of no consequence. Of course, the same might be said of your women here in Britain. You just need to look at Parliament, even at the BBC ... especially here in fact. It really doesn't matter what we women think.'

'Jahida? Is the Princess correct?'

She sat up slowly. 'Of course she's right. But not entirely.

Women *do* matter and we can and do make a difference. Not always directly perhaps.' She paused for a moment, seemingly gathering her thoughts. 'We can influence the men subtly and with much less noise.'

'With your feminine charms?' said Desai.

'Charms. Guile. Cunning. Subterfuge. Or just plain common sense. Call it what you will. Women in India support their men. They have their children and bring them up and, in some cases, prepare them to challenge their Imperial rulers. Women are as important to the Independence struggle as men. The men are helpless without the support of women.' Jahida replied firmly.

Bokhari sighed. 'I'm not sure this is getting us very far.'

'I agree,' Orwell said, surprised by Jahida's intervention.

'But you asked. Perhaps you don't really want to know what we women think,' Jahida said accusingly.

Orwell was unsure whether he should challenge Jahida? He was keen not to upset her any further and after looking at her and then at Bokhari, decided to divert the discussion.

'Z.A., we haven't heard your view.'

Bokhari looked uncomfortable. 'I'd like to hear the others' first.'

Baghat and Sahni immediately focused their eyes on the table.

'Mr Baghat, perhaps you would say a word,' said Bokhari.

Baghat looked up slowly. He appeared reluctant even to open his mouth. 'Bose is a hero to many in India. He has considerable support. And his message is most simple: get the British out by whatever means are necessary. Quit India as they say. The time has come. That is very clear from what we have heard. It matters little to most Indians whether it is the British or the Japanese colonialists that rule over us. We always suffer regardless.'

'Is that your view?' Orwell asked.

Baghat did not reply.

Orwell repeated the question.

There was an expectant pause.

'It is *a* view. I'm not sure it is relevant whether it's my personal view. I think that is my own business,' Baghat replied curtly, and returned to inspecting the table top.

'And Mr Sahni? Mrs Sahni?'

Balraj Sahni looked at the others and shook his head. Damyanti remained mute.

'Mr Sahni, do you have anything to contribute?' Orwell said.

'I agree with Baghat.'

'About what exactly?'

'That Bose is correct in some details. But—'

'Some details?' There was a scold in Orwell's voice. 'Please, expand if you will.'

It was becoming all too clear – his Indian colleagues were reluctant to criticise Bose and might even support his aims.

Sahni avoided eye contact and looked away without replying to Orwell. There was another uncomfortable pause. The Princess once more broke the silence.

'He, Bose, fails to mention the internal differences between Congress and the Muslim League. I think that is deliberate. Until those are sorted, India will not be ready for independence. That is my own view. Of course, it is also the view of the British government.'

'We can sort out our differences if we are left alone to do so,' Baghat suggested.

'I agree. We can. But what we really need is a true socialist party!' Anand said loudly.

'We need to hear the women of India,' the Princess continued.

Baghat jumped in again. 'We need the British out first! We don't need the British to tell us what's best for us. And we don't need either European socialism or communism! We Indians will find our own system, thank you very much.'

Bokhari appeared embarrassed and stood up. 'Enough! Gentlemen, and ladies, this is getting a little out of hand. I think we should all calm down.'

Orwell felt excited and tried once more to get Bokhari to declare himself.

'Z.A., we haven't heard your views yet.'

'I think we should stop now, Blair,' he said firmly and began to shuffle his papers. 'It has been most interesting and I thank you for your efforts. Perhaps we need more time to refine the process. Thank you all for coming.'

Most looked pleasantly surprised by the abrupt ending. Orwell waited for the room to clear before he apprehended Jahida.

'Thank you for your contribution. I thought it was very useful.'

'Don't patronise me George.'

' I didn't mean' Orwell felt awkward and changed the subject. 'Have you seen Rana? Do you know why she's not here?'

'I've no idea,' Jahida replied and quickly left the room.

PART II

11

THE CHEAP GERMAN ALARM CLOCK BARELY RATTLED INTO LIFE at 5am. The bell was tinny and the mechanism had a way of losing time, much like life itself for Inspector Charles Percy of Scotland Yard. As a result it was always later than the clock indicated. Punctilious to a fault, he had compensated by waking earlier than was necessary.

His wife, Vera, snored in the twin bed, oblivious to his and the clock's waking existence. At least, that was the impression she conveyed. The room was cold in every respect and there was now a permanent frost in their relationship. For the past ten years they had shared a bedroom, the chill and little else. Although they had the kiddies' room, the absence of any such kiddie left it spare for occasions when he came home late or their arguments boiled over. Percy much preferred it but insisted on maintaining at least a semblance of conjugal normality by occupying the same bedroom as Vera. Plus, he knew that his early-morning departure annoyed her immensely.

His withered left leg told him today was going to be a Bad Day as the limb was stiff and painful to the touch. He felt colder than usual and thought that he must have left his leg outside the blankets. Either that or she had pulled the covers off him. He cursed Vera, his luck, all London's Dockers, their trade unions and the Labour Party.

The General Strike of 1926 was forever inscribed on his body. Sixteen years ago he had been a young, fit and naïve constable who had had the misfortune to be in the wrong place at the wrong time and the stevedores had not spared him. Now, at forty-one, and beginning to feel it, his smashed leg was a daily reminder of the power of the labour movement, collectivism and physical force in general. His permanent disablement had been sustained as a result of a multiple fracture – in truth, it was 'bollocked-up' by an incompetent police surgeon. Yet, he had long since convinced himself that the quack was less responsible than the strikers who had precipitated the initial injury.

The reasons for the General Strike were also of no consequence to him – the ends could never justify the means. The men who had crushed his leg were to blame. It was their choice, intent and actions that had caused his impairment and sealed his fate. But for them, he might not be living in this police house in Poplar, in the heart of an East London slum, with an unforgiving wife. On a Bad Day the Red Bastards had a lot to answer for. He would never forgive them.

His leg had been the subject of many a dispute outside of his marriage. That the force had kept him on was partly to avoid litigation surrounding the employment of the unqualified surgeon and, belatedly, recognition that he was indeed something of 'a clever dick'.

Despite his limited education, he was in a job unsuited to his innate intelligence and his approach to solving cases was different to that of his peers. For this reason he considered himself an artisan among labourers. And, like an artist, flashes of insight came to him seemingly from nowhere and at times he least expected. He could not explain how these visions came to him. Others might have suggested that his prescience was, more often than not, simply in comparison with the incompetence of the general herd of policemen. Percy begged to differ. He attributed his knack of seeing what others failed to see to some new faculty developed by way of compensation for his twisted leg, in much the same way as the hearing of the blind was said to become more acute.

After three years recovering on half-pay, he had been assigned to a desk job. Within a matter of months his combing of unsolved cases had led to new leads, a number of arrests and several successful prosecutions. He was thus promoted to CID and rose to detective sergeant in just five years. In the six years that followed, he barely left his desk.

As with all true artists, Percy eventually hit a barren period and his creative juices dried up. The unsolved cases on his desk began to mount and this coincided with the onset of his marital problems. Soon, his effectiveness began to be questioned. His stupid leg was also giving him hell. It was time for a change and it came not of his own making.

On the very day Britain went to war – 1st September, 1939 – he was summoned to his commander's office and ordered to report to the Missing Persons Section the following Monday. He'd had no idea that such a section even existed in Scotland Yard. The incentive was a promotion to detective inspector. Reluctantly but realistically, he accepted.

Percy was in charge of two officers: Detective Constable Harold Baines and Police Constable Wilfred Taylor. How Baines had come to be in the police was itself something of a mystery. Although he was twenty-three, he looked and acted like an overgrown adolescent. He had none of the expected qualities of a detective, save that he did not wear a uniform. Someone, somewhere, had finally recognised that his necessary skills were missing, and this probably accounted for his assignment to Missing Persons.

Baines' original promotion to detective had also been the consequence of an accident. A newspaper article had placed him at the scene of an attempted bank raid where he had helped foil the robbers and apprehend them almost single-handedly, or so the story went. In fact, he was just an off-duty constable who happened to be in the bank as a customer. The robbers had entered armed with pick-axe handles and demanded the teller hand over the cash. Baines, not knowing what to do, had run out of the bank and blundered into the lookout, sending him sprawling on the pavement. Baines always carried his newly acquired police whistle and gave it a loud blast. There had been no need. The raiders had been followed into the bank by armed flying-squad detectives and the fallen lookout was in fact a policeman. The Metropolitan Police were embarking on a recruitment campaign at the time and it was felt that Baines's 'heroics' would be conducive to their efforts. A friendly reporter did the rest and Baines was swiftly promoted. However, once out of the public eye, his transfer had been equally meteoric.

PC Wilfred Taylor was nearing retirement. There was nothing exceptional about him. He had done his time and Missing Persons was his pre-retirement home. He had only months to serve and the higher-ups felt it was better for all if he was out of harm's way. He had accepted his fate magnanimously and settled into the note-taking and filing duties without complaint. At his age, he did not miss pounding the beat.

Missing Persons was hidden on an out-of-the-way stairwell in Scotland Yard and no one seemed to either know or care what it did. Before the war, missing persons had nearly always been considered absent by their own volition, even very young children. In any case, everyone knew that the Salvation Army's missing-persons operations were more effective. The section's main task was to record cases and occasionally return to those who had cared to inquire if they had heard anything. It was the equivalent of lost-and-found, only with no claimants and very few founds. Exceptionally, they would be asked to check the details of bodies retrieved from the Thames to see if they matched any on their files.

Percy soon found himself standing in this tiny stagnant pool of meaninglessness. In effect, Missing Persons had no call for his talents. He was a detective with nothing to detect and an inspector with nothing required inspection. As he was the principal, he decided unilaterally to change the unit's remit and operation. He knew that no one would notice or even care.

Before he could initiate the change, a surge in cases resulting from the Blitz had brought about an unwelcome flow of work, one that threatened to overrun the section. It was only now, fifteen months into the job and with the recent lull in the bombing, that he could set about transforming his entire working existence. It was to be a new beginning.

Most of the cases were simple runaways or wartime relocations, but a few were more problematic and might even have involved foul play. He tried to identify the differences by developing an algorithm. Cases were to be filed according to a new grading system and the more interesting or serious ones would become the focus of the section's work. Wherever possible, this entailed connecting the missing person to incidents or other crimes. Almost inevitably, this meant confrontation with those investigating such cases and who, more often than not, thought his interventions both unnecessary and unhelpful. Soon, he was known as Inspector Hop-along.

Then, in early January 1942, everything changed.

12

'Is it Blair or Orwell?' Two men stood looking quizzically at the twin nameplates on Orwell's open office door.

'It depends on who's doing the asking,' said Orwell.

'Scotland Yard.'

'In that case it had better be Blair. Good morning, gentlemen. How may I assist you? It's one and the same by the way. I'm both Blair and Orwell. The latter is my nom-de-plume.'

The younger of the two men looked confused and turned to the older man.

'Nom-de-plume. The name he writes under,' said the senior in an aside and turned to Orwell. 'Good morning, Mr Blair-Orwell. I'm Inspector Charles Percy. And this is Detective Constable Baines. May we have a word?' Both men removed their hats.

'By all means. Please sit down. How can I help?' Percy was immediately struck by the sound of Orwell's voice. Its gravelly, high pitch seemed totally at odds with the substantive character in front of him.

There was only one chair and the senior policeman quickly seconded it, leaving Baines standing.

Recognising the junior rank's predicament Orwell said, 'You'll need to get a chair from next door, Constable.'

'It's *Detective* Constable sir.' Baines looked at Percy, who gave him a doleful, dismissive look.

The young detective paused, then said, 'That's all right, I'll stand.' He then moved dutifully behind Percy and took out his notebook. Orwell noticed how he sucked and wetted the end of his pencil – a substitute teat – in nervous anticipation.

Orwell shuffled the papers on his desk and rolled another cigarette. He kept his natural antipathy towards policemen in check. If they really were the long arm of the state, there was little to fear as they looked decidedly clueless.

'How can I help you, Inspector Charles?'

'Percy, sir. It's Inspector Charles Percy.'

'Sorry, I must have misheard you. My apologies, Inspector.' Orwell pretended to smile and focused on rolling his cigarette.

Percy gave a quick shake of the head and a pretend smile. 'Easily and often done.' He looked at Orwell. 'I'm sure you are aware that one of your members of staff has been reported missing.'

'A Miss Rana Muk-ur-jee?' said Baines.

Orwell immediately looked up. 'This is about Miss Mukurjee? Yes, certainly, I'd heard she was absent.'

'More like *missing*, sir.'

Orwell had known – Rana had not met him on the Thursday as arranged. At first, he had thought nothing of it, assuming she was either unwell or it was the time-of-the-month thing. After a week, he began to worry and made tentative inquiries. Jahida had been particularly unhelpful, making it clear what she thought of his pursuit of Rana. But she had promised to look into the matter. A few days later, she reported that Rana had disappeared from her digs and that nobody had seen her for some time. Bokhari had been informed.

'Not bad news, I hope.' Orwell was concerned and was now fidgeting with his cigarette.

'Why do you say that?' Percy turned and gave Baines a knowing look.

'I just assumed—'

'What did you assume, Mr Blair?'

'I just assumed it might be bad news, Inspector. That's all we seem to have lately. And the very fact that you're here, an inspector from Scotland Yard, also suggests something might have happened to her.'

'It has, sir ... she's gone missing.'

Orwell continued to fiddle with his roll-up. Only on the point of lighting it did he look up.

Percy continued. 'Apart from those particular assumptions, have you any other reason to think something untoward might have happened to her?'

Orwell placed his cigarette in the corner of his mouth. 'No, of course not. But we are at war, Inspector, and London is a dangerous place at the moment. One naturally assumes the worse in such circumstances. I should imagine a lot of missing people remain unaccounted for.'

Percy did not respond and Orwell dragged on his cigarette and immediately began to cough. Percy waited for him to finish.

'How well did you know Miss Mukurjee?'

'She worked for ...with me. She was very good, very committed and very bright.'

'And what did she actually do?'

'She was a production assistant.'

'Was?'

'Is, Inspector. She's a production assistant.'

'Producing what exactly?'

'Radio Talks.'

'Is that what you do here? I was told you're an author of some sort.'

Orwell wondered whether the words had been chosen by the inspector or someone he had spoken to.

'This is the BBC, Inspector, and we make and broadcast radio programmes. That's what we do.' His belief that all policemen were either inept or stupid was very close to being affirmed.

Percy looked at Orwell and wondered how anyone could listen on the wireless to Orwell's voice for very long. The high-pitched squeak was grating. 'And when did you last see the young lady, Mr Blair?'

Orwell was obviously thinking about how to answer and knew that if he wasn't careful he might incriminate himself in some way.

'I'm really not sure. I'd need to check with my secretary. I think it might have been on the Tuesday morning, ten days or so ago.'

'And in what capacity was that?'

'Sorry, what do you mean?'

'Was it here – at work? Were you working with her here, in your office?'

'Yes, and in the studio, of course. Where else would we be?' The inference that he might have had more than a working relationship with Rana was patently obvious.

'And did she appear to be her normal self?'

'I'm sure she was. I can't say that she was any different. I'm sure I would have noticed otherwise.'

'Nothing untoward then?'

'No. Not that I recall. Nothing *untoward*.'

'Did she have any close acquaintances here at the BBC? Any friends?'

'I really don't know, Inspector. You'd have to ask others.'

'And what were you producing that Tuesday, Mr Blair?'

'I really can't remember. We have a very busy itinerary. I'd need to check.'

'With your secretary?' There was a hint of disparagement in the policeman's voice.

'Yes, Miss Parratt. She's just next door. I could ask if you really need to know.'

'That'll not be necessary. I can see this war is keeping you very busy, producing radio entertainment.' The mocking tone continued. Percy looked around the bare-walled office and as he turned towards Baines, he seemed pleased his entertainment gibe had landed.

'Yes, Inspector. We're very busy with the war effort. We do our bit. As you do yourself no doubt.'

The mutual antagonism was already palpable. Orwell looked at the Constable who was clearly on a different wavelength to his senior.

'And how long have you been working with the young lady?'

'Miss Parratt?' Orwell replied, deliberately obfuscating the question.

'No, I meant the missing woman, Miss Mukurjee.'

'Two or three months, I should say. Certainly no more.'

'Not long then?'

'No, not long. I could check?'

Percy straightened the rim of his hat while Orwell

arranged some papers on his desk. There was a long pause in which both men appeared to be thinking. Eventually, Percy spoke, 'And how would you describe her?'

'As I said, very committed. She was very helpful and very bright.'

'Young and attractive, as they go, would you say?'

'*As they go*, Inspector?'

'You know, for an Indian woman, if you like that sort of thing.'

The Inspector was now deliberately provoking him.

Orwell ignored the bait. 'I presume you know her age, Inspector?'

Baines flipped a page in his notebook. 'Yes, sir. Twenty-one.'

'Then I'd say she was – is young, Inspector.'

'And attractive?'

'That depends, as you say, if you like that *sort of thing*.'

'I'm asking for your opinion, Mr Blair.'

'And I'm saying it's a matter of taste, Inspector, and that is entirely subjective. Therefore, what I may or may not think will have no bearing on your understanding of what I might mean by attractive, if indeed I were to tell you. One man's notion of attractiveness is another's ugly girlfriend or even his wife perhaps.'

Percy turned around in his seat. 'Did you get that, Baines?'

'I think so, sir.' Baines was still clearly confused and avoided direct eye contact. He was now chewing on his pencil.

Turning back to Orwell, Percy sat forward. 'So, I can take it that she was attractive?'

'Shouldn't that be *is* attractive, Inspector? I'll have to leave you to decide for yourself. Have you not got a photograph? The Personnel Department might be able to provide you with one. Then you can make up your own mind.'

'We have all her details, sir. Isn't that so, Baines?'

Orwell jumped in. 'Can I ask who reported her missing?'

Baines consulted his notebook. 'Mr Bo … Bok Harry.'

Orwell helped with the pronunciation.

'An Indian gentleman, I presume,' said Percy.

'Yes, he's my boss here at the BBC. I take it you've already seen him?'

'No, not yet. His secretary, a Miss Thomas, reported the Indian woman missing. It's a strange world we now live in, wouldn't you say? Indians as bosses and all? Or is that just here at the BBC?'

'What do you mean, Inspector?'

'Well, the BBC is well known for being a bit different. A world of its own, some might say.'

'I grant you, a world of its own, but different? In what way exactly?'

'You tell me, Mr Blair. Having an Indian for a boss is different, I'd say. Wouldn't you, Baines?'

'Definitely, sir. There's none at the Yard. Never has been. Never will be, I should say.'

'You don't mind that, Mr Blair?'

'No, Inspector, I really don't mind.'

An uncomfortable silence followed during which the two men eyed each. Percy blinked first.

'Are there any other Indians?'

'Here in the department?' Orwell decided some deliberate facetiousness was in order. 'Yes, this is the Eastern Service and I'm the only English person in the India Section.'

'The Eastern Service?'

'Yes, Inspector. We broadcast to the East … not East

Anglia I might add. Our programmes go to India and beyond.'

'The Orient?'

'Yes, but mainly to India. Hence the my Indian colleagues.'

'And what exactly do you broadcast, Mr Blair?'

'As I said, radio Talks. They're about all sorts of things but mainly British culture, our way of life, literature and science, that sort of thing.'

'Sounds like high-class stuff. Obviously not for the likes of me or Baines here.'

'I wouldn't say that, Inspector. We cater for all walks, even policemen.'

For a moment, Orwell appeared to think that he had overstepped the mark and as a result ducked behind the desk to re-tie an already tied shoelace.

'And Miss Mukurjee? What did she do as a production assistant?'

Orwell popped his head up from behind the desk. 'She helped organise the broadcasts.' He finished with the lace and looked directly at Percy.

'And what did she actually do in that regard?'

'She contacted the speakers, prepared the scripts and researched the subjects of the programmes.'

'And she did that *under* you?'

The crude double entendre was meant to infuriate Orwell and it did. 'Yes, I'm the Talks Producer. I'm responsible for the broadcasts. And she worked *with* me.'

'Pleasurable work, I'd say. Especially given the times – the war and all.'

'It can be very interesting, as is looking for missing persons, no doubt.'

Percy understood the slight and took a deep breath.

'And where were you on that Tuesday evening, Mr Blair?'

'I really can't recall, Inspector.'

'Perhaps your secretary would know?'

'I was most probably at home with my wife. Either that or on duty.'

'On duty?'

'I'm in the LDV, a sergeant in the Home Guard. I can check my roster, or you can check it if you wish.'

'You said, most probably? Would your wife be able to confirm that you were at home, sir? She would know your whereabouts?'

'Most certainly. Am I some sort of suspect, Inspector?'

'And your wife's name, sir? And your home address, if you please.'

'Eileen Blair. 111 Langford Court, Abbey Road, St. John's Wood.'

'Have you got that, Baines?'

'Yes, sir.'

'And you've no recollection of seeing Miss Mukurjee after that Tuesday?'

'No, Inspector. One day is very much like any other at the moment.'

'You don't recall noticing her absence at all?'

'Of course. We work quite irregular hours and there are quite a few production assistants. I may not have noticed the length of time she hadn't been here. We've been terribly busy of late.' Orwell paused. 'Have you any idea what might have happened to her?'

Baines looked up. 'We—'

'We can't say at this moment, sir,' said Percy.

'It's a damned business, Inspector.'

'What is?'

'London. The chaos and—'

'Yes, sir. It keeps us all very busy.'

'I'm sure it does, Inspector. I'm sure it does.'

'Is there anything else you'd like to tell us, Mr Blair?'

'No. I don't think there is. If I remember anything—'

'You know where to contact us, sir. Whitehall 1212. Ask for Inspector Percy in Missing Persons. If I'm not there, you can leave a message with Baines here or a Constable Taylor.'

'Thank you. Will that be all?'

'For the moment, Mr Blair … or is it Mr Orwell?'

'For you, Inspector, it's Blair. Eric Blair.'

Percy stopped on his way to the door. 'Might I meet Mr Orwell sometime? Perhaps we could discuss his books.'

Orwell almost broke into a smile. 'I'll let him know you're interested.'

Baines gave Orwell a cursory wave and Orwell saluted him in return. Percy turned again and caught Orwell's eye. There was a frisson of mutual understanding – that this meeting was not going to be their last. They had something in common, even if in that moment they did not understand what it might be. Orwell sat back in his chair and re-ran the meeting in his head. He was clearly anxious as a result of Percy"s questioning and even more so by involvement of Bokhari. Why had he reported Rana missing without telling him? Had he said or done anything to raise any suspicions in the policeman's mind? And what if he had?

13

Percy had taken an instant dislike to Eric Blair and his upper-class smugness. He thought Blair wore a sense of his own superiority too easily. And then there was the way he dressed, the grubby untidiness, which stood out. The upper class don't even bother to look smart to be taken seriously, he thought. Above all, Percy had a feeling that Blair was not what he projected himself to be. Gut instinct also told him that Eric Blair might be Jekyll to George Orwell's Hyde, and it was the latter he was now keen to investigate.

Despite being an intelligent man, Percy didn't quite know where to start. He was an occasional reader but no-one would call him a bookworm. At school he had been force-fed Dickens and Kipling, and since then some of Conan Doyle's Sherlock Holmes had stood him in good stead. He was a policeman after all. Once in a while he picked up a Tuppenny Dreadful and on the odd occasion he had purloined a Penguin pocket edition from some missing person's house or flat. He justified the latter as evidence - an important ingredient in getting to know the victim.

Orwell was the first writer he had ever met and, not

being well read, their meeting had sparked a self-consciousness. He was curious to know more about this odd man and his writing. Was it instinct, experience or prejudice that told him George Orwell was implicated in Rana Mukurjee's disappearance? But where should he start? His intelligence approach demanded a methodology. He knew he had to read Orwell's work.

'Baines!'

'Yes, sir?'

'I want you to go to Westminster Central Library and get me all the books you can by George Orwell.'

'But I don't belong to the library, guv ... had no need.'

'Go. Show them your warrant. Tell 'em it's for an urgent police inquiry and refer them to me if they cause any trouble.'

'What sort of books would they be, sir?'

'What d'you mean? They'll be BOOKS!'

'But what sort, sir? Stories and the like, or big books?'

'Big books! Just get me anything by George Orwell. Now go!'

BAINES RETURNED forty-five minutes later and appeared to be empty-handed.

'Well?' The inspector looked anxiously at his underling.

Baines reached into his pocket and withdrew a book. 'They didn't have any, sir. Nothing by Orwell or Blair.'

Percy looked at the book Baines was holding. 'Then what's that?'

'I went to the bookshop in Victoria Street and found this.' It was a copy of *Burmese Days* by George Orwell.

Baines's initiative shocked Percy and he was about to

compliment the young detective when Baines said, 'The girl in the library said I should go there if it was so important. She even gave me a list of books.' He scrambled in his raincoat for his notebook. 'It's here somewhere ... *Burmese Days* – that's the one I got there. *Down and Out in Paris and London* – that doesn't sound too good, does it? *A Clergyman's Daughter* – not my cuppa tea. And *Coming Up For Air*. Oh, and *The Road to Wigan Pier*. Is Wigan by the sea? And here's another – *Homage to Cata-Cata-lonia*, wherever that is. And *Keep the As-Asp* or something or other *Flying*. I've no idea what that is when it's at home! He's written a lot, hasn't he?'

'Give me the list, Baines.'

'Can I have some money for the book, guv? I had to buy it and it's cleaned me out. Here's the receipt.'

Percy reached into his pocket and gave Baines whatever change he had. 'You'll have to wait for the rest.'

14

VERA WAS STILL IN HER DRESSING GOWN WHEN PERCY returned home. It was nearly six o'clock in the evening and he was early for once. He tried to never be at home before six, especially in the summer. The drawing-in of the nights made it more bearable and by late-January he was able to face her.

He couldn't recall when it had gone wrong for them. It was as if he had awoken one day to find an almost complete stranger lying next to him. She had metamorphasised into some sort of alien creature. The start of the Blitz had probably been the catalyst for the total dissolution of their relationship, although it had been teetering on the brink before that. Now they were just an addition to the many unseen casualties of the war. In eleven years, Vera had transformed from being a polite, engaging and rather pretty young woman into something else. Something quite grotesque in many ways. Physically, she was spreading in all directions. She was untidy and self-centred and seemed to care about nothing and nobody. Percy wondered whether she hated him and everything he represented. She invariably raised his disability in their arguments and used it as a weapon; his weakness was her strength. She called him the cripple and under his breath he called her a whore. Of course, she was no such thing, but he couldn't find a word that would penetrate the carapace of her self-regard. They had not made love for over twelve months because she hated sex with him and his withered leg. Added to which, she was now chain-smoking.

He came into the kitchen and laid a pile of books on the table. Vera lit her cigarette from the gas stove and her dressing gown came loose, exposing half a breast as she sat down at the table. As usual, she wore no makeup and her hair was unbrushed and matted in greasy clumps. She noticed his long look and pulled her dressing gown closed.

'What's this? What's with the books? I don't read. And you certainly don't?' She drew heavily on the cigarette and blew the smoke towards him.

'Work.'

Vera sneered. 'So, you're a librarian now? I'd say you're better suited.'

'It's a case.'

'A missing person is somewhere in one of the books?'

'You wouldn't understand,' he said, and went to put the kettle on.

Vera moved an arm towards the books and was about to take one. 'What books are they?'

'Leave 'em!' Percy shouted.

She ignored him, took one from the top of the stack and slowly read the cover. '*Coming Up For Air* by George... Orwell. Never heard of him!' She dropped the book back onto the pile and fingered the books below. 'They're all by him! All by the same bloke?'

'Yes.'

'Who is he? He's gone missing has he? Fell into one of his books did he?'

'Why d'you want to know?'

'Because his bloody books are sitting on my kitchen table. That's why!'

'I told you, I'm working on a case and he's involved.'

'Oh, involved, is he?'

'Why are you pretending to be interested in what I do all of a sudden?'

'Why the hell 'ave you got all this stuff? You don't read books. Can't see you reading all them! You fall asleep reading the bloody 'paper.'

Vera's working-class London roots surfaced whenever she raised her voice in anger. The louder she became, the more cockney she sounded and the more distasteful. By the time she reached a crescendo, she was the genuine article and her 'North and South' bellowed like a common washer woman. It frightened him to think that other people might see him in her company. She shamed him.

It hadn't always been that way. Once upon a time, he had loved her and she him. They had wanted to be together, despite his leg. Vera had been happy. They had been happy. She never said anything about his limp, the scar, the constant complaints and the aches and pains. It was all invisible and they managed. In fact they more than managed. He had a steady job – a respectable position with a good pension – and she worked part-time in a drapery store on the Caledonian Road. She had ambitions to be a seamstress to the rich and famous and thought she could do this from home, once the children were born. But of course the children never came.

Vera had become convinced that Percy's leg was the cause of his impotence. She brought it into every dispute, no matter that his other vital parts were in full working order and had been proven to be so. Something internal must have been damaged, she believed, and he needed to have 'the test'. At first Percy objected to the idea of masturbating into a vial under the scrutiny of strangers. He told her it was disgusting and he couldn't and wouldn't do it under any circumstances. It would be too humiliating and no self-respecting man would submit to such embarrassment. But he eventually gave in for the sake of peace. She had got her way through relentless nagging and bitter asides, including the threat of denying him his 'husbandly rights'...forever. That had been enough to make him succumb. He went on to pass the test and was proven to be fully operational. Breaking the news to Vera had been worse than the test itself and she immediately collapsed on hearing the verdict. After resuscitation, she insisted they must have messed up the examination or swapped the samples. It was a mis-trial and she was not guilty. All the women in her family had been fertile – babies falling out of them every nine months, twins and all. Despite the evidence, it had to be him and his leg, she insisted. As a result, he had long since lost his 'husbandly rights'.

Then the Blitz came and Vera's accusations went with them to the Underground shelters for nine months of hell. One night, some of the more itinerant refugees from the Luftwaffe had even formed a queue to resolve the fertility problem. Percy arrived just in time with his warrant card and threatened to have them exposed to Hitler's bombers unless they moved on.

Months later, when the bombing had paused, Vera remained in the prison of her moods and the pointlessness of her existence. He could never give her what she most wanted and for this he had to pay.

15

Had Betty reported Rana's disappearance and had she done so under Z.A.'s instruction? Or had he shattered Betty's dreams of a life together and now she had reason to seek some sort of revenge? He had mistreated her in the worst possible way and ditched her for Rana. At the time he had begun to feel very little for Betty. Nevertheless, he did not want to hurt her. In his mind there had been little choice, or so he continued to tell himself. He knew she had plans, dreams, that were never going to materialise and they were never going anywhere except to bed and even there the pleasure had evaporated. He could no longer satisfy her and his lungs were telling him to stop. And, yet, he had taken a younger, prettier and more educated woman. Had he really crushed Betty?

Orwell's rationalisation was that there could be no Pygmalion type of transformation of Betty. She was never going to be an Eliza Doolittle and he was no Professor Higgins. He couldn't save her from the working-class life that had shaped her and out of which she desperately longed to escape. He had tried but the books he had given her to read appeared to remain unread as she had had nothing to say about any of them. It was as if they were a foreign country and she didn't have the language or indeed a passport to cross the frontier into his world.

Their sexual compatibility had been just about bearable and it clearly delineated the border where they met. For all that, she was genuine and very much alive, her joie de vie was unrehearsed and unabashed. Betty didn't appear to think before she spoke or showed her emotions. She was life as he sometimes wished it to be and had provided him with moments when he too didn't have to think or analyse anything. Unfortunately, as a writer, he also felt that that was not his prerogative, especially in the dark times they were living through.

That Betty had been promoted on his fulsome recommendation and was now Bokhari's secretary, Orwell hoped she would have an affair with her new boss and thereby diminish his guilt. It was difficult to say whether this had come to fruition and it seemed somewhat unlikely in any case. Orwell couldn't imagine them making love. Bokhari appeared to be as ascetic in his relationships as he was catholic in his taste of programme content. Betty was obviously not Bokhari's sort, he thought, unless of course Bokhari was also in the game for some carnal diversion.

In so many respects Bokhari remained an enigma to Orwell. He was not unattractive. He was clever, if not witty, and he was alone in London. There was no evidence of any commitments back home in India. Furthermore he was well paid for what he did, or so Orwell presumed. Betty had also previously admitted an eye for 'exotic' gentlemen. But had she acted on it? She was a woman on the rebound and may have been open to Z.A.'s entreaties, if in the unlikely event he had made any. It was therefore quite possible she had put

Blair behind her and may even have forgiven him? That was what Orwell hoped.

———

UNKNOWN TO ORWELL, he had indeed hurt Betty and to begin with she had been very angry with him. But now she was content to move on and the promotion had helped. She no longer held any real resentment towards him. Like many married men who overstep the line, she thought that he had seen the error of his ways and had returned to Eileen, especially in her time of need. In Betty's mind that had been the right thing to do and she now respected him for that. In any case, Orwell had recently become less than impressive beneath the sheets and, once or twice, she had worried about him actually dying on top of her. But his taking up with Rana had jolted her and some simmering resentment was still inhabiting her.

However, Bokhari was a good, hard-working boss and she was getting on with him 'famously'. Unlike Blair, he was unproblematic, charming and always grateful for her efforts. She had to get things just so all the time and, unlike Blair, Bokhari had asked for discipline and order in everything she did. Only perfection would do and Betty had risen to the challenge and was thriving on it.

It was Bokhari who had asked her to report Rana missing. Office rumours had begun to circulate and at first Betty thought the idea that Rana was having an affair with Blair was preposterous. Why would a divine, intelligent creature like Rana be attracted to that grizzled and bad-tempered old man? Rana Mukurjee could have her pick of men. Indian men in particular would fall at her feet if she so desired. Betty even wondered why she herself had been attracted to

Blair or even Orwell? Nevertheless, when Bokhari had asked her to report Rana missing she had become really worried and hated to think anything bad might have happened to her as a consequence of Blair's advances.

It dawned on Orwell that the ghosts of his literary imagination had come to haunt him in the most perverse fashion. Betty was the reincarnation of Ma Hla May, Flory's prostitute in *Burmese Days*, and Rana was the translucent Elizabeth Lackersteen. They had somehow swapped their race and much else besides. It was as though he was looking at a photographic negative of the two women, added to which their personalities and that their roles had been transmuted in some sort of mishap of translation. Forsaking Betty for Rana, he hoped, would not have the same deadly outcome as that of the book. He had also come to the conclusion that Rana had been right, Flory was a coward.

Just as Elizabeth Lackersteen had been to Flory, Rana was Orwell's idea of a perfect companion – a more complete and young version of Eileen. That Rana might hate the British Empire and all it stood for only elevated her in his estimation. She was antithetical to his Englishness and his attempts to enculturate her into the mysteries of the 'common people'. She had largely rebuffed or denigrated his efforts. This he put down to a combination of his poor teaching and her unwillingness to learn. Despite her age, she had well-formed and deeply ingrained positions on most subjects. She was educated rather than intelligent, he thought. She rarely changed her mind and seldom made room for any opinion that might contradict or challenge her own. Her unflinching, unemotional shell was not just a protective coat, it was a weapon and he had loved the challenge of trying to disarm her.

He also thought of her as an ally, albeit one that joined

him on her own terms and for her own ends. In so many respects, she reminded him of Jahida.

Orwell made his way to The Cut and sought out Crow. He wanted to question the landlord about Rana. The journey was as normal as normal could be in times of war. The streets were in a state of continual repair and disrepair and militarisation had converted London into one great encampment for the various Allied soldiers, sailors and airmen. Although he had wanted to be part of the war machine, he felt himself peripheral to the effort and sacrifice that was going on all around. He scuttled apologetically between the mass of uniforms and eventually arrived at the Emporium.

The shop was shut for a holiday. He used the back entrance and hurried to the room. There was no sign of life or any recent visitor. There was no note. He quickly left by the back door and for most of the journey home he had a feeling of being followed. He put this down to his shadow called guilt.

16

Percy had not expected the call – in fact a written summons to attend Tottenham Court Road police station. There was little information, just that he was to report directly to Detective Chief Inspector Edward Mackie of the Criminal Investigation Department. The name was enough for him to comply without complaint or hesitation. Mackie's reputation went before him and he was the quintessential detective's detective. Percy was in awe of the man, the master and fellow artist in criminal investigation. This was a Calling and he was about to become one of The Chosen.

Percy stood at the open door of Mackie's office and watched his idol. The man was almost exactly as he had imagined – big, late-middle-aged, with broad shoulders, a full head of shiny black hair and an expansive taste in suits. He sat at his desk and puffed contentedly on a large cigar as he studied a copy of the *Sporting Life*.

Mackie must have sensed he was being observed because without looking up he said, 'I'm busy.' He had a deep, baritone voice to match his square jaw and granite features.

'Percy, reporting for duty, sir.'

'Percy? On first name terms now, are we?'

'No, guv. Inspector Charles Percy, Missing Persons.'

'Missing what?'

'Persons.'

'Well done, you've found me, and I didn't even know I was lost! You with the Sally Army?'

'No, guv. The Yard. And I was told to report directly to you.'

'Why? What have you done or what do you want?'

'To be honest guv, I've no idea.'

'Can't you see I'm busy? Who the hell told you to come here?'

'I just had this note, guv.' Percy felt like a schoolboy reporting to the headmaster as he handed the note to Mackie.

Mackie glimpsed at the paper and threw it onto the desk. 'Oh that ... everyone should have had one of those. You're from the Yard? A detective?'

'Yes, sir. DI. I'm in charge of the Missing—'

'Done any murders?'

Percy was momentarily stumped by the question and paused before answering. 'No, guv, not personally.'

'I meant ... you know what I meant! Have you worked a murder?'

'No, guv.'

'In that case, I can't use you. I suggest you go back to the Yard and find yourself a few more missing persons. Stop wasting both our times.' Mackie resumed studying the form of the racehorses.

Percy turned to leave. He was so near to his hero, yet so far. He felt as he would if he had found a counterfeit five-pound note in his wallet. There was no way he was going to leave without at least trying. He stopped as he approached the door.

'What I lack in experience I can make up for in intelligence.'

'Intelligence? That's the first time I've heard that out of the mouth of a copper! I don't need intelligence. I need experienced detectives!'

'You need to know what to look for. And how to look, guv.' Percy turned back to face Mackie and nodded towards the *Sporting Life*.

Mackie acknowledged the inference and closed the newspaper.

Mackie pointed with his cigar. 'Are you lame? You hobble. What's wrong with your leg?'

'An accident ... while on duty.'

'When?'

'When I was a constable ... '26, during the strike.'

'What happened?'

'It got crushed and the doctor ...' Percy was reluctant to apportion blame.

'Ballsed it up?' Mackie finished the sentence.

'The dockers did it,' Percy said quickly.

'But the quack buggered it.' Mackie drew on his cigar and blew a massive cloud of pungent smoke into the air.

'How did you know?'

'You just told me. It's written all over your face. I can also read between the lines, and the fact that you're still in the force ... if Missing Persons counts! What else do I need to know?'

Percy wanted to applaud the fabled detective's powers of deduction but was also intent on changing the subject. Before he could think of a response, Mackie was once more on his case.

'Can you walk?'

'I'm here, guv.'

'So what can you do with your *intelligence*?'

'Use it. I've developed some new ways of systematically assessing and evaluating evidence. Finding and putting together the tiniest and most insignificant pieces of evidence and connecting them to the big clues. Anyone can collect the big stuff – male, five foot three, sixteen stone, with brown hair etcetera. But I'd ask, where does he get his trousers, his braces, his belt? What sort of job would he do if he were as big and short as that? Would he be able to ride a bicycle? You need to think like him, live his life, put yourself inside his head. It's at the microscopic level that we need to work. It's the small things that really matter.'

'Clues! Micro...bloody...scopic blooming clues! Whatever next?' Mackie's tone was distinctly dismissive. 'What do you think this is, some bloody Agatha Christie nonsense? Or Sherlock Holmes perhaps?'

'More of a Doctor Watson, I'd say.' He was perilously close to insubordination and tried a more submissive approach. 'I'm here to assist if you need it, of course.'

'Doctor bleeding Watson now, are you? This isn't bleeding fiction, Percy! This is for real, sonny Jim. You've never done a murder and you're here to *assist* us? I know there's a war going on but what's the bloody force coming to? Have you ever seen a body, a murdered one that is?' Mackie blew more smoke up in the air and waved his hand to disperse it.

'No, guv, but the principles are the same. Murder or missing person, you take the smallest clues and fit them to the largest obvious or known ones. It's like having a jigsaw puzzle with no picture, different-size pieces and not even straight edges. Others can collect the pieces and I'll put them together.'

Mackie seemed to be thinking.

'But can you run?'

Percy declined to answer.

'I thought not. How the Dickens are you supposed to catch criminals if you can't run?' Mackie paused. 'I know ... intelligence!'

'There's plenty of nimble constables, guv. I can tell them where to go and who to catch.'

Mackie seemed pleased with that answer and rose from his chair. 'Come with me and keep up ... if you can.'

Percy looked at the the name on the office door – it was not Mackie's.

'It's not your office?'

'I'm on loan from the Murder Squad. They called me in to take charge. We have a multiple.'

'A multiple?'

' Murders. Three so far.'

'And the same MO?'

'Looks like it. And that's why you've all been called in – all detectives with a rank that is. And that might be my biggest mistake.'

As they made their way swiftly down the corridor, others pinned themselves to the walls as if Mackie was parting the waves with Percy in his wake.

'He's still out there and we need to find him ... fast. If the Jerries don't get you tonight, he might ... only he goes for women, so you should be all right. Unless you like dressing up that is. You're not one of those, are you?'

Percy smiled and averted his eyes. 'No, guv, I'm married.'

'Notice you didn't say happily!'

Percy didn't appreciate the remark but smiled benignly.

Mackie led them into the Incident Room. It was packed with detectives and uniformed officers who became silent almost immediately. He walked over to a young constable pinning papers to a board.

'Hold on to that,' Mackie said, handing the young policeman his cigar. 'All right, you lot. Listen up.'

He stood imperiously at the head of the room and waited for complete silence. Percy stood at the back and was impressed by Mackie's power to immediately command the space.

'So far ... victim one. On Sunday morning, the body of a woman was discovered in an air-raid shelter at 8.40 am in Montagu Place in Marylebone by one Howard Batchelor, an electrician. Constable Miles called it in at 8.51 am. The scene was attended by DDI Clare of D Division, Albany Street nick. DSC Fred Cherill, Sir Fingerprints himself, later attended, as did a Dr Baldie, the local police surgeon. He confirmed she'd been strangled. Her handbag was presumed stolen – we don't know what was in that bag. We do know that she is, or was, one Evelyn Hamilton, but other than that we know next to nothing about her. We need to know what she was doing there.'

Mackie pointed to the large map on the board behind him and placed a pin on the location already marked with an X.

'Victim two. On Monday, the body of thirty-five-year-old Mrs Evelyn Oatley – also known as Miss Leta or Nita Ward – was found naked in her flat on Wardour Street. A former Windmill girl and actress, and lately a lady of the night. She was found by Messrs Charles Fuelling and George Carter, meter readers with the Electricity Board. She had been strangled, her throat had been cut and she'd been mutilated. Fingerprints suggest the strangler is left-handed.'

Again, he pointed to the board and a set of particularly gruesome photographs. He placed another pin on the location.

'Three: yesterday, a forty-three-year-old prostitute, Mrs Margaret Florence Lowe – also known as Pearl – was murdered in her flat in Gosfield Street, Marylebone. This one was called in by DS Blacktop. Are you here, Blacktop?'

The detective sergeant raised his hand. Mackie continued.

'Like the others, she'd been strangled with a silk stocking and her body mutilated with a variety of implements including a razor blade, various kitchen knives and a candlestick.'

Mackie walked to the board and stared at the photographs before placing a third pin.

'There's no evidence yet to connect the first with the others, but something tells me they are.' He walked to the back of the room and looked Percy straight in the eye. 'Percy here will find out how, won't you, Percy?'

Percy nearly collapsed and took deep breaths. He could feel himself breaking into a sweat.

'So what have we got, Percy? What does your *intelligence* tell us so far? Perhaps I should explain, gentlemen – this is Detective Inspector Percy from the Yard no less, and he's an *intelligence* expert. And I'm not being familiar – Percy really is his surname! Yes, intelligence ... a rare thing among you lot. And Percy here has kindly brought some to help us find our killer.'

Mackie was setting him up to knock him down, that was clear. He had a choice: play along or show them what he could do. He limped over to the photographs, thinking fast.

'If the cases are related, I think the first victim was probably a trial run that went wrong for some reason. He didn't have time to do what he wanted in the open air – the sexual assault and mutilation. He was probably disturbed in the act. Apart from that, there's little in common between the first and the other victims. We don't know if she was on the game like the other two. Unlike the governor, I don't think we should assume the cases are related. I wouldn't rule it out, but I wouldn't rule it in either.'

He had crossed the rubicon by disagreeing with London's most famous detective and had no choice but to continue.

'So far, you've concentrated on the obvious – we nearly always do. The fingerprints and abrasions tell us he's a left-handed strangler who likes to cut his victims with whatever's to hand. He's improvising – not prepared – and that makes him what's called an opportunist. Which means he's not planning to do what he does, or how he's going to do it. That's probably what we should work on. He's not in control and he's bound to leave clues.'

Percy waited and gave himself time to think before speaking again.

'He could be a Londoner, a local, or at least someone who's living near to London. He can make it in and out of town on a daily basis. Either that, or he's here temporarily, a visitor, travelling salesman, or a serviceman. Whoever it is, he's been staying or based here all this week.'

He paused once more and tried to gauge the reception. The audience looked blank. Some turned towards Mackie, who sat at the back, head down as if inspecting his shoes. Percy needed to break the near-silence and resumed.

'Sex would appear to be the main motive, not robbery. And if it's sexual, it's doubtful that he's finished. He's some sort of addict. He'll not stop till we – *you* – catch him.'

He paused again, thinking about what he had just said.

Unconsciously, his application to join the case had just slipped out. Fear and exhilaration coursed through him.

'These are just the big pieces, the bleeding obvious, you might say. At this stage I'd need to look at all the evidence – the small pieces, the fragments – before I can add anything further.' He surveyed the still blank expressions on the faces of those in front of him.

Mackie got up and walked to the front of the room, smiling as if congratulating himself on having embarrassed Percy, who now thought his once-upon-a-time hero had transmogrified into the devil himself. He had to rescue the situation. Before Mackie reached him he blurted, 'We have two Evelyns! And they were found by either an electrician or employees of the London Electric Company. Might be a coincidence. We don't know.'

The association had been spontaneous and involuntary. It was as if his brain had independently computed the evidence and directed his mouth to speak. Just like when he had first been consigned to his desk job. He was beginning to rediscover the art.

Mackie retrieved his cigar from the young constable, relit it and watched the smoke rise to the ceiling. 'So, nothing we don't already know,' Mackie said sarcastically, playing to the gallery. 'So much for Percy of the Yard and his *intelligence*! So we'd better warn all the Evelyns out there! Tell them to watch out for the sparks, electrical types, cos they'll be in for a nasty shock!'

This was met with guffaws from the assembled.

Percy ignored Mackie and, feeling emboldened, turned his back and began to study the crime-scene photographs. Mackie had not noticed that there were two Evelyns and an electricity connection. But even if it was irrelevant, he had made his point: everything needed to be re-examined, no matter how trivial. He smiled and savoured the small victory.

As Mackie was about to go back to his office, Percy stopped him. 'I'll need to go to the scene of the second murder. Would that okay, guv? And I'll need to review all the evidence and notes, yours included, for any small details that might be relevant.' He might have tried not to sound impudent, but had failed.

Luckily, Mackie was still in knockabout mode. 'I only take relevant notes, sonny. Do what you have to and just stay out of my way.'

Percy felt elated. He had surprised himself. For a moment he had forgotten about his leg and Vera and how he was seen by others. He felt rejuvenated, reborn and a real detective at last.

After collecting copies of the murder photographs, he went to Margaret Lowe's ground-floor flat in Gosford Street. On the way he called Baines and asked that they meet at the scene. He arrived to find an auxiliary constable guarding the premises and flashed his warrant card with a new insouciance as he entered.

The blackout curtains over a small window in the kitchen were still drawn and Percy had to turn on the hall light to see his way. The door to a room just off the kitchen was open and he entered. The smell was overwhelming. Although the body had long gone, the bloody mess was everywhere, most noticeably on the crimson-stained mattress. Percy took the photographs from his brief case and tried to locate himself as if he were the camera. The eiderdown and blankets that had partially covered Margaret

Lowe's body had been removed so he discarded the first photograph showing her head emerging. He took a second photograph, one that showed her mutilated torso, and held it up. Momentarily, he had a vision of Vera as the dead woman, and closed his eyes, forcing himself to think of something else. A knock on the door saved him. It was Baines.

'Guv, sorry I'm late. Are you all right? You look a bit—'

'I'm okay. Good to see you for once.'

'A real murder case and all.' Baines caught sight of the photographs. 'Holy Jesus Christ! Shit ... Look at that! I think I'm going—' He rushed out of the room. Percy heard him retch and found Baines doubled over the kitchen sink. He ran the tap.

'Sorry, guv ... I've never seen—' He doubled over once more but nothing came out of him.

'Take a glass of water,' Percy said. 'I need to go back in.'

'I'll be with you in just a mo, guv. I just need a sec.'

'Take your time.'

Percy returned to the bedroom and resumed his examination. There was scant furniture or furnishings: a chair, a night-table, an antiquated wardrobe and a tatty old rug had made up the boudoir of Margaret Lowe. He studied a black-and-white photograph of the murder weapons, four in all, whose handles had been conveniently labelled with their different functions – bread, vegetable, table and, what? He couldn't figure what the black-handled knife might be used for other than slicing the thighs of an ageing prostitute.

There was a separate photograph of a poker, the handle of which appeared to have snapped off during the violence. An anaemic-looking Baines came into the room and watched as Percy meditated on the remaining photographs.

'Is that a candle, guv?' Baines asked, indicating one of the victim photographs. 'Between her—'

'Yes,' said Percy. 'From this.' He showed Baines a photograph of a candlestick and the young detective ran back into the kitchen and retched.

'There's no clock!' Percy suddenly exclaimed. 'It's a bedroom. So where's the clock?'

'Lady of the night, guv – p'raps she didn't need one,' Baines shouted back.

Percy started to search the bedroom. The table had but one drawer and there was nothing in the wardrobe apart from a few clothes. With difficulty owing to his leg, and careful not to disturb the clotted blood pools, he checked under the bed.

'Ah, there it is! Pros, like taxi drivers and lawyers, always like to have a meter running.'

The clock had stopped at 3.40 but there was no way of telling whether this had been in the afternoon or early morning. He picked it up with his handkerchief and placed it on the bedside table, then took an evidence bag from his case and dropped it in.

'When did it happen, guv?'

'Monday. And he's struck again since.'

'Sorry?'

'It's a multiple. That's why they called us in. All hands to the pump.'

'You mean a Jack the Ripper—'

'Something like that. Only he's taken a few days off now. He started on Sunday, killed here on Monday and again on Tuesday, and nothing since. He's due, I reckon.'

'Do you think he drinks their blood, guv?'

'He's not Dracula! And it's not some bloody fiction! This is for real, sonny!' Percy imitated Mackie.

'Sorry, guv. Are we done 'ere? I'd like to get some fresh air. Oh, we've had a development in the Indian case.'

'Let's go. I don't think there's anything else,' Percy said as if he had not heard the young detective.

They closed the front door behind them and saluted the auxiliary, who was sheltering from the rain just inside the building.

'A development?'

'Yes, guv. I forgot to tell you. It's this Orwell fella. He's been telling porky pies by the looks of it.'

'What about?'

'An affair.'

'With the missing woman?'

'Looks like it. He not just a writer, it seems. He's been dipping his pencil where he shouldn't.'

Percy shook his head. 'His pen. You don't dip a pencil.'

Baines's forehead creased and he looked at Percy blankly. 'Oh, and he's got a record. Well, a note on file. He was visited by the Vice boys a couple of years back. Indecent or obscene publications, or something like that. Apparently, some dirty sex books from France were seized and he was given a warning. He's not what he seems is our writer.'

'Keep quiet about Blair-Orwell for the time being,' Percy said. 'I'd like to follow it up myself.'

Baines, looking pleased with himself, tipped his hat, winked at Percy and walked off with a swagger.

Percy thought for a moment and shouted after the detective, 'Baines, how do you know?'

There was no reply. Baines was already lost to himself and the noise of the traffic.

BACK AT TOTTENHAM COURT ROAD police station, Percy inspected Margaret Lowe's belongings. Her black handbag contained all the usual ingredients of a working woman's everyday existence: a neatly folded handkerchief, two flattened cigarettes, a postage stamp and a gramophone-needle tin containing an assortment of coloured pills. In a side pocket he found two folded one-pound notes. He noted the serial numbers. Two more notes were lying at the bottom of the bag and he recorded their numbers. After making inquiries as to the location of the handbag, he was told that it had been partially concealed and that the killer had probably not seen it. He assumed that ladies of the night routinely did this to prevent being robbed by their clientele.

The door to the evidence room opened and a voice boomed.

'Oi, you, Percy, get your skates on and come with me! We've got another one.'

It was Mackie.

THEY DROVE through the darkened streets with the bell of the police car ringing out to alert pedestrians, as road accidents were becoming commonplace in the blackout.

It was the first time Percy had been in a fast-moving police car and he tingled with a guilty excitement. They arrived without incident at 187 Sussex Gardens, Paddington, at 10.30 pm.

As they entered the bedroom of the flat, Percy grabbed Mackie's raincoat to prevent him stepping on two used condoms lying just inside the doorway. Next to the condoms lay a copy of the *Evening Standard* from 12th February on which a condom wrapper had been placed. Mackie moved to examine the body on the bed and Percy inspected the room.

'Look at this, Sherlock. Not a pretty sight. Not squeamish, are you?' Mackie almost touched the body with his nose as he examined the wounds. The woman was almost translucent, save for the bloodied mess around her breasts and genitals. A stocking around her neck was knotted below her chin and there were various incisions to her torso, including a large gash stretching from her navel to her groin.

'It's the same killer. Left-handed. Same butchery,' said Mackie.

Percy had already seen enough and continued his examination of the room. On a table in the corner, a bloodied razor sat among various manicure devices. He moved his head to prevent his shadow falling across the table, and noticed the layer of dust covering everything. A closer examination revealed two distinct outlines of objects that had been disturbed or taken. There was also a small purse containing just pennies and a couple of Aspirin. It had been ransacked by the killer.

Mackie watched Percy as he went about his business. 'Well, Einstein, anything?'

'Whoever it was, she must have let him in through the front door because there's no other entrance. It's only this flat that uses the door from the street. In other words, he must have been invited in.'

'And?'

'He's taken some things from the table. And I'd say he's been through her purse because there's no notes. But I don't think he was out to rob her.'

'Do we know who she is? Was she on the game?'

'It looks like it judging by the Johnnies. I'll ask.' As Percy went to the door he spotted another used condom on the floor and pointed to it. 'Mind your step, guv.'

A constable stood outside the bedroom.

'PC Payne, sir,' said a still clearly shocked young policeman.

'You discovered her?'

'Yes, guv.'

'Do we know who she is?'

'Mrs Doris Jew ... Jouannet. The husband is Henry Jouannet. Sorry, sir, I'm not sure how to say it. It's J-O-U—'

'That's all right. Just make sure you get it right in your notes.'

'Her husband is the hotel manager at the Royal Court in Sloane Square. Apparently, they didn't really live together. He has a room at the hotel and said he came here every night just for his supper. He kept saying 'He told her not to do it. That's all he kept saying.'

'Do what?'

'Walk the streets, sir. He thinks she was on the game.'

'Thanks, Constable. Stay here, will you?'

Percy returned to the bedroom. Mackie sat on a chair, scouring the horse-racing results in a discarded *Evening Standard*.

Percy looked at the small bedside stand to the left of twin beds that had been pushed together. A cigarette butt lay in an ashtray – it was a Craven A. Next to this was a packet of Elastoplast. Some of the plasters had been roughly torn off. The hands of a clock had stopped at eight – but, again, this could have been day or night.

By the time Percy returned to the station it was well past midnight and he had no intention of going back to Vera. He was strangely enlivened. For once in his career, he felt he was doing something significant and doing it well. Despite the horror of the scenes he had witnessed, he was charged with a new sense of purpose.

Struggling to sleep as he lay in the duty cell set aside for officers in the bowels of the station, he started to read *A Clergyman's Daughter*. Despite the clamour from some drunken squaddies in the next cell, he ploughed on reading what he already judged to be 'not his cup of tea'.

Eventually he came across the rather strange twist in the novel: Dorothy Hare, the downtrodden daughter of the eponymous clergyman, after having rebuffed the advances of Warburton, a middle-aged atheistic lothario in their small East Anglian town, inexplicably develops amnesia and surfaces in the Old Kent Road. Furthermore, whilst attempting to escape Warburton's clutches, Dorothy had been seen by the village gossip-in-chief in what she thought was an 'embrace'. It didn't take Percy long to ponder the possibility that Rana Mukurjee may have had something of a similar experience. Substitute Warburton for Orwell perhaps?

17

The tentative knock suggested a juvenile hand. For a moment, Orwell thought someone had simply touched the door in passing. It was repeated and he rose from his desk stiffly, relit the roll-up that had died in his mouth, and opened the door.

'Mr Blair-Orwell?'

Orwell looked at Baines askance. 'You know it is, Constable.'

'Detective Constable Baines of Scotland Yard, sir.'

'Missing Persons, if I remember rightly. You'd better come in. I presume this is about Miss Mukurjee.'

'Correct, sir.'

'Is there any news?' Orwell sat at his desk and indicated to the young detective that he should pull up a chair.

'Not exactly, sir.'

There was a pause and the young policeman, after removing his hat, took out his notebook, sucked his pencil and turned some pages.

'What does "not exactly" mean, Constable?'

'*Detective* Constable, sir. This is a rather delicate

matter—'

'Delicate?' Orwell had heard that word a lot recently and had some idea of what might follow.

'We've recently received some information concerning yourself and Miss Mukurjee.'

Orwell smothered a cough welling in his throat.

'Suffice to say, sir, it concerns your relationship with the young lady.'

'Miss Mukurjee?'

'Yes, sir. And I'm here to clarify matters.'

'Miss Mukurjee was ... is my assistant. I think the word "relationship" is probably misleading in this instance.'

'No other sort of ... Might you just be friends of a particular sort?'

'What sort did you have in mind, Detective?' said Orwell, sensing the young man's embarrassment.

'Outside of the BBC for instance.'

Orwell had had enough of the game. 'What are you getting at? What have you been told?'

Baines closed his notebook as if to prevent Orwell seeing anything he shouldn't. 'I'm not in a position to divulge anything as yet, sir. I'm only intent on getting your side of the story.'

'Story?'

'Your version, if you will.'

'I've told you my version already.'

'Yes, sir. But I just wanted to check.'

'My version in comparison to this other version that I'm not to be privy to?'

'As I said, sir, I can't—'

'Divulge anything. Not even when and how you received this information?'

'Not at this moment, sir.' Baines paused and reopened

his notebook. 'So, you had an entirely professional relationship with Miss Mukurjee, you would say?'

'Yes, I would say that – entirely professional. Is that all? I'm pressed for time and really don't think I can help you any further.'

'You've a warning on file, Mr Orwell. From the Vice Squad, I believe?'

Orwell was momentarily taken aback.

'A misunderstanding. It was nothing. Henry Miller in case you're interested. I had to import his—' Orwell had lost the detective, that much was clear. He eyed the door.

The officer pocketed his notebook, put on his hat and placed his pencil behind his ear, then rose to leave.

'Your senior ... what's his name?' Orwell asked.

'Percy, sir. DI Percy.'

'Oh, yes, Percy. Thank you.'

Jahida appeared at the door. She nodded at the young man and waited until he had left, then entered the office. 'I've seen him before somewhere.'

'He's with the police. Missing Persons.' Orwell returned to his desk and began to roll another cigarette.

Jahida sat in the chair Baines had vacated. As usual, she was dressed in a riot of colour and her sari hung like a rainbow-coloured waterfall.

'They get younger every day! He looked as if he should be in school. What did he want? It must be Rana. Had he any news?'

Orwell continued working on his cigarette. 'Yes ... or rather no. It was about Rana, but no news, I'm afraid.'

'Then what did he want?'

'Nothing really. He was just keeping us informed.'

'Us? You? Why you? And just to tell us there was no news? Haven't they got better things to do?'

'I presume he was here because she worked for me.'

'She worked for the BBC, George. She didn't work for you.'

'With me then. And it should be *works*. We need to keep it in the present tense.'

'Of course.'

He lit the roll-up and decided to dig a little deeper. 'What do you know about Rana?'

'She's hard-working, intelligent and eager to get on I'd say.'

'No, I meant her background. Where she comes from for instance. Has she any family?'

Jahida looked away abruptly. 'I don't really know.'

There was a long pause. Orwell sensed she was was reluctant to answer.

'When she arrived, you warned me off her. Why did you do that?'

Jahida considered her answer before replying, 'I did it for your own good. I know you, George.'

'If I remember rightly, you said she was trouble. Why did you say that? You knew something, didn't you? What sort of trouble?'

Jahida nervously adjusted her sari. 'I was right. Look at us now ... with the police here and all.'

'But that's not what you meant. You know something about her.'

'She's young, pretty and strong-minded. That's all. And that's enough to spell danger, especially for an Indian woman. I should know.'

There was another strained pause and Orwell stared at Jahida as she continued to fine-tune her sari.

'And her family?'

'Why do you ask?'

'I'm just curious. She's not mentioned anyone.'

'Just curious?' Jahida was on the offensive.

'Has she any siblings?'

'I believe ... I might have heard ... there could be one.'

'In India?'

'Yes, I believe so. What does it matter? What business is it of yours?' said Jahida, increasingly irritated.

'A brother or sister?'

'A elder brother I believe. Is this an interrogation? Are you back to being the colonial policeman?'

He ignored the barbed remark. 'And her politics?'

'Oh, George, you, above all others, should have gathered those by now.'

'In fact I haven't ... couldn't. She was ... is ... an enigma. I can't make her out.'

'In what way?'

Orwell thought for a moment and relit his cigarette. He blew out some smoke and rubbed his thigh.

'She was so certain, emphatic even, about so much. Which is odd for someone so young. She seemed to have a set opinion about most things. But I can't make out her politics exactly. Like the rest of us she wants an independent India. But, she' s not spoken about how that is to come about. Do you know? She's unlike any Indian woman I've ever met, apart from yourself of course.'

'Now you're being both a racialist and a typical male bore!'

'I didn't mean it like that and you know it.'

'Do I?' Jahida cast her best matron face.

'All I was trying to say is, she's extremely mature for her years. She sometimes comes across as schooled, or trained in some way. Her arguments sound as if they are second-hand, as though they weren't her own.'

'Is that what you thought? She's some sort of ventriloquist's dummy? Just like me?'

'No, I'm not saying that at all.'

'It sounded like that – as if she has no mind of her own. That she couldn't have her own ideas or opinions ... like most of us Indian women, perhaps?'

'I didn't mean that at all, and you well know it. Why do you insist on perverting everything I say?'

'I'm not. It's what you sound like. For someone who is supposedly renowned for plain speaking, you can be incredibly vague.'

'Where might it have come from, that directness?'

There was another momentary silence and they stared at each other.

'Struggle, George, struggle. We women have had to learn how to get our voices heard. Like the rest of us, she probably learned through struggle. We have to grow up quickly in the circumstances we find ourselves in ...at home in India. Women have to, just to survive.'

'You do know about her then?'

'She must have been born into struggle. And like many others, her life has probably not been easy. But unlike many others, the vast majority in fact, she has done remarkably well to get this far. That's all I will say.'

Orwell noticed the hesitance of Jahida's remarks and their generality.

'And her disappearance? Do you have any idea what might have happened to her?'

' George I need to go. We have a meeting with Bokhari in 1-01.' Jahida lifted her sari and with her back to him waved for Orwell to follow her.

'Jahida!' he shouted after her.

She was gone.

18

Percy awoke with an insight: he needed to check on recent assaults on women within a two-mile radius of the murders. This had been overlooked – murder squads tend to concentrate only on murders.

Without bothering to clean himself up, he asked the reluctant duty sergeant to initiate a local audit. Invoking Mackie - it never failed to deliver compliance - the sergeant duly but reluctantly obliged.

Four hours later and just before Percy was about to go to lunch, the duty sergeant reported back.

'West End Central and Paddington Green nicks. Two attacks reported in the past two days, and both involve servicemen. Could be one and the same?'

Without informing Mackie, Percy left for Paddington Green.

The first incident report concerned Catherine Mulcahy – a prostitute who plied the streets of Piccadilly and kept a room for business in Marble Arch. On Thursday, 12th February, at 10 pm she had been propositioned by an airman and they had taken a taxi to her place of work. He gave her two pounds and even proceeded to try to get his money's worth whilst still in the cab. She said she'd had a 'funny feeling' about him all along.

A wonderful thing is hindsight, Percy thought.

The report described in explicit detail what had followed. Mulcahy, or the constable who had taken her statement, was either a budding writer of erotica or had read too many Tuppenny Dreadful rags. The description of Mulcahy, naked on her bed, save for her boots, and engaging in some rough foreplay when attacked, seemed overly gratuitous. Yet it was also precisely the sort of detail he thrived upon. The description of the attacker was rather vague but sufficient: five foot eight or nine, medium build and wiry. Greenish-grey eyes. Pale and looked like he had been wearing glasses. Well-spoken and clean-shaven too. He had also told her he was thirty-one. In all, he had paid her ten pounds in one-pound notes – two in the cab. The rest he had thrown on the floor as he escaped. The money was taken as evidence and a carbon copy of the receipt was attached to the report. Percy went to the front desk and requested the evidence bag and copied down the serial numbers of the notes.

West End Central police station was the next stop.

The second report concerned Mary Heywood, thirty, married but separated. She had been due to meet her new army-officer boyfriend at the Brasserie Universelle in Piccadilly between eight and nine on the night of the attack. By all accounts she was a 'just regular girl' in search of a steady relationship. The boyfriend failed to show but she did not take this to be unusual due to his regularly revised schedule. She sat alone in the bar and was approached by an airman, who offered to buy her a drink. She described him as blond and scruffy. He spoke with a refined accent. Despite being wary of his advance, for some reason she agreed to accompany him to the Trocadero for something to eat. At the restaurant she began to question his motives when he failed to take off his greatcoat and looked anxious. He then pulled out a wad of money and counted it out in front of her. There was thirty pounds in all. To escape, she agreed to give him her telephone number, COL6622. It was false. She left at 9.05 pm.

Halfway back to the brasserie, the airman offered to show her the way, via Jermyn Street. Mary knew this was not the correct route, yet again for some unknown reason she continued to follow him. She took out her small night torch to light the way down the blacked-out streets but he suggested she put it away in case an ARW saw them. The Air Raid Wardens were often frustrated ex-police or invalided servicemen from some time past and exercised their new found authority with gusto. The couple soon entered St. Alban's Street and it was there that he suddenly attacked her outside the nearby Captain's Club, kissing and fondling her against her will. As she attempted to get away, he grabbed her by the throat and began to strangle her, saying over and over, 'You won't, you won't.' Then his grip tightened and she lost consciousness.

The report included a statement from Mary's saviour, a young night porter named John Shine. At 9.45 pm he was making his way to work along St. James's Market when a flicker from a torch down an alleyway caught his attention. He heard a noise that sounded like a scuffle and went to investigate. The torchlight flickered a few more times as he approached and he came across Mary Heywood lying in a doorway. He heard someone running off and the sound of something dropping onto the pavement. The victim's torch was later recovered at the scene. Shine attended the woman, who was semi-conscious and incoherent. He tried to summon help but none was forthcoming. He managed to get her to her feet and saw the contents of her handbag strewn on the floor. Next to them lay a respirator. Thinking it was Mary Heywood's, he rescued it and they made their way to Haymarket.

Police Constable C46 James Skinner's statement was next: 'I approached the couple. It was just after 9.54 pm. Having ascertained the nature of the incident, Shine surrendered the respirator to my custody. I then accompanied them both to West End Central police station. I then returned to No. 1 St. James's Market and recovered some more of the contents and the bag of the attacked woman, Miss Mary Heywood.'

Percy asked to see the respirator. From its case, it was identified as belonging to a member of the RAF Regiment – number 525987.

'Have you contacted them yet?' Percy asked the duty sergeant.

'Yes, sir. Did it myself. I've been in touch with the RAF Police and asked them to check the number. In fact we've just heard.' He scrambled for his notes and retrieved a piece of paper. It was the wrong one. He looked again and found what he was after.

'The mask belongs to Leading Aircraftman Cummins of 14/32 Flight. I took the liberty of asking the RAF lot to detain him.'

'Good work, Sergeant.'

'Thank you, sir.'

'Send DC Bennett and one of your boys to pick him up. I'll be downstairs.'

Percy sat in the canteen of the station and took out *Down and Out in Paris and London*. Had Orwell really done all this or was it fiction?

19

'THAT WOMAN! THAT STUPID EF'ING WOMAN!' ORWELL WAS unable to contain himself. Even at half volume, everyone in the ante-room must have heard him. 'Either she goes or I do! That useless, stupid, stuck-up cow!'

There was an embarrassed silence and everyone averted their eyes. Only Jahida looked at Orwell and gave him her best matron face. The veins in his forehead bulged and he had turned a bright shade of pink. No one had seen or heard him like that before. He swallowed a rising cough and threw his script onto the control table.

'Z.A., I mean it. She has to go.'

'We heard you!' Jahida said. 'Calm down and watch your language!'

'Blair, please—' said Bokhari as Sir James Sutton, permanent secretary in the War Office and husband of the 'stuck-up cow', entered the room.

Short, portly and balding, the pin-striped suited mandarin looked older than his years, whatever they might be. His squinty eyes were hidden behind thick-lensed, horn-rimmed spectacles and Orwell couldn't help but notice how he immediately filled the room in every sense.

'Good show, Bokhari! This is excellent stuff you're doing here. Lady Sutton is having such a good time doing these little talks. Keep it up. Keep it up!' he said as if he were the team captain.

It was all Orwell could do to stop himself punching the patrician square on the jaw. The others hid their embarrassed smirks and swallowed their giggles. Bokhari, forever the diplomat, came to the rescue.

'Thank you, Sir James. I think you flatter us. And Lady Sutton, I think there's still room for some improvement,' he replied diplomatically and looked directly at Orwell,.

'Improvement? Really? Well, good luck old chap. And a little advice: I wouldn't ask her before changing anything, if I were you. Just go ahead and change it. I always find it's best that way with Gertrude. She doesn't always listen to good advice, you know. It's like training a cat. Sometimes she goes off on a bit of a detour. Perhaps you've noticed? Can't keep to the blinking script at all! She never knows when to stop. Overruns in everything she does. Probably not good for the wireless, eh?'

Sutton's voice reminded Orwell of the ack-ack guns. His short bursts were fired off more in hope than accuracy and only sporadically did they hit a meaningful target. He continued spraying the air.

'I pity you poor fellows trying to rein her in. If you find the secret, let me know!' He guffawed and waited for the expected approbation. It was not forthcoming. Orwell could restrain himself no longer and, looking directly at Sir James exclaimed, 'An absolute blinking disaster!'

The mandarin remained silent and simply smiled.

There was an awkward pause, then Bokhari attempted to recover the situation and stepped in once more.

'The situation in India and Far East. It is no doubt a disaster.'

'A disaster? Not yet,' Sir James replied, looking directly at Orwell.

'It's useless. She's lost! And it's all a bloody mess,' Orwell mumbled.

'I fear Mr Blair has very strong views about situation in India,' said Bokhari.

'I thought for a moment you were referring to my wife!' Sir James chuckled and again looked Orwell directly in the eye. There was a moment of mutual recognition and they both knew something had just transpired.

Bokhari shuffled his papers to signal the end of the meeting.

As he was about to leave the studio ante-room, Sir James turned to Orwell. 'Might I have a word, Blair, in private?'

Bokhari and Jahida moved to leave the room, Jahida signalling to Orwell that he should button his mouth.

Sir James waited until the room was cleared, and said, 'Lost? A bloody disaster?' He averted his eyes and dusted something invisible off his lapel.

Orwell stood motionless and said nothing. A cough was tunnelling its way through his windpipe. He swallowed it.

'I agree, she *is* hopeless.' Sir James reached into his breast pocket and took out a silver cigarette case. He flipped it open and offered it to Orwell.

'She's absolutely bloody useless at the broadcasting business. Any damn fool can see, or should I say, hear it. The empress really has no clothes, so to speak. Only, I think you should be a little more guarded about letting everyone know. Gertrude might get to hear and that would be that. I'd be forced to have a word with those upstairs. You get my drift, Blair?' He took a lighter from his jacket pocket and lit both their cigarettes. 'I'd have to get you sacked or something like that. Now that would be a disaster, I'd say.'

Orwell didn't know whether he was being supported or threatened? There didn't appear to be any menace in Sutton's tone and his civil-service demeanour made it difficult to discern any emotion in his voice. Yet Orwell detected that something was in the offing.

Sutton went over to the studio window and stood with his back to Orwell. A plume of smoke enveloped him as if he were disappearing into a typical London fog. He turned around.

'You see, Blair ... dammit man, can I just call you Orwell?'

'Of course. Whatever you find—'

'I find an awful lot to admire in your work. I've actually read one or two of your essays. I particularly liked *The Road to Wigan Pier* and more recently I was particularly taken by *The Lion and the Unicorn*. Are you surprised?'

Orwell felt a distinct thaw in the air and his shoulders dropped in relief. 'Yes, I certainly am. Thank you. I'm ... what can I say? I would never have thought. A man such as yourself.'

'And what sort of man is that, do you suppose?' Sutton took a step towards Orwell.

'Part of the Tory Establishment.'

Sutton smiled broadly and shook his head. Almost whispering, he added, 'Part of the Establishment? How little you know me, Orwell. Part of the Establishment indeed! And for the record, I've never been a Conservative. Yes, I'm in the higher echelons of the ... well, call it the Establishment if you will. But I'm first and last a civil servant and as such I try to maintain a meticulous impartiality in all matters political. I'm an organ-grinder, not one of the elected monkeys.' Orwell grinned in appreciation of that phrase.

'And unlike the politicians, I pride myself on getting things done rather than just saying or promising to do something. And, of course, the monkeys seldom get around to actually doing anything meaningful without our say so.'

Orwell stood transfixed, sure that Sutton had more to say. He wasn't disappointed.

'Like you, Orwell, I consider myself a plain-speaking man. I've come quite a long way in life. Worked my way up, as they say. I have few, if any, pretensions and I'm known for telling it as I see it. I think that's why Churchill likes to have me around. You see, we do have that in common, at least.' Sutton looked around to see if they were being overheard. 'I'd also say that I know excrement when I see and smell it. And this job of yours, here at the BBC, to my eyes and nose at least, is full to the brim of, excuse my French, *merde*. Pumping this stuff out by the square yard must be most unedifying for a man of your talent, Lady Sutton's efforts especially. So I can empathise with you on that score. You see, I too am dictated to by political imbeciles and incompetents such as ... well, that would be saying.'

Sutton took a long drag on his cigarette and once more patrolled the room on the lookout for eavesdroppers. 'Returning to the essential point, and the reason I wanted to talk: India is doomed if Churchill and the people I work with have their way. It'll indeed be a disaster of biblical proportions.'

Orwell was now hanging on every word. 'Churchill?'

'Yes, Churchill, Amery, Linlithgow, all of them in fact. The Establishment.'

'I'm sorry, but I don't see what this has to do with my

assessment of your wife's ability as a broadcaster. We seem to have strayed somewhat —' Orwell interjected.

'Yes, I was afraid you wouldn't see the connection.' Sutton paused and appeared to be in two minds as to whether to continue. He looked Orwell in the eye as if searching for a signal that he might be trusted. 'It occurred to me earlier, when you said "disaster" and Bokhara tried to divert the subject. That the future of India is our common ground. You and I are like Emperor Neros, we're both fiddling while Rome - or India in this case - burns. You're putting out wireless programmes about poetry and those diatribes of my good wife and they're supposed to save India! But for what, or more important, for whom? Where I was brought up, they'd say it was, excuse me, a load of bollocks. No amount of Tennyson, Byron, Wordsworth, or indeed my Gertrude will save India from a disaster of our own making. I think you and I both know that.'

'Yes, of course,' said Orwell. 'You'd have to be a damn fool to think otherwise. But what is one to do? The die is cast. That India is most likely lost to the Japanese. It will have to fend for itself sooner or later. Perhaps a little poetry might provide some solace to someone, somewhere out there.'

Sutton moved closer – the short civil servant looking up at the towering Orwell.

'Perhaps it might, Orwell, but poems, no matter how insightful, will not save India. I certainly agree, it would be most regrettable, a catastrophe even, if India was to be lost to the Axis. But in fact that's not really the most pressing problem. No, you see, more important ...' Sutton paused, as if considering what to say next. 'You might not know this but I spent five years trying to sort out the finances of the government of India. I was responsible for setting their budget. I know exactly how that country's run. I can give you pound, shilling and penny farthing of how much we have plundered those people for our own gain. It's now facing a disaster entirely of our making. There will be millions of deaths in the coming months. Yes, millions, and we shall be responsible. And with your help I want to prevent that happening.'

'Millions of deaths? Why are you telling me all this? Surely it's—'

'Secret? Yes, top secret. But I'm telling you because ... I need to tell someone. And I know you care about India, as I do.'

'But you're far better placed than I to do something about it.'

'Perhaps, but I'm not entirely sure. In fact, I think you might be better placed in some respects. I'm bound, you see by being part of the Establishment. Once they have you, they have you. There's no escape. Not that most care to escape in any case. I'm bound you see and I'm no Harry Houdini.' Looking at his pocket watch, Sutton quickly made for the door. 'We need to resume this conversation. I have to rush.'

'This conversation?'

'I'd like to finish what I was saying. I'd like to have another word ... before it's too late.'

'I'm sorry?'

'There have been some developments, in cabinet, and I need to ... talk. My club? No, perhaps not. Somewhere a bit more private. I'll be in touch.'

Sutton moved towards the the door.

'When? When shall we meet?' Orwell called after him.

Sutton stopped and turned. 'How about tonight?'

Orwell was surprised by the suggestion.

‘Is that suitable? I’d really like to pick your brains before—’

‘Yes.’ The words emerged almost involuntarily. ‘But you need to telephone me or my secretary this afternoon. I’ll see what I can do. I’m afraid there’s a bit of a flap on at the minute. One of our assistants has gone AWOL.’

‘Yes, I’d heard. Gertrude said something about not getting her script on time as a result. Not that she ever keeps to it! She thinks we can’t rely on the new breed of Indians. She’s always thought that ... even about the old-school wallahs. In her estimation these young, modern types are even more unreliable. Quite put out about the script she was. I’ll telephone you this afternoon.’ Sutton nodded and left the room.

Orwell stood dumbstruck. A very senior civil servant had just unburdened himself of some state secret. It was extraordinary, even surreal.

20

Meeting Sir James Sutton turned out to be fraught with difficulty. Eileen was due 'a Laurence' and Orwell knew he ought to be on hand to pick up the pieces. He was also expected to attend his Home Guard station to answer a charge that he had endangered a recruit by exploding a device without permission. The disciplinary panel should have taken precedence but his journalistic instincts impelled him to meet Sutton instead. He compromised and asked that they had a high tea rather than meet in the evening. That would enable him to report to the tribunal and then return to Eileen before the full force of her grief had taken over.

They met at a restaurant across from Waterloo station. It was neither salubrious nor the proletarian greasy spoon that Orwell would have preferred. As had been the case with many foreign-owned businesses, a rapid change of name and an underplaying of the origins of the restaurateurs had been undertaken. Ristorante Azzuri was now the Blue Café and Enrico and Maria Conti had become Henry and Mary Prince. The place was now devoid of anything

Italian and from 4.30 pm every afternoon, excluding Saturdays and Sundays, they served an English high tea with scones and jam - but no cream.

Orwell entered, thinking that the once Italian café was entirely in keeping with the senior civil servant's character – neither highbrow nor lowbrow and under the surface not at all what it seemed.

Sutton was already waiting in a seat away from public view. There was just one other customer.

Orwell had not had time to change into his Home Guard uniform and instead carried it in a large brown paper bag. He made his way towards his nervous-looking host.

'Sir James.'

'I'd prefer you not use my name,' Sutton replied softly behind his hand. 'Everyone calls me P.J. Is it to be Orwell or Blair this afternoon?'

'Just call me George,' Orwell whispered, his hand to his mouth in mimicry. Sutton appeared not to appreciate the humour.

'Thanks for coming, George. I wanted to see you—'

Mary came and stood by their table, awaiting their order.

'High tea for two, please,' Sutton ordered and she left as swiftly and silently as she had come. 'I wanted to talk about —' he looked around nervously and indicated the only other customer. 'Do you think we can talk here? What I have to say is rather—'

'Delicate?' Orwell almost smiled before a cough welled up.

'It's more than delicate, as you put it. It's about our conversation earlier and the catastrophe that is shortly to happen in India.'

Relieved that the subject of Sutton's wife was off the

agenda, Orwell reached for his tobacco tin. Sutton reciprocated by taking out his silver cigarette case and insisting Orwell take one. They were Player's Weights and Orwell thought twice before accepting, then placed his tin on the table and fumbled one of the cheap cigarettes out of Sutton's case.

'I'm a straightforward man, Orwell – sorry, George – and I know one when I see one. That's why I think I can trust you. I believe you're an honest man, sincere in your beliefs – most of which, from what I can gather, I strongly disagree with. Still, I take you to be fundamentally on the side of truth, decency and most important your country. Am I correct?' He lit their cigarettes with a monogrammed lighter.

Orwell took a drag on the cigarette and stifled a cough. 'I believe in saying and, wherever possible, doing the right thing for my country. Yes, in that regard, I suppose I am honest. But my beliefs are also an essential part of that and I can't separate my political views from what I see as good for the country. They are one and the same in my book. I'm an English socialist.'

'Yes, that's obvious enough. But you're no friend of either the fascists or the communists, or indeed the Conservatives, I gather.'

'You're well informed.'

Sutton acted as though he had not heard and Orwell decided not to pursue the matter.

'And yourself? Do you have a political persuasion? A secret one perhaps?' Orwell asked mischievously.

'Categorically not!' Sutton had raised his voice and immediately reverted to a whisper. 'I'm a civil servant and I sometimes think I was born to be one. I've never sallied into political theorems of this or that. I've no ideology and I was never brainwashed at school. If anything, I'd say I'm apolitical. I've seen the political class first hand and it's a club I've no wish to be a member of. I consider myself independent in the true meaning of that word. I serve my country. I serve my ... our people, regardless of politics and the politicians. I simply serve my country the best I can.'

For some reason Orwell did not believe Sutton and took a moment before replying.

'Regardless? What happens if, or when, Hitler arrives? Would you serve him? My Country, Left or Right ... will there be a fence left for you to sit on if that day ever arrives?'

'I thought it was *Right or Left*? I particularly liked that piece of yours. Yes, certainly, I'll continue serving my country, Left and/or Right. In any case, Herr Hitler doesn't look like arriving just yet.'

Mary returned with a pot of steaming tea and two scones, margarine and a red paste that was a poor imitation of jam. She said nothing and once again disappeared as quickly as she had arrived. Sutton watched closely until she had negotiated the kitchen door.

'You were saying? India?' said Orwell.

'Shall I be mother?' Sutton poured the tea.

It was too weak for Orwell's taste and he insisted on taking it black. He also dispensed with the greasy margarine and spread the jam-like substance liberally on the crumbly, day-or-two old scone.

'India. Yes. Now, what passes between us here must remain strictly confidential. In fact, it is top secret. I take it you understand what that means?' He turned towards the man in the corner and waited to see if there was any reaction.

'In that case, don't tell me anything. Why do you need to?' Orwell replied.

'I need to tell someone before it's too late,' Sutton said.

They were the same words Sutton had used in Portland Place.

'Too late?'

'Before Churchill causes the death of millions more Indians.' Sutton kept an eye on the other customer, who appeared to be engrossed in his newspaper.

'Millions ... how?'

'By dividing India. His strategy for stalling any sort of independence is the oldest in the book – divide and rule. He believes that as long as the Indian nationalists are divided between the Hindus and Muslims, we can maintain their governance. It's a powerful and perhaps the most persuasive rationale for the continuation of our rule. Only now, what has been an implicit policy is about to become explicit.' Sutton looked around, then whispered, 'India is to be partitioned...only after the war is won.'

Orwell was taken aback by the word.

'As in Ireland or, at least, something similar. But on an immense scale. Churchill's believes that just as we held on to Ulster, we can hang on to India for the duration. He hopes that by setting Hindu against Muslim, we can limit any cession of our rule for the time being. We are going to propose something that falls a long way short of full independence. Dominion status or something akin. Of course it will be rejected by Congress. So while they haggle, we reap the benefits of having India as a bulwark against the Japanese.'

Sutton sipped his tea and lit another cigarette without offering one to Orwell. 'Of course, it's also a recipe for a pogram. It's just stoking up trouble. Imagine the chaos, the carnage of what will inevitably be a bloody division. There will be inter-communal conflict, conflagration, war even, for generations. It's almost guaranteed. It's well known that Churchill has scant regard for the Indians, especially Ghandi, and this is testimony to his profound ignorance and bigotry.'

Orwell finished his scone and lit a cigarette, one of his own Turkish shags. Sutton's disapproval was evident.

'But what if the Japanese get there first? All this will be made redundant.'

'We believe – the government that is – that the Japanese have no real interest in colonising India. In any case, Churchill is adamant that, come what may, they must be held back and that we must save India ...for ourselves. I've seen the figures. India will be protected because we're dependent upon it for raw materials and men. That country is paying the price for *our* war. We're already sequestrating their food and as a result there's a famine in Bengal unlike anything we've seen before. Bihar will be next. And that's why a disaster is pending. Hundreds of thousands, millions perhaps, will die as a consequence of what Churchill is proposing. In all conscience, I cannot and will not be party to it.'

The hollow civil servant had metamorphosed into a man of substance. There was unfamiliar emotion in his voice and his cheeks had the colour of the jam-like substance on the plate in front of him. Orwell found himself warming to the man.

'And we're doing this in the name of freedom and democracy. The very things we're denying the Indians.' Orwell paused, took a sip of his rapidly cooling tea, and said, 'I still don't see why you're telling me all this. What can I do? I can hardly broadcast it. The censors are all over my work. Security and policy etcetera.'

'Of course. Of course. I recognise that you can't say

anything on the wireless ... even write anything. No, I just need you to spread the word to your colleagues in the India Section. Let them know. Inform them of Churchill's folly, but subtly of course so as to not spook them into thinking it's just your notion. Gertrude tells me they're proper chatterboxes. They'll spread the word to those who matter most in India. We know they have a direct line to the top.'

'We? How do you know?'

Sutton appeared ill at ease and took a moment to gather his thoughts.

'I've seen the reports. You have some rather strange bods working in the BBC. Half of your section are not to be trusted, it seems.'

'Me included, no doubt,' Orwell replied.

'Yes, very much so.'

That he was not trusted by the authorities pleased him. It was something of a badge of honour.

'But *you* trust me?'

'I do, but somewhat reluctantly, I must say,' Sutton replied, smiling.

'So what happens when the word gets out? Will they be able to trace it back to you or me?'

'They will, but by then I shall be Secretary for War. Churchill suggested as much this morning. No one will then suspect me of speaking out of turn. That, by the way, is also secret for the time being.'

Once again, Orwell could hardly believe his ears. Sutton now sat more upright, as if a considerable weight had been lifted off his shoulders.

'Secretary for War? That's a cabinet position. I thought you were a civil servant.'

'Yes, I am. I also need to do best by my country. The PM took me aside this morning and told me he's replacing that fool Margesson. That man is useless and I'm am only too willing to take his place and get things done. To serve my country.'

'And India?'

'Yes and India. But don't get me wrong Orwell – the interests of my country come first. What I see as an injustice for India is nothing compared to the incomparable harm the Churchill plan could also have for our own people. Our dependence on India and all the other territories, dependencies, colonies and the like, is such that we're bound to be tipped into the abyss should Churchill succeed. It will incite rebellion, if not revolution, elsewhere and everywhere.'

'Rebellion? More like calls for freedom, I would suggest. And of course we're no longer capable of settling the natives with gunships.' Orwell replied.

'It will be the end of the empire – something I know you'd love to hasten. But at what price both home and abroad? Of course, if millions die in India it will be most regrettable, but the destitution and suffering wreaked on my, your, fellow countrymen is also my concern. I'll not apologise for that. Our whole economy could be economically and socially ruined. It would be a step into the unknown. Britain without an empire. That's why I need your help. Churchill needs to be stopped.'

'My help? I never imagined that saving the empire would fall to me.' Orwell smiled at the thought.

'No, but spreading the word about the impending disaster is and you have a way with words.'

'Perhaps. On occasion the pen is indeed mightier than sword. But would they shoot the messenger?'

'I'm told they do. So you and I need to be very careful,' Sutton looked once more towards the man in the corner. There was a pause and both men averted their eyes.

Orwell tried to replay the salient points in his head. He thought about the Section and the probability that he was surrounded by 'untrustworthy' types'. Desai? Perhaps Baghat or the Princess? Bokhari even?

'And the government spies in the BBC? Won't they soon pick up the gossip?'

'Most certainly. That is the whole point. They will know that the Indians in India know Churchill's plan.' Sutton replied assuredly.

'In that case do you have the names of the people I shouldn't pass the time of day with?'

'No – all the reports I've seen are coded.'

'So it could be anyone?' Orwell said.

'It could be the whole crowd and they wouldn't know about each other.'

'These informers, spies, are they all Indian?'

'Yes, from what I've seen they must be, although they're generally considered unreliable by our Intelligence people. Some are known or suspected to be double agents. But there are others – their British Intelligence contacts.'

'You make it sound like the BBC is infested with spies.'

Sutton raised his eyebrows, lit another cigarette and summoned Mary. 'Another pot please, my dear,'

The mute woman collected the tea plates and cutlery, gave the table a cursory wipe and, spilling crumbs onto the floor, made her way back to the kitchen.

Sutton offered the faintest of nods in the direction of the solitary customer reading his newspaper. 'Is it really safe here, do you think?'

Orwell looked around at the stranger in the corner and suddenly shouted, 'Excuse me, have you the time?' The man ignored him or didn't hear. He tried again. 'Excuse me, have you the time?' This worked.

'Scusi ... Mi dispiace, ma non parlo l'inglese. No speak l'ingles,' said the man over the top of his newspaper.

'Italiano?' Orwell asked.

'Si, Italiano.'

Orwell turned back to Sutton. Although clearly impressed with his initiative, the man was still far from settled.

'Italian ... that could be a problem.'

'A problem?'

'May I remind you that we are at war with them,' Sutton began to shuffle in his chair. A droplet of perspiration formed on his forehead.

'Are we at war with all the Italians who live in London? I believe there are quite a few,' Orwell said cynically.

'No, I meant—'

Mary returned with a fresh pot of tea and cups smelling of soap suds. She placed the pot on the table and made her way to the kitchen. As she passed the other customer, she nodded subtly. Orwell, too, was now a little suspicious but thought it best not alert the increasingly paranoid Sutton.

'You're married?' Sutton asked, indicating Orwell's wedding ring.

'Yes.'

'Happily?'

Orwell, genuinely surprised by the sudden personal turn, paused and wondered whether and how to respond.

'We're quite normal, I suppose. We have our ups and downs. Why do you ask?'

'You've never had call for – how shall I put it – extra-marital services?' Sutton inquired over the rim of his tea cup.

Orwell swallowed his laughter. 'Have you?'

'I only ask because, well, damn it man, Gertrude and I ... we're no longer simpatico, if you know what I mean.'

'Yes, I think I do.'

'And we're unfruitful.'

Orwell could barely disguise a wry smile. 'You've no children, I take it?'

'Quite, though why, we have no idea. We've tried, but that was some time ago. How about you? Have you any?'

The confessions of the almost simpering senior civil servant had suddenly stopped being amusing. Sutton had somehow struck a raw nerve and Orwell thought it best to precis the truth.

'No, we're far too busy and I'm far too selfish and it's far too insecure in the writing business. It's a precarious existence. Children would just ... well, they'd get in the way.' He looked to see if Sutton suspected his lie.

'And your wife feels the same?'

'Yes, Eileen feels pretty much the same. Have you been reading my file?'

Sutton neither affirmed or denied and just shuffled in his seat. He then leaned over.

'I'm getting on now, George, and I'm about to be in the public eye as never before. I'm in need of ...let's say... servicing. I need to see if the locomotive can still leave the station. Just once, for myself. As a man, I was hoping you might appreciate my plight.'

Sutton was clearly embarrassed. The colour of his cheeks had now gone beyond that of the smudge of jam paste that remained on his plate. It was unlikely the man had made such a revelation before and must have taken some will, nerve or simply desperation. A wave of sympathy suddenly and unexpectedly overcame Orwell.

'Oh, indeed, as a man, I can certainly sympathise. I

honestly believe us men have needs that women sometimes fail to appreciate. But what do you want to do about it?'

'That's where I thought you might also be able to help. Though since you're happily married, perhaps not?'

Orwell suspected Sutton also knew more about his affairs than he was letting on. But something else struck him – Sir James did actually want him to procure a 'service'.

'I'm afraid I can't help, old boy. Not my ... not my line of work. Call me lucky, but I've had no call for it except once in Burma. That was a long time ago and I was in the flower of youth you'll understand.'

Sutton looked despondent. 'Of course. I was rather stupid to ask. Please forget about it. Only I'd heard you were 'a man of the world', as they say. Please, please forget I even mentioned it.'

Sutton had read his file. Orwell knew it and was intrigued. Quite illogically, he felt the need to go along with the request and to see if he was being set up in some way.

'I could however make some inquiries. The BBC has its faults, but knowing what's what, who's who, even where's where is something it does rather well. I can ask, discreetly of course.'

Sutton's eyes lit up. 'Would you? Please, I don't want you to get into any trouble. But if you could, I'd be most grateful.'

'I take it that this is something that would be both dangerous and extremely damaging for a person in your position, if it were to become known?'

'That goes without saying.'

'Yet you trust me?'

Without hesitation Sutton replied, 'Yes, for some reason I do. I must admit I don't really know why. Sometimes, contrary to my approach to most things, one simply has to follow one's instincts. I think I'm doing that with you. It's totally irrational, I admit. You probably stand for a lot of things I violently disagree with and I don't share your politics one jot. You could also end my career if what I told you ever came out. But for some reason I believe that will not be the case. I want to trust you because … you're George Orwell.'

'I'm also Eric Blair.'

'So you are. So you are. But George Orwell is someone I feel I can trust.'

Sutton's estimation was flattering but Orwell was still wary of what he was letting himself in for. The plight of India and the fulfilment one man's sexual craving were hardly equivalent. If he undertook the latter in the pursuit of the former, he might perhaps be able to live with any consequences.

'I'll ask around. Out of town?'

'No, I can't leave London. I'm under orders from the PM. It'll have to be in town.'

'I can't promise. As I said, it's not my usual line of business.'

'I'm sure you'll do your best.'

Orwell forced a smile and raised his tea cup. 'For the country!' He then turned to the Italian. 'For England!'

The man ignored him. Reaching for his bag, Orwell paused and turned to Sutton. 'I also have a favour to ask. I have to dash as I'm being charged with blowing up a dentist! You see, I'm in the Home Guard and, well, it's a long story, but I accidentally ignited a small charge in a demo I was leading. Unfortunately, some debris hit the dentist fellow full in the mouth. Quite apposite but painful nevertheless. He only acquired a small cracked tooth and everything seemed fine and dandy. I presumed he could fix it himself.

We christened it a war wound and that was that. But now, apparently, word has got out, and tonight I'm to be charged with ... well, I don't know what exactly. Hence the uniform in my bag. As I said, I'm due there shortly.'

'And the favour?'

'Oh, yes, well, should I be thrown out, I'd like you, as soon-to-be Secretary for War, to step in on my behalf. Would that be possible? You'd be doing me a tremendous *service* in return.'

'That would obviously be quite improper. However, in this instance, I think I might find a way.' Sutton almost smiled.

'Quits then?'

'By that I assume you'll also spread the word on Churchill's idea of partitioning of India.'

'I'll try.'

Orwell picked up his bag, helped himself to a cigarette from Sutton's case and went to the lavatory to change into his uniform. By the time he returned, Sutton had paid the bill and had left.

21

It had been relatively easy for Orwell to secure an escort for Sutton. Too easy in fact. Nearly every man he had asked, under the pretext of research for a new novel, had at least some idea of where he might procure a 'service'. Such was wartime. After some difficult negotiations, a hefty *fee* and solid assurances as to their discretion, he arranged to meet 'Diane' from the unlikely named Esher Ladies' Circle under the clock at Waterloo station.

Diane arrived punctually on the 2.14 train from Esher. Tall, rather slim and of an uncertain age, she was dressed as one might expect an Esher lady to be dressed – in a neat, well-fitting two-piece suit adorned with a fox-fur ruff, a leather handbag, white leather gloves and what appeared to be real silk stockings. For all the world she looked as if she had stepped out of *Tatler*. Despite being a stranger, she made a beeline for Orwell.

'How did you know it was me?' he asked.

'It's my job,' she replied in a very upper middle class drawl.

'You understand the arrangements? You know it's—'

'For a friend of yours, yes, I understand,' she replied curtly.

Orwell was jittery about the whole enterprise, especially taking her to Crow's dingy digs.

'It's difficult but ... this is a rather delicate matter. It's most important that you observe—'

Diane stopped and looked him in the eye. 'Strict confidentiality? Don't presume to tell me how to do my job, Mr Smith?'

'Yes, no ... well, of course. I know you will. It's just that—'

'Shall we go?'

Diane marched ahead. Despite his stride advantage, Orwell struggled to keep up and stifled a cough lingering in the back of his throat.

'I'm afraid that the accommodation might not to your usual standards,' he said, wheezing as they sped along.

'My standards?'

'It was the best I could do in the circumstances.'

'I'm paid by the hour, not by the state of the furnishings,' she tartly replied.

'I understand, but just to warn you.'

He looked around nervously as they made their way out of the station. Diane walked ahead with all the aplomb of a finishing-school graduate and not a few men, mostly soldiers, threw leery glances as she passed. Some even wolf-whistled and offered suggestions as to how she might wish to spend the night. As her obvious companion, Orwell felt his ego being boosted by the squaddies' envy and he returned the soldiers stares with interest. Diane appeared to take the notice for granted.

'There's something I wanted to ask. The Esher Ladies' Circle?' It had been on his mind since they left the station.

'We're ladies from Esher,' she replied simply.

Orwell conjured a vision of bored middle-class housewives or the wives of army officers on their own version of 'active service' and transformed in Jekyll-and-Hyde fashion into escorts or high-class prostitutes for the duration of the war. He thought that it could not be for the money as these women were obviously looking for something else to enliven their otherwise comfortable suburban existence. He let his imagination run away with the thought of these promiscuous ladies from Esher and Diane suddenly took on a new dimension. As a result he began to feel less concerned about her standards. Might she relish the roughness and squalor, something by way of contrast with her own cosseted home life?

They turned into Short Street and Crow's Emporium came into view. Orwell broke into a sweat and began to cough violently. He discreetly checked his handkerchief for signs of Joe.

'I'm sorry,' he spluttered between the hacking.

Diane disregarded him, as if steeling herself for the encounter.

They entered the junk shop and the shop bell rang. Crow, perched on his stool at the counter, looked up from an artefact he had been examining with a large magnifying glass. The lens remained over one eye, turning it into a huge cyclops-like appendage that covered half of his face.

'Ah, Mr Smith.'

'Mr Crow.'

'I told you, it's Dick to my friends and to you. Others call me different, of course.'

Crow lowered the magnifying glass and playfully used it to reconnoitre Diane. 'And what do we 'ave 'ere? A beautiful vision I'd say! A fine piece, if I might be so bold.'

Diane turned away, seemingly repulsed. Orwell nodded

at Crow and he and Diane quickly passed through the curtain to the stairs.

The room was moderately improved by Orwell's cursory clean-up the previous day. He had even placed a small vase of sweet peas on the window ledge and the fire was primed. Two glasses and a bottle of wine had been provided at cost. Diane sat on the only chair by the fireplace, inspecting her glossy polished nails and straightening her stockings. She appeared not to be overly concerned with the state of the place. Orwell stood awkwardly at the window, struggling with what to say.

'Have you been doing this long?'

She looked at him dismissively but remained silent.

'Sorry, I shouldn't have asked. I'll have to go soon. My friend, colleague more like, will be here any moment now.' He moved towards the door. 'I'll be back later. By five at the latest.'

He descended the stairs to the back entrance, unsure, even a little disconcerted, about leaving Diane alone in the room. He had forgotten to tell her the whereabouts of the WC. He thought he heard Crow calling and decided to ignore him.

At the agreed time, Sutton arrived on foot. He had dressed down for the occasion – flat cap, large scarf and tweed suit of some bygone age. Apart from his horn-rimmed glasses, he was barely recognisable.

'Orwell.' He gasped for breath. 'George, I've been thinking.'

'She's upstairs.'

'I'm not sure this is really—'

'She's waiting. Her name's Diane and she's very, very pretty.' This was not the word he had meant to use. *Desirable* would have been better. He held the back door open and shuffled his client into the shop.

'Up one flight. The room's on the right. The toilet's one floor up from that. I suggest you light the fire and pour yourself a drink before … well, you know.' He then reached into his pocket and placed a packet of condoms in Sutton's hand. 'Johnnies. I have no use for them myself.'

Sutton looked shocked and nearly dropped the gift. 'Oh, of course.' He had obviously not come prepared. It was as if his change of attire had transformed the authoritative figure into a quivering adolescent virgin.

Orwell watched as Sutton tentatively made his way up the stairs. Then he closed the door and headed for The Cut. He had nearly two hours to kill and the Blue Café would do nicely.

When he returned to Crow's, the room was empty. The fire was unlit and the wine untouched. More telling, the bed remained made up. It appeared that something, or rather nothing, had happened. Orwell was both intrigued and baffled, and made his way down to the shop.

Crow had his head down in his hands on the counter. A snore trembled from somewhere within. Orwell touched his arm. The junk man awoke with alarm and grabbed an antique cricket bat from under the counter.

'Shit! Don't be doing that! I could have killed yer!' He held up the bat. 'Bradman, 242 not out. The Oval or was it Lords? Interested?'

'I'm sorry. I didn't think. No, I'm not that keen on cricket.'

Crow relaxed and shuffled on his stool. 'Your rent's due.'

Orwell feigned not hearing. 'Did you see her?'

'See her?' The old man salivated.

'Just now, this afternoon. The woman I was with here earlier.'

'Yes, course I did. And very, very desirable she was too. I bet she was a pretty—'

'I meant did you see her leave?'

'I did. You were quick, I thought. Got a problem downstairs, 'ave yer? Either that, or the meter was running, if you know what I mean! She looked the expensive sort.'

'No, I don't know what you mean.'

'Well, she wasn't here long, was she?'

Orwell thought for a moment and decided to leave the old man with his own perverse version of events. As he was about to leave, Crow once more raised the issue of the rent.

Orwell returned to the counter and lit a cigarette. 'What about the other young woman I was with? Has she been?'

'The brown one? No, I've not seen her. Not since I last saw you at any rate. When was that?' The old man scratched his head, then his chin. 'Must 'ave been at least a week or two or more I'd guess.'

Orwell pulled out his wallet and handed over his only ten-shilling note. Lubricating the man's palm might get him to talk.

'Here's your rent. She's not been when you're out?'

'How would I know that? Psychic I ain't'. Crow picked up a small eyepiece and began to examine the note.

'She's not left a message or anything?'

'Nope. Nuffink. Lost her, 'ave you? Run off, has she?'

'Could you let me know if she turns up?'

'And how am I supposed to do that? Send you a pigeon?'

Searching his wallet, Orwell spotted Burgess's card and handed it Crow. 'Phone the number on the card.'

Crow looked at the card through the magnifying glass.

'Oh...BBC is it? And should I say Mr *Smith* wants to be contacted? Is it just John Smith? In which case, will they know which John Smith? It's a very popular name in these parts.' Crow smirked and gave Orwell a knowing wink.

'No, say it's Blair.'

'Blair? That's your real name is it? That's you?'

'Just say it's Blair.'

Orwell watched in silence as Crow went about his business. He wanted to stay and see if Rana appeared, but knew that that was improbable, if not downright absurd. After a long pause, Crow spoke.

'She wasn't here ... but another bloke was. Another brown fella.'

'An Indian? What did he want?' Orwell's voice, already squeaky, became tremulous with the bombshell. He took a long drag on his cigarette, only to immediately convulse with a fit of coughing.

Crow watched on apathetically.

'Did he say anything? What did he want? What did he look like?' Orwell almost choked on his questions.

'He was brown all right. Black I'd say. A Darkie. In fact he was the darkest I've seen 'round here. Young with a big mop of hair. It needed a cut, definitely. He was scruffy like, and oily.' There was no hint of irony in Crow's description.

'Did he say anything?'

'Nuffink. So I got him to buy one of these.' Crow reached for a paperweight with the Tower of London captured in the preposterous snow-like fluid. 'He loved it. D'you want one? Only a bob. G'on – eleven pence ha'penny to you.'

'Did he say why he was here?' Orwell said, vexed by Crow's lack of concern.

'Told yer, he didn't say a dicky.'

'When was this?'

Crow scratched his head and rolled his eyes. 'Oh, I dunno. The other day. I can't keep up with it. The days just—'

'Did you tell him anything? Did you mention the one I was with?'

'Nope. How many more times? I already told yer, he didn't say a word, apart from how he loved the—' Crow held up the paperweight.

'Did *you* say anything?'

''Bout what?'

'Anything.'

'You, you mean? The room? Nah, course not. I never ever speak about my tenants. You never know who's listening. Strictly private and confidential I am. It's their business what they're up to, not mine. As long as they pays the rent, that is. And you just have.' Crow pulled the ten-shilling note out of his breast pocket and placed it in a box behind the counter.

'You'll contact me if she turns up? And the Indian too?' Orwell's voice was becoming a desperate squeal.

'Her big brother, is it? After you, is he?'

'Her brother? What makes you say that?'

'Obvious, innit? Or is he her boyfriend from back there? Eloped, 'as she?'

'As you say, that's my business.' He stared at Crow and decided to leave. 'Just get in touch if she or anyone turns up looking for me. On that number.'

'And Blair, is it? I'd better write all this down.'

'Let me write it.' He snatched back a card and hurriedly wrote 'Blair' on the back.

'And who do I charge it to, the telephone call, if I make it?'

'I'll see you right.'

'In that case, I might be in touch Mr *Blair*.'

Orwell left the junk shop panicked and confused. The reappearance of the mysterious Indian had not been a coincidence. He fitted the description of the Wallington stranger – it must have been the same man. But how was he connected to Rana's disappearance? She must have been followed and that meant their affair and the room was known. As he negotiated The Cut, the full calamity of organising Sutton's liaison dawned upon him.

More circumspect than ever, he made his way back to Portland Place, all the while checking whether he was being followed.

'Afternoon, sir. It's a bit brass monkeys out there.' Arthur, or perhaps Godfrey, the BBC commissionaire greeted him at reception. Orwell ignored him and rushed to the lift. Its doors opened, unexpectedly and shockingly revealed the corpulent figure of Sir James Sutton in his usual three-piece pinstripe suit.

Orwell made way for the passengers stepping out of the cage. 'Sir James.'

'Blair, just the man I wanted to see. I was just in your office.' Sutton's acting was abominable.

'I'm terribly sorry, Sir James. I had an errand to run.'

'Don't worry, old man, I've found you now.'

When they were alone, Sutton almost collapsed into Orwell's arms.

'What happened?'

'Nothing. Nothing happened, thank God. I couldn't go through with it. I paid her and she left. I went shortly after. These are yours.' he whispered and handed Orwell the packet of condoms.

'Did anyone see you?'

'No, how could they? I left by the back door as instructed.'

'Did you say anything ... to her, I mean?'

'Yes. Well, no, not exactly. I just said I'd changed my mind and thanked her for her time.'

'What did she say?'

'Just that the price was the same, so I paid her and she left. I think she went down through the front entrance. Is there a problem? Might she recognise me? My God. What—'

'That won't happen. She's very professional. She wouldn't say anything.'

'How can we be sure?'

'We can't. But that was always the risk. In any case, nothing happened.'

Orwell could not bring himself to reveal the fact that the room might have been under surveillance. The entire episode was an unmitigated disaster, one that was rapidly spiralling out of control.

Sutton, like a naughty schoolboy, made his way to the reception desk, looking back only as the lift doors closed on Orwell.

22

The Blackout Ripper was invented on Saturday, 14th February – St. Valentine's Day. News of the murders had broken and the press's inevitable invocations of Jack the Ripper turned out to be even more lurid than anyone could have imagined. Like many who had become inured to the mass killing on the real battlefields, Vera couldn't get enough of murder stories. She sat in the tiny kitchen in a fog of smoke and drinking what only looked like tea.

'Serves 'em right.'

'Serves who right?' said Percy, making himself a proper cup of tea.

'Them girls. The Ripper murders! Where 'ave you been?'

'I don't know what the bloody hell you're on about. Jack the Ripper is hardly news.'

'The Blackout Ripper, you wally! It's 'ere on the front page. He could 'ave murdered half a dozen it says. Half a dozen! Who needs the bloody Germans?'

Percy was shocked. How had the press got hold of the story? He continued to make the tea until, unable to resist any longer, he inched up behind Vera and read the newspaper headlines over her shoulder. She turned and blew smoke into his eyes. He retreated, opened a small window over the sink and stirred his brew. His job had just got a lot harder. Mackie would be incandescent with rage and everyone would be in the man's sights. There had been an agreement with the press not to publish anything that might start a panic or forewarn the killer. Now someone had gone and blown the case.

'Anyway, serves 'em right is what I say.' Vera got up from her chair and closed the window over the sink.

'Why do you keep saying that? You don't know anything. No one deserves what they went through. No one.' Percy reflected on his words. No, not even Vera deserved what had happened to those women.

Vera lit another cigarette and Percy reopened the little window again. She seemed not to notice.

'They were asking for it ... being on the game and all.'

'How d'you know that? Does it say that?'

'No, but it says one of 'em worked for herself ... self-employed it says 'ere. And we all know what that means!'

'No one deserves that. It doesn't matter what they did for a living.' Percy retrieved the milk from the sink. It had curdled so he decided to go without.

'What's it to you? D'you know what 'appened to 'em?'

'I heard.' That she didn't know he was working on the case gave him a perverse sense of pleasure. He hadn't wanted to share his newfound sense of importance and job satisfaction; it was for him alone. Now her obvious but warped interest in the case only served to enhance his delight.

'You heard? You should be finding the bloody Ripper. That's what you should be doing – instead of standing 'ere like a spare whatsit! It ain't safe for us to go out while he's on the loose.'

'You don't go out!'

'You should be out there, not in Missing bloody Persons or whatever it is you do! What good you doing there for Christ's sake?'

Vera was now winding up for her coup de grâce – he could feel it.

'Course, you couldn't catch him with your leg anyway!'

'You can be a right ...' Percy swallowed his curse.

'Say it! G'on, say it!'

Percy turned to leave. 'I'm going to work.'

'That's it, run away ... or should I say, limp along?'

'Why don't you just button that foul mouth of yours and say something sensible for change?' A woefully inadequate parting salvo, but it was the best he could do at that moment.

BY THE TIME he arrived at West End Central police station, Percy had exorcised Vera. The duty sergeant greeted him with the news that the suspect, Cummins, was in detention. DC Bennett was waiting outside the interview room with a gas mask and an envelope containing Cummins's possessions. Percy stopped to inspect them: a cigarette case, a leather wallet and a comb with some missing teeth. He opened the wallet and asked Bennett to note the serial numbers on two one-pound notes. Alongside a few stamps and photographs of what appeared to be family members was Cummins's RAF identity card. Percy tipped the wallet upside down and shook it. A crumpled scrap of paper fell to the ground. He picked it up and carefully unfolded it. What appeared to be a telephone number – COL6622 – was scrawled in pencil.

'And the respirator?'

'He insisted we bring it.'

'Insisted?'

'Yes, guv. He wouldn't leave without it.'

'Let's have a look.'

Percy opened the gas-mask case. Inside was a wristwatch with a brown leather strap that had been repaired with Elastoplast. Eight one-pound notes were stuffed into the flap of the case.

'Get the numbers.'

Mackie appeared, near to boiling point as expected. 'Where is he?' he bellowed.

'Who, guv?' said Bennett, naively.

'Adolph bloody Hitler! Who d'you think? The suspect, knuckle-head. Where is he? Now I'm here, I'll do this myself.'

'He's in here, guv,' said Bennett as Mackie opened the door and entered the interview room. Percy and the young DC followed sheepishly.

'Well?' Mackie looked at Percy and waited for a response.

'But I thought you were going—'

'Who do we have here?'

Cummins smirked and sat back in his chair.

Bennett read from his notes. 'Gordon Frederick Cummins. Leading Aircraftman based at St. James' Close, Flat 27.'

'And?' said Mackie.

'Has he been cautioned, Bennett?' asked Percy.

'Yes, sir. I read him his rights.'

'Carry on, Detective,' Percy replied.

Bennett resumed reading from his notebook. 'Someone answering Aircraftman—'

'Leading Aircraftman,' said Cummins, and smiled broadly.

Bennett continued. 'Leading Aircraftman Cummins's description assaulted a woman last night around 9.45 pm. The attack took place in St. Alban's Street in Haymarket. A respirator with LAC Cummins's regimental number was found at the scene. That's all, guv.'

Mackie stared intently at Cummins, who looked down at the table.

'So how do you explain that, sonny?' Mackie barked.

'And who are you?' Cummins said.

Percy thought the chief was going to smack the suspect but Mackie just remained staring at Cummins.

'This is Chief Inspector Mackie. I'm Detective Inspector Percy. And you've already been introduced to DC Bennett here.'

'Percy? That your surname?' Cummins smiled and ran his fingers through his hair.

Before Percy could reply, Mackie pounced. 'So, now that we're acquainted, sonny Jim, how do you explain your gas mask being at the scene of the assault?'

Cummins looked up. 'I lost it ... or it was taken. By mistake or not, I don't know. But I ended up with someone else's. The one I brought here.'

'He insisted, guv,' said Bennett. 'It's not his. It belongs to another airman. We've checked and it was reported lost this morning.'

Mackie sat back in his chair and took out his lighter and a cigar, which he twirled in his hand but did not light. 'So tell us your story,'

Cummins said he had been drinking with a fellow

airman in the Universelle in Piccadilly and had started a conversation with a woman. He had lost count of how much he'd had to drink and only remembered walking out with her. He had no recollection of where they went or of assaulting her. If he had, he was most sorry and willing to compensate her.

'Compensate her?' Mackie growled.

'For any damage caused,' Cummins said.

'You want to *compensate* her for attacking her? So you admit it then?'

'No, I just thought ... Look, I don't remember anything. I don't remember touching her.'

'Did she give you her telephone number?' Percy asked.

'No.'

'Then how come her number is in your wallet?' Percy threw the scrap of paper onto the table.

'I was too pissed, drunk I mean. Perhaps she did give it to me. I don't remember.'

Cummins's previous assuredness seemed to be quickly evaporating.

'So how do you explain how your respirator was found at the scene of the assault?' Mackie asked again.

Cummins looked directly at Mackie and in a faltering voice replied, 'I told you, I've no idea. All I know is, I came home with the one I brought here today and it's not mine. I didn't assault her and whoever took my mask left it there so you'd nab me.'

Mackie shook his head and rubbed his cigar. He obviously didn't believe a word Cummins had said.

'Write it down. All of it. What you just told us,' said Mackie.

Bennett passed him a pencil and some paper and he began to write using his left hand. Mackie stopped him.

'What happened to your hand? Show me.'

Cummins held out his hand. There were scratch marks on it, some still quite moist.

'Oh those. Nothing really. Caught them on an engine at the station last week. For some reason they won't clear up. Must be the cold weather or the grease, or something.'

'Carry on. Write up your story.' Mackie lit his cigar and blew the smoke high into the ceiling. He then got up and turned to the detainee. 'We forgot to tell you – we're from the Murder Squad.'

Cummins looked up slowly, raised his eyebrows and resumed writing.

Percy followed Mackie out of the interview room, leaving Bennett to supervise.

Mackie turned to Percy. 'Cocky little bugger! He's our man, I can feel it in my water. What do we know about the respirator he brought in?' He seemed calmer and back in the senior-investigator mode.

'We found these.' Percy gestured to the wristwatch and money. 'We've taken the serial numbers.'

'Do you think he put them there just for us?'

'Looks like it, guv. Either that or he's a bit stupid. But he doesn't strike me as that. I agree, he's too cocky. He thinks he's clever. The fact that he insisted on bringing it with him suggests he wanted us to find them. The Elastoplast looks the same as that we found in the Jouannet flat.'

'That's what I think. And his hand?'

'One of the early assaults – the Hamilton murder most likely.'

'That's also what I thought.' Mackie took a drag on his cigar and pushed the smoke slowly through his nostrils. It seemed to signal some sort of satisfaction that they had indeed got their man.

'Get over to his digs and see what else you can find. By the way, Percy, you're doing a good job.'

'Thanks, guv.' Percy could scarcely hide his elation. Remembering his leg, he smothered an impulse to skip along the corridor.

PERCY WAS quick to locate Cummins's room at the RAF barracks. A tunic hung on the bunk bed. He searched the pockets and found a fountain pen with the initials 'D.J.' He checked his notes – it had to belong to Doris Jouannet. Inside the airman's kitbag were a blood-stained shirt and towel.

In the block's kitchen he found a cigarette case bearing the initials L.W. pushed to the back of one of the cupboards. Inside the white metal case was a photograph of a woman he didn't recognise so he checked his notebook. The initials corresponded with those of another victim – Leta Ward, or Evelyn Oatley as she was also known.

Back at Tottenham Court Road police station, Percy presented his trove of evidence to Mackie. While impressed, the senior man continued to argue that the case against Cummins was circumstantial – solid but not watertight. They needed something else.

EXHAUSTED, Percy returned home to find Vera asleep in the sitting room. A bottle of sleeping pills lay on the floor and he checked to see if she had taken too many. He was half-relieved to find that bottle was still mostly full. As she was comatose, he luxuriated in being able to move about the house without interference and occasionally wished that she had taken just a few more of the tablets.

He sat in his armchair and considered the chasm between home life and work. His day had been exhilarating and the plaudits from Mackie were still ringing in his ears. Then, he had to come home to this, to her. How could he change his life? What must he do to salvage his existence? Should he tell her about his success? Would she believe him? Would it make any difference? One thing was for sure: he had had enough, could take no more. He needed to leave her.

By the dying embers of the sitting-room fire, he resumed reading *Down and Out in Paris and London*. Suddenly and as if in a sharp pain Percy swore loudly, 'Shit!' Vera snored on, oblivious. He read the passage aloud twice over, 'I pulled her off the bed and threw her onto the floor. And then I fell upon her like a tiger.' This was Charlie, one of the tramps, recounting to Orwell his savage attack on a prostitute. Percy found the coincidence disturbing and closed the book.

23

'SINGAPORE HAS FALLEN,' BOKHARI ANNOUNCED SOLEMNLY. 'Thousands of Indian troops have been captured.' He paused, assessing the reaction of those gathered.

'Bose has already been on the airwaves. He's saying that – I quote ...Bokhari began to read from a teleprint sheet. "*The fall of Singapore means the collapse of the British Empire ... the end of the iniquitous regime which it has symbolised and the dawn of a new era in Indian history*."

The room fell silent and Orwell detected a certain excitement, even satisfaction, amongst his Indian colleagues. Bokhari continued. 'Furthermore there are reports from Bengal that attacks by fifth columnists have already started.'

What seemed to Orwell like an embarrassed silence followed. The dream of an independent India appeared to be coming to fruition and here they all were, Indians in London, trying to decide how to respond to the threat of the Japanese 'liberating' them. No one dared break the silence. Broadcasting poetry and literary criticism seemed even more ridiculous than usual. Yet, by way of a diversion, that is what the Planning Committee went on to discuss.

After the meeting, Orwell returned to his cubicle and found Burgess sitting in his chair, waiting for him. He suspected Burgess had been rifling through the pile of papers he had left on the desk. Once again, there was the overpowering smell of Burgess's aftershave and Orwell had to catch his breath as it hit the back of his throat.

'You've heard the news?' Burgess stood up, and adjusting his tie and tugging on his immodest cufflinks, moved aside. Orwell circled the unwelcome intruder and seated himself at his desk.

'About Singapore? Yes, Bokhari just informed us.'

Orwell tried to signal his unwillingness to start a conversation and began to sort through his rummaged papers. Burgess dismissed the gesture and sat down opposite. He offered his unwilling host a cigarette from a monogrammed silver case.

'And?'

Orwell broke off the filter tip. 'And what?'

Burgess produced a slim lighter and leaned over to light Orwell's cigarette. 'How did the Indians take it?'

Orwell thought for a moment before answering. 'How d'you think?'

'I somehow doubt they were too upset,' Burgess said.

'Why do you say that?'

'Because, like you, I know they want us out. And if the Japs help them, so be it. The sooner the better as far as they're concerned. Even if it means we end up losing the war.'

'That may be the case but it's not what they all believe, or even want. Replacing us with the Japanese will not help

India or the Indians, and most of them know it, even if they don't or won't always say it.'

'I almost agree. But, as someone once famously asked, "*What is to be done*?" Burgess smirked, blew a smoke ring and lanced it with his finger.

Orwell did not answer and just shuffled the papers on the desk once more. Burgess watched him move the same file from from one side of the desk to the other and back again.

'Lenin's "*What Is To Be Done*?" Have you read it?

'Lenin?' said Orwell, surprised by the reference. 'You know your Lenin?'

Burgess smiled. 'Doesn't everyone around here?'

Orwell stared at Burgess. He disliked everything about the man yet there was something intriguing, even appealing, about him, despite the fact that he was obviously homosexual. Burgess certainly gave an air of knowing something, But what?

'How's your assistant, Miss—'

'Mukurjee,' said Orwell.

'That's right. A real cutie.'

'She's ... you've not heard?'

'Heard...what?' Burgess feigned.

From his intonation Orwell knew Burgess' already knew about Rana.

'She's missing.'

'Gone AWOL has she?'

'Yes. We've not heard from or seen her for ... some time now.'

'She's just disappeared?'

'She's missing.'

'Are the police involved?'

Again, Orwell suspected Burgess was being less than candid.

'Yes, the police have been notified.'

'And have they any theories?'

'No. Not yet.'

'Was she involved ... in some sort of relationship? A lover's tiff perhaps?'

Burgess was fishing and Orwell's suspicious grew.

'Why do you say that?'

'No reason. I just thought —' Burgess raised himself from his seat and went towards the door, 'Let me know if I can be of any help. I do hope they find her.'

As he was about to leave, he turned and, as if by way of an aside, announced, 'Oh, by the way, there's going to be a cabinet reshuffle. There's to be an India Committee headed by The Major – dear old Attlee no less. There's even talk of our ex-man in Moscow, Cripps, being dragooned into some sort of mission or other. It's all rather hush-hush, but I'm sure I can trust you.' Burgess produced an exaggerated wink. He sounded like a schoolboy sneak.

'As an Old Etonian? Still wearing the tie, I see,' Orwell said.

'Yes, it works. You should try it. You'd be surprised how many doors it opens.'

'You don't really expect me to keep mum on that basis, do you? That we went to the same school?'

'Why not? I'm told you loved the place.'

'For once you've been terribly misinformed.' Orwell dragged on his cigarette and agitated the papers on the desk once more.

'Really?'

'Yes, really.'

'Oh, and I nearly forgot, your friend Sutton, he's going to be Secretary for War.'

'My friend?'

'Yes, I've heard you get along swimmingly, especially with Lady Sutton!' Burgess said sarcastically.

'You hear a lot it seems. Your ears must be constantly ringing.'

'Just tittle-tattle, chit-chat. Have you seen the posters? *Tittle-tattle lost the battle!* And *Careless talk costs lives!* No one in Whitehall seems to heed the message it seems. Sutton will also be on this new India Committee. I'm told Churchill offered him a seat in the Lords but the silly bugger actually declined it. Furthermore, as he's not in Parliament, they'll have to find him a safe seat. So that means a by-election. Winston didn't know what he was doing by all accounts. He hadn't a bloody clue. Amery is the architect and is directing matters. It's all quite extraordinary, don't you think?'

Orwell coughed to cover up any indication of his foreknowledge of Sutton's promotion.

'Sir James, or P.J. as he likes to be known – a certain over-familiarity I'd say – has something of a reputation, you know,' said Burgess.

'I don't know him but I've met him here. A reputation, you say?'

Burgess returned and stood by the chair opposite Orwell. 'He's a real stickler, apparently, and he doesn't suffer fools gladly. The story is, he made his way up ... humble beginnings and all that. So no doubt he has a chip or two on his shoulder, or at least a point to prove. All his types do. Either way, he seems very eager to please and Winston obviously needs him for some unknown reason. No one can really fathom it, as by all accounts they're chalk and cheese.'

Burgess raised his eyebrows, tilted his head to one side and left the office.

Orwell could not shake off the feeling that something was not quite right about what had just occurred. Burgess was too well-informed and too willing to gossip. The man knew far too much for a mere Talks Producer at the BBC. So why was this bird always singing?

24

Percy had not slept, despite taking to the kiddies' room. The case against Cummins was almost but not quite watertight. Mackie's reputation was at stake since his trademark was based on the fact that he had never lost a case. As such, there could be no weak link in the chain of evidence mounting against the accused.

Percy also felt that a vital piece of the jigsaw was still missing. As he opened his wallet to purchase his lunch it struck him – the bank notes. In the statements from the women who had been assaulted but not murdered and his RAF room-mates, Cummins had been described as ostentatious or 'flashy' with his money. Most spoke of his fondness for displaying a wad of notes. Percy sensed that it had to be the bank notes that connected the cases. Forgoing lunch, he set off again for the barracks.

Percy reviewed his notes. Two of the bank notes in the Mulcahy attack had consecutive serial numbers: M.87 D

397808 and 09, suggesting they had been distributed at the same time and that would have been on a pay day. The officer in charge of payment explained that the process was carried out by surname alphabetically. The notes distributed the previous Thursday had all been new and numbered consecutively. Percy requested the pay book and scoured the records. Prior to Cummins were Corporals Critchley, Crook and Crozier.

'Can I speak to any of 'em?' Percy asked.

'Only Critchley is here.'

Percy found the corporal in his bunk-room. Critchley still had three of his four notes. The serial numbers were M.87 D 397799, 800 and 801, which meant that the spent note had to be either 798 or 802.

According to the pay book, Corporal Crook had been paid three pounds and Air Cadet Crozier two pounds, both in the new notes. This suggested that Crook's notes were 803, 804 and 805. Crozier's would have been 806 and 807. Cummins had received two pounds so his notes must have been 808 and 809 – which corresponded with the serial numbers on the notes given to Catherine Mulcahy.

Percy had his missing link. It was time to report back to Mackie. Case closed?

LATER THAT AFTERNOON, Mackie returned from Brixton prison after charging Cummins with the murders of Evelyn Oatley, Margaret Lowe and Doris Jouannet. There was insufficient evidence to charge the airman with Evelyn Hamilton's murder. The Operations Room at Tottenham Court Road police station broke into spontaneous applause as the celebrated detective entered, smoking his customary cigar.

The burly chief inspector raised his arms in triumph and walked to the front of the room. The applause grew in strength as he savoured the moment. Percy stood at the back and pretended to clap enthusiastically.

'Thank you. Thank you,' Mackie shouted above the din. 'Job done. And …' The room hushed. 'I want to thank all of you for helping me solve this case.'

Percy was immediately struck by the *me*.

'It just goes to show that experience – my experience – and your hard work … well, killers beware!'

The room broke into another round of applause.

'I've been in this job long enough to know that instinct is what you need. That, and a bit of luck now and again. But it's all about having a nose for the wrong'uns and, if I say so myself, you only get that with experience. Okay, there's new-fangled ways of doing things, so-called intelligence stuff, but it's having a gut feeling, using the knowledge picked up along the way that really counts. And that's how I got the Ripper. Good old-fashioned detective work … and a lot of leg-work by yours truly!'

Another round of congratulations burst forth. Mackie milked the plaudits.

'Now, I've gotta go. Murder waits for no man. Another case to solve. Thanks again and good luck!'

As he made his exit, Mackie spotted Percy and winked at him knowingly.

Percy was aghast. His hero was a fraud, a charlatan. There had been no recognition and certainly no truth in the account he had just heard. His own hard intelligence work had not been acknowledged and had, in fact, been denigrated. His was a non-existence. It was as if it had all been a bad dream and he had not been involved in the case at all. He had no choice but to wake up and get himself back to Missing Persons.

25

Anand was waiting in Orwell's office. The normally well-turned-out socialite looked quite bedraggled and his serious expression suggested their meeting was not to be the usual lunchtime sojourn to the Wheatsheaf public house. He was smoking too – always a sign that something was troubling him.

'Mulk, what brings you here? I wasn't expecting you.' Orwell sat at his desk and proceeded to empty his briefcase and shuffle some papers in a less than half-interested way.

'I need to talk,' Anand said, sitting in front of Orwell. He fidgeted in the chair, rocking back and forth, crossing and uncrossing his legs.

'Why, what's happened?'

'I ...I'm not sure about the baby. There, I've said it. I'm not sure I want to be a father at this moment. And in the middle of a war.'

'And Kathleen? Why, I thought you were lovebirds? You were made to have children together.' Orwell was genuinely troubled by the confession.

'We were never that. Let's just say it was convenient to be

seen as such.' Anand stopped rocking and stared at Orwell. He dragged on his cigarette and spluttered.

'Convenient?'

'Yes. But... I ...we ...had no plans to beget children. Our work came first. That was what we agreed. Now it's too late and I'm going to be stuck with a child.'

'Stuck? It was an accident, I take it.'

'Most certainly. The product of a rare interaction. More than somewhat rare of late.' Anand's gaze shifted over Orwell's shoulder at the blank wall beyond.

'What do you plan to do about it? Now, I mean.'

'That's why I'm here. I need your help and some advice. What can I do, dear friend? What should I do? Tell me, please, what would you do?'

'Is she intent on keeping the child? Is it too late to ... you know?'

'Most definitely. She wants the child.'

'Good, you know my views on that score. Perhaps you'll change your mind once it's born. Once you see it, you could ... you might change your mind.'

'I very much hope so, I really do. But I'm not prepared to be a father.'

'What's the problem exactly? Just the timing? Or is it that you just don't want children ever? What are you afraid of? The responsibility? The commitment?' Orwell stared at his friend. 'Is it because it will be half-caste?'

'You bastard! That is a most unfortunate and, if I might say so, highly inappropriate term. It will be of no caste. Mixed race, Eurasian, if you must ... but that, I assure you, is not the issue. I have no problem with that. Not at all,' Anand said indignantly. 'The fact of the matter is, I'm not sure I still love Kathleen. That is the crux of it. And I have no wish to spend the next dozen years or so bringing up a child. It would be a disaster – not just for me but for all concerned.' Anand focused on the floor and then the ceiling. 'I keep praying that the Nazis will solve my problem but they appear to have run out of bombs.'

'Don't say that! She doesn't deserve that!'

'I meant for myself, you idiot! She's carrying my child. I wouldn't want her hurt. I was hoping the Nazis would save me.'

'Sorry, I thought ... You know that Eileen and I have been trying. Is there any chance Kathleen might change her mind? We would take the child if ... she wanted to give it up. Are you sure she wants to keep it?'

'Most certain.' Anand resumed his rocking motion in the chair and waved the cigarette rather than actually smoking it.

'Kathleen doesn't strike me as being cut out for being a housewife and doing the motherly thing or the chores. What about her career? Has she no plans to go back to acting?' Orwell was trying to console his friend.

'If the truth be told, she was never very good at it. I think even she's now realised that to be the case. She thinks she has no talent in that direction, none at all.'

'That doesn't seem to deter some!'

'There are no opportunities in any case. The war has seen to that. She needs something to do. But I don't think she actually realises what's involved in being a mother full-time.'

Orwell began to roll a cigarette. Anand reached into his pocket and threw a packet onto the desk.

'Take these. Damn it, I don't smoke. I hate it! I don't know why I even bought them.' He stamped his cigarette out on the floor before Orwell could hand him an ashtray.

Orwell helped himself to one of the cigarettes and lit it.

It was not to his liking and he twirled it between his fingers, suspiciously inspecting its properties. As permitted among good friends, there was a long silence while both men gathered their thoughts.

'Shall we go to the pub? Perhaps a pint will inspire.'

Anand nodded and rose from the chair. 'Why not?'

ON THEIR WAY to the pub Orwell considered reciprocating his friend's confidence and disclosing his own troubles regarding Rana. Unusually, he felt the need to unburden himself of his guilt. Yet, as they neared their destination, he decided against it. This was Anand's moment of need. Nevertheless it was the perfect opportunity for his Sutton mission and Anand was a perfect conduit – he could normally be relied upon to spread such news far and wide.

They sat in the saloon with their pints and for what seemed like an eternity nothing was said apart from the initial toast: 'Cheers! Down the hatch!'

Both writers were in a contemplative mood. Eventually, Orwell broke the silence.

'Rumour has it that India could be partitioned.'

'Partitioned?'

'Ulstered. Split up between the warring factions, or 'communities' as they quaintly call them.'

'And where did you hear this? On the BBC? If so, it's probably nonsense.'

Anand's reaction was not what Orwell had been expecting. The man had managed to sound almost disinterested in the one subject that mattered most to him.

'No. I have my own sources.'

'Your own sources?'

'Yes, my own sources. And they are entirely reliable. They say that Churchill is in for the long game. He wants to hold on to India, especially for his war aims. And after the war what he's proposing will inevitably see it divided between Hindus and Muslims. In the meantime, we should be able to continue to pillage your country. One consequence of all this is that there's already a dreadful famine in Bengal and Bihar, as you know.'

'Everyone knows about that. The price of British imperialism. Indians count for nought. Your sources tell you this about partition?' Anand was now engaged and inquisitive.

'Yes. There's more ... far more important, there's to be a cabinet-level ministerial mission to India and it's to be led by a renowned figure, someone your people might trust. Stafford Cripps. However, the terms of any agreement are doomed to fail ... or should I say, designed to fail. They will be totally unacceptable to Congress and perhaps even Jinnah's Muslim League. The whole plan is to split the independence movement and keep India under our control for the duration of the war. Only after that there is likely to be some sort of partition. India will be divided up in such a way as to ensure its continued dependency on Britain. All this might take years.' Orwell sipped his pint. 'What do you think?'

'Why would they do that? Why would Churchill offer something that is unacceptable from the start? Surely that will play into the hands of Congress and those wanting to stir up trouble. And what about the immediate threat from Japan?'

'It's all for public consumption and, more so, the Americans. Roosevelt put Churchill in a real jam with the Atlantic Charter, promising freedom, democracy and self-government to all peoples who have been invaded or conquered. It was Roosevelt's big idea and one that Churchill felt compelled to sign up to. Who knows, he was probably the worse for wear at the time.'

'Drunk, you mean?' Anand's face furrowed. He again seemed unsure whether to take the story seriously.

'He's certainly a bit ga-ga by all accounts. The fact is that Churchill had to renege on a promise he made to Roosevelt last year and stand up in the Commons and say it didn't apply to the colonies or dominions, and especially India. That was tantamount to a slap in the face for the Yanks. Now he has to make amends by being seen to be offering something, anything rather than nothing. Churchill has no intention of giving India full independence. He doesn't want to be the prime minister that lost India and will do anything in his power to see that that doesn't happen. That's why he's deliberately targeted millions of Indians as expendable.'

'George, my dear friend, what are you going to do with this information?'

'Nothing. I can't. It's—'

'A secret or simply chitter-chatter, gossip?'

'My source is impeccable. It's going to happen. I can't say a word on the wireless. I can't even write anything about it. It'll never get past the censors.'

'You just told me!'

'So I did. And it's your round.'

Anand looked distracted as he went to the bar. Had Sutton's seed been planted? Orwell knew he could rely on Anand to propagate the issue and embellish it if need be.

26

Percy wearily climbed the stairs to the forgotten Missing Persons Section and was considering the fate of George Bowling in *Coming Up For Air* which he had just finished reading. Like Orwell's fictional protagonist, Percy's escape to a world of 'what might have been' had ended in stasis. Now, after his excursion to the Golden Country of real detective work, he found himself back in the mire of Missing Persons. And, like Bowling, he had experienced profound disappointment in his role model. The classicist academic Porteous had turned out to be entirely ignorant of the contemporary world and woefully divorced from reality. Mackie, on the other hand, knew how to manipulate the real world and used others to ruthlessly enhance his own reputation. Despite his initial dismissal of the novel, Percy found himself admiring Orwell's ability to capture the frustration, boredom and outright meaninglessness of everyday life for those, like himself, in the middle-lower reaches of respectability. It was a numbing existence made all the more painful by brief interludes of doing something different – George Bowling's trip down memory lane and his own spell on a real murder inquiry. Such breaks from trough of routine inevitably demand a return to normality; only it comes with a heightened sense of alienation. Recognition of one's imprisonment in the drudge of daily life exposes the fact that there is little or nothing one could do to change things. By the time Percy reached the section door he was more determined than ever to avoid this depressing scenario.

As he entered the office, Percy felt like one of those missing persons who are found when they didn't want to be.

'Guv! Welcome home!' Baines said, broadcast so loud that Taylor, next door, must have been able to hear.

'Baines. Get me a cuppa, will you?'

Percy went into his office and hung up his hat and coat. Normal service had been resumed and by the time Baines reappeared with a mug of tea, he was already assessing the pile of cases on and around his desk.

'What have you been playing at while the cat's away? How come there's so many cases here?'

Baines looked at Percy quizzically. 'The cat, sir?'

Percy was already annoyed with his subordinate.

'What have you been doing while I was away?'

'We just had a flood of cases. Got swamped and—' Baines sucked on the end of his pencil.

'And?'

Baines produced a piece of note paper and passed it to Percy. 'And this.'

'What's this? Your resignation, I hope!'

'No, guv, I'm not ... It's about him ... the writer fella. Blair-Orwell.'

Percy read the note, looked up at Baines and then re-read it.

'When did you get this?'

'I tried to tell you. At the dead woman's flat ... remember? The place I was throwing up.'

'I remember you puking but nothing about this.'

'I tried to tell you but you said it had to wait.'

'How did it get here?'

'In the post. It was addressed to you but I opened because it didn't say it was personal or confidential or anything like that.'

Percy was almost apoplectic. 'Am I hearing you right? You opened my post?'

'I thought ... well, I thought it might be something to do with a case. As it turned out, it was.'

'Anonymous. Where's the envelope? Did it have a postmark?'

'I-I threw it in the bin, guv. You see, I opened the letter and didn't think.'

'For God's sake! Have you learned nothing? That's basic stuff.'

'No, it wasn't like that, guv. You see, I got called away and, by the time I returned, I realised I needed to keep the envelope to check the postmark but the cleaners had been. The bin had been emptied. I chased the cleaner but she'd gone. So I lost the envelope. Sorry, guv.'

'I bet you are!'

Baines retreated from Percy's desk and was about to leave when he turned and bleated, 'But I did go and see him ... Orwell. I went—'

'You did WHAT?' Percy nearly levitated from his chair and his bad leg remonstrated with a sharp pain.

'I went to interview him, guv. I thought—'

'What were you thinking, you stupid, bloody idiot?'

'I thought...I thought it would help if I just confirmed some facts with him.'

'Facts?'

'About his relationship with the Indian woman.'

There was nothing Percy could do or say that could retrieve the situation. He shook his head and was thinking.

'What did he say? Told you to bugger off I bet.'

'Nothing really, guv. Just said he worked with her and nothing else was going on. So I knew he was lying 'cos I had the letter.'

'You didn't say anything about the letter? Did you mention the place in Wallington, the cottage, in the letter?'

'No, I don't think so.' Baines rustled through his notebook.

'You don't think so?'

'No, guv. I'm pretty sure I didn't say anything about his other place. It's called The Stores, by the way.'

Percy held up the note. 'If this is true, he's been lying all along. But is it? Whoever it is would have to know him and probably works at the BBC. How do we know it's not just a pack of lies from someone who's vindictive or doesn't like Orwell? An ex-mistress for instance. Or just someone who doesn't like his books.'

'That's what I thought, guv, so I followed him.'

Percy could not believe what he was hearing. His poor leg pulsated in tune with his rising blood pressure.

'He didn't see me, guv. I made sure of that.'

'Have you any idea what might have happened if he had?'

'But I found out he was at it. He has a room in The Cut where he takes 'em. It's above a junk shop. He met one and took her there. I saw them with my own eyes. He could have taken her there ... the one that's missing.'

'And the one you saw him with?'

'Smart, I'd say. Proper lady. Not Indian.'

'A place in The Cut?'

'Less likely to be seen or known down there, I'd say. No one would know them and no one would bother 'em either. That's the sort of place it is.'

Percy's fury subsided. He was now intrigued and ready to follow up. He sensed that this was his opportunity to do something meaningful.

'Did you go into the junk shop?'

'Ah, no, guv. I thought about that and followed the woman when she left. I figured since we knew Orwell's whereabouts I'd try to find out who she was. She went to Waterloo station and caught the Esher train. The 4.06.'

'You followed her all the way to Esher?'

'I didn't know she was going all the way, but she did. She went to a house …' Baines started to read from his notes. 'Rosebud. That's the name of the house. Park View Gardens, Esher. I found out her name as well.' Baines looked at Percy as if expecting of some sort of commendation for his initiative. It was not forthcoming.

'Well?'

'Broadbent. Mrs Cynthia Broadbent. She's married to a solicitor, Reginald Broadbent. They've no children. They're both members of the Conservative Club and obviously neither of 'em has a record. He plays golf, or did do before the war. She's not a writer as far as I could find out …unless she uses another name like 'im.'

'A pen name.'

'But I couldn't find anything to connect her with Orwell. Not a sausage.'

'You definitely saw this Broadbent woman go with him into the junk shop?'

'Most definitely, guv. I tailed them from Waterloo to The Cut and they went into the junk shop together.' Baines consulted his notebook again. 'The Emporium it's called. Run by a well-known fence – one Whittington Crow. Commonly known as Dick. She came out before Orwell. Less than half an hour at the most, I'd say. It wasn't long.'

'Half an hour?'

'Less than. I thought that was strange. I've heard of quickies but that was, well, a half-crown job, if you ask me.'

'And no sign of our Indian woman, Mukurjee?'

'No guv.'

Percy rose from his desk and hobbled to the hat stand. 'I need to look inside that junk shop.'

'Shall I come with you. guv?'

'No, I think you've done enough already. More than enough.'

'Thank you, guv.'

PERCY COULDN'T WAIT to be out of the office, away from Baines' infuriating naivety. He went directly to The Cut and found a way through the miserable throng in the market before entering Short Street. From a distance, he studied Crow's Emporium for any sign of life. A light glimmered faintly – his signal to enter. The shop bell rang as he opened the door.

Crow was nowhere to be seen. Percy inspected the spoils of war and the stash of looted or stolen goods. Every item conjured an image of a loss, it had either been left or taken from someone's home and now it was here – amongst the junk. Each piece no doubt had a story to tell, an attachment or a memory that was now lost forever. It saddened Percy to think that this was its fate.

'Anything take yer fancy?' said a voice from nowhere.

Percy was slightly spooked by the disembodied inquiry. 'Not really. I'm looking for someone.'

'I don't do people. I only 'ave what you can see.' Crow raised his head above the counter and examined Percy.

'An Indian woman. I'm looking for an Indian woman.' Percy approached Crow.

'I don't do Indians, red ones or any other colour. Anyway, most of the tarts hang about the station. You'll get one there most likely. If that's what you're looking for, that is. Sorry, I can't help yer.'

'No, she's Indian. A young Indian woman. She's not a tart.' Percy was already thinking he'd like to bang Crow up ...for...anything. He had already gathered that he was a horrid creature.

'Lost her, 'ave you?'

'She's missing.'

'Aren't loads? Missing that is.'

'You've not seen her?'

'Not round 'ere. Anyways, what's it to you? A friend, is she?'

'Friend of a friend. I think you might know him.'

'And who might that be, your friend, the one I might know?' Crow moved from behind the counter and stood in front of the shop door.

'His name's Blair. Tall, funny moustache. Squeaky voice.'

'Blair? A friend you say?'

'Yes, Eric and I go way back.'

'And what makes you think I'd know him?'

'He mentioned your shop.'

'A recommendation, eh? I get a lot of those. And who might you be when you're at home?'

'The name's Bowling. George Bowling.'

The *Coming Up For Air* character must have made an

impression on him – it was out of Percy's mouth before he could stop himself and there was no taking it back.

'Anyways, I don't know your mate Blair. I've never heard of him and I've never seen him or your Indian girl. It's the war. People go missin' all the time. That's what 'appens. Why don't you see if the Sally Army can help?'

Crow turned his attention to his stockpile of junk. 'I don't suppose I can interest you in anything else while you're here? I got some lovely things. Something for the missus perhaps?'

'No. Not at the moment.' Percy replied.

A lie for a lie.

27

THE ANONYMOUS CALL HAD COME. BURGESS COULD HARDLY contain his pleasure at having something on Orwell at last. His secretary had answered. Despite its brevity – 'Tell Mr Blair someone's been asking' – Miss Tompkins deduced that the caller was 'definitely a Londoner, Cockneyish and sounded old.' Why the message had come to Burgess was less obvious, although it gave him an opportunity to ask Orwell who it was doing the asking. First he needed a pretext for a meeting.

'GEORGE, I'm glad I caught you. Any news about Bernal?'

Once again, Burgess had claimed a seat in Orwell's office without being invited. Orwell frowned at the intruder's presumptuousness and took a long drag on his cigarette.

'Sit down, won't you?'

Burgess ignored the reproach and sat forward. 'Bernal? Any news?'

'Our so-called Red scientist? No, but we're having lunch.'

'Lunch? You should have called. I could join you. I was hoping we might share him.'

Orwell could hardly hide his contempt for the audacity of the man!

'I could mention you to him, if I remember, that is.'

'Please do.' Burgess shuffled in the chair. 'Oh, by the way, I got a rather strange telephone call. Someone left a rather oblique message for you.'

Orwell sat upright. 'When was this?'

'Just yesterday, I believe. I was out so my secretary took the call.'

'The message?' Orwell's high-pitched voice crackled and he stifled a nervous cough.

'"*Tell Mr Blair someone's been asking.*" That's all. Any idea who it might have been?'

'No. What did he sound like?'

'Miss Tompkins thought he might be an older man. A Cockney.'

Orwell began to roll a cigarette. 'Probably Warburg from my Home Guard platoon.'

'It seems rather odd that he didn't say who he was. And why did it came through to me? It's all rather odd to say the least.'

Orwell feigned searching his desk drawers to stall the interview but Burgess was in no hurry to leave.

'That's probably Warburg. He has some strange ways about him. He knows I'm a Talks Producer here. I presume the switchboard just went by that.'

'I checked with them,' said Burgess. 'He had my direct number.'

'I have no idea why Warburg might do that. As I said, he has his foibles and he's getting on, if you know what I mean.'

'Where do you think he got my number from? He said 'someone was asking' but didn't say who.'

The interrogation was becoming a bore and Burgess's intent seemed all too obvious. 'I'm sure it's not that important,' said Orwell. 'He'll call back if need be. Thanks all the same. Presumably your secretary gave him my number.'

'But it's odd, don't you think? Most people would say who they were.'

'I'm also a journalist and we protect our sources. If you'll excuse me, I have some work to finish before we record a talk.'

'Yes, of course, old boy. Just thought I'd pass on the message. Oh, and if you see Sage – Bernal – will you say hello for me?'

'Yes. I'll mention you, if I remember.'

Orwell waited for Burgess to disappear along the corridor then headed out. He had to see Crow.

As he stepped out of the lift Percy approached him.

'Mr Blair. Just the man I'm looking for. Well, Mr Orwell to be precise.'

'Inspector?'

'You remember me?'

'Inspector Percy, isn't it?'

'That's correct,' said Percy, and Orwell thought the inspector seemed flattered that he had been correctly remembered.

'I'm in rather a hurry, Inspector. Is it important?'

'It could be, sir.' Percy stood across Orwell's path. 'I'd be grateful if you could spare me a minute. I'd like to check some things with you.'

'Your boy already did that.'

'Baines, you mean?'

'Yes, he came to see me.'

'Yes, I know. I'm afraid he was a bit quick off the mark. I've already told him as much.'

'Well, Inspector, how can I help? I really must be going,' Orwell made to look at his watch, only to find he was not wearing it.

'Shall we go somewhere more private?'

'How about the canteen? It's so bad that no one in their right mind uses it, especially at this time of day.'

A stench of boiled cabbage and two-day-old fish hung in the air. They collected two cups of thrice-boiled tea and found some seats in a remote area. Orwell noticed Percy's limp.

'Have you hurt yourself, Inspector?'

'No, it's permanent, I'm afraid. The consequence of an incident ...on duty.'

'Really, I'm sorry. Now, how can I help? I presume this is regarding Miss Mukurjee.'

'Yes, it is.' Percy sipped the tea and winced. 'Blimey! I thought the Yard's tea was bad!'

Orwell poured some of his into his saucer and Percy looked bemused.

'Miss Mukurjee? Orwell asked.

'Yes. I was wondering whether she'd been in contact.'

Orwell shook his head.

'Did you see Miss Mukurjee outside of work, before she disappeared, that is?'

'Why do you ask?'

'A straight yes of no will do.'

'Baines already asked me that, Inspector. No, I can't recall seeing her outside of work. I'm still not sure why you're asking again.'

'Let's just say that some additional information has

come to light. It suggests that you and Miss Mukurjee were closer than you're letting on.'

Orwell reached for his tobacco tin and began to roll a cigarette.

'And this information has just arrived from a reliable informant, Inspector? Out of the blue, so to speak.'

'I thought you might be able to confirm whether that's the case.'

'How would you define *closer*? Is one really close to one's wife, for instance?'

'I'm not sure that's really relevant, Mr Orwell. My relationship with my wife is my own affair. It's certainly not part of any police inquiry. But I'd say that *closer* infers an intimate relationship of some sort.'

'You mean sex?'

'Yes. Were you having an affair with Miss Mukurjee?'

They were now like two dogs circling each other in the street.

'No, I was not. Do you really think a young, pretty woman would find me that attractive?'

Orwell's face creased in a self-deprecatory chuckle. 'Now, I really should be going.' He shuffled in his seat and finished his tea. 'The informant, did you speak to him ... or her?'

'I can't say.'

'Can't or won't? Either way, I'll take that to be no. Did Baines? Is that why he came running?'

Orwell lit his cigarette and the smell of the strong shag smothered the stench of the canteen.

'I can't say, sir.'

'So it's my word against whoever told you this?'

'Pretty much ... as things stand.'

'And who do you believe, Inspector?'

'I'd rather not—'

'Say?'

'Exactly.'

'Is there anything else? I must rush.' Orwell rose from his seat, towering over Percy, and turned to leave.

'Miss Dorothy Hare?'

'She's fictional, Inspector, is she your informant?' Orwell said, laughing loudly.

'I know that, sir. I've read *The Clergyman's Daughter*.'

'*A Clergyman's* ... It's *A*.'

'Sorry. It's just that it got me thinking. Could Miss Mukurjee have lost her memory, just like Dorothy Hare?'

'It could well be. Anything could have happened to her. London is a very dangerous place at the moment, what with the Blackout Ripper and his kind stalking the streets.'

'You've read about that case?' Percy looked pleased.

'Hasn't everyone? A ghastly business. Tell me, Inspector, what's happening to the good old English murder? Once upon a time, we had the likes of Dr Palmer of Rugely, Joseph Smith and even Dr Crippen. Now it's all, well, like this Ripper fellow.'

'What about Jack, the original Ripper?'

Orwell nodded. Then realisation dawned.

'You don't think Rana ... Miss Mukurjee could have ... Oh my God! You suspect—'

'No, sir. I don't. Not at all. We've caught the Ripper and, as far as we know, she wasn't one of his victims. I had a very close involvement in the case myself.'

'Really? I thought you were just—'

'Missing Persons? Yes, sir, but I was seconded to the case on special duties,' Percy said proudly.

Time to burst the inspector's bubble of self-importance.

'And now you're back.'

'Yes. Back at Missing Persons.'

'With plenty of time to read my books, by the sound of it.'

'Yes, I've read more than one.'

'I'm flattered, Inspector. And what did you make of them?'

'I have to admit, they're not to my taste, sir. Not my cup of tea as they say.'

'What is your cup of tea, Inspector?'

'I like a good yarn. Detective stories mostly.'

'Of course,' Orwell replied dismissively.

28

Orwell made his way to The Cut hoping for the best but fearing the worst – that Rana had been to the room and the mysterious Indian had reappeared. He was frantic.

Crow greeted him like a long-lost debtor.

'Who was it? Who was asking? Was it the Indian?' Orwell gasped as he pushed through the door.

Crow took his time, closing the ledger he had been studying oh so slowly.

'For pity's sake, man, tell me!'

The door slammed shut and the bell rang out like that at a boxing-match about to start.

'This Bowling, a friend of yours, is he?'

'Bowling?'

'That's what he said. Look, I've even written it down.' Crow took a scrap of paper from his handkerchief pocket and handed it to Orwell, who stared, mouth agape.

'What did he look like?'

'Nuffink really ... just ordinary-looking. Suit and tie. Fortyish. Mousy hair and no 'tache. Oh, and a limp – a real bad one. Anyways, he said he was a friend of yours and that you knew him from way back.'

'Anything else?'

'I told him I didn't know yer, as I always do. And then he says he's looking for an Indian lady, your one, I presume. Blimey, I thought, she 'as a lot of blokes after her! She must be very pop'lar.'

Crow's leery eye appeared and he rubbed his hands before picking up his magnifying glass and running it across the counter.

Orwell knew immediately that Bowling was in fact Detective Inspector Charles Percy. And the only person who could have told Percy about the room was the mysterious Wallington Indian. Orwell paced the shop floor, his mind in turmoil. This also meant Percy knew about Rana's visit to Wallington. In which case, his lies had been discovered and that made him a prime suspect in her disappearance.

'Do you know this bloke Bowling?' Crow asked.

'Yes, I know him very well.'

Orwell allowed himself a rueful smile over Percy's alias.

'If he comes back, should I tell 'im you've been?'

'No, do as you always say you do – say nothing.'

Orwell paid the rent and sixpence for the telephone call, and hoped that he would never use the room again. He left Crow smirking as he pocketed the ten shilling note.

ORWELL ARRIVED at Langdon Court with his mind made up: he would confess to Percy his affair with Rana. It needed to be as soon as possible and in the hope that the policeman would then understand why he had not told the whole truth.

Eileen was asleep in an armchair. She looked prettier tonight, at peace, and he wished it would last forever. It wouldn't if she found out about Rana. His previous affairs had been tolerated, even condoned in her support for his 'artistic' endeavours. She had accepted that creative types needed free rein and she hadn't seen his flings as a threat to their relationship. Indeed, he had always wanted her more after an affair had ended and had pledged his undying love on such occasions.

Eileen stirred and, sensing something was off, asked him what was wrong. Orwell fobbed her off with a story about his bête noir, Gertrude Sutton, and that seemed to appease her.

He was becoming an accomplished liar.

ORWELL TELEPHONED PERCY AT 9AM, saying they needed to meet as soon as possible.

Percy replied, 'I thought you might.'

They settled on the Blue Café for high tea. Orwell arrived to find Percy waiting outside the restaurant inspecting some graffiti and damage to the shop front.

'Local yobs – they've got it in for the Eyeties. Did you know it was an Eyetie place?' Percy asked.

'Yes, I know they're Italian. Shall we go in?'

Maria came out from the kitchen. She had a black eye and a bandage around her wrist. Orwell asked her what had happened but she shook her head and remained silent. They ordered two high teas.

'You've been here before?'

'Yes, with a friend.'

'A Mrs Cynthia Broadbent by any chance?'

Orwell shook his head, bemused. 'Who's she?'

'Come on, Orwell. I thought you'd called this meeting to tell me the truth.'

'I have, but I've no idea who you're talking about.'

'And you're sticking to that?' Percy looked Orwell in the eye. 'Perhaps we should both stop beating about the bush. You were recently seen with a Mrs Broadbent entering the Emporium junk shop in The Cut. It appeared that you and the lady from Esher knew each other.'

Orwell shook his head. 'Esher?'

'Yes, Esher. She's married. An affair with a married woman ... and you being married and all?'

So it was Diane the inspector was referring to. 'No, it's not what you think, Inspector. I didn't know her name, or at least her real name. I was just helping a friend, doing him a favour. A delicate matter, if you follow my drift.'

'And who might this friend be?'

Orwell said nothing.

'Perhaps an imaginary friend. Or one of your fictional characters. George Bowling perhaps?'

Both men smiled, and for the first time Orwell had a sense of something shared with Percy.

'I really can't tell you who it is, Inspector.'

'Now why might that be?'

Orwell scratched his ear. Something had to give. 'Let's just say he's a public figure and it would not be in the national interest were it to come out.'

'The national interest. I didn't see that one coming, especially from someone who calls himself a socialist. It doesn't really add up, Orwell.'

'You *have* done your homework. Socialists can love their country Inspector. We just have a problem with those in charge.'

'Would you say you're patriotic then?'

'If that's wanting the best for all working people, yes.'

'Then why do your socialists go on strike and harm innocent people and the country?'

'I take it you don't share my politics. Have you ever met a socialist?'

Percy looked down at his leg.

Orwell sensed that there was obviously a story there, something about his injured leg.

'No one was seen entering the junk shop while you and Mrs Broadbent—'

'Diane, that's what she called herself. I've no idea what her real name was. She trades from something calling itself the Esher Ladies' Circle,' said Orwell.

Percy's shook his head in what looked like disbelief.

Maria returned with the high teas. The scones looked smaller and the paste was barely a shade of pink. The whole thing looked decidedly uninviting, yet Percy attacked the ersatz offering and finished with a sip of the tea.

'No one apart from you and this *Diane* were seen to enter the junk shop. She left after thirty minutes or so. I put it to you that there was no such public figure and that the only interest you're protecting is your own.'

'I'm telling you the truth, Inspector.'

'If that's the case, how do you explain that no one else was seen entering? Was your man already there?'

'Yes, he was there.' Orwell paused, relishing the rather obvious explanation he was about to deliver. 'It's quite simple, Inspector. There's a back entrance.'

Percy looked coy and somewhat embarrassed.

'Am I being watched? Have you been following me?'

Percy stared at Orwell. 'You were seen, sir. That's all I can say.'

'By whom? Was it Crow? It must have been Crow.'

'No, it wasn't Crow. For someone in his trade it's more than his life's worth to be seen talking to the likes of us.'

It then occurred to Orwell that there was an alternative.

'Was it your informant? An Indian?'

'Why do you say that?'

'Because I think you know that Rana Mukurjee and I were—'

'Having an affair? Yes, I thought as much.'

'And your informant told you this. Which means you also know about Wallington and The Stores.'

'Yes, we have good reason to believe that you and Miss Mukurjee met previously in Wallington.'

'The same informant I presume?'

'One of your work colleagues perhaps?'

Orwell pushed aside his scone, took out his tobacco tin and rolled a cigarette.

'I very much doubt it.'

'Then why do you suppose it was an Indian who informed on you?'

Orwell lit his cigarette and closed the tin. 'You see, Inspector, both at Crow's and in Wallington, an Indian was asking about Rana. It must be the same man. He's your informant. And he must have something to do with her disappearance. He's the one you should be looking for.'

'Any idea who it might be?'

'My guess would be her elder brother.'

'Did she tell you she had a brother?'

'No, not at the time. But I found that out from a colleague.'

'Why didn't she mention him?'

'I don't know, Inspector. I really don't.'

'And why would her brother tip us off about you and his sister?'

'I don't know that either.'

Orwell stifled a cough and blew a stream of smoke towards the ceiling. Percy looked around and signalled Maria to replenish their tea pot.

'What do you think's happened to her?'

'Your guess is as good as mine Inspector.'

'Why should I believe you now? You've been lying to me ever since we met.'

'Because I've just told you the honest truth.'

29

Percy travelled to Esher. It was a relief to get away from London and he was hoping he would make some headway on the case. The train was filled with the recently enlisted recruits heading for various Surrey encampments. He stood out in his civvies and a feeling of physical inadequacy nagged at him. These young men were destined to be heroes, no matter that Dorking, Esher, Guildford, Reigate and Box Hill were less than propitious destinations. He wanted to bare his scarred and withered leg, his own medal of service, as if that might legitimate his right to sit in the same carriage.

Esher appeared almost untouched by the war. By the time he arrived mid-morning, the drizzle and a blustery wind had rendered this sleepy dormitory town on the green fringe of London virtually deserted. It was difficult to find anyone who knew the whereabouts of Park View Gardens. He had little choice but to make his way to the local police station and request directions. He was discreet, saying he was investigating a case concerning a client of the local solicitor, Reginald Broadbent. The local desk sergeant was only too willing to break from the torpor of Esher crime fighting and provided a car to the Broadbent residence.

Park View Gardens was everything Percy imagined suburbia to be. Most of the houses were detached and built in a mock Tudor style. Their poor cousins were the semi-detached 'villas', segregated on the opposite side of the road. They had a block-like functionality onto which their inhabitants had attempted to graft various overtures to the classical traditions of Greece and Rome. Doric and Ionic columns, plaster-cast lions and eagles, all resembling set props from some ghastly Hollywood B-movie, were appended indiscriminately. They stood defiantly, facing their faux medieval counterparts that had been inspired by British silver-screen epics. There appeared to be some sort of competition as to which carried more historical or cinematic kudos. The grander houses, those on the right-hand side of the road, had uniform gravel paths leading to front-door porches invariably submerged under some sort of climbing plant. Even the lattice lead-work of the windows was camouflaged with bomb shatter tape – the only evidence of global hostilities. Nothing, it seemed, was meant to suggest that Esher was actually at war. This could have been any time between 1920 and 1939. The occasional sound of a fighter plane or bomber overhead was the only reminder that something else was going on beyond the trimmed lawns and hedges of Park View Gardens.

Percy limped from the police car to Rosebud and imagined himself mowing the lawn and pruning the roses. He would get a car just so he could park it in the integral garage, whose doors he'd leave open so that those across the street could envy his success. It would definitely be Vera's idea of heaven on earth.

By the time he reached the front door, the vision had

cleared. This was not for the likes of him and it never would be.

The chimes of the bell were still ringing when the door opened. Cynthia Broadbent's head appeared around the door. A cigarette dangled from her lips and her hair was collected in a tight turban.

Percy raised his trilby, realising she had taken him for a salesman of some sort. Before she could say 'Not today', he produced his warrant card.

'Detective Inspector Charles Percy of Scotland Yard. Mrs Broadbent?'

'Yes, I'm Mrs Reginald Broadbent. How can I help you, Inspector?'

'May I come in? It would be more ... private,' Percy said, looking around to see if any of the neighbours' curtains had twitched.

'Will it take long? I'm rather busy. Is it my husband you need to see? Has something happened to him?'

'No, it's you I'd like to talk to, Mrs Broadbent.'

She opened the door and let him in. She was still in a dressing gown.

'Do you need a minute to get dressed?'

'Thank you. I think I should. Please, Inspector, make yourself comfortable in the sitting room. I'll not be long.'

The room was a riot of floral motifs on the carpets, curtains and even on the settees. The sideboards were adorned with great vases crowded with all manner of exotic flowers, none of which Percy could name. He sneezed and his chest began to tighten.

Cynthia Broadbent reappeared a few minutes later in a green two-piece trouser suit. Her auburn hair hung loose in long flowing curls that covered her shoulders.

'Oh, I'm sorry, Inspector. I sometimes forget that some people are allergic. Please, let's go to Reginald's study.'

The study had the atmosphere of a cell. The walls were bare and the curtains half-drawn. Books were strewn all around. He suspected it had not been used for some time.

They sat facing each other on two leather armchairs.

'Is your husband at work, Mrs Broadbent? Are you expecting him?'

'No. Mr Broadbent is in Edinburgh. He's not due back until sometime next week, I believe. I'm never quite sure about Reginald's movements. Now, what's this all about?'

'Do you know a Mr George Orwell?'

'Can't say I do. The name doesn't ring any bells, I'm afraid. Should I?'

'Or a Mr Eric Blair?'

'No, I'm sorry. The name is not familiar.' She paused, seeming to think for a moment. 'Ah, but I did once know a Jacinta Blair, at my boarding school. Fat girl, always eating ... but I'm not familiar with any man of that name. Jacinta's father, perhaps? I don't think I ever met him.'

A broad smile covered her face. She was playing games and Percy decided to up the ante.

'Have you been up to London in the past few weeks?'

'Could you get to the nub of the matter, please? I have a lunch date.'

'Yes, certainly. I'm investigating the disappearance of a young woman and I have reason to believe that she may have frequented a place that you, yourself, recently visited.'

'And where might that be?'

'The Emporium. It's a junk shop in The Cut near Waterloo station.'

Cynthia Broadbent smiled, lit a cigarette and went to a drinks cupboard. 'Can I tempt you, Inspector.'

'No, thank you.'

'Too early? Or not while on duty, as you say?'

'The latter.'

'A junk shop in Waterloo. I can't say that's my usual place to shop! Perhaps it's a case of mistaken identity,' she said, pouring herself a drink.

'Are you saying it wasn't you?'

'I'm not sure how my presence or absence really helps in your search for this unfortunate woman.'

That confirmed Percy's suspicions.

'What if I say that you were correctly identified by a very reliable source?'

Cynthia Broadbent took a swig from her glass, took a drag on the cigarette and blew out the smoke. 'One of your own, I presume?'

'Yes, one of my officers,' said Percy, delighted by the elevation of his command.

'Then I would have to say I may well have been the woman shopping for bargains, as one does in these times. Whether it was called the Emporium, I can't say I noticed.'

'So you admit to visiting the shop.'

'Admit?' She grinned again. 'You make it sound as if I'm guilty of something other than shopping, Inspector. Yes, I admit I may have visited a shop in Waterloo. A junk shop one might well call it. But I was simply killing time while waiting for my train.'

'And who were you with?'

'Oh, I was seen with company?'

'Who was the gentleman you were with, Mrs Broadbent?'

She sat down and adjusted herself.

'A Mr Smith. I met him at the station and he suggested

an antique shop he knew. He volunteered to show me the way.'

'A Mr Smith?'

'Yes, that's who he said he was and I had no reason to doubt it.'

'And did you purchase anything in the *antique* shop?'

'No, most definitely not. It was indeed just junk. I had been misled.'

She got up and pulled the curtains back fully. It was still raining but it didn't detract from the the manicured garden.

As she returned to her seat she remarked casually, 'And the little man – the Jew who runs it – was obnoxious in the extreme. So I left as soon as I could.'

'And how long were you in there?'

'I've really no idea. But hardly any time at all I recall.'

'Five or ten minutes, say?'

'Ten perhaps. Why don't you ask your officer?'

'He estimated thirty minutes, half an hour at least. You then left, alone.'

'It seemed a lot less. Yes, I left alone. Mr Smith, or whoever he was, said he had business with the Jew, so I left and made my own way back to Waterloo.'

'And that was the sum of your expedition to The Cut?'

'Hardly an expedition Inspector. I was quite disturbed by the whole experience. I wanted to get back to Esher as quickly as I could. I admit, I foolishly allowed myself to follow a complete stranger into a place that no respectable married woman should have ventured. I was angry with myself for being such fool. Who is this Smith man? Does he and the nasty little Jew have something to do with the woman you're looking for?'

She'd made the connection. Percy was impressed.

'You took the owner to be a Jew? Why? Do you have a problem with Jews, Mrs Broadbent?'

'Everything about him. I think they got us into...this war.'

Percy had no wish to be sidetracked and ignored her anti-Jew comments.

'Did you tell your husband about your experience?'

'I went on a shopping trip and I got waylaid by a man, a complete stranger. It's sometimes best not to admit to such things. No, I didn't say anything to Reginald and I'd be grateful if you'd do the same.' She lit another cigarette and took another quaff of her drink.

'Would you recognise this Smith again?'

'I'm really not sure. I've tried to forget what happened. I'd rather not think about it anymore.'

'He had no distinguishing features?'

'I'm sure your officer has a description.'

'Indeed, but I'd like yours, if you please.'

'Well, as I recall, he was tall, lanky even. Rather thin. And he had a funny little pencil moustache, French style, I believe. A terrible cough as well. I should say he was ill. In his forties, but could be older. Lots of wrinkles. He was shabby but well-spoken – like a true gentleman. Hence the reason I took him at his word.'

'That's a very good description. Did you tell him your name?'

'No, of course not. I called myself Daphne or Diane ... something like that. I was quick-witted enough to do that at least.'

'Diane?'

'Or something similar. Was I followed back here to Esher by your officer? How else would you have known where to—'

'Yes, I'm afraid it was necessary.'

'My husband needn't know anything about this, I hope.'

'No, at the moment there's no need for him to know what happened.'

'At the moment?'

'Unless you prove to be a witness.'

'To what exactly, Inspector?'

'To the disappearance of the young woman I'm looking for. One last question – was there anyone else in the shop apart from you, the owner and Mr Smith?'

'Not to my knowledge. That's why I wanted to get out of there as quickly as I could. I'd just been reading about the ghastly Ripper case and realised what a fool I'd been.'

'The Ripper case?'

'Yes, this so-called Blackout Ripper.'

'I don't think you'd have been in danger. He had a penchant for ... women of the night.'

'Prostitutes, you mean?'

'Yes, and, in any case, we arrested him some time ago.'

'Well, with hindsight, my fears may have been misplaced. But at the time I felt I was in danger from this Smith and his Jew friend. They were both rather scary once we were inside that place. Will that be all, Inspector? I really must be getting along,' she said, rising from the chair.

'To the Esher Ladies' Circle by any chance?'

'Why, whatever's that? I've never heard of it. Is there such a thing? And how would *you* know, Inspector? No, I'm off to the golf club for lunch. They do a rather good fresh-fruit salad and you just can't get that anywhere else. I shouldn't say this, especially to a policeman, but I'm sure they have their contacts in the black market!'

'I'm sure they have.'

'Good luck with your search and I'm sorry if I've not been much help.'

'You've been very helpful, Mrs Broadbent, very helpful. Thank you and have a good lunch.'

Percy made his way down the gravel path, then turned back towards the house. Cynthia Broadbent was on the telephone.

30

The atmosphere in Room 101 was even more tense than usual. Clearly, Anand had done what Orwell had hoped. The rumour mill had been working overtime and news of the impending government mission to India now appeared to be common knowledge. That the mission was destined to fail had also permeated the ensemble. All save Bokhari seemed deflated, though even he stated that that 'truculent damsel, Miss Nationalism', needed to be kept at bay in this dire situation. Jahida and the Princess objected strongly to the sexist inference. Orwell tried to work out what the remark had meant. Was Bokhari for the status quo, or did he feel that there was no point in engaging in talk of independence whilst the war was still being waged? Or had he too heard that Cripps' mission was designed to fail and there was no point discussing independence at this juncture? Either way, it was the first time Orwell had heard Bokhari express a view on the future of India, albeit a cryptic one.

Then, as the meeting came to a conclusion, news came through that Sir Stafford Cripps was indeed to be the government's envoy. That Burgess had told him some days earlier meant that he had to pretend ignorance. Anand was also knowingly perturbed and was shaking his head furiously. After the meeting, they stayed in the room.

'It's set-up as you suggested. Cripps has no chance and Churchill will scapegoat both Cripps and the Indian leadership for the failure,' an irate Anand exclaimed. 'You were right George, it's the same old story: Indian divisions being used to maintain British rule. But Cripps? A vegetarian, teetotal devout Christian and friend of Nehru! Jinnah and the Muslim League won't like that. Some are even suggesting Cripps could be a future prime minister if he pulls it off! Has Churchill done it to get him out of the way? No matter, he's only been chosen to sweeten the pill. It's a disaster for all concerned, both India and Cripps. He's been set up by Churchill. Everyone will see the failure as his personal responsibility.' Anand demanded a cigarette from Orwell.

'Then why has Cripps taken the task? That's what I don't understand. Why, if you and I can see what's happening, can't he? Maybe the terms are better than your source suggested? Perhaps Cripps has got something up his sleeve? Might he have something better to offer?' Orwell rolled a cigarette and offered it to Anand, who was in no hurry to light it, leaving it lying on the desk. Orwell took it back and lit it for himself.

'Did your source get it wrong?' Anand replied.

'He could have been deliberately misinformed. A case of pricking the balloon of expectation after it's been inflated. Expecting the worst and getting second-best might then be taken as some sort of success. We should have known, we're in the propaganda business after all. Everything depends on the terms Cripps has been given to work with. Does he know about Churchill's plan for partition after the war?'

'The bastards just want to keep India under their yoke for the duration and Cripps is their patsy. In which case he can't really have anything to offer, certainly not immediate independence that Congress is demanding.'

Orwell sighed and Anand left without saying another word about India or the baby.

Contacting Sutton was now imperative. Had the man deliberately propagated the disaster story, only for there now to be some form of compromise settlement? For a moment, Orwell didn't want to believe that Sutton had been anything other than sincere.

Even before the announcement of Cripps's mission, Orwell had wanted to tell Sutton that he and Diane had been followed and that the police were investigating Crow's room in relation to Rana's disappearance. He felt responsible and wanted to reassure Sutton that his identity was safe, even though he could no longer vouch for Diane. However, Sutton was not answering his calls and all attempts to catch up with him at the BBC and elsewhere had come to nought.

Gertrude Sutton had said her husband was very busy in his new position as Secretary for War and no longer had time to escort her to the studios. She had taken a message but this, too, had gone unanswered. Perhaps Sutton had been spooked and was trying to distance himself. Orwell wanted to let sleeping dogs lie, but Sutton was still the only person who could provide the one ingredient that could stymie Churchill's plan, the actual terms that Cripps was to put to the Indians. If the true nature of these were to be made public before Cripps's departure, rather than the inevitable anodyne declaration of intent that would be propagated, there might be some hope of avoiding the looming disaster, the future partition of India.

A thought struck him: maybe there was an alternative source. Inviting Burgess to lunch with Bernal, while unwelcome, might be the answer. If anyone knew Cripps's terms of reference, it would be Guy Burgess.

BERNAL WAS NOT what Orwell was expecting. The 'Red' scientist was tall, well-presented, even debonair, something of a matinee idol, and quite unlike any of the communists Orwell had previously met. Having a significant thatch of hair was the only thing they had in common.

While having taken an interest in scientific developments, Orwell could not begin to comprehend some of Bernal's expertise in crystallography and latterly assessing the impact of high explosives. He soon realised that he would have to confine the conversation to generalities and the administrative arrangements associated with the planned programme of talks. Discussion of politics and Bernal's avowed support for the Soviet regime were to be taboo.

As Burgess was late, Orwell took the opportunity to ask Bernal about Burgess.

'Have you known Burgess long?' Orwell asked, as if it were nothing more than an innocent aside.

'I think we first met at Cambridge,' Bernal said in a pronounced Irish lilt.

'How so? I thought he was doing History or the like?'

'Probably at a party or reception. There were so many, I can't honestly recall.' Bernal seemed uncomfortable. 'Were you at Cambridge?'

'No, I went to Burma after school.' Orwell sounded somewhat apologetic. 'I made the mistake of joining the police there.'

'A colonial apparatchik?'

'You could say that. I'd say I was more of a colonial servant.' It was Orwell's turn to feel uneasy and he needed to return to the subject of Burgess. 'Have you seen much of him since?'

'No, I wouldn't say I have. We bumped into each other some time back ... at a mutual friend's house, Victor Rothschild. I believe Guy now rents a flat of his. Do you know him?'

'Rothschild? No.'

'Another Cambridge man.'

'Of course.'

The conversation drifted along from the fishing in Ireland to potatoes, then back to rationing and the price of a pint. Bernal appeared bored and drank more than his fair share of the wine Orwell had provided courtesy of his BBC expenses allowance. By the time Burgess appeared, the two men had exhausted their stock of trivia.

'Sorry, so sorry!' Burgess burst in, already worse for wear. He tossed his hat, scarf and coat onto a spare chair. 'You'll never guess what I've just seen. A bloody great hammer-and-sickle flag flying from the roof of Selfridges! I thought the bloody revolution had arrived! What are we drinking?'

'It's been there for weeks,' Orwell said dryly. He knew this because his mother was actually working in the store.

'We've started on the wine Mr Blair ordered,' Bernal said.

'Blair? My dear Sage, don't you know? This is George Orwell! The famous, or perhaps infamous, writer?'

Orwell immediately thought that their familiarity appeared to belie their supposed acquaintanceship.

'Sorry. I thought ... You signed everything Blair. I can't say I've read—'

'Of course. Why should you have? I've not read anything of yours either.'

'I damn well have! I've read some of George's stuff.' Burgess almost shouted. 'The Burmese what d'you call it? *Burmese Days*. And, *Homage to Catalonia*. I'd suggest you are not the biggest supporter of the Communist Party after that one George. And I'm not sure you'd get on with that one, Sage.' He glanced knowingly at Bernal. 'Now, drinks!' Burgess spun in his chair and demanded attention from the waiter.

'Guy, I think you should lower your voice.' Bernal gently tugged on Burgess's sleeve. 'You're being a bit of a boor.'

Orwell's suspicion that the two men knew each other well was now confirmed.

'I just need a drink, Sage. Waiter! Is there anyone serving in here?' Burgess bellowed.

The waiter came over with an empty glass. Burgess ordered a Bloody Mary – equal parts vodka and tomato juice – and another bottle of wine. 'This one's on me, I insist! Have you eaten, by the way? Let's not stay here. Let's go to the Café Royal? They always fit me in. If not, I'll get Victor to buzz them. What d'you say?'

Burgess's condition was both an opportunity and a problem. If Orwell could get him alone, he may be able to find out about Cripps's terms but further inebriation would make that unlikely. Eating therefore seemed a good idea. In any case, the Café Royal was not to be missed, especially if Burgess or, more likely, the BBC was paying.

While they were finishing off the wine, the conversation

turned to politics. At first, Bernal seemed reluctant to say anything and returned a non-commital observation when asked about the ending of the Hitler-Stalin Pact. Bernal suggested that the Soviets would defeat the Germans by Christmas. Burgess lightly berated him for being such an optimist but concurred that the Russians would succeed in the long run because the Nazis had over-reached themselves. Orwell could not determine whether their sparring was for real. It all seemed rather theatrical and he found himself unwilling to contribute.

'Everyone knows you're a genius Sage but that doesn't extend to predicting the future!' Burgess almost shouted across the table.

'Now, George, you tell Sage how you'd sort this country out. George, you see Sage, is a proper socialist! Tell us, George, what's your recipe?' Despite his condition, there was condescension in Burgess's tone. Perhaps he was not as drunk as he appeared.

'I think we need to get the war done first,' was all Orwell could muster in response.

'Well, I'm assuming that with our Soviet friends we shall win. Don't you agree, Sage? And after that, what will this country look like? Will you still be working for the BBC George? Or will you go back to your books and a quiet life in the country perhaps?' Burgess was no longer slurring or shuffling around and his intimation of Orwell having a place in '*the country*' had not gone unnoticed.

'I'll go back to my books almost certainly. The BBC is an asylum and I would have done my time.'

'Only, the lunatics are already in charge, my dear fellow. Surely you've discovered that. I've been told – and you'll not believe this – that we're still paying Hitler royalties for *Mein Kampf*! Apparently, they go through Sweden or some such place. Can you believe it?' Burgess broke into a loud laugh.

'Nothing surprises me about the BBC.' Orwell replied.

Bernal fidgeted uncomfortably during the conversation and continued to contribute very little. He sipped the last of his wine and made his excuses – something about getting back to his laboratory to supervise someone or something or other. He was satisfied with the arrangement for his talk and would be in touch. He quickly bade them farewell. The abruptness of his departure was troubling but Orwell recognised his opportunity.

'Right George, the Café Royal? Let's go,' Burgess said.

Orwell feigned some reluctance. 'I really...really must be going,'

'Nonsense, George. I'd like us to have a bit more of a chat. In fact I have some news you'll be interested in.'

'News?'

'About India ... and Cripps. I know you're most interested in that. I've picked up a bit of gossip down the line. We can chat over something to eat.'

Burgess's willingness to volunteer his information had taken Orwell by surprise. It was an unexpected opportunity. They finished their drinks and set off for the Cafe Royal.

After a minor altercation with the Maître d', they were allowed into the establishment. The upper classes were still at play while the working class cowered in the Underground shelters not a hundred yards away. The notion of 'us all being in this war together' was just another lie, Orwell thought.

They made their way to a deserted table and Burgess

acknowledged waves from a few of the clientele. Dressed as he was, Orwell felt like an outsider and was actually relieved to think that that indeed was the case. Burgess, on the other hand, looked entirely at home, although his initial remarks suggested otherwise.

'These people are the reason we're destined to have a revolution before the end of this war! Look at them, on their fat arses! The only fighting they do is with their appetite. I'm with you, George. They should be put up against the wall! But there again, that would probably be the waste of a good few bullets!'

The outburst was entirely unexpected and Orwell protested that he had never said or wrote any such thing. Despite its pretensions, Orwell found the Café Royal's food was decidedly unappetising and he couldn't hide his disappointment with the minuscule rubbery pork chop he'd been served. Burgess insisted he complain but Orwell had no intention of causing a scene. He had more important matters on his mind.

The conversation began benignly enough. It was mostly about the BBC and the nature of the propaganda they were producing. Cripps's mission was studiously avoided until after the last spoonful of what was more 'sticky' than 'toffee' pudding. Brandies were ordered and Burgess insisted they have a Corona too. Orwell, who had not smoked a proper cigar since the start of the war, forsook the state of his lungs and accepted the offer.

Once settled, Orwell confronted the issue at hand.

'Cripps?'

Burgess looked sheepishly over his brandy glass and puffed gently on his cigar. 'Oh, yes, I was wondering when you'd get round to that. I didn't want to spoil your luncheon, but it seems the chef had other ideas!' Burgess then leaned across the table and half covered his mouth with his hand.

'Cripps ... well, yes he's doomed I'm afraid, or so I'm reliably informed.' Burgess made sure he had Orwell's full attention before continuing. ' Do you know, I had a vision when I heard about Cripps. I was reminded of my childhood of all things. You see, when I was eleven, I had to extricate my mother from the clutches of my dead father. He'd died on the job, if you know what I mean. And when I thought about the Cripps mission I couldn't help but think that our relationship with India is pretty much of the same order. The dying empire atop the nubile bride. Only I can't see Cripps in my role, can you? I can't see him dismantling the Raj and liberating Mother India. Not least with the terms I'm told he's been given.'

Orwell drew back in shock at the analogy and took a drink. 'Do you know what the terms are?'

'Of course. Contacts. Chums. Old boys. The usual.'

'And what are they, the terms?' Orwell asked.

'Why do you want to know? What would you do with the information?' Burgess offered a cold, piercing stare from beneath his floppy hair. His near-permanent grin had all but disappeared. He looked different – older and sterner than he had been just minutes earlier. This was a delicate situation.

'Just curiosity.'

'You expect me to believe that? Come now George, we all know curiosity killed the cat. Everything has consequences, even the most trivial of affairs.'

Burgess seemed to be angling so Orwell reversed the questioning. 'What do you think I would do with it?'

'Release it to your radical Indian friends perhaps?'

'And why might I do that?'

'Because it would most likely scupper Cripps before he even sets foot in India. It might force the coalition's hand and they'd have to lay more on the table. In which case Churchill might even resign if that was to occur, or so I'm informed. The consequences for the course of the entire war might then be entirely disastrous.'

'Then it all depends on what Cripps has to offer.'

'Indeed. But my sources tell me there's very little for the starving Indians to feed on. In fact, I'd go so far as to say they'd be hard pressed to find anything on the menu that suits their palate. We appear to be offering Jinnah and the Muslims a plate of pork and Gandhi one of beef, if you follow my drift.'

'Then why is Cripps even bothering? What's in it for him?'

'That's a good question and one that bothers me and a lot of other people. To be honest, no-one has any real idea. He can be a loose cannon by all accounts. He's certainly no friend of Churchill.'

'The terms? You've still not told me what they are.'

Burgess paused, took a swig of his brandy and stared at Orwell. 'Oh, one more thing. Sutton. Have you seen him lately?'

'No, why do you ask?' Orwell swallowed the cough that he had been harbouring since he first inhaled the cigar.

'No reason. I just thought you and he seemed to be getting along. Apparently, he's fallen into line over the terms. I'm told they thought he might resign at one point. Then he went and had some form of Damascene conversion it seems. Either that or Winston has got something on him. That's usually the case. Anyhow, I'm told he voted with the rest of the cabinet. In fact the vote was unanimous by all accounts.'

Sutton's sudden submission was disturbing. Did Churchill know about Sutton's attempted infidelity? If Sutton had really capitulated was there any reason for him to continue to seek out the terms of the mission? Orwell decided the cause was still just and the fate of millions in India was still at stake.

Burgess leaned over. 'And Miss—'

'Mukurjee?'

'Yes, your Indian girl. Any news?'

'No. She's still missing.' Orwell shuffled in his seat and finished off his brandy. The lingering cough finally surfaced and he smothered it with his handkerchief. There was a trace of Joe's blood on his handkerchief and he quickly pocketed the signal.

'I might have some news on that score as well.'

'What?' Orwell coughed again. Burgess waited until he had cleared his lungs.

'She has a brother. He was at Cambridge ... until he too disappeared. No one has seen hide or hair of him for, well, weeks. Apparently, he's also something of a loose cannon and got into all manner of scrapes up at King's. A Bose man they say. Probably gone on the run. Could well be back in India by now ... or Berlin more likely. Might I suggest you damp the cigar? Save it for another time. Those coughs sound rather serious.'

Orwell ignored the advice. 'How do you know this?'

'Contacts.'

'Of course.'

Orwell headed for the WC. His lungs and his bladder needed relieving. He found an empty cubicle and thought about his luncheon partner. He had realised by now that Burgess obviously had no intention of divulging the terms of the Cripps's mission, if indeed he knew them. The invite to the Café Royal had been a ruse, but to what end? Why was he saying a lot, yet not disclosing anything in particular? Was it Burgess's way of letting him know he was being watched ... that his every move was known? Burgess seemed to know everything, but how? What might he do with his information? And of what interest could he possibly be to Burgess? More important, did Burgess know what had happened to Rana? He also knew about her brother.

Of one thing Orwell was now certain: Burgess was not to be trusted.

He returned to the table to find Burgess had gone and, being a gentleman, had paid the bill, no doubt out of his BBC expenses account.

31

'It ain't half quiet up here. There's a war on, you know! Is there anyone at home? All gone missing, have yer?'

'So this is where they send you when you've done yer time! The arse end of nowhere.'

'P'raps we need a Missing Persons Squad to find Missing Persons!'

In less than a few minutes, the two cocky young detectives from Mackie's team announced themselves by denouncing the Section, street beggars, homosexuals, conscientious objectors and vegetarians. Baines and Taylor sat speechless. The intruders were loud and most unwelcome.

On hearing the commotion Percy walked into the front office. 'How can I help you gentlemen?'

'DCs. Ponting and Borlock, Murder Squad. DCI Mackie sent us. We were told to ask for Percy. We haven't got his second name. He thinks this Percy might be able to assist us in our enquiries.'

'That's me, and that's my surname.'

'Percy?' Ponting looked at his partner and raised his eyebrows.

'DI Percy to you. Now, how can I *assist*?'

'We've the body of an Indian bloke. Stabbed and thrown in the river by Hammersmith Bridge, or at least that's where he washed up. The governor thought you might know who he is. One of your missing persons perhaps?' Ponting sniggered.

'Indian?'

'Well, a darkie, from the East. Looked Indian, Gunga Din like, but he was almost white by the time they dredged him out.'

'Two knife wounds. One to the neck, the other to the heart. Dead by the time he hit the water, the governor reckons. Splosh!' Borlock spoke almost gleefully while making a diving motion with his hands.

'Young? Old?'

'Youngish, tho' it's difficult to say with the darkies.' Ponting smirked and sought acknowledgement from his confederate.

'And no identity papers,' Borlock said.

'We think he might have come off a boat.'

'An Indian, male, with a knife in his neck?' Percy's first thought was of Rana Mukurjee's brother. Baines seemed about to say something so Percy quickly intervened, 'As far as I'm aware, there are no Indian males on our books, but we'll need to check. I'm sorry, gentlemen, that's all we can do for now. It'll take a day or two to go through the records.'

'That's all you can do?' Ponting shook his head dismissively. The two detectives began to fidget uncomfortably. They were no doubt thinking that Mackie would have been expecting them to come back with something more.

'Give my regards to DCI Mackie and tell him if he needs some *intelligence* to let me know,' Percy replied cryptically.

'Intelligence?' Both Borlock and Ponting replied in harmony.

'Yes. Make sure you tell him exactly that. Now, I'm sure you're very busy.' Percy showed them to the door.

As soon as they had left, Baines followed Percy into his office, question marks etched on his face.

'It's got something to do with her, hasn't it? That's why you didn't say anything.'

Percy smiled. 'Well done, son. At last, you're getting hang of this.'

'Why?' Baines looked even more perplexed.

'Because, well, I reckon they'll be back. And by then we might be able to tell them what they don't know, which is obviously quite a lot.'

'*Intelligence*, it's a code: Mackie will know you know something.'

'Very good! You got the message. Perhaps he will. If not, we'll just have to make our own enquiries. Why, for instance, is the Murder Squad interested in a dead Indian?'

'Because he's been murdered?' Baines said innocently.

Percy shook his head. 'I doubt it. They've plenty of other fish to fry. I can't see a dead Indian being top of their case list. And Mackie wouldn't be involved. He'd leave it to those numbskulls who were here just now. So why were they here? How often have the Murder Squad come to us?'

'Never.'

'Precisely. Something's up and it's no accident that Mackie has contacted us.'

'You, you mean.'

Later that day the call came from Mackie and Percy made his way to Fulham Police Station. He found Mackie in a cigar-smoke-filled office reading the *Sporting Life*. A sense of déjà vu overcame him.

'A tip-off.' Mackie put aside the newspaper and relit his cigar. 'I meant to get in touch before now. To apologise for not acknowledging your efforts in the Ripper case.'

The admission was totally unexpected and out of character. Not knowing how to respond, Percy just sat and listened.

'I need to keep up appearances for the sake of the force. It needs strong characters, leaders, old-school coppers. I'm what they call a role model, someone to look up to. Anyways, this tip-off means I might repay you.'

He sounded contrite but Percy didn't really believe a word he said.

'What was the tip-off?'

'Just that you might know the Indian we pulled out the river.'

'Do you know where it came from?' Percy asked.

'Not a clue. Out of the blue we got a telephone call. I didn't put two and two together at first. Then the penny dropped. I couldn't believe it was you she mentioned.'

'She?'

'Well-spoken, the desk sergeant tells me. Not your usual nark. That's why I was interested.'

'So you sent the monkeys over.'

'No, that was just to get them out of my hair. Sorry.' Mackie took out another cigar and clipped its end. 'So, do you know who he might be, the dead'n?'

'I have an idea.'

'So?'

'I need to ask a few questions before I can say for sure. I also need to see the body or at least some photographs.'

'But you think you might know. *Intelligence*?'

'Intelligence.'

32

Percy entered the lift at the same time as the elderly man. His fellow traveller seemed suspicious, more so after they went to press the fifth-floor button at the same time. Percy quickly withdrew his hand and stepped back against the cage wall. The lift shuddered and rose. No sooner had it cleared the first two floors when it came to a halt. The old man did not look unduly alarmed and pressed the button again. As if regaining its breath, the lift rattled into life. They arrived at the fifth floor and Percy volunteered to open the gates. The old man failed to acknowledge him.

'And thank *you*!' Percy shouted.

A woman opened the front door.

'Mrs Blair?'

'Yes, Eileen Blair.'

'Inspector Charles Percy, Scotland Yard. Is your husband at home?' He held up his warrant card.

'No.'

'Are you expecting him?'

'What's this about, Inspector?'

'May I come in?'

Eileen opened the door wider and allowed Percy to pass. He made his way into the sitting room. Books lined the walls and littered the floor in tottering piles.

'Please sit down if you can find a space! I'm sorry about the mess. It's George. That's how he works. Now, how can I help?'

'Has your husband told you about his missing BBC colleague?'

'No, I've no idea what you're talking about.' Eileen looked bemused.

'One of his assistants, at the BBC, has gone missing and it's been some time now. Her name is Rana Mukurjee. She's Indian.'

'I've never heard of her. George hasn't mentioned the name I'm sure.'

'Yet he's been working with her for months. Why might that be?'

'Perhaps it slipped his mind. He's rather preoccupied at the moment. Perhaps he did say something, only I've not taken it in. Who knows? There are such a lot of horrible things happening, it's difficult to focus on anything. I think it's best to leave things at work and not to talk about them at home. George is the same. He tends not to bring his work home with him. How about you, Inspector?'

'I agree. Although it is good to share one's problems and it's nice to have someone to come home to and talk about, well, anything.'

'Are you married, Inspector? Do you talk about your work?'

'Yes, I'm married. And, no, I don't talk about my work, if I can help it.' Percy looked away, feeling embarrassed by the frank admission.

'Happily? Are you happily married?'

'It's difficult in my job. We don't have much time to be ... and what with the war and all. It means I'm really busy. Is anyone happy anymore what with everything going on?' Percy took a moment and focused on the case. 'Rana Mukurjee's her name. Your husband hasn't mentioned her disappearance?'

Eileen shook her head. 'Have you any children?' she asked. Percy paused before answering.

'No, we've not been blessed on that score. But we were trying before all this ... the war that is.' Perhaps just to unburden himself, Percy found himself voluntarily talking about his personal situation.

'I can sympathise with you on that score Inspector.' Eileen replied.

'You've none then?'

'No, George and I have not been *blessed*, as you put it, not yet, at any rate.'

'Forgive me for asking, and it's none of my business, but are *you* happy Mrs ...Orwell?'

'It's Blair. And you're right, it is none of your business, Inspector.'

Eileen's hand shook as she lit a cigarette. After taking a long drag she exhaled to one side. 'It's such a stupid little word, isn't it? *Happy*. Don't you think?'

She looked away and Percy thought she might be about to cry. He didn't reply. He had never considered the meaning of words and simply took them as given. He had certainly never considered whether 'happy' was a silly little word. But now, looking at Eileen, he had no doubt that it was. It should have been placed in quarantine for the duration of the war, he thought. He vowed to himself never again to ask anyone whether they were happy, at least not until the hostilities had ended.

Eileen recovered her poise and turned to Percy. 'To be perfectly honest, I agree with you. This is not the time to be happy about anything. I lost my dear brother last year, in France. We were very close. He would do anything or go anywhere if I needed him ... quite unlike George. I think of him every day and miss him dreadfully. I'm not sure I'll ever really be happy ever again.'

'I'm sorry for your loss ... they say time is a great healer.'

'Thank you, Inspector, but I've often wondered who *they* are. The great British public who put up with everything? Can I get you some tea? Everything feels better with a good old cuppa they also say! I sometimes think it's George's answer to everything.'

The offer was unexpected but welcome. 'Actually, if it's not too much trouble, that would be very nice. Thank you very much.'

Eileen went to the kitchen and Percy picked a book off the floor – H.G. Wells's *War of the Worlds*. He thumbed through it and was struck by the underlining and comments pencilled in on nearly every page. After a few minutes Eileen returned with a tray of tea and a biscuit tin.

'Has he really read all these?'

'Oh, yes, all of them. Some many times over.'

'I wish I had read more. I've never been one for the books. I think I was put off at school. It was always a chore. I couldn't see any pleasure coming from it. I'd rather be out kicking a ball ... or another boy. Have you read many yourself?'

'Yes, for my degree. I'm a psychologist by training.'

'A trick cyclist? Sorry.'

'No, that's psychiatry. I studied psychology and how young children begin to read.'

Percy sipped his tea. Eileen looked distant and sorrowful.

'Do you think he'll be much longer?' Percy asked, hoping Orwell would not show for a while because, for some unknown reason, he felt very comfortable in Eileen's company. He had not spoken like this to anyone for such a long time, if ever, and desperately wanted their conversation to continue.

'I don't think so. But he might have gone to the pub ... for the news broadcast. They have a wireless and he likes to hear what's going on ... and have a pint, of course. It's rather ironic, given that he works at the BBC that we don't ourselves have a wireless. Why have you come here tonight, Inspector? How can George help you with your enquiries?'

'I'd rather talk to your husband, Mrs Blair. I wouldn't want to be bothering you.'

'It would be no bother. In fact, I'd like to help if I can. I'd certainly like to know what's going on.'

Percy thought about Orwell's infidelity and knew he could not reveal the relationship with Rana. Instead, he broached the subject of The Stores.

'Have you been to Wallington recently?'

'You know we have a place there? The Stores.'

'Yes, your husband told me.'

'No, I've not been back for some time. To be honest, I have no intention of going back. It's quite primitive – which is why George loves it. But it's not for me. I much prefer my home comforts.'

'Has your husband been back?'

'Is this still to do with the missing woman? If so, why not just tell me?'

This was getting awkward and he was beginning to tie himself in knots.

'As I said, I'd rather speak to your husband.'

'I'm not daft, Inspector. Are you suggesting my husband and the missing woman were together in Wallington? I can put two and two together you know.'

'I'm not suggesting anything, Mrs Blair. In fact, it's not just the woman that brings me here. A young Indian man was seen in Wallington. We think he may be related to Miss Mukurjee, but we have no idea why or how he came to be there.'

'And George might?'

'Yes...' said Percy, relieved to have explained away his line of questioning. 'It could be something political. I know your husband is involved in broadcasting to India.'

'Yes. Of course, it might well be something to do with his broadcasts.' Eileen offered Percy the biscuit tin.

'It's something we need to look into, given what's going on with the Indians at the moment. The independence business.'

'And you suspect that George is somehow involved?'

'It would appear so. That's what I need to talk to him about.'

'More tea, Inspector?'

Percy sat back on the settee and looked intently at Eileen. Had she believed him? She turned away from his stare.

'What does your wife do Inspector?'

'She's a seamstress.'

'A seamstress? How practical. I sometimes wish I had those skills'

'But she's not worked for a while.'

'The war?'

'No, she's not been well.'

'Oh, I'm sorry. If I may, what's—'

'The doctors can't make up their minds. Truth is, I don't think they really know.'

Eileen shuddered and Percy wondered if she had recognised her own predicament.

'Is it physical?'

'It is now, but I think it was mainly in her head to begin with. She was very down. Only now, she's ill. She's not looking after herself. She's let herself go. Look I-I shouldn't be burdening you with all this. I'm sorry.'

'No, I'm sorry I asked. I had no right to.'

Percy took a moment to compose himself. 'It's the children thing. Not coming and all.'

'She blames herself?'

'No! Not a bit of it. She blames me entirely. In fact, she blames my leg.'

'Excuse me! Your leg?' Eileen let out a small giggle.

'Yes, believe it or not. I had an accident while on duty, which is pretty much why I'm here and not with the boys at the front. It was smashed during the strike of '26. Vera reckons, well, she thinks it's caused the problem. Which is nonsense because I've had everything checked out. According to the quacks, I'm all right, you know... But she's having none of it. It's my leg that prevents us ... anyway, that's what she's got into her head. Biology was never her strong point.'

'I'm sorry.'

'No need to be. If I may say so, you don't look too well yourself.'

'You're right, Inspector, I'm not.'

'And your husband, he's not in the best of health either.'

Eileen's eyes brightened. 'No, we're a very sorry couple, aren't we?'

'We all have our crosses to bear.'

'In your case, it's your leg.'

'I was thinking more of Vera, my wife.'

They both chuckled.

'I'm sorry, Inspector. George must have gone to the pub otherwise he'd be back by now.'

'Perhaps I should go there. Which one is it?'

'The Fox and Horses, just by St. James' Underground. Please don't detain or arrest him. In fact, tell him to come home.'

'I will.' Percy made his way to the door. 'And thank you for our little chat. I very much appreciated it, as well as the tea and biscuits, of course.'

'So did I, Inspector.'

The old man was back, waiting for the cage to descend. Despite his leg, Percy decided to walk down the stairs.

33

ORWELL LIKED TO OBSERVE THE WORKING CLASS AT LEISURE, or outside of work at least. They were mostly middle-aged or older men in various states of despair and disrepair. Either too old or too infirm for the war, or even for cleaning up its consequences. He felt an affinity with their non-combatant status, but little else. There but for the grace of God he thought. He had Eileen, a relatively comfortable home, work at the BBC and his writing, although none of that made his pint taste any better. It was remarkable – no one seemed to want to listen to the news on the wireless, which he was straining to hear above the din of the near-full pub. Despite having full access to the BBC's monitoring reports, he still wanted to listen to the broadcasts. The spoken word somehow felt more visceral, and being in the company of strangers and gauging their reactions somehow added, or negated, the veracity of the announcements.

Percy found his man in the public bar. Spotting him had been all too easy. Orwell's glass needed replenishing, so Percy ordered two pints of bitter and made his way over to the corner table.

'Inspector!'

Percy pulled up a chair. 'Mr Orwell, I bought you a pint.'

'Thanks. Not on duty then?'

He looked at his watch. 'I went off duty two minutes ago.'

'Is this your local? I've not seen you in here before now.'

'No, I was looking for you.'

'How did you know where to find me?' Orwell lit a roll-up and sipped his beer. 'Cheers.' The froth covered his pencil moustache and for a moment he looked as if he had aged or had a convulsion of some sort.

'Your wife directed me.'

'Eileen?'

'Yes, she said you'd be here listening to the news and you are.'

'Not that I can hear a word above the din. Is no news good news, Inspector?' Orwell sounded disconcerted.

'There's been a development in the Mukurjee case.'

'You've found her?'

Percy removed his hat and shook his head. 'No. But we have found a dead Indian man. Murdered.'

It was Orwell's turn to shake his head. 'Murdered?'

'Yes, stabbed and thrown in the river. It could be your man, the one who's been following you. He certainly fits the description.'

Orwell stopped his glass half way towards his mouth. 'You don't think—'

'I don't think anything Mr Orwell.' Percy took a swig of his beer. 'Other than he may have been following you and

Miss Mukurjee. Have you had any more thoughts as to why? Could he be Miss Mukurjee's brother?'

'He might well be. But who would want to kill him? And why?'

'That's what I intend to find out.'

Neither spoke for a moment. Some of the men in the bar were gesturing in their direction and huddles were forming. Two men sat at a nearby table were clearly intent on eavesdropping.

Orwell lowered his voice. 'What did you say to Eileen?'

'Only that the Indian might have been following you ... just you. I told her it could be something political.'

'And she believed you?'

'She appeared to find it credible, which it might be, given your record.'

The two eavesdroppers craned their necks. One dropped a penny on to the floor. It rolled away in the opposite direction from Orwell and Percy's table. None the wiser, they returned to the throng at the bar.

'You didn't tell her anything else?'

'There was no reason to.'

'Thank you, Inspector. You see, she's not well, and knowing about Rana, Miss Mukurjee, wouldn't help her condition.'

'I could see that for myself.' Percy looked at Orwell accusingly.

'So what happens next?'

'We need to concentrate on finding Miss Mukurjee. She's obviously the key to all this. Do you think any of your Indian colleagues might be able to help?'

'Miss Doshi – Jahida possibly. She has her ear to ground on most things. I could ask. Should I say anything about the brother?'

'Not yet. We've still to make a positive identification. All we know is that we have a dead Indian male on our hands.' Percy looked around. 'May I ask you a personal question?'

'Delicate is it?'

'Yes, sort of, but I'll ask it anyway. How do you feel about cheating on your wife? How could you do that to her?'

Orwell seemed taken aback by the charge and cleared his throat.

'Cheating?'

'What else would you call it?'

'A sort of mutual arrangement. We tolerate it. Or, should I say, Eileen tolerates it.'

'So she knows about your affairs?'

'No, not exactly. We agree not to talk about what each other does in that regard. They're not really affairs in any case. More like diversions.'

'Call them what you will, she must know that you're seeing and doing it with someone else.'

'That's one way of putting it, I suppose. Yes, I suspect she knows ... but we agree not to make it an issue.' Orwell sipped his beer and made another roll-up. He began a cough and smothered it with a handkerchief.

'Why does she tolerate it?' Percy obviously couldn't understand the arrangement. It was far beyond both his experience and moral landscape.

'I suppose it's because she's devoted to me or something of that sort. Love even. She also knows it's necessary.'

Percy nearly choked on his beer. 'Necessary?'

'As a writer I need the freedom to express myself and, well, sex is part of that. You see, we don't much care who sleeps with whom. Without being too precious Inspector, what really matters to us is being faithful in an emotional and intellectual sense. I'm sometimes unfaithful to Eileen and I know I treat her very badly on occasion. Buy I also know she has been unfaithful to me. Nevertheless we have a proper marriage in the sense that we've been through some awful struggles together and come out the other side all the better for it. Do you know that she was with me in the war in Spain? She was there for me and she understands my needs.'

'What about hers? Do you have any idea about her needs?'

Orwell shook his head 'Is it really possible to understand a woman's needs Inspector?'

Percy shook his head, and looked even more pained. With Vera it felt more like he was simply at war, not in one together. Orwell had described another world and Percy couldn't even begin to imagine such a relationship.

'You don't believe me, Inspector?'

'Are you normal, for your sort that is?'

'Writers you mean?'

'Yes.'

'I wouldn't say it's normal, but it's not entirely unknown.'

A loud cheer went up at the bar and Percy guessed that a football result had been announced rather than a battlefield victory.

'And what about you, Inspector? How's your love life? Even policemen have a love life of some sort, surely.'

'Why do you want to know?'

'For the same reason you asked about mine.'

'I don't think I have much in common with you, Mr Orwell. I really don't.'

Orwell raised his glass in salute. 'We're both men, Inspector.'

'That's probably as far as it goes. But we're very different men, I'd say. I get a distinct impression that you really don't care for women, with your so-called diversions.'

'Nothing could be further from the truth.' Orwell laughed loudly, again drawing the attention of the regulars.

'I've seen it in men before, and I got that feeling from reading your books. Whereas I actually like women. Well, most,' said Percy.

'Which ones? The books, I mean.'

'The Burma one.'

'*Burmese Days*?'

Percy was reluctant to say any more, but didn't want Orwell dismissing him as just another ignorant policeman. He took a large swig of his bitter. 'For example. Your main man—'

'Flory.'

'He buys the Burmese girl and treats her terribly. Yet you say hardly anything about it. And Elizabeth, she's empty-headed and has nothing to say. And Dorothy in *A Clergyman's* is so simple-minded, if I might say so. Then there's Bowling's wife.'

'Hilda.'

'Yes. Although I have to admit, I actually know one like her. But she's not typical by any stroke.' Percy looked Orwell in the eye. 'My wife, Vera, she's as joyless as Bowling's Hilda. But she's not typical of all women.'

'By that I take it you don't ...?' Orwell finished his drink and tilted his glass back and forth.

'Perhaps I'm a George Bowling,' Percy replied, resigned.

'There's a lot like him about, Inspector. Another pint? I'll get them in. They'll be calling time any minute ... another victory for Hermann Goering! Watney's keep watering it down. It feels like you're drinking piss. Someone's making a profit by this war at least.'

Orwell went to the bar. The nods and winks of the locals were becoming more intense and he was almost encircled. The barman seemed reluctant to look his way and Orwell raised his hand and smiled benignly at the inquisitors. After eventually being served, he made his way back to Percy with their re-filled glasses.

'They think we're spies ... or nancy boys,' Orwell said, sipping from the near overflowing glass. Some of his beer spilt on to the already sticky floor.

'Why do you say that?'

'Just the way they're looking at us.'

Percy looked at the crowd.

'I can recognise it. It's the look I got in Burma. We could be Germans, or any foreigners, it doesn't really matter. They're all the bloody same to them.' Orwell rolled his cigarette between his fingers. 'I must say, you've done your homework on me, Inspector. I'm flattered. But I think you're wrong about the women in my books. Although I'm not at my best with the female characters, I grant you that. I've been told that before. But the truth is, some women are actually like the ones I describe ... You said your wife was joyless. Why's that?'

'She blames my gammy leg for her not being able to have children.'

Orwell laughed out loud and Percy shook his head and smiled.

'And yes, we don't ... you know. But I'm not the one that's falling short in that department. I've had the tests to prove it. When she was told it was her, she changed. Stopped being the woman I married. That's when she became joyless. Still is.'

Orwell sat ruminating. Percy waited to see if he would reciprocate.

'Eileen and I want to have children too but we can't. I think I might be the problem. But we're not sure. Eileen wants me to have the examination but I've refused. I think it's disgusting what you have to do.'

'I've done it,' Percy replied assertively.

'And?'

'It's a little embarrassing … but a pleasurable relief! I could have arrested them for the mags they gave me!'

Both men laughed and for the first time Percy was at ease in Orwell's company. The feeling appeared to be mutual.

'Really, there's nothing to it. You just—'

'I know what you do Inspector!'

Again they both laughed loudly and caught the attention of the onlookers, who appeared to be increasingly incensed by their very presence.

'Then do it. Get it done. Find out what the problem is or where it lies. For both your sakes.'

'I might do,' said Orwell. 'After the war. Then again, given Eileen's health, I might not. If she wanted to have children by someone else it wouldn't bother me, because I have very little physical jealousy. So what are you going to do about your joyless wife, Inspector?'

'I've been considering adoption, but I haven't told Vera yet. I'm not sure it would salvage the situation in any case. She's too far gone and she mightn't take to it if it's not her own. In which case … I might have to leave her.'

Orwell raised his eyebrows. 'I hadn't even thought about adoption.'

'There'll be hundreds, thousands even, of orphans looking for a home after this lot,' Percy said.

'I suppose you're right. It's worth thinking about, although I imagine Eileen would feel pretty much as your wife might. The child would be a constant reminder of her, or my, inadequacy and she'd probably not take to the idea of it being someone else's.'

'And if it is you that has the problem, would you stop playing around if there was a child?'

'I suppose I might have to.'

'Might?'

'Would ... most probably.' Orwell took a drag of his cigarette and blew the smoke high towards the already tarred brown ceiling. 'Then again, it's just 1942 and we've already had two great wars and the Wall Street Crash. If we both had children today, I've a feeling they might not survive the next forty-two years. Do you think they'll be sharing a pint in 1984? I have my doubts. The world will be a different place by then, that's for sure. But will it be any better? Should we be bringing children into such a world?'

'Who else is going to put things right? We certainly don't seem able to.'

Both men sat back in their chairs at the same time, looked at each other and then at their beer.

'Where do we go from here, with Rana I mean?'

'I believe the answer lies in your office at the BBC. Someone must have known about you and Miss Mukurjee. Somehow, the brother becomes aware of what's going on and follows you. Where she's gone and how her brother – if it is him – came to end up dead in the Thames, well, that remains to be found out. Start asking questions Orwell and find out what you can. Did anyone know about your room in The Cut, apart from your anonymous, influential friend and Diane or Mrs Broadbent, or whatever she calls herself?'

'He can't be brought into this. He mustn't be.'

'It's murder, not just a missing-persons case. What if your VIP is implicated?'

'That's highly unlikely, Inspector. Preposterous even.'

'Think about it, Orwell. Could he be involved in some way?'

'What do you have in mind?'

'The national interest, you said. Important and powerful people attract all sorts of enemies, as well as having friends in high places to sort things out.'

'I think you're going off the beaten track, Inspector.'

'That's where I like to be. You never know what you'll find and it's often the best place to look. It's where they don't expect or want you to look.'

Two auxiliary constables suddenly appeared either side of their table. Percy and Orwell looked at each other and ignored them, until one said, 'Evening gents. Can we see some identification, please?'

'Why?' said Orwell.

'Identification, please.'

'I'll deal with this.' Percy produced his warrant card.

'Oh, I'm sorry, guv. It's just that we had a report—'

'What did it say? Tell me, Constable.'

The constable hesitated and looked at his colleague.

'It said there were two strange-looking men acting suspiciously. We have to follow them up, all the reports. Really sorry to bother you, guv.'

'Did it say anything else?'

'Such as, guv?'

'I'm asking you, Constable. Do we look strange to you? Did it say anything about how we were acting suspiciously?'

'No, guv, not exactly.'

'Not exactly? Then how?'

'They obviously thought we were ... Mary-Anns. Do we look like a couple of queers? Orwell chimed in.'

One of the officers stuttered his reply.

'Well, I think that will be all,' Percy said, wanting to close the proceedings before Orwell said something else.

'Yes, guv. Goodnight and —'

The two constables beat a retreat watched by the crowd at the bar. They all looked disappointed.

'I think we should go. Your wife told me to send you home. Better late than never.' Percy rose and put on his hat. 'Call me if you hear anything. Anything at all. It's the smallest things that often matter the most.'

'I will. Thank you for the pint.'

Percy arrived home to find Vera had already gone to bed.

34

For the first time in weeks, the air-raid sirens sounded and everyone ignored them. People were carrying on in what now passed for normal in wartime London. Although anxious at first, Orwell looked skywards and shrugged. Obviously a false alarm or a practice of some sort.

He arrived at Portland Place to find Arthur or Godfrey standing outside on the pavement, scanning the sky for potential intruders.

'Thought for a sec Jerry had got up early!' he said in his annoyingly jovial way.

'Morning, Arthur,' Orwell said as he swung past the doorman.

'It's Godfrey, sir.'

Orwell ignored the correction and entered the lift. As the cage doors were about to close, Burgess pushed through, dishevelled and looking every bit like the morning after. He caught his breath, looked behind and shuffled between the other passengers towards Orwell.

'George, by Jove, I was hoping we'd meet. Look, I'm sorry

about the other day at the Café Royal. I had to dash. Couldn't be helped I'm afraid. I hope you don't—'

'Really, it's not a problem.'

Burgess spent the journey rearranging his clothing and trying to smooth his hair. Orwell caught a waft of his intense aftershave and bad breath and recoiled. They arrived at the India Section's floor and exited, Burgess seemingly by mistake. He looked around, as if checking they could not be overheard, and then turned to Orwell.

'By the way, Cripps's terms, I know what they are.' His voice suggested an illicit offer. 'India is to be given Dominion status. There'll be elections but only *after* the war. Meantime, we stay in charge of all defence matters. And – here's the rub – there's an opt-out.'

'Meaning?'

'The Ulster provision. If any of the Indian states wish to opt out of an all-India constitution, they'll be able to do so. You know what that means?'

'They've effectively given a green light for a future Pakistan. Partition.'

Burgess nodded and looked conspiratorially at Orwell. 'I'm told Amery insisted on it and Churchill readily agreed. I can also confirm what I think I told you the other day: the whole Cabinet, Atlee and your friend Sutton on the India Committee have signed up to it. It'll keep the Muslims on-side for the duration, and the Yanks off Churchill's back, which is probably what this is mostly about.'

'Will it? The whole thing is a recipe for division and disaster. Congress won't support it and Cripps will almost certainly fail. Churchill knows it. It's meant to fail. Congress will still demand immediate independence and, crucially, charge of defence.'

'Quite, unless of course Cripps has some sort of magic wand,' Burgess said cryptically.

Orwell had Burgess's attention and took the opportunity to change the subject.

'I meant to ask ... Rana Mukurjee's brother, have you heard any more?'

'Why?' Burgess said.

'It might help to find her.'

'She's still missing?' His tone was innocent but he fiddled nervously with his tie and collar as a gaggle of technicians passed them in the corridor.

'Yes, and it's not looking good.' Orwell replied.

'What do you mean?'

'What with this Ripper thing.'

'Oh, crikey. Of course. I hadn't thought. You don't think —' Burgess was still buttoning his waistcoat.

'Who knows? Anything could have happened to her. It's possible.'

'I suppose so. But haven't they caught the blighter? I heard—' Burgess was finally dressed and his hair was smoothed.

'Yes, but at the time she went missing they hadn't.'

Burgess shuffled his feet. 'I've not heard anything. As I said, he's probably scooted it to Berlin to join Bose. He was definitely of that ilk. If so, good riddance, I'd say. Perhaps she's gone with him?' Burgess walked several feet away, then turned round. 'Oh, by the way, George, have you heard from Bernal? Only I think he may have some bad news for you.' Burgess walked slowly back to Orwell. 'He's very busy and told me he won't have time for the talks you asked him to do. I'm sorry, old man. He's been asked to do some hush-hush stuff for the War Office apparently.' Burgess strolled off, again adjusting his tie and collar as he went.

Orwell stood motionless in utter disbelief. Burgess turned and appeared to be gloating as he walked off.

Orwell was fuming.

'Jahida, have you heard from Professor Bernal?' he shouted from his cubicle.

Jahida came to the door and watched as he threw papers across his desk. His hands were shaking and he gasped, fighting back the fit of coughing that threatened to overcome him.

'Don't shout at me like that!' she said. 'Yes, I heard from the university this morning. His secretary called. He's only got time for the Home Service programme he agreed to. He's very sorry but he can't do yours. He suggested we use the same recording for both.'

'Burgess!' Orwell, now incandescent, began to wheeze and cough. 'And that Red bastard! I knew there was something fishy going on between those two.'

'Calm down. What are you talking about?'

'No matter.'

You'll make yourself ill. I'll get you some tea.'

Orwell sat staring at the blank wall of the office - it was BBC policy not to decorate work spaces. After a few minutes Jahida returned. 'Drink it while it's hot.'

Orwell poured some tea into his saucer and decided to change the subject. 'Any news, of Rana?'

'No, I've not heard anything.'

'Or her brother?'

'No, why? Have you heard something?'

'No, I just wondered whether you'd had any more thoughts about him. Could he be involved in her disappearance?'

'Is there's something you're not telling me George? I can tell. You've heard something.'

Orwell thought for a moment before answering. 'Burgess told me her brother was at Cambridge and that he was a known Bose supporter. God knows how he knows, but he told me that.'

'A Bose supporter?'

'Yes, and quite openly it seems. Burgess has Cambridge contacts and hears an awful lot through his Old Boy's network.'

'And he knew about Rana's brother?'

'Yes. It's very odd, isn't it? Then again, Cambridge is a small world. It's like a gossipy village, or so I'm told.'

'It's a small world,' Jahida whispered.

'They say that the Cambridge crowd know everyone and everything that's worth knowing and Burgess appears to be very much a part of it.'

'Aren't you one?'

' I didn't go to Cambridge thank God. I'd have been a black sheep. A class traitor in their eyes!' Orwell wheezed and poured some more tea into his saucer.

'You do drink tea like a prole!'

How far could he press Jahida? He decided he had little to lose.

'Burgess thought the brother might have fled to join Bose in Berlin.'

'And taken Rana?'

'Who knows?'

'Absolute tosh. She wouldn't do that. She's definitely not one of Bose's. Definitely not. And she's not in Berlin, I'm certain of that.'

'How can you be so sure? Where is she then?'

'She had no time for Sanjit ... that's her brother. They had nothing in common. In fact, she thought he was a spoilt brat. She wanted nothing to do with him. That much I do know.'

'She told you that? What else?'

'Nothing.'

Orwell looked Jahida in the eye. 'What else, Jahida? It might help.'

'I don't know anything else.' She adjusted her sari and shuffled her feet.

Orwell sensed she knew more than she was willing to say.

'Are you sure? Nothing at all?'

'She's safe. I know it.'

'You know?'

'I know.' Jahida rose from her chair and left the office without turning back.

'Jahida!' Orwell shouted after her but there was no response.

35

Percy was now the only direct connection between the disappearance of Rana Mukurjee and the body of the Indian male. The tip-off had named him directly. However, it was only by establishing the identity of the murder victim that he could confirm the cases were in fact linked. Baines, armed with photographs of the dead man's face, was sent to King's College, Cambridge, to make inquiries. It took little detective work to verify that the corpse was indeed Sanjit Mukurjee. That narrowed the field to those who knew about Rana Mukurjee's disappearance and the fact that she had a brother. Orwell was one candidate and there had to be at least one other.

The tip-off had come from a well-spoken woman. So Percy went back to Portland Place.

Confronted by the evidence, Orwell decided he had little reason to protect Jahida if she would not confide in him.

'Miss Jahida Doshi, my assistant, knew Rana had a brother.'

'Anyone else?'

There was Burgess, of course, but he would contaminate everything. It might lead to further questioning, even revelations leading to Sutton, the new Secretary for War. Orwell had to lie.

'Not that I can think of.'

'Miss Doshi, is she well-spoken?' Percy asked.

Orwell looked at Percy quizzically. 'She's an announcer, so obviously she's well-spoken. It's the BBC after all. Why do you ask?'

'And you say she knew Rana Mukurjee had a brother?'

'Yes, I believe so.'

'Has Miss Doshi said anything about the brother since?'

'She told me Rana didn't get on with him at all and that it's unlikely she would have gone with him willingly.'

'Where to? Back to India?'

Reaching for his tobacco tin, Orwell again hesitated. 'It's complicated, Inspector. It's Indian politics – which are very messy at the moment.'

'Try me.'

'Well, if you insist., Orwell lit his roll-up. 'Rana's brother was a follower of a chap called Bose, a radical Indian nationalist who wants immediate and unconditional independence for India and he's willing to actually fight us for it. He's not in the Gandhi non-violence mould – far from it. He has an army of followers and he's thrown in his lot with the Nazis because he thinks that will help kick us out of India. He's broadcasting propaganda from Berlin. In a way, he's doing what we do here, only he lies more than we do! Rana, as far as anyone can tell, didn't share Bose's views. Yes, she was – is – a nationalist of sorts, but not a supporter of Bose. It's therefore highly unlikely she would have willingly followed her brother to Berlin. If that's where he was heading. Of course, we can't be sure.'

'Basically, the brother was a Nazi sympathiser.'

'I wouldn't say that. It was probably more a case of my enemy's enemy is my friend.'

'So a friend of the Nazis?'

'More their ally, I'd say. I doubt whether he shared much of their ideology and it's doubtful whether they would think much of him. But why look a gift horse? Hitler cosies up to anyone if it serves his purpose, and I suspect he sees Bose's nationalists as a useful thorn in our side.'

Percy seemed intrigued. This was all a long way from Missing Persons.

'So Miss Doshi knows all this?' Percy asked.

'I don't know. She probably knows nothing about what happened to the brother. I haven't told her anything about that.'

'And Miss Mukurjee's whereabouts? Do you think she knows where she is or what's happened to her?'

Orwell recalled Jahida's assertion that Rana was safe. 'You'd need to ask her that yourself.'

'Do you think she would tell me?'

'I really don't know, Inspector. Why shouldn't she?'

'Because we've been looking for the Mukurjee woman for weeks now and if Miss Doshi has known all the while, she's been wasting our time, and that's a serious offence.' Percy thought for a moment. 'Would she tell you?'

'I think she would have told me by now.' Orwell coughed. 'You still haven't answered my question: what has being well-spoken got to do with all this?'

It was Percy's turn to think before answering. 'We had a tip-off about the body of the brother. And, yes, we've confirmed his identity. Unfortunately it is Sanjit Mukurjee. The tip-off came from a woman and she was—'

'Well-spoken – she's middle-class in other words. Isn't it fascinating how the class system plays such an important role in English detective work?'

'Yes, she was described as well-spoken. She suggested I deduce who the dead man was. At the time I had no idea. But after a little thought it was obvious. She knew that I'm investigating the disappearance of an Indian woman and we now had a dead Indian male. It was then easy enough to put two and two together, even for a plod like myself. I'm the connection between the cases. Although, when we got the tip-off, I had no idea who he was or what his relationship to Miss Mukurjee might be, other than the bleeding obvious fact that they were or are, we hope in her case, both Indian. The informant knows I'm the bridge between the cases. Therefore, it's got to be someone who knew Miss Mukurjee had a brother and subsequently what has happened to him. The informant knew he was dead. Yet all we know is that this woman is well-spoken.'

'You suspect Jahida Doshi?'

'She fits the bill. Would she have told anyone else about the brother? Another well-spoken BBC woman colleague? I'm sure there are plenty around here.'

'She's not a gossip Inspector. In fact, I'd say Jahida Doshi is a secretary in the proper use of the term: a keeper of secrets.'

'Secrets?'

'Confidences, more like.'

'That you yourself have shared with her?'

'Yes, I may have.'

'Your *diversions*, for instance? Did she know about you and Miss Mukurjee?'

'I'm not sure where you're going with this.'

'I'm trying to establish whether Miss Doshi could have passed on her knowledge of Miss Mukurjee's brother to anyone – another well-spoken woman – here at the BBC.'

'How would I know?'

'Any guesses? Which other women on your staff might she have told?'

'I really don't think she'd have spoken to anyone else. What about Bokhari, my boss? Have you interviewed him?'

'I presume he's also well-spoken, but in case you haven't noticed, he's not a woman!'

'You're very observant, Inspector!'

'Cut out the sarcasm, Orwell. Might she have told Bokhari? Or he, her? He must have appointed Miss Mukurjee in the first place.'

'Yes, I believe so. But we've established he's not a woman, so he can't be the one who tipped you off.'

'Which brings us back to Miss Doshi.'

'Are you going to interview her?'

Percy thought for a moment and Orwell could see he was hatching something.

'No, I'd like you to ... share a confidence with her. I'd like you to tell her what's happened to the brother. Then tell me how she reacts. As an observer of the human condition, a writer, I feel sure you can do that.'

'You want me to be a snitch? A police informer?'

'Think of it as 'helping the police with their inquiries' as we say. Will you do it?'

'And if I decline?'

'Then I might have another chat with your wife about Wallington and the junk shop.'

'Are you blackmailing me, Inspector?'

'No, I'm giving you a choice, Orwell. I'm assuming you want to help us find Miss Mukurjee?'

36

Following Jahida was a madcap idea. One that made Orwell feel treacherous. Nevertheless, he had committed himself. As he had no recollection of seeing her in anything other than a sari, it took him some time to realise that the small, chubby woman wearing a headscarf and dressed in a nondescript khaki raincoat over everyday office clothes, was in fact her. She resembled every other woman heading home from work. But there was something about her walk – a distinct wobble – that gave her away.

He left Portland Place and turned right into New Cavendish Street. A couple of minutes later, he reached the porch of number 48, a block of nondescript flats.

'Are you following me, George?'

'Jahida, my God! I had no idea—'

'Don't lie, George. I saw you waiting before I set off. You're not exactly hard to notice. You'd make a lousy spy. Why are you following me?'

Orwell was flooded with guilt. 'I-I wanted to talk ... outside the office.'

'About something so important that you needed to follow me?'

'Yes, actually it is. I have some news about Rana, or at least, her brother.'

'Sanjit?'

'It's bad news, I'm afraid.' Orwell looked around and was feeling uncomfortable talking in the street. 'Do you live here? Can we go in?'

'Yes, I live here, but, no, you can't come in. Just tell me the news.'

'Can we go somewhere for tea perhaps. It's too early for the pub.'

'I don't want tea. Just tell me your news, will you?' Jahida snapped.

'He's dead.'

Jahida looked visibly shocked. 'How, when? How do you know? Who told you?'

'The police found his body. He'd been stabbed.'

'Murdered? Sanjit? Oh my God!' Jahida raised her hands to cover her mouth. A passer-by stopped and stared before moving along.

Orwell lowered his voice. 'They're certain it's him. They found him in the river sometime last week.'

'So that's why you were asking about him the other day. You already knew, but didn't tell me. You were trying to find out what I knew! That's low, George, even by your standards. That's low.' She waited for a response but he gave none. 'Why did the police tell *you*?'

'The policeman who's working on Rana's case, this Inspector Percy, I ran into him in my local.'

'And he just told you?' Jahida could not have looked more disbelieving.

'Yes, why not?'

'No matter. But why didn't you just tell me the other day at work?'

Orwell allowed another passer-by to get out of earshot before answering. 'They didn't know for sure. They just had a body. And it was because of what you said ... that you were certain Rana was safe. I took that to mean that you know where she is. In which case, she needs to know about her brother.'

Jahida shook her head Indian style. 'Perhaps I just heard she's safe. I wouldn't have to know where she is exactly.'

It had started to rain and they shuffled further into the doorway. Orwell lit his roll-up and coughed. Jahida half-turned away and shook her head in disapproval.

'Can you get the news to her?'

'Why should I do that, George?'

'Jahida it's her brother, for goodness' sake.'

'I told you, she had no time for him and I doubt whether he'll be missed, least of all by Rana.'

'But that doesn't mean she shouldn't know what's happened. Where is she, Jahida? If not for me, you need to let Inspector know. You're wasting their time if you don't, and that could get you into serious trouble.'

Jahida turned away and paused before asking, 'Have they caught anyone for the murder?'

'No, not that I've heard. Please, will you tell her?'

'Is that all? We're both getting wet out here and I need to go in.'

'To put the kettle on?' he asked in hope.

'Yes, but I'm not offering. I make too much tea for you at work. I have no intention of making you any out of it! Now, please go home to Eileen. It's after five. She'll make you some tea.'

'I can't come in?'

'No, George! Please, leave me to get on. Go home. Eileen needs you.'

Before Orwell could respond, she shut the door on him and was gone.

37

Eileen sat in the dark, wrapped in a blanket. The fire had not been lit. She had been drinking and smoking heavily. Something was wrong because she always became as quiet as a ticking bomb before exploding. Since the fuse was lit, Orwell tried some pre-emptive pacification by offering to put the kettle on. She said nothing.

Orwell returned to the sitting room with a cup of tea, took an armchair and placed it strategically so that she had no direct view of him. He rolled a cigarette and picked up one of the books from the floor. The first salvo duly arrived.

'Did you take her to The Stores?'

'Who?'

'You know who, George! Your missing Indian.'

'Did Percy tell you that?' He swallowed some congestion and felt Joe filling his lungs.

'Don't lie to me. DID YOU TAKE HER to Wallington?'

Orwell returned his book to the floor, sipped his tea and dragged on the cigarette.

'We had some urgent work and I thought it a good idea to get away from the office ... for some peace and quiet. Yes, we went to Wallington. I was still convalescing. I couldn't go in to work.'

'What do you take me for George? You're such a poor liar. Why don't you just come out and admit it?'

'Like you did with Georges Kopp? I don't recall you ever admitting it.' He regretted those words immediately. He closed his eyes and took a deep breath, holding it until Eileen spoke.

'It wasn't like that! Georges was very kind to me. He saved your life, for Christ's sake!'

'And I suppose that gave him a licence to sleep with you.'

'How can you be so cruel?'

'I was laid up with a bullet through my neck and you went off with my CO.' Orwell's voice rose in pitch. 'That's what it was like! Now that was being cruel!'

'It was NOT like that! He was kind to me and you know it. Georges looked after me.'

'Is that what you call it? Shagging a man's wife while he's fighting for his life isn't what one would usually call a kindness.'

'You bastard George! That's so typical of you. You have to turn everything around. This isn't about Georges, it's about *you*. Were you having an affair with this Indian woman or not?' Eileen threw off the blanket and lit a cigarette. She poured some wine and missed her glass. 'Oh, fuck it. Look what you've made me do!'

'Stop drinking.'

'When you stop fucking every woman that's daft enough to let you, that's when I'll stop. You were having an affair, weren't you? And it had to be a little Indian tart. *Burmese Days* and all that.'

'You're drunk.'

'No, George, I'm pissed ... pissed off with you. And it's

not just because you need to have other women. It's because you took her to Wallington. That's *our* place! You took her to *our* place and that's unforgivable. I've put up with all the others because they were ... out of sight. But taking her to Wallington, I can't forgive you for that. She must be something special to do that. Is she?'

'Don't give me that! You hate the other times. Anyway, she's now gone missing.'

'That's useful.'

'What do you mean?'

'How convenient – to get rid of her like that. I presume you had no long-term plans in any case.'

'She's gone missing, for Christ's sake!'

'And you've got something to do with it.'

'No, don't be daft ... her brother's been murdered.'

'Jesus! It gets worse. This is better than any of your books! I presume that's got nothing to do with you either. The police obviously don't think so, otherwise why was that Inspector here?'

'His name's Percy and, no, he doesn't think ... It's the Indian thing. The politics are getting very nasty but it's got nothing to do with Rana.'

'Rana?'

'Yes, Rana. That's her name.'

'Why her? What's she got that Jahida or the Princess haven't?'

Percy's word came to mind. 'Joy.'

'That's a strange notion, even for you. *Joy!* Is that what plain-speaking George Orwell calls it now? What's wrong with calling it a good old-fashioned shag?'

They looked away from one another and sat in silence for what seemed like an age. Orwell shook his head and whispered, 'It wasn't just that.'

'Not *just* that! So you did fuck her. Do you love her? My God, that would be a first!' Eileen fumbled for her cigarettes. Visibly shaking, she took a large glug of the wine and lit another cigarette.

'No, I-I love you.'

'You think you do, in your own way, but I'm not sure it's what most of us mean by it. Free love I believe your Bloomsbury crowd call it: anyone can have it – whoever, wherever and whenever. You're really a rank Tory in lots of things, George, but one thing's for sure: you're a true socialist when it comes to sex!'

'They're not my Bloomsbury—' Orwell stopped himself. Saying anything more would only make matters worse.

Eileen sobbed and drew her knees up to her chin under the blanket. 'I can't do this anymore, George. I can't stand the deceit, the sheer bloody hell of it all. I've walked the extra mile for you and all I get is this: I'm put in reserve. For *joy*. If that's what you're after.' Eileen untangled her arms from the blanket and took another drink. 'Everyone calls you "misery guts". You're the joyless one, George. In fact, you're a right miserable sod most of the time. If you want joy, stay well away from George – that would be my advice to all sensible women. You can be the most miserable bugger on this planet at times! I'd love to meet this Rana and find out how she made you feel *joy*. She must be a bloody miracle-worker!'

'You're pissed.'

'I have every bloody right to be.'

'I'm going to the pub.'

'That's it, run away! I'll still be here when you come back ... and you know it. No matter what, I'll still be here, damn fool that I am,' Eileen screamed.

Orwell slammed the door behind him.

38

PERCY ARRIVED HOME AT 6 PM. THE HOUSE WAS DARK AND felt cold, or at least colder than usual. He went into the front room and switched the light on. There was no sign of Vera. He went to the kitchen, made a pot of tea, then headed back to the sitting room to tend the long spent fire. There was no sign of her.

While the tea brewed, he kicked off his shoes and began to search for his slippers. Remembering he'd left them in the bedroom that morning, he went upstairs. Still no sign of Vera. He pushed his hands under the covers on the bed but there was no warmth. The bathroom was empty too. He called out her name in vain. 'Vera? Vera!' She must have left the house – for the first time in months – and it pleased him. Perhaps it was a sign of some sort of recovery?

Back in the sitting room he picked up his copy of *Keep the Aspidistra Flying*. Orwell's characterisation of the much-flawed Gordon Comstock impressed him. The struggles of the poet and his willingness to endure hardship while forsaking all others in his pursuit of recognition told him something about the author ... as well as telling him something about himself? Perhaps not. Comstock was a self-centred, opinionated and vain individual who used others and disowned materialism by choice. Unlike Comstock, would Orwell settle down if and when his wife became pregnant? And just like Comstock and Rosemary, would the Blairs end up with that icon of middle-class respectability, the Aspidistra, on their living-room table? That would certainly be the pinnacle of Vera's ambition, but it was never going to be his. However, might he, too, have to capitulate if she had a child? Of course, it was never going to happen because Vera was barren. The only question now was: should or could he leave her?

Vera did not return that night and he had the whole bed to himself. He was strangely untroubled by her unexpected and unexplained absence. It wasn't until breakfast time that it occurred to Percy to check the wardrobe. Their small suitcase was missing, as were most of her clothes. It was then that he began to digest the possibility that she had left *him*. It was a bitter-sweet moment.

On his way to the office, he remembered that Vera had an aunt in Bethnal Green – who was, as far as he knew, her only surviving relative. He decided to take a detour, if only to satisfy his curiosity. The old woman was a widow and it transpired that she had long since lost touch with both her niece and any sense of reality. She didn't recognise Percy and insisted he show her his warrant card before letting him into her tiny lodging. She had no idea where Vera might be and suggested he contact the police. He reminded her that he *was* the police, but she merely shrugged. He made a swift exit.

He stood on the pavement and wondered who Vera might have turned to. They had no close friends. He could only think that she might have returned to her previous workplace, the drapery store on the Caledonian Road.

He made his way there, only to find a burned-out shell. He asked around and discovered that the building had survived the worst of the Blitz and that the destruction in front of him was the result of a recent freak accident.

The irony of the situation was not lost on Percy; Vera was now a missing person.

39

The BBC canteen was only quarter-full and its general griminess seemed even more depressing than usual. Burgess had arrived at his table uninvited and, as usual, looked somewhat worse for wear.

'George, have you heard? Cripps is definitely going to India ... bearing the gifts that no one wants.' Burgess smirked. 'No doubt Winston hopes they will shoot the messenger.'

'So he's really going? Of course, we'll be told to dress him up in our broadcasts,' Orwell said wearily.

'Oh no. Quite the reverse. We've been told to show him up – as a crank, an extremist, a loose cannon.'

'So he'll be blamed for the failure?'

'Quite. Failure is not allowed to land on Winston's desk in any shape or form. Cripps will take all the blame ... along with the Congress of course. Everybody has to believe it's the Indians, as well as Cripps, who can't deliver, or so I'm told.'

The '*or so I'm told,*' made Orwell cringe.

'They've given Cripps enough rope to hang himself. The

poor bugger thinks he's got some room for manoeuvre, but as far as the Cabinet are concerned he's not going there to negotiate. Not a jot. He's just the messenger boy and the message is set in stone. We're not to give the Indians anything if they don't pull their weight in the war. That's why they haven't yet published any of the terms he's taking with him. A declaration of some sort.'

'Two million Indians in the army doesn't count as pulling their weight then?'

'A drop in the ocean old boy, given their numbers. Winston wants their full cooperation and Gandhi's still the problem on that score. Non-violence is all very well if you're fighting a civilised enemy, someone like us, but the Japs don't see it that way. They'll take it as a green light to do whatever they like. I don't think Gandhi understands that. We need the Indians to fight, not just hold their hands up and turn the other cheek. That's not resistance. We've seen what happened in Burma when the Japs arrived. They were welcomed with open arms. The same might happen in India if there is no compromise.'

For once, Orwell found himself nodding in agreement with Burgess, albeit reluctantly.

'But the Indians will already know Cripps' terms.' said Orwell.

'How?'

'These things have a way of getting out. If you know and I know what they are, I'm pretty sure plenty of others will. The Indians will have already got wind of most, if not all, of them.'

'Of course, but that's where Cripps's misunderstanding comes to the party. The Indians will trust him and think that he has some room to revise the terms of a settlement. And that's what Cripps most likely believes himself. Why else would he go? Everyone will be led to believe that there's scope for compromise and the whole exercise, his mission, will look genuine. In which case Churchill and the British government will appear to have been the honest broker with regard to what they will call extortionate Indian demands. This is entirely for American consumption, of course. When Cripps's mission comes to nought, we'll have to carry on being in charge for the duration – which, in reality, is what this is all about.'

Burgess made it all sound like a game, a jolly caper of some sort. Had he forgotten that there were millions of human lives at stake?

'And when the war is over, what happens then? Who'll be around to pick up the pieces?' Orwell asked.

'Not us I hope.' Burgess stifled a giggle. 'The cat will already be out of the bag and they'll be left to fight among themselves, Gandhi or no bloody Gandhi. Let's just hope we've won the war by then. We don't want to be seen letting India go when we have our tail between our legs!'

Orwell sipped his tea. 'You sound pretty sanguine about it all.'

'History tells us it has to happen: the rise and fall of empires and all that. It's our turn of the wheel, and it's long overdue, some might say. From what I've heard about your views, you'd agree with that.'

Orwell waited before answering.

'My views? Everybody knows what they are. I believe India should have her freedom but I'm not sure she's in any condition to defend herself right now. That's my fear in all this. I've made it abundantly clear that I'm not an imperialist, but—'

'But India needs our paternalism? That's pretty conservative of you. The Indians will want control of their defence regardless of whether or not they are capable of it. It's bound to be a major sticking point in Cripps' negotiations.'

'If we go too soon, who knows what might happen?'

'And if we stay?'

'There maybe just a chance that Cripps will be able to work things out,' Orwell optimistically suggested.

'The hand grenade of independence is about to be thrown George. And anyone with an ounce of knowledge about India knows that once we offer an opt-out to the Muslims there will any number of others – Sikhs, Tamils, Kashmiris, Nepalese, Burmese you name it – all demanding their independence. India will implode. Churchill, Amery and even your friend Sutton knows it. That's why we need to get out - to Quit India - as Congress demand, but only after the war.'

Burgess offered one of his know-it-all smiles. The air still reeked of his aftershave after he'd left.

40

Percy wasted no time in getting to Portland Place as Jahida Doshi had requested the meeting, stressing that she had some important information regarding the whereabouts of Rana. They met in the BBC canteen and found a deserted corner of the ever-bleak canteen.

'Inspector, Rana Mukurjee is safe. I thought you should know. She's quite well and in no danger.'

Percy had half-expected the news. 'How do you know?'

'She's staying with me ... in my flat.'

'And how long has she been there?'

'All the time. She was never missing. I've been looking after her.'

'But you didn't inform us?'

'That's right. But I did it to protect her.'

Percy took a moment to digest the information.

'Protect her? From Orwell?'

'Good heavens, no, though God knows, I tried. I meant her brother, Sanjit.'

'Miss Doshi, you know he's dead? He's been murdered.'

'Yes, I know. Orwell told me. That's why I can tell you she's safe.'

'But why did you need to protect her from her own brother?'

Jahida shook her head and looked Percy straight in the eye. 'Do you know *anything* about Indian customs, Inspector?'

Percy shook his head and shrugged, then sipped the soapy tea. He suddenly realised that this was the first Indian woman he had ever talked to.

'She was due to be married – back home in India.'

'But she ran away. She eloped?'

'No Inspector, she *escaped*. She had other ideas about her future.'

'So she didn't want to marry?'

Jahida shook her head. 'You *really* have no idea, do you? To put it mildly, she was *sold*, along with several goats and a few acres, to someone she had never met and who was a lot older. Quite rightly, she was terrified and ran away. I think I would have done the same, if I had her courage. Luckily, I avoided that fate. And, as is the custom, her brother was told to take her back to India ... or else.'

'Meaning?'

'He was to make sure she never married anyone else.'

Percy looked confused. 'And how was he supposed to do that?'

'How do you think?'

'I really don't know, Miss Doshi, you need to tell me. Are you're suggesting he'd have harmed her in some way?'

'Much worse, Inspector, much, much worse. She'd brought shame on the family. Sanjit was ordered to get her back or ...kill her ... or get her to kill herself. It was his duty, for sake of the family's honour.'

'Is ... is that what happens?' Percy was aghast.

'It's the way of the world where I come from. Family comes first and last. Family honour counts above everything else. Not like here, where whatever goes, it seems. Marriage seems to count for very little in my experience.'

The comment hit Percy hard but he couldn't help but think of both his own and Orwell's current circumstances.

'You might be right about what happens here, but how on earth could anyone murder their own sister just because she didn't want to marry someone? Someone she'd never even met! It's unbelievable. It's ...if I may say so, uncivilised!'

'Where I come from *we* are the *civilised* ones and it's you and your plastic families that are seen as not so. We have centuries of tradition. Family is the core, the bedrock of our society ... something your society is sorely lacking I suggest.'

'How come you got involved? Are you related?'

'We are family. I'm Rana's aunt.'

'Are you married? Do you have any children?

'No. Nor do I have ambitions in that direction. That's why Rana came to me.'

'Does your sister know her daughter's with you?'

'Yes. In fact it was Sunita who asked me to take Rana in ... to save her. You see, the same thing happened to my sister, only she couldn't escape. She knew what it was like and she wanted to spare Rana the ordeal. So we arranged for Rana to visit me in London before the wedding.'

'And she was never going to go back. You even got her the job at the BBC?'

'Yes, she was to take my place as Orwell's assistant ... only he went and protested too much about getting rid of me. Our programme controller, Mr Bokhari, managed to find room for us both, providing Rana wasn't paid. I've had to support her from my own pocket.'

'And Sanjit? You knew he was in Cambridge?'

'Of course. He's the apple of my brother-in-law's eye. He told the whole of India about getting into Cambridge. My sister was also very proud of him at first. He could do no wrong as far as they were concerned. Sunita and I thought he would side with Rana when she ran away, look after her here in England. Instead ... well, he had his own problems up at Cambridge. Then the Bose thing happened. Do you know about Bose?'

'The Nazi sympathiser in Berlin? Yes, Orwell told me about him.'

'Yes, well that's all a load of nonsense. With Sanjit, the Bose thing was all a diversion. He had no real political inclinations or ideology... he had only debts. He was never into politics. He was always more interested in himself and having a good time. He was the spoilt brat you'll find in most Indian families. He's a boy, you see.'

'He had debts?'

'He gambled and led the high life. I'm told it's very easy to do that at Cambridge. He was up to his neck in debt. He tried to get money off me, only to realise that working for the BBC was hardly going to make me a goldmine. I told him as much. So when he got his orders about Rana, from his father's family, I think he saw it as an opportunity.'

'To do what?'

'Blackmail. Somehow he must have discovered Orwell and Rana were having an affair. It was almost common knowledge around here in any case, although George didn't seem to realise it. He seldom does. The whole section knew or suspected as much. When Sanjit contacted Rana and threatened to expose Orwell, she panicked and we decided it was best if she disappeared.'

'But Orwell doesn't have much money either. If he did, he too wouldn't be working here.'

'Sanjit must have been desperate. He told me his creditors were lining up. Anything, no matter how little, would have been enough to buy him some time. Orwell was to be told about Rana's predicament and he would feel compelled to save her. He would have no choice and would have to come up with some money to buy Sanjit off. That, I believe, was Sanjit's plan.'

'And that's why he's been murdered? Hang on, are you saying Orwell—'

'Of course not! George had nothing to do with Sanjit's death. He knew nothing of the blackmail. Rana never told him and neither have I. So when Rana went missing, Sanjit's plan was dead in the water, literally as it turned out. Orwell would no longer be able to help her.' Jahida drank some tea and waited to gauge Percy's reaction. He looked confused.

'I've no idea how Sanjit came to be murdered. I can only hazard a guess it was something to do with the gambling debts. He owed a lot of people a lot of money.'

'Can I see Miss Mukurjee? I'll need to corroborate what you've just told me.'

'Of course. Do we need to say anything to George?'

'I'll deal with Orwell once I've seen the young woman. Leave that to me. '

'And me, Inspector? Will I be charged with obstructing the police or wasting your time?'

'I'll also deal with that later. It's no longer just a missing-persons case, Miss Doshi. We now have a murder on our hands.'

Percy left Jahida staring at the stains on the table.

It was the silence that struck Percy. His home was empty in every respect. At first, he had revelled in the quiet and the solitude but he was now beginning to miss the arguments and temper flares that had formed the constant background noise in his domestic life. Now, the only disturbance was the clamour from the immediate neighbours, something he had barely noticed under the din of his and Vera's own making. Next door's quarrels sounded every bit as dreadful as his own had been. Only the howls and screeches of their children stood out as a discordant choral accompaniment to the parental racket. Children, it seemed, were not the antidote to marital conflict.

He warmed some broth on the stove and settled down with his notebook to review the Mukurjee case and started to go through the sequence of events. Something was still troubling him: had the brother sent him the note, and if so, why? How would that fit in with the supposed blackmail?

41

Percy and Baines waited in the Emporium for Crow to materialise from behind his ever-increasing piles of war booty. A small child's rocking horse caught Percy's attention and he moved closer to inspect it. He ran his hand over its head. It had an ear missing and its real horse-hair mane was singed. He wondered about its little owner and hoped the child had been evacuated to some rural idyll in Devon or Cornwall. The reality was probably less benign. The forlorn-looking object looked every bit an innocent casualty of the war and its presence here somehow made the whole situation even more depressing.

'Don't tell me – Bowler, isn't it? The old man took off some pince-nez spectacles and wiped them on his sleeve. He then clipped the glasses back on to his nose and said, 'Rozzers! I knew it!'

'Mr Crow, I'm Detective Inspector Percy and this is Detective Constable Baines. We're here to ask you a few questions about the room upstairs. The one you let out to a Mr Eric Blair.'

Crow thought for a moment and went back behind the

counter. He tried to sound nonchalant. 'Nah, never heard of 'im. I've got no renter by that name. Never 'ave. I'm very sorry, gentlemen, but I can't help you there.' Crow squinted and again removed the glasses. He looked at Percy closely. 'Wasn't you calling yourself Bowler or something last time you were 'ere? Whoever you are, I can't help yer.' He replaced the glasses once more and flipped over the page of a newspaper.

Baines looked bemused and mouthed *Bowler?* as they advanced on the shopkeeper.

'This is a murder case, Crow. I warn you – if you withhold any information pertinent to our investigation, you'll be charged with assisting and abetting a murder. Does that help jog your memory at all?'

The old man sat up with a start. 'Murder? Who's been murdered? Not something to do with this Ripper, is it?'

'Why do you say that?'

'Well ... they was all working girls, or so I read. Just like old Jack's.'

'And?'

'Some of my tenants have been known to *support* those sorts of ladies in their need. I don't say anything. It's not my business. What they do in the room up there is up to them. I don't pry. I don't wanna know. It's not my—'

'Business? Allowing your room to be used for and profiting from prostitution *is* illegal. I'd say it's a good business at the moment, wouldn't you, Baines?'

'Yes, guv, what with all the squaddies in town. A booming business by all accounts.'

'I don't know if they were prostitutes! I wasn't up there. All I know is they *looked* like prozzies. That's all I'm saying. They could have been their girlfriends, mistresses or sisters for all I know. Perhaps not sisters! I never ask.'

'And Blair?'

'I told yer, I don't know anyone by that name!'

'That's strange because the constable here saw him coming and going from this shop and I suggest he wasn't buying your junk. Do you mind if we look around? There's a lot of stuff here. Is it all kosher?'

'Gentlemen, please. Now look, let me help you and you help me. Everyone will be 'appy that way.' Crow grinned broadly and held up his palms in supplication.

'Mr Crow, tell us what you know about Blair and we'll see what we can do.'

'That's more like it. Smith, that's what he called himself. Well, at first he did. Then it was Blair.'

' Who did he bring here?'

'A young Indian woman ... very young and very pretty. You couldn't help but notice her. And then, later, he had some very pricey bird. She wasn't 'ere long tho. Very quick she was. A bit snooty if you ask me. I didn't take to her at all. But I see what he might have seen in her. She was a wrong'un for this sorta place, I thought. Pricey.'

'Pricey?'

'The real classy type. More West End than East End, more Park Lane than Pimlico, if you know what I mean.'

'Any others?'

'No, not to my knowledge. Tho' he 'ad a key to the back door so there could have been others as well. He's not the Ripper, is he?'

'No, he's not the Ripper.'

'Thank Gawd for that! I'd never live with that on my conscience.' Crow took out a stained handkerchief and mopped his brow furiously.

'Did anyone else come looking for Blair?'

'Only an Indian bloke, but I'm sure he was looking for

the Indian woman. I told Smith ... Blair... about 'im. Oh, and you of course – Mr Bowler as you were then. And then I telephoned his friend and told 'im about you snooping around here asking about 'im. And he's never paid me for that call. Tight he was.' It was, of course a lie. Orwell had already paid him for the call.

'Who was this friend?'

'I dunno, some bloke at the BBC. Hang on, I've still got his card somewhere – let me find it for you.' Crow went behind the counter and opened a small money drawer. 'Burgess, that's the fella. I phoned 'im and spoke to his secretary. At the BBC he is. I said you were snooping around. And I said that to Blair when he came 'round, after I'd phoned that is.'

'Can I take the card?' Percy said.

'Be my guest. Can't say I'll be using it again. Nice, isn't it? Very posh. You should get some made up like that, Inspector. Is that what the BBC spends our money on ...fancy cards? Now, will that be all gents? I've a living to make and I'm sure you're very busy as well. You know where I am and I'm always here if you need me. Only too willing to scratch your back, if you know what I mean.'

Percy turned the card over. *Blair* was written on the back.

'Does anyone ever buy this stuff?' Baines asked.

'You'd be surprised, young man. It takes all sorts. The Indian fella bought one of these.' Crow reached for a glass paperweight of Tower Bridge in a snow scene. 'Would you like one? Only one and six to you. Something for the girlfriend.'

Baines took the ornament. 'I quite like that. What d'you think, guv?'

Percy swiped the object out of Baines's hand and handed it back to Crow.

'You'll be hearing from us. Don't say a word to anyone about our visit. If you do, we'll put it out that you've been helping us with our inquiries. I think we all know what that means around here.'

Crow said nothing and just opened the shop door. As soon as the door had closed behind them the sign flipped to CLOSED and Percy heard the bolts and locks being applied.

'Baines, have you come across that name Burgess in all this?'

'No, guv, it's a new one to me.'

'And me. Why didn't Orwell tell us about him? I wonder what this Burgess knows?'

'He knows you were looking for Blair - Orwell ... or someone called Bowler was.'

'It was Bowling, George Bowling. So does Burgess know about the junk shop?'

'He could do.'

They walked down the street. The women gossiping at their front doors appeared to be able to tell that they were officials of some sort, either from the council or the police, and shuffled inside as they approached.

'Crow phones Burgess after I visit the shop. And soon after that Orwell comes to me and confesses his affair with the Indian woman. But he makes no mention of the call or this man Burgess. Why?'

'I dunno, guv.'

'Neither do I, Baines. Only Orwell can tell us ... and this Burgess of course.'

42

'MISS DOSHI *IS* VERY WELL-SPOKEN, BUT SHE DIDN'T TIP US off about Sanjit Mukurjee,' Percy sounded certain.

Orwell said nothing and just chewed his lips nervously.

'Someone else here at the BBC knew you were having an affair with Rana Mukurjee *and* that she had a brother. I'll ask you once more: who do you think that might be?'

Orwell looked uncomfortable and fumbled for his tobacco tin. He wheezed and took deep breaths. His shallow eyes seemed almost to have receded into their sockets. 'Bokhari perhaps?'

Percy watched Orwell struggle to contain a cough before asking in an understated manner, 'Do you know a Mr Guy Burgess? I believe he works here at the BBC.'

Orwell looked surprised and the cough he had been sheltering made its escape.

'Yes. He's a Talks Producer, in the Home Service. We sometimes work together, or at least, we attend the same meetings. Why do you ask?'

'Would you call him a friend?'

'No, certainly not. We have our differences, you might say.'

'Differences?'

'On working matters. We don't necessarily see eye-to-eye on the content of the Talks – that sort of thing.'

'So you wouldn't invite him home for dinner?'

'Not out of choice, Inspector. I've no time for the fellow. He's not my sort, although I have a feeling that my wife, Eileen, would probably like him.'

Percy reached into his pocket and produced Burgess's card. 'So how is it that you asked Crow to call Burgess on your behalf, if he's not a friend, that is? Did you write your name on the back of this?'

Orwell hesitated. 'Yes, I did. It was just one of a number of BBC cards I have. I pulled it out randomly I recall and I suppose I didn't really look. I'm not so illustrious as to have my own and I couldn't remember the telephone number here. So, yes, I wrote my name on it.'

'Not Smith?'

'Or Bowling.'

'Touché.' Percy half-smiled. 'You didn't want Crow to know who you really were, so you gave him your real name? That doesn't sound too clever. Why didn't you just copy the number from the card?'

'I wasn't thinking. I was in a hurry and he wouldn't have been able to contact me by calling a Mr Smith at the BBC.'

'Then you had him call Burgess in order to relay a message. Again, that seems a rather odd thing to do.'

'As I just explained, it was one of a number of cards I had on me with the BBC's number. I wanted him to call the switchboard. Burgess has nothing to do with this. That was purely coincidental.'

'Are you sure? D'you know, Orwell, I've come to the conclusion that you're not very good at lying.'

'Is that supposed to be a compliment, Inspector?'

'In most walks of life I suppose it would be. But, for a professional propagandist, I somehow doubt it.'

'Propagandist? I've never really come to terms with that description. But, unusually, on this occasion I find myself agreeing with you.' Orwell paused and wrote something down. 'You see, all propaganda is lies, even when one's telling the truth.' He looked up from the desk. 'Now, does that make me a good or bad propagandist? I'm not at all sure.'

'So, this Burgess? What might he know?'

Orwell laughed. 'Everything! Oh my goodness, Inspector, he knows everyone and everything!'

'I'm not sure I'm following you. Are you saying he knew about the junk shop and Sanjit Mukurjee?'

'About the unfortunate brother, almost certainly. He told me he knew of him from his Cambridge contacts. About Crow's shop, I can't be certain, but it wouldn't surprise me. As I said, he knows everything about everyone. And I wouldn't be surprised if that even includes yourself, Inspector.'

'So he might also know about your mysterious VIP.'

'I wouldn't put it past him, but I sincerely hope not. Burgess has a lot of important contacts, so I'm told.'

Orwell coughed and inspected his handkerchief, looking, Percy now knew, for tell-tale signs of his illness.

'Are you able to carry on?'

Orwell placed the handkerchief to his mouth and nodded.

'Why might Burgess be interested in George Orwell or even Eric Blair?'

'Intelligence, subversion, treason, consorting with the enemy? Who knows? I can't believe he's just interested in my writing. He's also a homosexual.' Orwell said.

Percy smiled as Orwell's use of his favourite word. 'Intelligence?'

'Yes, I think he's something to do with the War Office, Secret Intelligence or whatever, but I can't say for sure.'

'He's spying on you?'

'Not just me I'd wager. In my case I presume it's because I'm considered some sort of threat to national security. I fought in Spain – on the wrong side as far as they're concerned. And of course I'm a socialist. That's reason enough it seems. I've long thought I'm being watched. Perhaps we all are.'

'And your friend, the VIP? He'd be suspected of being a Socialist sympathiser?'

'No, far from it. But given his important position, consorting with me probably makes him what they call 'a risk'. If that's the case, I think both of us, you and I, may well be out of our depth, Inspector. You need to be careful not to tread on anyone's toes, especially in Intelligence.'

'Let me worry about that Orwell. So, what's the connection with Sanjit Mukurjee? Was he also a subversive like yourself?'

'I'm not sure I'd consider myself a subversive as such. I think those who run this country are the real subversives. I've no idea about Sanjit Mukurjee. All I know is, he was a Bose man. That would be enough for Intelligence to take an interest in him. He'd certainly be considered a threat to national security.'

'Miss Doshi believes the Bose thing was all a sham. He had other problems – money mostly. He was a gambler and he owed a lot of people a lot of money.'

'Then perhaps someone caught up with him. But what about your well-spoken informant? Why did she want you to connect the cases?'

'Cynthia Broadbent?' Percy almost left his seat on hearing his own voice. Her name had entered his consciousness from nowhere.

'Yes, Diane or whoever she really is. She's very well-spoken I recall.'

'Quite.' Percy felt light-headed. 'Tell me, how did you come to know about the Esher Ladies' Circle?'

Orwell scratched his head and pulled on his ear lobe. 'I was given her number by someone here at work. I asked one of the chaps. Desai – he's on loan from the Ministry of Information – I think he gave me her contact details.'

'Is Desai a colleague of Burgess's?'

'Yes, of course.'

'Have you still got the number?' Percy asked.

'I'll look.'

'You see, Orwell, I don't believe there is such a thing as an Esher Ladies' Circle and Diane is not what you'd call a lady of the night. Why would she be on the game? I've been to Esher. I've seen her house. She doesn't strike me as your usual prostitute, or even an 'escort' as they are sometimes called in polite company.'

'Bored housewives looking for a bit of excitement perhaps, Inspector? *While the cat's away* and all that. In war, stranger things happen.'

'Even so, my instincts tell me, Mrs Cynthia Broadbent is not what she may have appeared to be.'

'Are you suggesting I was being set up?'

'It's beginning to look that way.' Percy replied.

'By Burgess? The Intelligence people, our own Secret Police?'

'Possibly. But are they after you or your VIP? I think that is the question.'

Orwell shook his head and reached for his tobacco tin. 'This may sound odd, Inspector, but I'd like to think it's me they're after. It would be something of a badge of honour to be considered as a threat to the Establishment, don't you think?'

Not really knowing what to think, Percy just shook his head. 'By the way, I think I know who your VIP is. A Lady Sutton is a regular presenter of your talks, is she not? Her husband has just been made Secretary of State for War. Again, one didn't really need to be a genius to work out that connection.'

'You missed your vocation, Inspector. You should have been in Intelligence yourself. There was I thinking all policemen were—'

'Stupid? A bit slow? Most maybe, but not all, I assure you.'

Orwell looked at Percy with what seemed like a new found respect.

'So what happens now? Do you arrest this Mrs Broadbent and or Burgess?'

'On what charges do you suggest?'

'Accessories or conspiracy to murder? Sanjit Mukurjee was murdered and Burgess must be in the frame.'

'I don't think so, Orwell. We have nothing to connect them to Sanjit Mukurjee's murder, other than the call. We still have no idea as to why he met his maker. It looks like someone called in a loan and he was caught by one of the sharks. To be honest, I think we'll probably never know. I doubt the Murder Squad will put themselves out to find out who killed an Indian. Although—'

'But you might?'

Percy did not answer.

'What about Rana Mukurjee? We seem to have lost sight of why you're here in the first place Inspector. Any news?'

'I've been assured that she's safe and well. The case will therefore be closed as soon as we can verify for certain that she is safe.'

'Did Miss Doshi tell you that? Have you seen her? How do you know she's safe?'

'Orwell, my advice would be don't get involved any further. Not least for the sake of your wife.'

'And how's your own marriage, Inspector?' Orwell snapped back.

Percy paused before answering. 'Vera's left me.'

'Oh, I'm sorry. Really, that was rude of me, I shouldn't have asked.'

'I'm not sure I am, sorry, that is. My further advice to you, for what it's worth, is get yourself a child – adopt if necessary – and stick to writing your books while you can. No more *diversions*. You need to look after your wife. She needs you as much as you need her.'

Percy rose from the chair, put on his hat and walked out without looking back.

43

'FOUND HIM!' PERCY SHOUTED. 'I'VE BLOODY WELL FOUND him!'

In the bowels of Scotland Yard he had taken a file from a shelf. The cover read: *Guy Francis de Moncy BURGESS*. It was a charge sheet. He read through the paperwork.

'Soliciting: improperly soliciting a man in a public lavatory. He passed a suggestive note under the door. He claimed he was reading *Middlemarch* and the note had come from the other cubicle. The case was dismissed on the grounds of insufficient evidence' It was dated 10th January 1939. Just as he was about to close the file, a sentence popped out from the page. *Solicitor for the accused – Mr Reginald Broadbent.* Percy stared in disbelief. Burgess's connection to Diane was looking right back at him.

PERCY TELEPHONED CYNTHIA 'DIANE' BROADBENT. In return for not involving her husband, she agreed to meet at the Blue Café as it was convenient for trains into Waterloo from

Esher. At 4.30 p.m., he sat and pondered the possible links between Diane and Sanjit Mukurjee's murder. The well-spoken woman had to be her, but why?

As usual, the café was near-deserted – just a young couple who looked as if they were on their first date and a middle-aged man reading a newspaper. Maria was sullen and failed to recognise him. He told her he was waiting for a friend and they would have the high tea when she arrived.

The door opened and a rather dishevelled man walked in. He surveyed the scene and lit a cigarette before approaching the loner reading the newspaper. He asked the man something and Percy heard a foreign response. This was followed by a vigorous shake of the head. The man then made a beeline for Percy.

'I'm Guy Burgess. I believe we need to talk. You're Inspector Percy, I presume.'

Percy caught the full blast of Burgess's aftershave and winced. 'I am. But I was not expecting *you*.'

'But we do need to talk, Inspector. Mrs Broadbent is otherwise detained. Shall we have tea?'

Burgess took off his camel-hair overcoat and hung it over an adjacent chair. He offered Percy a cigarette, which he declined.

Maria delivered the tea. The scones were even smaller and the jam was now a tiny puddle of pink matter. There was no butter or margarine. Burgess took one look at the meagre offerings and pushed his plate away. Percy was about to pour the tea when Burgess placed his hand on Percy's.

'Let it brew.'

Percy quickly withdrew his hand and wiped it on the tablecloth. He couldn't recall being touched by a grown man like that.

'What's your relationship with Mrs Broadbent?' Percy asked.

'Relationship? Oh, it's not what you think, Inspector. I have no inclinations in that direction.'

'So I'm told ... So why are you here Burgess?'

'To help the police with their inquiries. You see, Inspector, or should I call you Percy? The world today is rather complicated and people are not what they seem. I'm sure you'll agree. To be blunt, you're in danger of wandering well beyond your neck of the woods.'

'You don't just work for BBC I take it?'

'You've worked that out. Bravo! So who do you think I work for?'

'The Intelligence Service?'

'Did you arrive at that conclusion yourself?' His condescension had returned with interest.

'And Mrs Broadbent – Diane?'

'One of our finest.'

'A prostitute?'

'Aren't we all, in one way or another? No, you see, she uses her womanly attributes for the good of the nation. A true patriot, one might say. I'm told she's very good at it.'

'Does her husband know?'

'I really can't say. Have you met Mr Broadbent?'

'No, but I know you have.'

'Really? I can't recall. How do you know?' Burgess tried to look innocent and a smirk appeared on his face.

'Your court record. He represented you three years ago. How could you possibly forget?'

'Oh that. Was that him? How serendipitous is that?' Burgess looked amused.

Percy was beginning to feel uncomfortable with Burgess' cockiness. He decided to cut to the chase.

'An unbelievable coincidence some might say. Are you here to warn me off?'

'Let's just say it would not be a great career move on your part to pursue your investigations any further. I'm told Miss Mukurjee has been found alive and well. I suggest you close the case and get back to finding those who remain missing. You seem to have a talent in that direction.'

Percy ignored the put-down. 'And Sanjit Mukurjee?'

'An unfortunate end by all accounts. It would appear the bookies have wiped his slate clean.'

' So why did Mrs Broadbent inform the Murder Squad about the connection between his murder and myself?'

'Did she?'

'You know she did. Why? And the first note – was that also your doing? Who else, apart from you, knew about Miss Mukurjee and Orwell having an affair?' Percy asked.

'Miss Doshi and, by all accounts, nearly the whole of the India Section at the BBC.'

'So it was you or your people who sent the tip-off. Why?'

'To put the cat amongst the pigeons one might say.'

'To send us off on a wild goose chase more like.'

'Yes, that didn't go quite to plan. Your young colleague—'

'Baines.'

'Well, he wasn't supposed to act on the note. It was meant for you. He rather upset the apple-cart by tailing Mrs Broadbent. We rather underestimated your Missing Persons colleague on that score.'

'You wanted us to think Orwell was somehow involved in the young woman's disappearance? Why?'

'Orwell? Well he's also not all he appears to be. He's made some strange bedfellows over the years and let's just say he is a person of interest to us. I would also suggest he's not one to be trusted on any account. So, as we knew that he has cheated on his wife and has had quite a few affairs with other women, he could well have had a hand in the death of an incensed brother. It's quite a plausible motive, don't you think?'

'You'd like me to think that. To cover up something else going on? You must also know about his VIP, Sir— '

'That was just fortuitous. It's amazing what a business card can do sometimes. In any case, that is a matter of national security Percy. You are under strict orders to forget everything about that. So, draw a line under the case Inspector. That's the advice from the very top. If you carry on digging, it will be your own grave you'll end up in, metaphorically one would hope. It's time to put the case to bed. And of course, this conversation has not taken place, that goes without saying. Shall I pour?'

44

Percy was now in something of a no man's land. The Missing Persons Section had been rediscovered by the powers that be and he had been called to account. He suspected Burgess's hand was also in this.

Baines had since volunteered to join the army and was waiting for his call-up, and Thomas had served his time. As a result, there was every likelihood they'd be closed down and the work given to the Salvation Army.

And there was an added domestic problem: Vera had returned. Inquiries as to her whereabouts had been met with silence, as had her decision to return. Hostilities resumed and Percy retreated to the kiddies' room. Any semblance of a conjugal relationship became a distant memory. They were still at war.

For Orwell, life at home had continued pretty much as usual. Eileen remained depressed and sickly, although the prospect of moving from MinInform to the Ministry for Food had enlivened her.

The blimps in the Home Guard had also rejected Orwell's call to develop their skills in guerrilla warfare as the prospect of a German invasion had all but evaporated.

The war was continuing elsewhere however. Relations with Jahida had collapsed and Bokhari had become even more insistent on rule-keeping. The atmosphere in the India Section was muted and sour and this was reflected in the Talks being broadcast. As a result, Orwell had become deeply depressed at the prospect of continuing in this vein. More than ever, he wanted to get back to his writing.

He arranged to meet Rana in Regent's Park. She looked different, older, and her vibrancy had dissipated into what he thought was a premature world-weariness. The air-raid shelters, sandbags and a rising early-morning mist only added to the gloom. The anti-aircraft batteries and search-lights were being cleaned and readied for the next raid. Most Londoners were still in their beds, if they still had one.

They did not embrace. Instead they walked, observing each other through the silence. They stopped near the bandstand that had been requisitioned by half a dozen squaddies on a sleep-over. A smell of beer and urine filled the air and Rana asked for a cigarette. Orwell obliged by rolling her one of his own and the strong Turkish shag did not take long to incite a splutter and cough.

'You'll soon sound like me and Joe,' he said.

'It's your filthy habit I've picked up,' she replied and smiled, her mood lifted momentarily.

'That'll teach you not to hang around with the wrong types.'

'I know,' Rana said, handing him back the cigarette. She looked up at the grey clouds. 'When will this all be over?'

'The war?' he asked.

'Yes, the war. What did you think I meant?'

'Us.'

'It's already over, George. You have Eileen. You always have. She needs you. Please, let's move on.'

They resumed walking. A gaggle of what looked like secretaries, typists and Whitehall clerks approached and giggled as they passed.

'And you don't...need me?' Orwell asked.

'No, I don't need you. Not now.'

'But you did before?'

'I did in a sort of way. I'm sorry, it was a terrible mistake.'

'In a sort of a way?'

'I meant ... I don't know what I meant. I can't seem to think anymore.' Her voice sounded choked and she turned her back on him. 'I had to do what I was told. I had no choice. I didn't want to.'

Her body shook and Orwell realised she was sobbing.

'I don't understand. Who told you? What—'

'I was told to befriend you.'

'That's an odd way of putting it.'

'I was told to gain your confidence. I was told to have an affair with you.'

Orwell stood still and appeared to be shocked. He took a long drag on his cigarette and blew the smoke skywards.

'My God! You were spying on me! This has all been planned. It was a set up. Everything was a set-up. Is Rana even your real name?' Orwell began to cough violently and bent over double.

'George, please, listen to me. I had no choice. I promise, I didn't intend it ...us...to go as far as we did. But I think ...it just happened. I didn't mean to but—'

'An affair?' Orwell gasped for breath and spat into his handkerchief. Joe was out in force.

'George, you'll make yourself ill. Please, just listen. They threatened to let Sanjit ... he was going to have to kill or maim me, or do something that would make me ...well, unlikely to get married to anyone else. There was no way I was going to go back to India with him. Then, he suddenly changed and gave me a choice. He asked me to befriend you and report back to him what we talked about and anything else on the others in the Section. Either that, or he'd carry out his threat. He was caught up with the Intelligence people. They recruited him at Cambridge and were supposedly going to pay off his debts if he could get me to spy on you and the Section.'

'You could have told me. But you didn't. Instead you *befriended* me. Why?'

'I did it because I was scared and because he was so desperate. He would have hurt me. The bookmakers were after him. He did what they asked in return for his debts being paid off. He was in danger and it was his only way out.'

'It obviously didn't work.'

'They reneged on the deal when I went into hiding. Sanjit was of no use anymore. I wasn't giving them anything. Sanjit did what they asked but they...let his bookies deal with him. I suppose it was my fault in the end. I couldn't do it any more because of how I felt about you.'

'Nonsense. It was of his own making. But why would anyone ...they, whoever *they* are...want to spy on me? What could I possibly know or do that would be of any interest to whoever it was controlling your brother?'

'I can't say.'

'Do you know?'

'Yes, I think ... Look, I'm sorry George, but I don't think *you* were their main interest. It was the whole Section. But later they must have found something else about you in particular.'

'Sutton!'

'Sutton?'

'Sir James bloody Sutton! But how could anyone have known about Sutton and myself? He paced around in a tight circle. 'It had to be Burgess. He set me up. They were on to Sutton. But they still made him Secretary for War! Churchill and Burgess have something on him and they can use it any time they choose. They've used all of us. All the time, Burgess knew everything from the very beginning.'

'George, I've no idea what you're talking about. All I knew was his wife and her ridiculous broadcasts. I had no idea you and he ... did you do something for him?'

'It's not important. You've no need to know. It's finished in any case. I've been stupid all along. I should have smelled a rat.'

'Why did you get involved with Sutton?'

'That's a long story. I doubt you would believe me if I told you.'

'Try me. I'd like to know.'

'I was trying to prevent millions of men, women and children being killed.'

'What?'

'I said you wouldn't believe me. Sutton told me about Churchill's plans for India. I was to pass them on to those in the Section who would contact their friends in India. The plans would then be exposed and that might stop them in their tracks. The lives of millions of Indians might be saved as a result.'

'How?'

'By preventing India being partitioned. If that happens there will be an inevitable conflagration of the Muslims and Hindus. India will be split up and communal conflict will be inevitable. Churchill's plan is to hold on to India for the duration of the war and then offer some sort of independence. Only that independence will entail the option of establishing a Pakistan. That's when it will explode. And by then we will be out of it.'

'So that's why they are interested in you?'

'Presumably. Only we...I failed. It looks like the Cripps mission - do you know about that? Cripps will fail to bring about any meaningful result. The Congress and the Muslim League will reject what he has to offer and Churchill's plan will remain on course. India will be partitioned after the war. Millions could die but Churchill doesn't care about that. Perhaps it was a nonsense to think we could stop it. Sutton is now on board with Churchill. He's been turned and I think I know why.'

Orwell walked on ahead. From behind him, Rana shouted, 'I was really fond of you, George. Please believe me, it wasn't an act. I fell for you, silly as that sounds. It was genuine.'

Orwell stopped and turned. 'We both fell ...only into the spider's web.'

He relit his cigarette and stared into the distance. A fighter plane roared overhead.

'What are you going to do now?' Orwell asked.

'I've been offered a place at Edinburgh. I'm going to read Politics.'

'Are you sure? It'll be cold up there.'

'I know. I've been told to wrap up. Have you been to Scotland?'

'I can't stand the Jocks.'

'You really are a racialist!'

'Will I see you?'

'If you come to Scotland.'

'I might just do that one day.'

'Yes, I mean, no I don't think that would be a good ... Oh, I don't know what I mean. I have to go, George. Aunt Jahida is waiting for me in Selfridges.'

'Yes, I heard. *Aunt* Jahida.'

'Don't blame her for looking after me. I didn't stay with her all the time. Sanjit would have found me if I did. Aunt Jahida found me a place out of London.'

'I shan't blame her, but I could ... I would have looked after you.'

'No, you couldn't. They're too powerful. In any case, you have far too many things on your plate. Get on and write your books. You'll be famous one day, I'm sure of it.'

'And pigs will fly. Look, I always meant to give you this.' Reaching into his pocket he took out a small carved wooden box. 'I've been carrying this around for an age. But now it's become something of a parting gift. Something to remember me by perhaps.'

Rana smiled, took the box and stood on her toes to kiss him gently on the cheek. Then she began to walk away. Almost immediately, she turned and said, 'By the way George, I've also got two names. My real name is Riju. It means something like... innocent. I thought you should know.'

He dragged on his roll-up and coughed some phlegm into the grass, inspecting it closely for signs of Joe. He then turned and walked in the opposite direction. It had started to rain.

EPILOGUE

'*I* REOPEN THIS DIARY AFTER AN INTERVAL OF ABOUT SIX MONTHS, *the war now in a new phase.*

The actual date of Cripps's departure for India was not given out, but presumably he has gone by now. Ordinary public opinion here seems gloomy about his departure. A frequent comment – 'They've done it to get him out of the way' – is also one of the reasons alleged on the German wireless. This is very silly and reflects the provincialism of English people who can't grasp that India is of any importance. Those better-informed are pessimistic because the non-publication of the government's terms to India indicates almost certainly that they are not good. Impossible to discover what powers Cripps has. Those who know will disclose nothing and one can draw hints from them only indirectly. For example, having been instructed to give Cripps a build-up in my newsletters, I present him as a political extremist. This draws the warning: 'Don't go too far in that direction.' Which suggests the higher-ups haven't much hope of full independence being granted to India.

I have now been at the BBC about six months. Shall remain if the political changes I foresee come off; otherwise, probably not.

Its atmosphere is something halfway between a girls' school and a lunatic asylum, and all we are doing at present is useless, or slightly worse than that. Our radio strategy is even more hopeless than our military one. Nevertheless, one rapidly becomes propaganda-minded and develops a cunning not previously held.'

George Orwell's Wartime Diary, 14th March 1942

AFTERWORD

22nd March 1942 - Sir Stafford Cripps left for India
7th April 1942 The Congress Working Committee rejected the British Declaration.
25th June 1942 Gordon Cummins was hanged
14th May 1944 The Blairs adopt their son Richard
29th March 1945 Eileen died aged 39 under anaesthesia
18th August 1945 Subhas Chandra Bose died in a plane crash
14th-15th August 1947 Indian Independence Bill
14th-15th August 1947 The creation of Pakistan
21st January 1950 George Orwell died aged 47
May 1951 Guy Burgess fled to Moscow

It is estimated that around 1–2 million people died and 15 million were displaced during the partition of India.

ABOUT THE AUTHOR

Peter Hodgkinson lives in Norfolk in the UK.
You can contact him here:

orwellcalling@gmail.com
facebook.com search **PeancoBooks Peter**
twitter.com **@peancobooks**

Printed in Great Britain
by Amazon